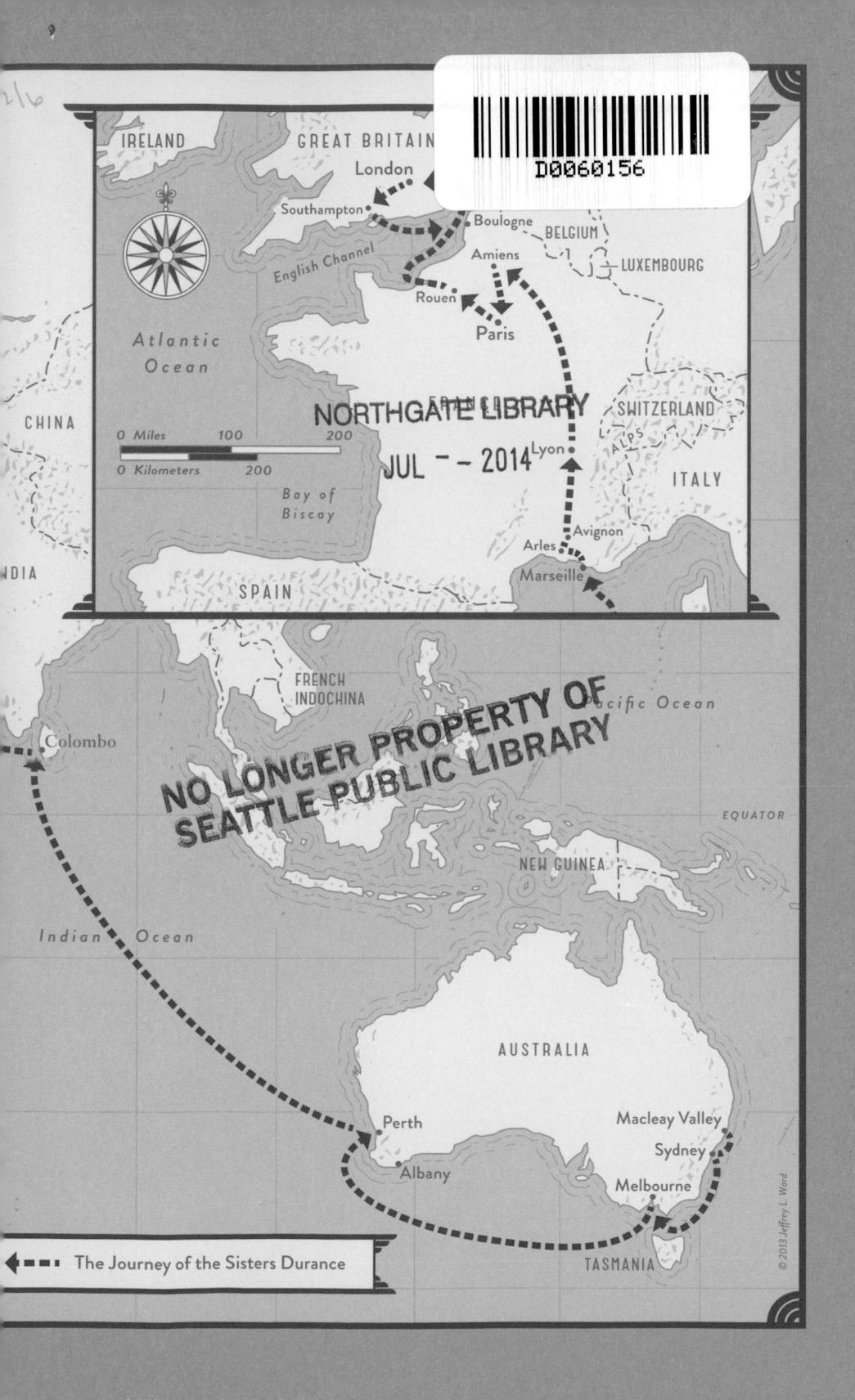

IRELAND

GREAT BRITAIN

London

Southampton

Boulogne

BELGIUM

LUXEMBOURG

Amiens

English Channel

Rouen

Paris

Atlantic
Ocean

0 Miles   100   200

0 Kilometers   200

SWITZERLAND

ALPS

ITALY

Lyon

CHINA

Avignon

Arles

Marseille

Bay of
Biscay

SPAIN

FRENCH
INDOCHINA

Pacific Ocean

Colombo

EQUATOR

NEW GUINEA

Indian   Ocean

AUSTRALIA

Perth

Macleay Valley

Sydney

Albany

Melbourne

INDIA

TASMANIA

© 2013 Jeffrey L. Ward

◀ ▪▪▪▪ The Journey of the Sisters Durance

THE
DAUGHTERS
OF MARS

Bettany's Book

Office of Innocence

The Tyrant's Novel

The Widow and Her Hero

The People's Train

NON-FICTION

Outback

The Place Where Souls Are Born

Now and in Time to Be: Ireland and the Irish

Memoirs from a Young Republic

Homebush Boy: A Memoir

The Great Shame

American Scoundrel

Abraham Lincoln

A Commonwealth of Thieves

Searching for Schindler

Three Famines

Australians

FOR CHILDREN

Ned Kelly and the City of the Bees

Roos in Shoes

THE DAUGHTERS OF MARS

A Novel

THOMAS KENEALLY

ATRIA BOOKS

New York   London   Toronto   Sydney   New Delhi

ATRIA BOOKS

A Division of Simon & Schuster, Inc.
1230 Avenue of the Americas
New York, NY 10020

First Atria Books hardcover edition August 2013
Originally published in Australia in 2012 by Vintage Australia

ATRIA BOOKS and colophon are trademarks of Simon & Schuster, Inc.

For information about special discounts for bulk purchases, please contact Simon & Schuster Special Sales at 1-866-506-1949 or business@simonandschuster.com.

The Simon & Schuster Speakers Bureau can bring authors to your live event. For more information or to book an event, contact the Simon & Schuster Speakers Bureau at 1-866-248-3049 or visit our website at www.simonspeakers.com.

Designed by Dana Sloan

Manufactured in the United States of America

10 9 8 7 6 5 4 3 2 1

Library of Congress Cataloging-in-Publication Data has been applied for.

ISBN: 978-1-4767-3461-3
ISBN: 978-1-4767-3463-7 (ebook)

To the two nurses,
Judith and Jane

Author's Note

The punctuation used in this narrative might seem occasionally eccentric, but is designed to honor that of the forgotten private journals of the Great War, written by men and women who frequently favored dashes rather than commas. Many of the smaller locations and institutions in this novel are fictional, though based generally on the medical installations of the period.

The incidents involving the hospital ship *Archimedes* are based broadly on what befell the hospital ship *Marquette,* in which valiant New Zealand nurses served. I hope New Zealanders will forgive my appropriating some of the *Marquette* material for my own purposes. As well, the involvement of an Irish regiment in these matters is fictional, and not meant to cast reflection on any venerable regiment.

The clearing station at Deux Églises did not exist (though one existed at a small village named Trois Arbres more or less in the same location). Similarly, the clearing station of Mellicourt is fictional in name, but not in terms of the labors undertaken there by nurses. The château named Baincthun never existed, but, in a similar location, the prototype of the formidable Lady Tarlton of the novel—in real life a woman of lively intelligence and great beauty named Lady Dudley— ran a similar Australian voluntary hospital. I hope these few liberties do not detract from the enjoyment of this tale.

BOOK I

Murdering Mrs. Durance

It was said around the valley that the two Durance girls went off but just the one bothered to come back. People could not have said which one, since both the girls were aloof and looked similar—dark and rather tall. There was confusion even in the local paper. And they weren't the sort of girls whose names were called across streets—girlfriend hallooing girlfriend in the excitement of Kempsey's big shopping days. Before the war it was the younger one—wasn't it?—who stayed at home with her parents. The slightly shorter one, anyhow. And it was she who took her mother, Mrs. Durance, to visit the surgeon in Sydney. But what could those Macquarie Street doctors do?

After a choppy night's passage down the coast aboard the *Currawong*, Mrs. Durance finally fell asleep off Broken Bay, only to be woken, as the steamer entered the Sydney Heads, by a steward bearing tea—Sally being on deck at the time for the experience of the approach to Port Jackson.

Mother and daughter had time for another cup of tea at the wharf in Darling Harbour before Sally took the exhausted Mrs. Durance to the surgeon's rooms in Macquarie Street. After an examination by this eminent man, she was sent from his office to Sydney Hospital for X-rays. Then she and Sally met up with Naomi, the other daughter, the one who was considered a bit flash—Macleay District Hospital not good enough for her—who'd been in Sydney a few years.

They went that afternoon for a bang-up tea at Cahill's, while they waited for the expert men who read the body's inner secrets from photographs to discover what was wrong with Mrs. Durance. The sisters knew their mother had understated her pain to them. They knew she was secretive about the scale of her bleeding and the urine coming out of the wrong opening.

That night, Naomi put them up in her little flat in Bondi Junction— Mama sharing Naomi's bed, Sally on the sofa. They could have all stayed at Mrs. Durance's younger sister Jackie's place at Randwick, but Mrs. Durance didn't want to share news of her health problems with her sister yet. Both Sally and Naomi woke several times to their mother's choked-down groans. But unblunted ambition seemed to declare itself the next morning in the briskness with which Naomi put on her uniform and her scarlet cape to go to her duty at Royal Prince Alfred Hospital.

There had always been something larger than her beginnings written in Naomi Durance's gestures and her long bones. Her parents knew it. She had left them for the city, but in so far as they were boastful, they boasted of her. Sally worked a mere three miles from home, across the river, at the Macleay District Hospital. Merit in that, no one denied, and loyalty. But it was news of Naomi that made eyes shine on the Durance farm.

It was cervical cancer, the surgeon told Mrs. Durance the next morning. There was no option of an operation, for it would be a very long, painful, and dangerous procedure, and could not hope to get all of the proliferating cancer. Surgery was to be recommended chiefly in the early stages, whereas metastasis had already occurred, as the X-rays showed. If she rested well and ate lots of fruit, he said, she could expect to live at least a year. She was a dairy farmer's wife? Well, no more butter churning, he said, and no early morning milking. He would give her a script for pain medicine, he told her. He would also be writing to her doctor in the Macleay so that he could keep her comfortable.

You are fortunate to have two daughters who are registered nurses, he told her.

I am, she said, glowing with pride but hollowed by pain.

She and Sally caught the regular outward journey of the *Currawong* home the next night. Naomi saw them off at Darling Harbour, in the shadow of those shameful slums of the Rocks. From them bubonic plague had come boiling forth in the girls' childhoods and been carried north on the *Currawong* by a rat nestled in a furniture case. Naomi waited in their small cabin until the last call to go ashore and then stayed on the wharf to wave a futile handkerchief, as if she were part of one of those heartbreaking paintings of emigrant farewell.

She's so beautiful, isn't she, Sal? asked Mrs. Durance, leaning on the railing from pain rather than as a gesture of languid seafaring. She has a lot of grace, doesn't she?

As they reached on a black tide for Dawes Point, the handkerchief still waved, more luminous than Naomi's face. Bush people did that handkerchief-waving stuff and it gave them away as hayseeds. But worldly Naomi risked that tonight. She had promised she'd come up as often as she could and help Sally out. But that she would remain a city woman was not questioned.

It was a brisk night, and Mrs. Durance developed a cold on top of all else. She again fell asleep late. Again Sally came on deck at dawn and looked out at the blue surge of the tide breaking on the yellow sand of Trial Bay and making enough water at the river bar to allow the *Currawong* to enter.

For six months Mrs. Durance ate her fruit and sat in sumps of sunlight on the veranda. But the cancer owned her by night. Sally still worked the day shift at Macleay District but now slept on call in the same room as her mother, her father having moved to a lean-to at the back of the homestead. Sally was to administer a sixth of a grain of morphine hypodermically when brave and reticent Mrs. Durance confessed, one way or another, to agony. Naomi took her holidays and came home on a visit and gave her sister a break from the regimen. In between, Mr. Durance paid their neighbor Mrs. Sorley's girl to sit with Mrs. Durance by day and was attentive himself. Since Mr. Sorley had been killed by a native cedar—which when cut had slipped sidewards rather than forwards—the Sorley kids were ever ready for employment.

Sally noticed more clearly now that though her father and mother were souls of decency, Eric Durance moved about the bedroom as if he and his wife were acquaintances only. He seemed to fear he might be seen as an intruder. There had always been that distant courtesy between her parents. Sally knew they'd infected Naomi and her with it too. It might be one of the reasons Naomi had cleared out—in the hope that on a different stage she might have a franker soul.

Mrs. Durance suffered so much night pain that she frequently told Sally she was praying to God for death. These were remarkable and dramatic things for her to say and—since she had always had contempt for overstatement—would be forced out of her only by the fiercest anguish.

In the seventh month of it, Naomi came back from Sydney again to sit with her mother by day and share the night watch. The second night she was home, Sally slept in her own room while Naomi took up post in Mrs. Durance's room on the camp cot, a surface of canvas no blanket could soften. Naomi was meant to wake Sally at four so that she could take over, but did not come rapping on her door till near dawn. Naomi was in a dress and boots and her eyes looked smeared after gales of tears.

Mama's gone, she said. I'm sorry, Mama's gone. I ran over to the Sorleys' and asked their boy to ride into town to get Dr. Maddox.

Sally stammered with a confused and bitter grief and went to go off at once down the hallway. Naomi took her shoulders and gazed at her, straight into her face. Naomi's eyes seemed full of conspiracy. To Sally she had the eyes of a co-murderer. At that instant their shared mercy and their crime drew them together so utterly that they were no longer city and country nurses but sisters once more of the same womb.

You didn't wake me for my shift, said Sally.

It wasn't necessary, Naomi asserted, frankly, with her gaze on her. She went before it was time to wake you.

Let me see her.

I washed her and laid her out.

Without me?

I wanted you to sleep. I burned her nightdresses and the rags she used and took all the tonics and pounded the bottles to dust. Especially that rhubarb concoction Mrs. Sorley swore by.

There was indeed still a taint of smoke in the air.

Naomi led her sister by the hand and they walked down the hallway to the plain room they had both been conceived in. Blackbutt walls hemmed in the dim corridors they loved and hated, which seemed to pull Sally closer to home but which had proved to be escape avenues for Naomi.

There was her mother—gray-faced, prepared, serene—the girl she had been at some time visible again in these features delivered of pain.

Sally heard herself howl and went to her mother's body, kissing the face. The skin of the dead yielded differently. They were beyond pain but past affection too. She kissed the hand. It smelled of the scented soap Naomi had washed the corpse with. This too was proof of death. The living mother smelled of workaday Sunlight soap.

Sally found herself on her knees, still caressing the hand, Naomi standing behind and above her. Naomi, who always presumed to do things first. Sally did not know whether to hate her, to attack her eyes, or fall flat in gratitude and wonder. Standing with a purpose in mind, she noticed the hypodermic needle, the morphine solution they had made up of pills actually prescribed by Dr. Maddox, and the unused bottled tablets in case the old doctor wanted to inspect them or return them to stock.

She went to the dresser, was poleaxed with loss by the mother-of-pearl hairbrush with strands of her mother's hair in it. She knew the little drawer where her mother kept her subdued pink lipstick and her beige face powder.

Yes, said Naomi, you should put some color on her poor face.

It was a prayer—not an order—and Sally set to.

The stolen reserve of morphine she had put together to finish her mother had been in the towel and linen cupboard in the hallway. How had Naomi found it? You could bet the solution Naomi had made up and injected for mercy's sake had been poured out, and the spare illicit tablets Sally had filched from Macleay District consigned to fire with the rhubarb tonic. To Sally—putting rouge and color into her mother's cheeks—it seemed knowledge grew between Naomi and her without them looking at each other. Yesterday they had been near strangers. Now they were altered. A different kind of reserve was imposed on them, and a different intimacy.

Is Papa up? Sally asked. Does he know?

Not yet. I was frightened. Will we tell him in a moment? Perhaps let the poor fellow rest a few more minutes.

For he would need to do the milking even on the morning of his wife's death.

But she finds it hard to face him, Sally perceived. Naomi—who had tried to avoid the weight of home and its taint of illness—had certainly assumed the weight now. She'd taken up station on the far side of the bed, across from where Sally, on her knees, put reasonable Methodist coloration on the poor, released features.

Naomi said, I didn't have any idea till I came home that it was as bad as that. Her pain was the whole world to her. She could see nothing but it. Well, not any longer.

Sally was engrossed with her mother.

It was easy, Mama, to steal what you needed. I cut out two pages from the drugs record book. Former nurses who had managed the drugs register had done similar excisions because they did not approve of some missed or untidily written entry. Then for your dear sake I copied the dosages on fresh pages, adding an extra dose of an eighth of a grain of morphine in this case and that, until I'd created a phantom two grains, which I then fetched from the drugs cabinet and brought home to you. It's unlikely a doctor or matron will remember a specific dose as months go by. But I don't care if they do.

She had kept the tablets hidden behind the bed linen in the hallway dresser. These two grains when mixed in solution and injected would bear away disease and the fuss of enduring all useless treatment. They would reach deep into the body and halt the mechanism of agony. And had now.

She kissed her mother's brow before gracing it with the powder. Eric Durance would be astonished by his wife's beauty in death.

Naomi declared, I gave her half a grain and we kissed and held hands, though I had to be careful—a touch would break her bones. Then she went.

You were standing over her? said Sally.

They both knew how rare it was that a patient expired while the nurse was standing there to observe and hold a hand. The dead went almost secretively.

By good fortune, said Naomi without flinching but without bothering to look at her sister. By good fortune I was there.

Again, Sally's astonishment that Naomi had done the right, fierce, loving, and hard thing Sally had meant to do! Even in this she was not to be outshone, the half-mad Sally thought. But Naomi was there because she had found the secret cache and took the burden of soothing her mother's breath down to nothing. A solemn loss and rejoicing were the day's order—Mama's freedom now from a world she had never since their babyhoods seemed accustomed to. As for her children, they must now get accustomed to something new. To new love and new hate and mutual shame.

The roads being firm just then, Dr. Maddox arrived by motor at midmorning. The town—ignorant of medicine—loved him for his kindliness and punctuality and a lack of airs in a place where a doctor could easily play the grand wizard. But the hospital staff knew he was one of those tosspots who could carry it off well; that some unforgettable and disabling past event drove him to it. Though he performed surgery only when the other town doctors were not available, he was still a better surgeon when sober than most country doctors. It was peripheral things he was negligent at—paperwork, including death certificates. His method with the town at large was to hide it all behind an air of universal brotherhood and to breathe an impeccably mentholated breath over the sickbeds of the shire.

That Saturday morning Dr. Maddox came to lower his face over Mrs. Durance and to ask Naomi about the last injection and how many grains, and to accept what she said and then breathe, Good woman—good, poor woman. Then he prepared a medical certificate, which he showed Naomi and Sally and which said Mrs. Durance had died of cancer, nephritis, and exinanition. There were in the valley many people Dr. Maddox had certified as dying of nephritis and exinanition. Nephritis and exinanition was the cited verdict all along both banks of the river and inland to the blue, wooded hills where the timber workers camped and always died of nephritis and exinanition, unless a tree fell on them. Farmers who had taken poison to escape the bank had their death certificates compassionately marked by Maddox with that saving formula.

This morning of the death, over tea Sally made while keeping her eyes from straying to Naomi, Dr. Maddox sat at the kitchen table and spoke for a while to the girls' father. These were very much men's mutterings, half-embarrassed and platitudinous. Their father wore large, mute features, the same he brought to his labors. They had not yet crumbled in grief but somehow promised soon to do so.

Sally had less reason to stay in the Macleay Valley now. She was maybe a year beyond the age girls left home for marriage. Her sister had returned to her Sydney duties. Mr. Durance took sturdily to his work and employed the Sorley boys when needed. But Sally did not yet feel entitled to go. To flee would be obscene. It would be an insult to her mother's spirit. Her sister could escape because escape was her forte. She'd managed the trick before. But while it was easy for strangers to declare Eric Durance independent—a freestanding fellow—he did not seem so rugged to Sally.

The country hospital had its own retaining power too. On the Wednesday following her mother's funeral she found that a fourteen-year-old boy with peritonitis she was nursing had died in the night, and she believed her stinging tears were a debt paid to her mother and a sort of tax paid to the valley. So by horseback, or more often by sulky, she continued traveling in her uniform—along the broad yellow-earth road and unreliable bridge over the river—to and from the home at Sherwood. She was a figure located essentially amidst the green paddocks, one who could not glibly get away.

It was in the corridors during her night shifts that the mercy they'd given her mother took on the demeanor of a crime never to be argued away. Did I do it because I was tired? Fed up with all-day working and all-night watching? In the nurses' cubicle at the end of a public ward which contained—with all injuries and diseases there present combined and counted—no pain such as that of her mother's, Sally wept without consolation, since no night pleadings from an entire hospital of patients seemed to come close to the daytime pleadings she'd heard from her dead but eternal mother.

This young woman of twenty-two—or near twenty-three—years was considered by those who bothered to see her to be possessed by a wistfulness which some people thought represented that greatest crime of bush towns: aloofness, flashness. Either that, or she was a cause for sympathy. A spinster-in-training.

Voluntary

Then—after eight months—the thunderclap. It would alter earthly geography. It altered the geography of duty and it enhanced all escape routes. It was not the thunderclap of war—at least in the clear and direct sense. It was not the declarations of the prime minister or the news that the enemy was in Samoa and New Guinea, and his flotilla of cruisers and raiders was already at sea, or about to take to it and make the Pacific and Indian Oceans perilous. It was not the rush to make a full-blown army out of a mere framework of weekend militias. It was not a renewed awareness that the valley was numerous in Bavarian Catholic cow-cockies, now likely to be less loyal even than the Irish. It was a letter addressed to her father and her by Naomi in Sydney.

> There is a call for military nurses. Unless you have sharp objections, I'll apply. But any acceptance is unlikely. If Sally feels that she would be left without proper help, I will of course . . .

Recently Sally had begun to favor the day shift for its busyness, leaving the house with stew and potatoes bubbling on the great iron range fueled with the fallen branches of ring-barked trees. In her noon absence her father would eat some of this and when she returned at dusk always declared it had been top-class. It was good that he was not a complainer, that his hard-mouthed taste was not broad, and any food involving meat, potatoes, and green peas fulfilled his idea of nourishment, as long as it was served scalding. But even before the great change in the world, she had known in some secret chamber of the mind that she *was* readying herself for an escape, one all the more—not less—daring and reckless because it did not involve tunneling or scaling walls.

On the excuse she would be home too late from the hospital, she had started to get the Sorley girl to cook her father the evening meal. Many would see what was coming their way—the womanless homestead which would be his lot—and they would rant and plead. But Mr. Durance did not show any sign he intended that. He stated a thoughtful and unblaming awareness that in the end both the girls would go, for Naomi had already proved it to him. Neither love nor blood nor begging, he wisely and grievingly knew, could hold a man and his children under one roof and unto death. At some time the roof would change itself into a wheel which spun off the children. This month—if the occasional *Herald* which reached the farm could be believed—the roofs of the world had become a wheel for crushing the breasts of mothers and fathers. If Naomi could be shrugged off by this roof in the Macleay, then she, Sally, was fit also to be thrown out on a tangent over earth, and perhaps over oceans—whose scope might even reduce her crimes as a daughter to the size of an atom.

There was as well a problem she had with a farmer's son named Ernie Macallister—about whose suitability for her and her suitability for him it seemed a number of people had already decided. She'd let herself be taken to Crescent Head to swim and once to the flickers at the Victoria. The college of women—her late mother too—had just about chosen to allot her in their minds to young Macallister like real estate. The tedium of all this frightened her.

The federal letter calling for nurses arrived at the Macleay District the same day as Naomi's and was left in the nurses' room by the matron in case any of her four charges felt the drag of history. Sally approached her matron and told her that she would like to apply. It would probably be for nothing. The matron was, however, English-born and ardent on the Empire and the war, and she gave Sally leave.

Sally intended to try to fit the business of potential enlistment in Sydney into two days and two nights. She sent a telegram asking to stay not at Naomi's flat but at the more spacious Randwick house of her Aunt Jackie. She knew this would be considered by Naomi as a stringent step. That it would be correctly interpreted as resentment of the urban sister and an avoidance of the unease rising from the murderous succor they had extended to their mother. But something was rampant in Sally, something that said crazily that Naomi should not feel entitled to keep the whole of the war and leave Sally with the crumbs of a languishing peace.

In Sydney by morning and rushing by tram to Victoria Barracks, Sally entered a drill hall where other women stood half-bewildered, and filled out a form about her nursing career and her own medical condition. She queued for the interview at which she was to present two papers—her nurse's registration and a health certificate from Dr. Maddox—to an elderly militia colonel, whose manner was paternal, and a senior matron who sat with him at a table, whose manner was dry. The pressure of unconfessed murder nudged up around the edges of the two printed forms, and she was pleased to pass them over.

Even so, Sally suspected she would not be chosen. She might make this slight and feeble move and then go back tamed for years more to the duty of daughterhood. She suspected she might in fact go back with as much secret relief as disappointment. She was willing to go back. That forenoon as she left the hall, she resigned herself to return on the following night's coaster. The tin roof would not spin her far off and had already begun its pull inwards.

She spent the rest of the day with Jackie. The aunt was the better part of ten years younger than her mother and—married to an accountant—did not seem to possess that worn quality which ultimately marked anyone who associated themselves with dairy cattle. She was jolly too, and had a genuine gift for levity, whereas Sally's mother had maintained her silence and air of endurance rather than give way to irony. This afternoon was not marked by any particular urban excitement designed to comfort Sally for her imminent return to the bush. A journey to the Italian greengrocers; some wurst for her children's and husband's lunches. Though the powers of the earth had decided that wurst would be called "devon" now, the meat was still in the process of taking on that new, solid British identity. Then to the grocer's—Moran & Cato's. Dazzling metropolitan experiences!

It was four o'clock then. The children whom the aunt intended for university were studying in their rooms—they possessed their own desks, no homework on kitchen tables in this house—and Naomi Durance arrived. Her knock was answered by her aunt while Sally was reading a magazine at the kitchen table. Sally heard her arrival and settled herself for facing her sister. Entering the living room she saw Naomi wearing a white jacket over a light blue dress, and carrying a straw hat with a blue band. She managed with an easy, urbane air her clothing and her striking green eyes and long features and her mother's sweetness about the long lips. She was also fit to be feared and worshipped in the best of makeup. Even their aunt greeted her as if she were an exciting visitation. The kids came out of their rooms wearing smiles of anticipation. She had brought with her a box of chocolates.

When the kids had taken chocolates back to their desks to help them with Euclid, Naomi began. What a surprise I got, Sally, when the colonel and matron told me another Durance—yes, Sally Durance—was down here.

She spoke softly like a magistrate pretending it was pleasant information but really taking it as another instance of human folly for which Sally would need to pay. This brought out something unwished-for and sullen in Sally.

Naomi said, Why didn't you ask me, instead of bothering Aunt Jackie? I could have put you up.

Yes, Sally wanted to say. The two killing daughters together. What a happy arrangement!

I just wanted to make my own plans, Sally mumbled. No offense intended.

And who's looking after Papa? I was just wondering.

Sally looked up into Naomi's potent eyes. You aren't. I'm not. But I've made sure he's taken care of.

But how does he feel at the moment?

He doesn't say. I've set up the Sorley girl to cook his meals. But at least twice a week Mrs. Sorley herself comes over with the daughter and brings scones and fruitcake. He may be lonely but he doesn't say. Anyhow, all those who have grown children will feel lonely sooner or later, won't they?

Naomi looked at the aunt as if all this were a slight against her too. Then she asked, But don't you think one daughter away is enough?

I don't know why it's a law of the universe that it's you who's away, said Sally.

She knew this was another mistake. She was having too much of the fight before the fight had been declared. Naomi doesn't want me to go home for Papa's sake but because I am a walking reproach to her. As I am to myself, but I need the great distraction of distance and wounds to forget it.

I am older, Naomi said, soft but taut. That's an accident of birth. I came here when Mama was healthy and you were training by your own choice at the Macleay. There was not so much need for one of us to be home as there is now. If you had been the older sister, you would be in my position and I would be in yours and without resenting it. But I got set up here and found new obligations before Mama got ill. It's an accident of the situation prevailing when I came here.

Well, the prevailing situation now is this war.

Yes, and that is dangerous, you know. Father could lose us both. There are deadly ships out there, between here and France. Read the *Herald*. Admiral von Spee's ships from China are already snooping about somewhere in the Pacific.

Sally felt heat enter her face. You look after your own safety, she told her sister, and I will mine.

The pretty aunt was gazing at her hands. The conversation was wearing through its fake-pleasant fabric. Rawness was eating its way out.

I am just saying, Naomi continued, that your turn will come and will probably prove a better tilt at life than I've had.

When will that be though? When I'm forty-five? Of course I feel uneasy about it all, and Papa doesn't publish his feelings every morning so I don't know for a dead certainty how he stands and what he needs. But if needs exist, it's *his* right and duty to say what they are, not yours.

She had never debated Naomi in such hard terms before. Aunt Jackie was becoming anxious. It was wrong to wrestle like this in their aunt's home.

Let's not quarrel, Naomi, said Sally then, fearing the chasm all at once and unwilling to be sucked back into girlishness and surly debate. Let's have some tea, eh? Because they won't accept me in any case, so there's no argument.

Maybe they won't take me either. But if they do take us both . . . ?

Well, it's expected to finish by next summer. Your *Herald* said that. If it's right about German admirals then it's right about that as well.

Their aunt was now occasionally opening her mouth and framing her lips.

Aunt Jackie, Sally said, I didn't mean anything by calling for tea in what is your house.

No, said Aunt Jackie, firm at last. But I will make it now. No help required! You two sit and speak calmly, please. Because it is—as you said—*my* house.

Sally became aware that the young cousins had come from their rooms to linger at the end of the hallway and listen to their older cousins' exchange. They turned back to their study as their mother moved to the kitchen. Sally sat in an easy chair, Naomi in the center of the sofa. Naomi said softly, I suppose you can still withdraw. It's not like the army. You're not a soldier.

Neither are you, whispered Sally across the room. We're equal in that.

You're starting again, Naomi pointed out. And you barely have a smile for either your auntie or me.

I am still in mourning, said Sally. So are you. That changes what we say and do.

This was so close to admitting their conspiracy that she looked away and felt a demeaning moisture appear on each eyelid. She wiped it briskly away.

Naomi rose and came to Sally and leaned down to put her arms around her shoulders. It was a clumsy caress. Durances weren't good at broad gestures.

I always thought of you as safe back there at home. I don't think of you as safe when you're down here, planning on being reckless.

Sally was certain that her sister was nine-tenths genuine in what she said, and knew nine-tenths was a great deal. She rose, kissed Naomi on the spot where her black hair arched over the left ear. Sally thought as they embraced how their mother's rivers of blood ran in them but could not concur.

The next morning at the door of the hall at Victoria Barracks sat a list of nurses acceptable to tend to soldiers in far places. Both the Durance girls' names were on it, the name of the one who had expected to be and of the one who hadn't.

Inside the stone drill hall was a great echo of women, a shrilling with an only partly successful contralto attempt by some matron to settle things down. Young women crowded up to take out of the hands of two confused young men—the colonel's orderlies—a sheet of paper on which their required clothing was listed. Having received the form, some found its prescribed garments comic and read them aloud mockingly, hooting at items even as the orderlies suggested they cross the hall to a glum sergeant at a table who was issuing money orders to cover the cost of the uniforms.

At a further table, cloth bags containing buttons and insignia were handed out. These were inspected with more reverence than the list. A silver Rising Sun collar badge lay in there, to be worn at the throat, and silver jacket buttons on which Australia was depicted geographically, and two boomerang-shaped metal insignia which spelled out "Australia" on the tunic shoulders.

Sally had not laid eyes on Naomi until she saw her ahead in the money queue. This was made up of recognizable hospital types—the pretty young ones always in trouble with matrons because their beauty might render them flighty and attractive to registrars and interns. Then plump, wide-hipped little women, aged beyond thirty, medical nuns, in effect, supposed by stereotype to be sour-mouthed but in Sally's experience often triumphant in their unfettered singleness, and smiling now at the new prospect this milling hall promised. Some severer-looking older women of the rank of sisters, who hid often genial souls but had learned that a neutral face endeared them to doctors and matrons. And, suddenly, sui generis, as they say, Naomi in her good green suit.

It is no humiliation for me, thought Sally, to take the sergeant's money. But it was strange to see Naomi there—in line with the less august for a small sum of cash. On an impulse Sally asked the girls in front of her whether they minded if she joined her sister.

They flung their arms around each other with a force left unspent from yesterday's quarrel. And in its compass not all grievance was tamed but at least the residue was put to momentary rest. Naomi stepped back and shook her head.

From now on, Sally promised herself, I reserve the right to be a head-shaker too. I have as much right to be amazed by her.

Then Naomi got to the sergeant and signed for the money he doled out with creaky care from a cash box. He made her sign the accounts book. Next, Sally. Naomi now went to say hello to a friend from her hospital. Sally had walked back about ten paces across the hall, a little confused about what to do next—shop for war at once or go home to her aunt's for some tea—when she saw an oval-faced, pretty young blue-gray–eyed woman wearing an orange summer dress and a cardigan over it, with a yellow jaunty hat on her head, and her light brown hair piled up. The girl said, Miss . . . Nurse, I can do it for you for a guinea plus a quid for fabric. Both the jacket and skirt with the cape and the gray working dress and a pinafore thrown in. Got my own sewing machine. Good as shop-bought, I guarantee. No delays. Only got one other order. You've got your belt already, no doubt. Hat, veil, and shoes you'll have to get yourself.

I've got the veil already, said Sally, as if this would put an end to the commercial impulse of the woman in the orange dress.

The oval-faced young woman shook her head in apparently genuine bewilderment. These girls'd rather waste their money. I don't know what sort of homes they come from. Fathers must own a bank or all be country doctors, I wouldn't be surprised.

The broad, easy humor of the girl's face made Sally shy. Thanks, but my sister and I are actually on our way to Hordern's now.

Come on, said the girl, lowering her head, looking up under auburn eyebrows. Some would consider this undue push on her part. Others, businesslike determination. Come on, dear, she whispered. If you don't like what I do, I won't charge you for it. I need the quid for fabric, so you'll have to take the risk and give me that to begin with. I'll give you that back too if you aren't thoroughly delighted. I mean gray serge? I run it up all the time. I've done gray serge for nuns and they never complained.

Sally hesitated. But the absolute promise of refund fascinated her, and a suspicion of an energetic rectitude in the girl made the issue one of gambling on character as against the bewilderment and boredom of shopping. They both stood there, thinking each other over.

Look, the girl resumed at the end of a few seconds' silence. I'm the sort of person the shops'd use anyhow, if I wanted to slave on it full-time.

A pound as a deposit then?

No, scratch that, said the girl. I can tell you're a solid type. I don't need anything.

But then, as if she were checking up on Sally's bona fides: Where do you nurse?

Sally told her—a bit like a soldier from a poor regiment forced to admit its name. The other woman nodded though, finding no grounds for embarrassment in the words "Macleay District."

I'm St. Vincent's, she said. Nuns took me in on a scholarship. I'm Honora Slattery. Hate being called Nora though. I draw the line at that. *Honora*. Please observe.

Sally surrendered her name too. This was one of those Irish, Sally knew, who generally didn't understand the line between good manners and stubbornness. They would take Australia over and downwards, her father always said, with their horse-racing and their drinking and their hidden contempt for the King.

I absolutely promise, said Honora Slattery, as if to allay Sally's sectarian suspicion, I won't be doing more than three girls plus mine. You see, I want to lay a bit of money up for Mama and himself. The old fella's a waterside worker. Sometimes we're flush, sometimes we're eating kumquats and lard.

She winked.

And just in case the hospital ship sinks, Honora Slattery ended.

Sally laughed and shook her head at the foreshadowing of this unlikely tragedy. They exchanged addresses. You can call my aunt, anyhow, when you're finished, said Sally. She's got a telephone.

Mother of God! said Honora. I've blundered in amongst the aristocracy.

No, Sally said. I'm a dairy farmer's daughter. But, I tell you, you'd better be good.

For what mocking, corrective words would Naomi feel entitled to utter, inspired by Slattery's failure and Sally's own gullibility?

Honora Slattery said, You can put the house on it.

Now a woman with a foghorn—who described herself as Chief Matron Appleton—called them to order. She had open features and that easiness of command of such women.

She told them they must meet again in a week at eight o'clock in the morning to be instructed on the army, on issues of soldiers and military units. They would be introduced to the whole gamut of duties affecting orderlies and nurses—from the front line to the general hospitals behind it. For now, they would fill in one more form to entitle them to military pay, and then could return either to their homes or to their civil nursing duties until required. Those who had more than twenty miles to travel could apply for a warrant.

They all took final turns at desks with pens and ink to fill the pay forms, women of forty elbowing their way with twenty-year-olds barely past their exams. Each form was dropped at a desk at the front of the hall where, after an orderly scanned them, they were placed in a cardboard box. The women left uncertainly. The plain dismissal—and the cardboard box where they'd left the record of their years—seemed too flimsy and insignificant to contain the shift they had managed.

At the top of the steps outside, Naomi was waiting, pulling on velvet gloves. Sally thought the question of shopping for kit would come up. Well, Naomi said instead, we must send poor Papa a telegram. He ought to know tout de suite.

Who is going to send it?

I will. That's only fair.

So Sally pressed telegram money on her and then surrendered herself to the strangeness of looking out over the parade ground to the Georgian gatehouse, where two soldiers in their big hats guarded Victoria Barracks from the malice of the emperor of Germany. There, as well, young talkative men played around and waited in line for their chance to invade the military premises and offer themselves.

I'll go home for a few days, Sally said. Since the sergeant's paying. I have to square things with the matron and with Papa.

But first, for the measuring-up, Sally arrived at Honora's place in

Enmore. It proved a dim but loud home, many brothers and sisters, a thin but young-looking mother, a hulking, sullen father reading the *Australian Worker* in the kitchen, and beyond all a veranda set up as a seamstress's workshop.

And that night, it was back to the *Currawong*. Sally loved the great coastal reach and the strenuous swell now that her mother was safe from suffering it. And the angles headlands adopted to inland mountains—which told her just about where she was on the map. She got one of Kempsey's two charabancs which waited up the slope from the wharf and took passengers to addresses in town and round the river. At last it rattled over the Sherwood bridge. The house was empty, her father gone somewhere, and the dray gone. It suited her to walk the two or more miles over to Macleay District on its hill above the convenient cemetery and told the matron and was treated as a woman who had somehow managed an astounding stunt. She was back at lunchtime. When she faced her widowed father he answered her with a terrible uncomplaining. After all, he'd already had the telegram.

It's a good and valorous thing to do, he asserted, nodding and weighing. And the one stipulation is you take care of each other.

When she overexplained the permanent arrangements she would make to get Mrs. Sorley's daughter in to cook, he waved aside the idea. Then—in her fever of guilt—she rode over to the genial widow Sorley's house to tell her what had happened. Even the red-yellow dust of the road in between had a different nature, as if it was preparing itself to be sighted by her no longer, her departure written into its atoms, making it someone else's road. She was greeted with the widow's full-blooded praise, a jar of blackberry jam as a gift, and an invitation to drink tea. Mrs. Sorley had never seemed reduced to an air of frailty by that freak slippage of the cedar that crushed her marriage. An ax blow left or right might have utterly altered the fall of that great hammer—the one that unluckily toppled on her husband. But these speculations didn't fill the house.

Mrs. Sorley's daughter had already brought the news of the original telegram the Durance girls had sent home from Sydney, so Mrs.

Sorley was apprised—she said—of the gallantry of the Durance girls, and her fifteen-year-old son made muttering noises about wishing it was him. Sally assured the widow she did not expect her to take any special trouble—Papa had declared himself quite up to the business of sustaining himself. In many ways, Sally knew, he was as strong as when he was a boy. His grief as a bereaved soul was more somber than Mrs. Sorley's, but he had hammered out a deal with it.

Not only did her father see her off again at the wharf in East Kempsey but so did Mrs. Sorley, her daughter, and two sons. Mrs. Sorley presented Sally this time with two little sacks of lavender to keep the sisters' clothes fresh. There were a number of young men rowdy on the deck of the steamer, waving good-bye to friends and families from throughout the town and the valley. Their whistling and shouting almost swamped the hushed good-byes of her father. With this mob of overexcited recruits, escaping jobs in Central Kempsey or on some dismal farm, Mr. Durance's own loss of two daughters did not seem as singular. Shouting went up a pitch and women's voices from the wharf became shriller when the *Currawong* eased away from the pier and from the shore on which she had assembled the materials for her mother's killing. There were men still drinking in the pub above the dock—their shadows could be seen through windows—and from the balcony of the Irish-owned general store which served the east of the town, a girl of perhaps fifteen years gazed out with the half interest worthy of the regular steamer's going.

Already, separated from the riverbank and turned towards the greater darkness of the less-settled downriver reaches and swamps, Sally felt she was no longer held by the duty of memory and might now be free to forget who she was for long hours at a time. Concern for her father dwindled at once. She was confident again in his ruggedness. She had been taken off that subtle and self-manufactured hook.

The *Archimedes* I

The corps was of some thirty nurses who were put to work in civil hospitals, the military as yet having neglected to create even one of their own. Sally stayed in Naomi's flat and worked at the Coast Hospital, which she reached by tram, a conveyance that gave her thought time. She read war news from the opened *Herald*s and *Telegraph*s of other riders. She went to Honora Slattery's again, and the uniform and the on-duty clothes were splendid and neatly stitched as promised. And no alteration was necessary, at which Honora herself seemed unsurprised and smug.

It was not a great wait, however—perhaps a week—until they were given railway tickets to the golden city, to Melbourne—the other pole to Sydney's civic pretensions, the two cities holding each other in orbits of mutual contempt. On the railway south—especially when they changed from train to train at Albury on the great dividing river, given neither state consented to recognize the value of the other's rail gauge—committees of women fussed over them, ordered lumpish boys to carry their bags from the New South Wales carriages to the Victorian ones, and gave them tea and pounds of cake. Each cup of tea and morsel of cake Sally absorbed removed her further from the networks of duty and blame. Each cup was the cup of forgetfulness. For stretches of hours, she did not think of her crime or her abandonment.

The ship that would take them lay at Port Melbourne. Its name was *Archimedes*. They were driven to it direct by motorcar from Swan-

ston Street, without being able to test Melbourne's claim of being supreme in the Antipodes for public gardens and architectural splendor.
The *Archimedes* shone at its dingy pier. Here was a passenger steamer
painted white and banded in green with, amidships, a vast red cross.
The cross bespoke their right to transit oceans and to turn up in Europe or elsewhere—they were not told where—unmolested. It was
therefore unlike the convoys already departed which were vulnerable
and for whose sake many—including the prime minister, it was said—
held their breath. Nonetheless it was soon clear that even their ship
would be darkened by night, and sailors and medical orderlies forbidden to smoke on deck after dusk. The *Archimedes* was estimated by
Naomi—on whatever basis—to be sixteen thousand tons.

The women from New South Wales were first on board and thus
created the very first echoing steely cries of their own and the *Archimedes*'s new careers. Their four-women cabins were forward on the
same deck—one deck beneath the promenade—as a cavernous hospital space was created by the removal of partitions amidships. Here
medical orderlies would sleep in hammocks as they all steamed to the
conflict.

From the railing they watched women from other places come
aboard after assembling on the dock. They saw the stylish Victorians
in lower-calf-length skirts, and wondered in what other ways these
women might assert superiority. They nudged each other at the sight
of a dozen Tasmanians in long, hooped skirts which looked to belong
to the old century. Yet when these girls came aboard there were hellos
and swapped greetings and all the rest of the manic conviviality that
suited the situation.

The vivid afternoon on which the *Archimedes* pulled away from
the wharf, the patriots and families left behind waved with a startling
energy, putting all their sinews into it as if there were a law that said
the stronger the farewell the more certain the return. The band played
"Annie Laurie" and those unavoidable and glib songs of departure—
"Auld Lang Syne" and so on. They could still hear the plaintive brass

on the wharf as the swell of Port Phillip hit them, and as the *Archimedes* saddled itself for its real business with real waters.

The most casually worldly nurse—Sally had heard by dinnertime in the main dining room—was a girl from Melbourne named Karla Freud. She was dark-haired and had sung for that famous theatrical company in Melbourne, the Tait brothers. But her parents had somehow dragged her off the stage and set her to nursing. Glossy-haired, lovely Freud did not stick with the Melbourne girls but seemed to seek novelty with the New South Wales women and Tasmanians. She brought to conversations with them what people called "presence." Somehow it became known she was a soprano. Part by her own desire but part due to constant urgings that arise when an obvious "theatrical" appears in a group, she was soon singing in the officers' mess—"Sally, Sally, Pride of Our Alley" and "Believe Me If All . . ." And humorous songs with a flirtatious edge, such as "Gee! But I Like Music with My Meals"—songs utterly suitable for her energy, her taste for droll fun, and her sculpted, thespian face.

Just the same, nursing's won the fight with the Theatre Royal, she declared to her fellow nurses after returning to their table. Because I don't have the courage to be Sarah Bernhardt.

Well, now you're really stuck, said Honora, who suspected Freud of being a bit pretentious. Even the papers can't pretend that the right side's winning hands down. We might be busy for a few years.

Right, said Freud without rancor. If I take nursing as my rehearsal period, I'll just about be back onstage at the Royal by the time I'm fifty.

A fair-haired girl named Leonora Casement—a Melbourne nurse—was a year younger than Sally. She must have begun her training as little more than a child. Yet she had confidence and wasn't callow and was taken round the promenade deck by a tall surgeon named Fellowes. If you looked at them walk past, you thought, there goes an unblighted pair—no dishonesties, no oddities, and no out-of-control signs of attachment. Melbourne girls said these two had known each other before the war, at the Austin Hospital.

Then the great sea troughs took over—the mad pitching, yawing, rolling, and the spasms and exhausted torpors of mal de mer. The Bight that bit everyone, as someone said. By the time the ship skirted Western Australia without actually sighting it and reached north over the sweltering equator, injuries to the medical orderlies were routine in the ship's hospital. There was one man badly beaten. A tuberculosis case as well: a nineteen-year-old of good frame, yet who should not have been recruited. But the nurses were under-employed and many were inveigled by officers, as Leonora had been, into turns on the deck.

Sally met a confident nurse named Carradine—yes, she admitted, the federal politician Mr. Joe Carradine who was attorney-general was also her father-in-law. She was quite open to letting you know she was married. It had been a secret before but on the *Archimedes* she needed to make it known to others lest she be pressured into man-to-woman promenades. Carradine's reddish hair framed a bony but lively face, and her body was lean but full-hipped. Her husband was a lieutenant of infantry—in the very first regiment of the First Brigade—who had gone off on the convoy weeks before.

As Leonora Casement was an exemplar for girls' courting, Elsie Carradine was a model for the ordained fidelities. Elsie walked by day only and with groups, to ensure nothing in her might be let loose which—through no intent of her own—would call to men in a way from which the dignity of their polished belts and insignia could not protect them or her.

Naomi amazed her sister by walking the deck at any agreed-upon time with a bulky, broad-shouldered captain named Ellis Hoyle, an infantry soldier left behind by the first convoy, who was—contrary to the letter of international law—fetching a ride aboard the *Archimedes*. It seemed to Sally that Naomi was thereby showing something her sister had not known was there—a lightness, a social grace. Naomi would never have done this sort of thing in the Macleay, since people there observed any sauntering pair with knowing headwags and smirks, wanting to herd them towards inept marriages. Sally walked the main deck with Honora, Freud, and Carradine, still awkward at the sight of her sister. She was fascinated that Naomi could balance the murder of their mother with a stroll alongside an officer above the ocean.

Sometimes Sally's group were squired by medical officers. All parties were free here from the false distance which operated in civil hospitals. Sally gauged that for different reasons—larrikin raucousness in one, aloof whimsy in the other—the officers liked Honora and Freud.

Three matrons sat at the captain's table, and the third of them—the most junior—drove the pace of talk and caused men to laugh robustly. She had done a lot of traveling while bush nursing in the Western District, Gippsland, and the northeast of Victoria. Her name was Matron Mitchie. The other two matrons—more entitled to capture the conversation—smiled thin-lipped and shook their heads in a tiny, only half-approving way at Matron Mitchie's daredevil strut across the narrow wire strung between humor and vulgarity. They seemed to think Mitchie less than an appropriate matron and a poor exemplar for the girls. And yet where were they from? Sally wondered. Probably escaping some enslaving and skimping farm that yielded plenty after flood but was barren in drought. Their fathers, too, had in their day crept to the bank manager and feared that the big stock and station agents would take them over and send them as poor-paid managers back to their land or as less than full beings off to the city.

The reason she thought of farms was that Sally knew from her own example that country girls were fools for nursing. They believed it was the greatest thing open to them. They perhaps hoped to marry doctors. These three hadn't married doctors, but Matron Mitchie was having so much fun on her own terms that in her case it was just as well. When she made men laugh, the laugh was not a concession to quaintness but came gushing up from the area between the sternum and abdomen.

This Mitchie woman had waddled aboard, thick-hipped, in Melbourne. From the start her eyes darted as if the more faces she scammed the happier she'd be. Yet this was the sort of matron whose frown could break a girl's heart purely because young women would want to please her so much. Whereas the other two were in some ways what Sally wanted to become—unhumbled, immune from the normal shocks to womanhood inherent in household squalor and husbands and children, yet relentlessly careful and outside and above life. They were practiced in unmanning younger doctors and making nurses quake. Patients called them dragons, and Sally could understand how they applied and invested themselves into becoming dragons.

Across the table at which Sally sat, Honora was having on a small scale the same effect on Dr. Fellowes and other young medical officers that Matron Mitchie was having on the ship's captain and the colonels. Her liveliness was not muted at all by the fact that the dining rooms of steamers, and officers in Sam Brownes and leather leggings, were not familiar to her. She was a fast learner. At St. Vincent's, she told the young medical officers, they had the methylated spirits addicts in. These fellows fought each other in the park at Darlinghurst in the shade of the gaol and came into emergency wards in the early mornings displaying gashes they couldn't remember how they'd received. She had been dressing the leg wound of a derelict, she said, when he began having fits. She ran for help but when she returned with an intern she found the man recovered, sitting on a chair and drinking from her bottle of medicinal alcohol.

It was how she told it that worked, and their willingness to be amused.

Affection for Honora had more than crept upon Sally, and she knew her to be a woman of honor by such a simple test as her dealings over the uniforms. So well finished were they that other nurses asked Sally if she had been to a tailor instead of to Hordern's. A woman of her word, Honora! Of many skittering but honest words. She was one of those girls who said fairly frequently too, When I'm married . . . They didn't contemplate any other future state and did not even take into their calculations the idea they might live on, solitary but free.

Yet Honora was not anxious for doctors, or so she told Sally. Too conceited, she said. Too used to obedience from patients. Likely to bring the habit home!

That's the sort of thing Honora might say at table now. Promising MOs—as everyone called the doctors—that none of them was human enough nor the right kind for her.

To mark their transit over the equator, the captain and ship's officers ordered the creation of a big swimming pool of canvas on the open lower deck aft and filled it with seawater. It was to be the center of the initiation into equator hopping. Some of the others had already been across the line going to or coming from the northern world: a number of the doctors had come to Australia in the first place from Edinburgh or Dublin or the great hospitals of London and were returning to the hemisphere of their birth. But most medical officers and orderlies and nurses had been born in Australia and had thought—as Sally had— that the train between Melbourne and Sydney or the coastal steamer from Brisbane might be the greatest journey the world would ever offer them. Yet now here was *the* equator—the burning and unconsumed filament that divided the world of southern innocence from the world of northern gravity of intent, and the hemisphere of colonists from the hemisphere of the owners.

Around the pool men and nurses dressed as gypsies and pirates had water thrown on them and were ducked under and made to suffer other rituals. The nurses had actually sat in their cabins making costumes for this. When Sally, feeling that she was disqualified from this flippancy both by nature and the serious shadow of her mother's death, failed to apply herself to that business, Honora presented her with a passable Queen of Hearts costume in any case, the red hearts applied to the puff-sleeved blouse with small, expert stitching. The casual, rapid-working love that had gone into this fancy dress frightened Sally.

On the ceremonial day she dressed with the others and moved aft. But a companionway presented itself and she took the risk of swinging herself down it to the hospital level, the level on which—much further astern—the jollity would be staged. If she was seen, the others knew she had been seasick before, so she was entitled to a little flash of nausea. She excused her way past a number of wide-eyed orderlies, opened the double doors into the hospital and rushed through the empty spaces to the nurses' pan room a little way forward. Facing it was a further cabin which was unlocked. She entered it. This was meant to be a pharmacist's office. But wherever the ship's stocks of medicines were, they were not here. The empty shelves made it even more a hiding space. The Queen of Hearts closed the door. She could hear running on the deck above her. From aft arose mocking, willfully farting bugle sounds and shouts and the profound echo of men's laughter. There was no chair to sit on in here. But she stood willingly in her vivid dress amongst the blank shelves.

Someone was passing. She heard the door open. Mrs. Carradine was there. Her reddish hair tumbled out of an eighteenth-century sea captain's tricorn.

I thought I saw you creep down here, she whispered. Are you all right, dearie? Can I fetch your sister?

Sally's face blazed. No, thanks, she said, surly. Look, it's just I'm not good at all these geographical hijinks.

Carradine raised her bony nose and hooted, and Sally began gratefully to laugh with her.

I'll get up there and endure it for Eric's sake, Carradine admitted. He's three weeks ahead of me in his convoy. He's gone through something like it. Or maybe they won't even let them have a ceremony in the convoy. But I'll go through it anyway.

Could I ask you a favor? said Sally. Let me stay in here. I'll be brave next time. I'm sure Naomi will be up there anyhow.

Of course, said Mrs. Carradine. Naomi seems confident in all things.

Carradine stepped up, smoothed Sally's locks, and suddenly kissed her forehead through them.

You have lovely black hair, you know, she said. I wish I did, instead of this carrot mop. Just as well I'm married. I never thought I'd get away with it, given this head of hair.

She stepped back. Okay, Queenie, she said and then winked. She closed the door like a friend and was gone. Sally would say to Honora, I felt sick. There'll be other fancy-dress balls, Honora, where I can wear the dress.

Naomi indeed seemed confident in all things. Taller than Sally. Tallness often imbued confidence. Even before high school Sally felt subject to bemused comparisons with Naomi by teachers and other girls. Some of it was her own sense of being less. Some of it was real. Naomi was good at the outside world. It was only with the inner world of the family that she took on an air of distance and exile. She would have no trouble with a "crossing-the-line" party. Things would falter only the next time she and Sally met up.

Across glittering, tepid seas they put into Colombo. With sailors and non-officers confined to the ship, unruly orderlies climbed down the anchor chain at night to steal launches and go ashore. The nurses and medical officers were permitted to land. Met at the wharf by various British middle-aged gentlemen, who assured them that they were in the most beautiful segment of the world and that the Singhalese people were the most handsome on earth, they were taken through a city of stalls and temples and giant Buddhas rising above shops at the end of thoroughfares, and then out along a lovely coast, where women in vivid fabric and brown-faced compact men—machetes in hand—watched them pass. They walked on the ramparts of Galle as the middle-aged men expanded on the subject of the Portuguese, the Dutch, and now the British ownership of the bright-though-hazed reaches of the harbor, and drove away some poverty-grimed members of the most beautiful race on earth, who were trying to sell the nurses fake coins from Dutch wrecks. Lemonade on a hotel veranda of the Amangalla Hotel beside a Dutch church was different from Macleay lemonade—redolent of an extra layer of spice and strangeness.

Oasis

Sally wrote to her father every four days or so, letters replete with a relentless newsiness designed to mask any shame at marooning him on his farm. Now he could be charmed awhile—her theory went—by stories of alien marvels and puzzles.

I never thought I would see the strange things I've seen and it goes to show how many ways there are of being a human.

She used all powers of language and scene-making she could—casting Port Suez as a town of many-storeyed buildings and pink hills in the background.

The great Canal shone so sharp and blue in the midst of sand and all along encampments of Tommies and Indians—wandering amongst tents—who looked pretty bored and cheered us. In the Bitter Lakes in the middle of the Canal there was a crowd of ships moored there. Then we were back into the arrow-straight canal and came to the shady town of Ismaïlia—shaded by palm trees, of course I mean. There we moored and came ashore for the first time. A lot of good-looking Arab houses of stone, and mansions people in the know tell me look French. Older Egyptian women dressed in black but urchin girls running around barefoot in orange and yellow and blue tatters. Some women carry big bundles

*on their heads. You can't help thinking, what's your life like, Mrs.
Egypt? How does it match up to a farmer's life in the Macleay?*

*The train carriages look cranky old affairs with not enough
windows, but once you're inside they're comfortable. The village
houses on the way to Cairo are all mud-walled. They look flat
and unfinished as if they're waiting for another floor to go on top.
People laboring on green patches of earth—they have irrigation
from the Sweetwater Canal that winds for miles and into Cairo.
The camels mince along with lowered heads and when they rest in
shade you see their owners asleep on top of them.*

*You ought to see Cairo station! It has a great glass roof and
is very grand in an Arabic sort of way—though British built.
Orderlies carry everything for us except our valises. This is pretty
flash. They're like porters but you don't have to slip them a shil-
ling a bag!*

*Many beggars and it is a shock to the system. Blind children—
some tell me that their own parents get them blinded in one eye by
a hot noodle when they are just babies—all so they can beg. And
this in what they call the British Empire.*

*More soon, dear Papa. I hope the Sorley girl is looking after
you.*

That last sentence written with edginess and with eyes half-closed.

She could barely make a stab at writing letters about Cairo. It overflowed the borders of any possible letter. Here at the railway station
they were loaded by a transport officer—four at a time—into open
gharries, each one driven by a soft-speaking brown man in a tarboosh
and wearing a crisp white jacket over a jalabiya. They were carried
out in late afternoon into a frenzy of people and traffic. A city that
was everything, too many people moving with too many ambitions,
too many hopes and destinations. It was at the same time a glimpse
of moored riverboats on—could it be?—the Nile. (These were of-

ficers' clubs where Nubian waiters in red tarbooshes and long white robes glided along with drinks trays held high.) It was people carrying all possible items on their heads—a child's coffin new-bought, a lounge chair, a haunch of camel meat, a bed. It was camels and donkeys on pavements and the smell of their urine, and men seated by them on mats working with sewing machines or turning furniture legs on little lathes. It was car horns of the army and of the rich blaring at one time with the clang of trams and the trumpet blasts of tram conductors. It was street sellers leaning into your gharry trying to sell flyswatters and whisks, scarabs and lottery tickets, and passing British soldiers telling them darkly to clear out—*imshi!*—and leave the ladies alone. It was raucous native bands in unexplained processions booming and howling—brass and trumpet—and shoe shiners crying, "'Allo, George" to the soldiers, and the soldiers with cockney accents calling, "'Ello, sweetie" at the nurses' gharries. Whistles from Australian soldiers—wandering the streets like men used to the place—frosted the hubbub with levity. And then the strange sight of the dragoman—who could translate a letter into English or Arabic or Greek or French—trudging along with his portable desk, pens, and ink and looking for business without business looking for him. Effendis—Egyptian gentlemen in well-cut suits and tarbooshes—sat at café tables talking at an impossible pace yet like centers of calm in all the fury. There were acrobats, fire-eaters, snake charmers—all yelling out at passing Australian and British soldiers for baksheesh. Shocking beggars—young girls with infants, crippled crones, their hands stained pink and yellow, and every kind of blindness and crookedness of body and amputation—as if these people themselves were the ones who'd taken part in a recent and very savage war. And if you looked at the sky you saw kites circling above the putrid streets, waiting to descend to their abominable yet cleansing meals of flesh. Even amongst the more talkative women in the gharries making for their hospital across the city at Mena the chatter stilled a little.

All this just the surface anyhow, the visible part of the crammed ocean of life here that you were not equipped to deal with in any way other than by looking at it—if at all—at a tangent.

Dear Papa,
How can I tell you of what Naomi and I have seen . . . ?

As the city was crossed, the peaks of the pyramids showed up ahead in a dust-tainted twilight. They had been heavenly creatures from picture books, gigantic entities in everyone's imagination, and it was hard now to believe they were tethered to a specific patch of earth—that they could be casually seen and perhaps approached and then passed by as you'd pass a town. Sweat ran down the sides of Sally's face and she could hear girls even from other gharries swearing they would wear their straw hats full-time. Bare, hard ground led to groves where their hospital lay with the pyramids blue now and pressing closer, pushing their reality on the women. The palmed oasis ahead seemed flat as a stage painting and defied belief too. The road took them into the trees to a flat-roofed mansion with a red cross on its veranda-ed wall. Once a hunting lodge—they'd been told—where the kings of Egypt invited their friends to shoot gazelles. More recently a hotel. Now a hospital.

The women were quartered in small rooms with spacious windows on the upper floors. Three beds waited in the room Sally shared with Carradine and Slattery—with Naomi next door, since they still kept their distance. One large lowboy and one deal table and a chair completed the amenities of the room. For bareness, said Carradine, it put a boarding-school room to shame. Yet from these windows could be seen across treetops—in the phenomenal blueness of dusk—the pyramid of Cheops.

Eric Carradine was in the Mena camp out there in the desert and that evening turned up suntanned and handsome to visit his wife. His brow was a bit foreshortened, women said, but he was A1 apart from that. It was apparent that Elsie and Eric Carradine were the least striving, most relaxed of people, with the long frenzy of searching for each other behind them.

One of the senior matrons spoke to the nurses in their mess on the first night and convinced them that in these premises their conversation must not be above a murmur, their laughter suppressed, their talk with patients reduced to the minimum of politeness and information. The chief medical officer—whom they had never seen before but who had come in now—was very elderly, well over sixty. Well, welcome then, ladies, was all he said. Matron will tell you the rest.

He seemed to suggest: since you've insisted on presenting yourselves here, we'll need to have you amongst us.

The matron and colonel seemed at first to be brother and sister in their contempt for nurses. For the girls were set to work scrubbing with carbolic the big rooms which had once been perhaps hotel libraries or ballrooms, while orderlies smoked and mucked about with one another in the shade of trees. Then—more normally—nurses were set to air mattresses and wash down rubber mattress covers and make beds, ready for the brave, shaking out the linen with a thud in the hot, dry air, with a whiplash beneath which their restrained conversation and their muted laughter were permitted. Next they moved out of the house to do similar work in marquees—which the colonel called "brigaded tents"—set in the gardens. A sign, said Honora, that some lunatic thought the huge hotel might not be enough for the wounded.

On a dim path Sally's shoe slipped off the duckboard laid out to the marquee and her ankle was sprained. In her family little pains like this fell instantly under the dictum: if that's the worst thing that happens to you . . . But with her mother—she remembered acutely as she limped—the adage had run out of its capacity to help. With their mother the worst thing had happened and set up its nest in her eye sockets.

To attempt forgetting that, she had only to step out of the grove and she was in infinity. She was sure all at once that this was why the pyramids were built. To deal with the infinity the Egyptians saw in all directions. Desert and those towering objects were so simple and triangular and undeniable that they called up memory of other things that were elemental and undeniable—the sisters' mercy in their mother's bedroom at Sherwood—but also put them in place. To be an accomplice is sometimes to forget for hours that you were one. Utter guilt couldn't be maintained nonstop in a distracting place like this.

Within a day or two they had taken to drinking tea on the roof. There you could sit in clear, cool air since this was winter, and take the improbable but giant paper-cutout-looking pyramids for granted. But if it felt at all chilly up there they convened in the officers' lounge downstairs where Lieutenant Carradine would come visiting with a group of young officers.

The battle was in Europe. There was only a rumor of it in Palestine, where people said the Turks might be on their way to the Canal. But even now the hospital grew fuller than Sally would have expected until—though there were no aged, no children, no women—it took on some of the atmosphere of quiet bustle which was meant to be the mark of a civil hospital. In the absence of conflict men still incurred damage and illness. Because the nights were cold in their desert camps, some had even managed to catch pneumonia. A few were wounded in bayonet drill through clumsiness or the overenthusiasm of a friend they should have parried. There was a young curly-haired man who had broken his leg when a truck full of English soldiers struck him. He was in a plaster cast—the base of his bed raised, the limb hoisted jauntily to match his jaunty demeanor. My own stupid fault, Nurse. You ought to see the dent in that truck. Sorry, can't take you to the dance this Sat'day.

Two wounded Turks—an utter novelty in their strange uniforms— were brought in from Sinai and treated while armed guards stood by their beds.

Beneath a canvas marquee in the garden of Mena House, the phenyl smell of drying duckboards—that cleansing, heavy reek—subdued their conversation. But they were busy too, Carradine and Slattery working elbow to elbow in the canvassed-off pan room advising order-lies on what shelf to put the basins, bed blocks, pans, while they them-selves unloaded—from large, immaculate canvas bags—softer things: towels, sheets, pillowcases, rubber undersheets never used before and lacking the normal cloying smells which came to attach themselves to the best-cleaned sheets in normal wards.

Slattery could be heard giving orders. Hold hard, sonny Jim. That corner there. See!

In the similarly draped-off surgical dressing room near the other end of the tent there was no traffic of orderlies and less air. Along with the young Leonora Casement, a sharp-nosed, sallow young woman named Rosanna Nettice from Melbourne, whose body was—despite her sickly look—full of the promise of energy, was unpacking drugs into the drug cupboard and recording quantities on an appropriate sheet. "Leo" they called Casement. She possessed a breezy, unhaunted soul that would never suit a Durance. A woman already at ease—with her own uncomplicated charm and with a zeal for work.

By shelves of stacked and unopened surgical dressings in the nurses' office, Sally—wearing gloves—laid out and covered the day's surgical trays for treating minor wounds. They as yet had no autoclave. Sterilization depended on a brass spirit heater and a rustic-looking pan for the instruments. But out here the trays and the clamps and retrac-tors, the lancets and forceps would often go unused and unbloodied, the beds as yet empty.

The matron opened the canvas flap of the marquee. Years of gladly accepted authority hid the woman she truly was as it did other issues such as her origins and age. She said, with a pause between the words to combat curtness, You three nurses. Leave that now. Please join me outside.

Outside, the heat fell filtered through palms and weighed on Sally's shoulders. This was the cool season and yet there was no coolness in the glare beyond the oasis. The matron told them they were to follow her down the duckboards and gathered other nurses from other tents into their company as they went. Naomi was one of them and sent the whisper of a questioning smile Sally's way. Carradine was with them too, the patches beneath her eyes looking vacant white as if her faint freckles had been stewed away. Ten nurses in all were led a few hundred yards out into the full light to a fence of barbed wire which surely had not been there yesterday and to a gate where four Australian military policemen kept guard.

Freud murmured briskly, The wounds of Venus.

The gate was unlocked and they entered the space beyond. A tent large enough for a circus lay ahead and the matron led them past other armed military policemen and through a flap left open for ventilation. The place seemed crowded by contrast with the other tents erected around Mena. There were perhaps seventy men sitting on their beds— some bored, some raising younger, softer faces of the kind a person could guess had come from the city, from work indoors. These were suburban cherubs still, untempered by military exercises and desert maneuvers. About ten orderlies moved around the tent on sundry duties. Each of the patients here wore a white armband to declare some purity they had violated. Many held their roll-your-own cigarettes as the nurses passed across their gaze. But they did not cheer as soldiers did if you met them in the bazaars—no normal hellos or queries were called out. In any case, between the nurses and them was located a barrier of five tables, as if the men were to be interviewed.

The matron led the nurses now into a spacious, screened-off area where two large pans boiled above Primus stoves. Orderlies plied their lifters to extract syringes and needles and laid them on trays beside bottles of solution and cotton wool and medicinal alcohol. The matron made the smallest deniable nod to the bottles of clear solution and the rest of the equipment marshalled on the counter. She said, I know you will show no levity in dealing with this grievous business. The colonel's orderlies should ideally do this work but despite his high opinion of them neither will they do it well nor will they be as safe from the mockery of the men—or the men from theirs. It is bad enough that orderlies should be the ones who treat the lesions and chancres!

The two orderlies in the canvassed-off space worked on, extracting syringes and wide-bore, punishing needles from the makeshift autoclaves. They did not seem to notice the slur uttered against them.

You are not deaconesses but military nurses. What you see here, you must see as a military crime. It is not your business to display distaste on the one hand or familiarity on the other.

She weighed them with her eyes to make sure they bore the right degree of somberness. The matron spoke as if she had bought up all the real estate of comment on the issue. She continued.

Either way it is a dosage of 8 drams solution per patient. Those men wearing a tag marked "G"—and I am sure I do not have to explain what that stands for—will attend the furthest table to the right. The patients will approach in columns of two and receive injections of novarsonobillon. As for the others, have you heard of solution 606?

Salvarsan? asked dutiful Leo.

All the nurses knew of 606. If they had not administered it, its myth had fallen over them. Syphilis was the wages of sin and 606 and a course of mercury pills might relieve the sinner of paying those wages fully. Thus some moralists said it was an immoral juice. But then they had never nursed congenitally poxed children.

Will you kindly and without hesitation divide into teams of two? Do put on those rubber gloves.

Sally paired with Freud. As they collected their trays with the syringes and needles and—in their case—the 606 solution, they could hear the matron addressing the men in the main part of the tent and telling them which tables to present themselves to. Sally and Freud and the others passed through the canvas into the main tented ward and took a place at one of the tables for the syphilitics.

It happened that Sally was the one to swab the arms and change needles, Freud to give the injections. It fell out that way barely with-

out their discussing it—perhaps because of Freud's worldliness. By
her presence you could sense that she really knew things that were
still confusing to Sally—the difference between lust and, as they said
in novels, desire. Desire was a cleaner thing by all accounts. But not
clean enough to save you entirely—it seemed—unless desire was concentrated and fixed in place by a flurry of marriage vows. Sally barely
had time to think how interesting the question was and how instructive was this line of men whose plentiful sweat smelled little worse
than that of healthy men from the camp. Sally swabbed the arm of
one who looked ahead, and another who viewed the ceiling and a third
whose eyes were lowered and a fourth who wept and who shuddered
so that Freud was left to say, Please keep it still, will you?

Don't cry, Sally told him. This will fix it.

For this boy wanted the vows and not the blight. All the while
Freud's hand reached with a natural composure. Her movements were
those of a person unafraid of contagion. But even she, Sally noticed,
did not look much at the fallen soldiers who presented themselves,
the casualties of the Wazzir, the suburb of hell within Cairo where
the berserk arrack liquor and the women selling their diseases for baksheesh were domiciled.

But now they were all lambs before the punishing but necessary
wide-bore needle which must be driven in with force, the flesh making its resistance. No one said, Don't hurt a man, Sister. No one said,
Oh cripes, a hornet's got me. Nothing was said because they had a lie
to keep and any utterance might let it out. If—cured one day—they
courted some oblivious girl in Australia, they could not utter the news
that lay contained in this tent. But solution 606 could give you back
your body for the battle or for the distant Australian bedroom where
you might sleep a cured man and die as an honored husband and
cherished father.

Freud handed the syringe to her after brisk use and Sally replaced it from beneath the cloth on the bowl with a fresh one. In
that tent they were party to a military secret. People in Australia did

not know of these first casualties—that there was a desire greater than the desire for battle, that there was a bacterium as yet more grievous than machine guns.

Ellis Hoyle—with whom Naomi had sometimes promenaded on the *Archimedes*—was a man not much older than her who had been training in the vast camp out in the desert beyond Mena House and the pyramids. Naomi had asked Captain Hoyle why such displays were engaged in at two o'clock in the afternoon when the sun was—at least for that reputedly more lenient season—most blatant and when light bounced off the gravel and sands to strike the men in the face under the brims of their bushmen's hats. He said that the generals thought this weather steeled men for unspecified worse things.

In the evening—along with a number of other officers, including Carradine's husband—Hoyle was regularly down at Mena House having tea with the nurses on the hotel roof or on the veranda. He and his friends—young officers barely converted from their normal callings as farmers, bank clerks, sheep breeders, schoolteachers—arrived by commandeered khaki cars. There was even a journalist or two and a very determinedly jolly young Anglican minister from Melbourne who did not serve as a chaplain but as an infantryman.

Since the nurses were not overworked, they slept adequately and their faces gleamed with the strangeness and ease of things as they prepared themselves for these evening visits from officers. They had time to change into their uniform jackets and skirts and good shoes in case the evening developed and they all had dinner together or went on a jaunt after dining in the mess.

Captain Ellis Hoyle was a tailored young man, an inch too square in the jaw so that you could bet he'd turn jowly when he was older. His mouth was long enough for his fellow officers to nickname him Duck. He was a solicitor from the Western District of Victoria and he spoke as if he loved the area in a way that Sally and Naomi had never managed to like the place they came from.

All the young men—like Ellis—had been to Cairo tailors and had
light, well-cut uniforms of fawn which had saved them from the heavy
serge the government of their Commonwealth had first handed them.
Their conversation was by now that of men who knew much about
Egyptian gharry drivers, peddlers and tailors, of men in dirty jalabiyas
selling red roses for "the lady." No mention of the dens of the Wazzir.
These young men might recount amusing tales of this or that soldier,
the hard cases, the rough men from the bush. And all the chatter
called forth out of Sally unexpected laughter, as if they'd been sent to
teach her that old skill. By their energy as much as the force of parody
or satire they diverted both the Durance sisters—the conversation so
much livelier than anything Sally had ever known.

There was always though in the end the matter of where she came
from. Soldiers felt the presence of women couldn't console them unless geography was cleared up first. These young men were all from
more favored homes and places than the Durance sisters. However,
Naomi had the presence for their sort of company—the capacity to
carry it off and seem worldly and not to be overwhelmed by social
castes. By escaping the Macleay early she had rendered such matters
as of no importance. Sally had not learned the same skill yet. Naomi
looked like she could be some pastoral magnate's daughter. On the
strength of that she might one day grow into being a squatter's wife or
some such thing and no one would be able to sniff out that she was
born of a mere one-hundred-and-fifty-acre dairy farmer and had trod-
den in manure on the way to school.

One of the men would suddenly mention dinner in Cairo—at the
Shepheard Hotel or the Windsor or at the Parisiana. The idea was sure
to capture other officers and the nurses with the novelty of an invention. Nurses took the arm of a particular officer. Naomi willingly took
the arm of Ellis Hoyle. But some were left unattached, of whom—by
firm choice—Sally Durance was one and Nettice another. Freud too
was sometimes an unaccompanied woman since she possessed a dark
grandeur that scared men.

Then—at the end of dinner when the last of the wine was served—a proposal would arise that everyone go out by gharry and see the pyramids and the Sphinx by starlight. Drivers would bring up the cars later to take the party back to the hospital and the camp. All of them had of course been to the pyramids many times—all the nurses had hired horses at Mena and ridden out by late afternoon. But night-time was different and emphasized the stone eternity of the things. Naomi and Ellis Hoyle rode in the one gharry, engrossed. How strange to see Naomi prefer someone openly. For there was a bit of surrender in that—and Sally hadn't thought her sister was a girl for surrender.

Sally's own companion—though the gharries could carry more than two, the unuttered rule was that people should travel in couples—turned out to be a tall, rather florid officer named Lieutenant Maclean. He was well-built but not exactly muscular. His heavy body was a bit too present, though not objectionable. Sally wondered whether that meant he would make an easier target than the others. He draped a horse blanket over his knees because it was now cold. But Sally was too squeamish to share it and waved it aside when by gesture he offered it.

You see that, he said, pointing across her body—but his arm not too close—to the gutter full of cabbage leaves. See the leaves stirring there?

The leaves *were* stirring. Now she could see there were at least two children sleeping amongst the husks.

Poor little beggars! he said. It doesn't matter who wins, they'll still sleep out in cabbage leaves.

Though if the Turks came, Sally argued, things might be worse still.

Well, we like to think so, don't we? I wonder what *they'd* say if we asked them. In any case, the Turks aren't coming yet, it seems. Our masters marched us out there and told us to make the chaps dig trenches in the desolation of gravel. But the Turks didn't come.

He laughed but didn't seem angry enough to wish any great harm on Turks or the Ottoman Empire. Even here it was the Germans—advancing on Paris—who held the imagination.

They were on the edges of the city now and Maclean looked up at the dazzle of stars. You've seen more of the enemy than we have, he remarked dreamily. I've got to say, you're all real bricks, you girls. A credit to Australia. Whereas we don't know yet whether we're a credit or not.

Since his doubt seemed sincere, she assured him, I can see *you* striding on—no matter what.

Perhaps she had volunteered too much admiration of his coming warriorhood. For there he was turning to her and leaning forwards so that he could see her eyes, though they were not quite able to be studied under starlight.

Thank you very much, he said. That's a reassuring thought.

They heard laughter from the gharry ahead. Captain Hoyle, said Maclean. He's keen on your sister. You might find a brother-in-law there. Barring accidents.

This astonishing news did not raise or answer the question of whether Naomi was as eager for Ellis Hoyle.

A further tumbling laughter from ahead—but it flirted a little more with the limits of what was considered proper control. Honora. She was with a man named Lionel something-or-other. She was popular with men. Perhaps they misread her by thinking her Celtic loudness meant something else than it did. Sally could tell meanwhile that Maclean didn't laugh unless a walk into a closed door or the collapse of a chair justified it. He was what they called sober. This suited Sally. In the sport of jollity and chat she was by temperament and by her crimes a nonstarter.

Maclean said suddenly and with apparent embarrassment, That Freud girl? Did you know her before?

No. She's from Melbourne.

Jewish, isn't she?

Yes, said Sally and was surprised to find she was envious, in a remote way.

The chaps who were on the *Archimedes* say she has a top-rate voice. But what sort of girl is she? In temperament, I mean.

She is very much a city woman and very amusing. We're all pleasant people as yet, of course. We're on a wonderful journey and we see marvelous things. We haven't been stung so far by anything inconvenient. But I don't think Freud will get stung badly by anything.

Well, he said and chuckled as if he were happy with that degree of information.

She thought all at once it was a bad thing for a man to quiz one woman about another. He should not be allowed too easily to get away with it.

You didn't want me to be your stalking horse for Nurse Freud, did you?

Oh my God, no! Oh no, that would be a terrible thing for a fellow to suggest. Besides, my questions about Miss Freud were simply idle chat.

She didn't quite believe him. The triangles of blackness ahead were the pyramids as sharp as a knife in a brilliant night sky. To underline the central role of the Sphinx, someone—one of the drivers or a guide who slept out here all night—had climbed the paws of the great stone beast and was holding a sodium flare in his hand, so that the wonderful and frightening face of the thing glowed from beneath, more terrifying and more godly than by day.

This is definitely the way, said Lieutenant Maclean, to see the Sphinx.

She hoped he would not take those great, glowing features dominating the dark as a lofty mandate to reach out and attempt something. They were shoulder to shoulder and that was enough for her. Any closer and her warmth would turn to revulsion.

Do you know, he said, pointing towards the diminishing radiance of the Sphinx's features, that there are chaps in our battalion who came here just to see this and not to fight? They're quite frank about that. Chaps who wanted a trip. I bet they turn up at your hospital pretending to hernias and bad hearts.

Sometimes, she admitted, there've been pretend patients. Men pretending tachycardia. You know, irregular heartbeat. Men can mimic tachycardia by sniffing cordite.

A young red-headed medical officer on the wards, Dr. Hookes—a general practitioner from the Western District of Victoria, of which, like Hoyle, he was willing to speak as the region of the earth which gave all other terrestrial regions any radiance they had—would say, Nurse, go and get the Faraday machine. And to the patient, Your heart needs an electric shock. And Sally would turn away to fetch this dreaded machine. There was such a device, but malingerers did not need to see it wheeled in. They would reassure Dr. Hookes that they thought their heart had settled. But one young man—very fresh-faced, perhaps a year from school—came in with a fibrillating heart and died on the bed in mid-sentence.

I do enjoy your company, Miss Durance, said the lieutenant all at once but not without consideration on his side.

The statement did not seem to plead for some short-term gain. But why and how could he know enough to like her? They were not much more than walking distance from Mena House, and she felt an urge to excuse herself, dismount the gharry, and start off overland. It took her seconds to understand that this would be correctly judged as madness.

I like spending a bit of time with you, he went on, because you're not a light-headed girl.

There was a gush of laughter from the gharry shared by Honora and Lionel. Maclean gestured in that direction. You see what I mean? he asked.

She was beginning to feel sorry for Maclean's men. They would have no trouble seeming to agree with him and then probably mocking him rotten in the bars available for non-officers in Cairo. He wasn't a bad fellow but had not yet recovered from his school-prefect self. He might now have been able to sense that his strict principles were not charming her as he thought they might have been.

I mean, these girls, he said, they're fine girls. And earnest when it comes down to nursing. They just don't seem as reliable.

I'd say my sister was most reliable, she said, boasting despite herself.

But she has a decent reserve, he said. It seems to me a decent reserve is a family trait of yours.

I hate that word "reserve," she told him, just to rout him further.

So that was the end of the debate about shyness or reticence or whatever.

I don't think I should be hard on our chaps, he said—an attempt to win her back. But what should alarm us a bit and be a salutary lesson is that the men pretty much beaten at Mons are British regulars. Is an Australian militiaman-cum-citizen soldier worth three of such men—as our boast goes? The fellows in the camp think so, but I believe a man is a man, Australian or not. And no question but that our chaps are better types. But not trained, you see, and hating to train. They hate it.

From the hospital roof they look as if they're training pretty hard, she argued.

Yes. But half of them don't even think it's necessary. Just give them a gun and let them loose, they think, and off they'll go like so many dingo-shooters.

She could feel his hand reach out for her wrist with particular intensity now. But no vein of fear seemed to throb in it—nor was there any sweat. It was a dry, calm hand. She felt it would be churlish to object. She let it lie there, passive, as long as it did not become part of an argument or consider advancing itself further.

You see, he said, returning to his theme, I wouldn't talk that way to one of these other girls. I simply wouldn't. I certainly wouldn't voice them to the adjutant or the lieutenant-colonel. So that leaves you, poor girl.

She found herself laughing low.

Shall we get out and go for a stroll? he asked. The cars are over there.

He helped her down onto the rubbly floor the pyramids grew from. There would have been other couples out there in the half dark star-

ing at the great shapes as the flare beneath the Sphinx's chin burned
out and left them half blinded. They all hoped that this place would
elevate their evening jaunt in one way or another. But the conversation
between her and Lieutenant Maclean dwindled out here—there was
too much space for words to make a dent. Soon the nurses and officers
transferred to the cars which had followed them, and in a final burst of
squeezed-in merriment, they reached the hospital.

All the rumors were of something named the Dardanelles. Staff Nurse
Carradine said, It'll be better than France. Because in France, everyone knew by Christmas and New Year, there had been that great
sacrifice of young men and the near capture of Paris. It developed
that the Dardanelles were Turkish and closer to the seat of the Ottoman Empire than Sinai. And although all this evoked ideas of the
scimitar and the harem and the torture chamber, these old-fashioned
implements and places seemed to make the Turks less accurate and
less well-trained shots than the Germans—the malign Huns who had
molested Belgian nuns but clearly knew how to string out a battle.
    In the mauve dusk Sally and the others sometimes stood on top
of the flat roof of Mena House and looked at the battalions marching
back out of the desert to their tents, all in good order—ambulances
trailing behind as if purely for the experience of it. She watched the
light horsemen wheel in fairly modest plumes of dust, and the infantry
battalions surge—without effort, as it seemed—over empty spaces.
Gradually, distant band music entered the equation. Perhaps only a
hundred boys suffering from heat exhaustion had been carried to the
hospital for treatment lest their dehydration and core temperature be
allowed to affect their brain.
    The leisurely night excursions to Cairo were gone. When Lieuten-
ant Eric Carradine arrived to see his wife, his face looked older. So
did the other men who turned up in the evenings for a while and sat
in the cane chairs on the roof with the nurses. One Lionel Dankworth—who to his disgust had been made a gunnery officer—was

seen nuzzling the side of Honora's face, and handsome Ellis Hoyle sought Naomi's hand while—most astoundingly—Naomi at one stage yielded it up to him.

When do they do it, d'you think? Honora asked Sally over tea later. Elsie and Eric—when do they manage it? You don't see them sneaking out, do you?

Honora the earthy woman asked such lusty and practical questions. One day, during tea in the mess, little sharp-nosed Nettice teased Honora by asking her, did she tell her chaplain about all the officers she'd hugged and kissed.

Yes, she said. But I tell him I do it only out of mercy, not because I'm a low girl. It's work to make men brave, I tell him, and they can't be brave unless they're happy.

Sally and others were inside the venereal compound again. There were the new victims of overestimated Venus. And ones who out of shame or recklessness had neglected to present themselves till the thing was established in them. Some had become accustomed to their shame or bad fortune and seemed to enjoy their leisure. They passed newspapers around and rolled cigarettes and discussed race results from twelve thousand miles away at Randwick or Flemington. But one day even the most unrepentant began to look bewildered and displaced when the bugles—as in an opera—began to draw nearer from the direction of the camp.

The route march of some twenty-five thousand infantry and light horse brigades eastwards towards the Canal passed the oasis where Mena House and its medical tents stood. From the wards the confident boots could be heard in unison and the imperious orders of officers and of sergeant majors with the voices of near-mad dogs. The sounds were enormous and constant and drew one out of doors. Some of the afflicted men even emerged from the tents to watch hopelessly, and Sally and the others ended their work and were escorted out of the compound. On the fringe of the palms they saw how long it took for just one battalion to pass with its accompanying trucks and ambulances and cooks. And then another band would come behind—blaring on yet another battalion to triumph and getting effusive with "The British Grenadiers," "Song of Australia," "Hope and Glory," "Waltzing Matilda," "Rule Britannia," "Flash Jack from Gundagai."

Honora Slattery announced the battalions as they passed. One, the First, was the founding stone from which the glory or the tragedy would be built, and at the head of a company within—barely to be seen in the dusty atmosphere—Captain Hoyle. And somewhere in the mass, Lieutenant Maclean. Someone—Carradine perhaps—had an operatic duty to run into the ranks and cling to her unswerving beloved. Finding then her clasp weakened by the tide of men coming behind, she should reel disconsolate from the ruthless host and weep on the verges of the desert as the regimental glory swept by. Staff Nurse Carradine did in fact appear—pale under the sun with Nettice—and they scanned the myriad of men for a sight of Eric Carradine, for the Victoria brigade was passing. The artillery came last. Tall Lionel sat on a horse to wave flamboyantly and grin crookedly in the hope his smile might reach Honora. It continued and continued until wonder was blunted. By dusk they were all vanished, and the band music evaporated from the air. Somehow Carradine's Eric was not sighted in the distracting masses. It was because, Sally knew, he had been looked for with too much effort.

After a few days Carradine had a fevered glow in her eye and was calculating that by now her husband was—along with every man who had taken tea at Mena House—either off some perilous shore or on it. Some light horse officers still came to tea, though many of their brethren too had been sent off on the adventure. These ones, however, had to stay here to stop the Turks raging out of Sinai to take the Canal. They gave the usual reassurances that if the Dardanelles rumors were right, there would be no grief at all. Kaiser Bill had dumped all his defective arms on the poor Turks because he needed the decent ones in France and Belgium.

The hospital seemed empty—except for that outlying, guarded leper colony. New transports from Australia were imminent. But for the moment there was hardly anyone in the desert camp to be cut by wire or an unwise lunge of a bayonet. A light horseman had appendicitis, an orderly caught pneumonia even though the hot season and the blizzards of grit named *khamsin* were starting. And the matron was sent to another hospital. It was rumored she had annoyed the colonel whom they never saw by demanding menial work of orderlies that he thought "her girls" should do.

One noon scandalous Matron Mitchie, the being who had made colonels hoot aboard the ship to Egypt, arrived by car at the door of Mena House. Through the window of a ward Sally saw her disembark while receiving a halfway military salute from the orderly who had opened the door for her. Hampered only by a slight arthritic limp—as if there had to be some small imperfection in her or else the more humorless gods would be forced to take a yet more serious tax from her—she rose up the steps to the wide veranda. Later, Sally happened to be in the chief building nursing an unconscious officer whose mount had thrown him during a race, when an orderly arrived.

Miss, Matron Mitchie wants you to meet her in the parlor. *Toot sweet*, she says.

The parlor was reserved for medical officers—nurses were permitted in but had rarely taken the chance until recently when the season's first columns of sand rose in the deserts and were blown along in the khamsin. The room reminded Sally of pictures she had seen in the *Mail* of Sydney clubs—themselves based on the clubs of London. The overupholstered chairs and the small tables of mahogany or some such wood for waiters to place drinks on were left over from the hotel days of this building. So were the racks for newspapers, the spine of each newspaper screwed between two varnished rods and hanging heavy with the weight of tidings from France, Russia, Serbia, Mesopotamia. Now there were twenty-four women or so in the room. Sally's sister and Carradine and the sculpted Freud and Slattery and Leonora

Casement and prune-faced Nettice—all marvelously changed by the expectation of what would be said. Matron Mitchie was there not in the ward clothes she seemed to have been wearing seconds earlier but in her traveling suit with her gray cape. The transmutation might serve to show what serious powers resided in Mitchie.

Well, ladies, she said to them. New nurses are on their way, their ship just in at Suez. So you are hand-selected by arrivals and fate and what I know of you. Now we are to take ship. If you have any patients for whom you have a special concern, leave notes for those who are on their way. You must gather everything you have—your bedrooms now are marked for others. You may leave behind in a shared tea chest all your sandalwood camels and filigree work—everything you bought in bazaars. You should be dressed *comme ça*.

She indicated her own formal wear.

But you must pack your on-duty uniforms and other effects. The question arises—the question of *whither*. Well, I can tell you the start of that *whither*.

On the edge of illumination, the women still laughed at her.

She raised and consulted a paper she had in her hand.

Our new station is the hospital ship—our friend the *Archimedes*. Archimedes being a Greek who liked baths and who sank himself to displace water, let us hope he looks down upon his ship and its sisters with a gentle gaze. But *à propos* earlier remarks, let me assure you, you have been chosen for your sobriety and nursing skills. You must not depart from those strengths.

Honora cried out, Our destination, Matron? I mean, once on *Archimedes*?

Mitchie leaned towards them.

Because we are a hospital ship and there will be news of all that's happened there in days past in the papers by tomorrow, there is no prohibition placed on me against telling you it is to the region of the fabled Hellespont—the mouth of that passage where things have begun to happen, that gate running between the Greeks and the Ottomans.

Women frowned. The atlases in their brains were inexact on that geography.

The ancients knew it forwards and backwards, said Mitchie, but the world was smaller then. We'll nurse boys who come to grief there and who certainly don't know it any better than we do. The omens of the campaign have been excellent, and so, I warn you, it may be the Turk himself that you must nurse. His flesh is human too. He too is born of woman.

She looked around the room inviting contradiction of this humane theorem.

She made a motion as if clearing the room of small talk.

Wear your coat, for it will be cold tonight between Cairo and Alexandria and we should leave pneumonia to the soldiers, who have more excuse for it.

The charabancs took them through a city to which they had become so quickly habituated that it had begun to lose some of its power to startle and appall them. Men still—heedless of traffic—led camels loaded with firewood for sale, or donkey carts. The stubborn poor came close to hurling themselves beneath the wheels of military trucks, water wagons, the white limousines of the rich, and the women's vehicles in an attempt to sell something or to be compensated with a coin for some maiming they had suffered.

The light was still hazy from the recent unseasonal sandstorm. The sun had frayed into a ball of tasseled edges as the charabancs arrived at the central Ramses Station. This—despite its concessions to Arabic style—was built like a fortress against the Arabic world. But of course Arab peddlers had penetrated it.

A truckload of medical orderlies—themselves assigned to Alexandria and perhaps to the *Archimedes*—followed the charabancs in trucks with all the nurses' luggage. So Mitchie and her women carried simply their valises and their immediate needs as they entered beneath the archways and moved amongst soldiers, Egyptian businessmen, and the poor. A person could damn well get used to this, said Honora.

Carradine, Sally, Naomi, and Mitchie had a compartment. Naomi offered Sally a seat by the cramped window of the carriage which seemed as designed to keep the world out as much as to allow sight of it.

Sally said, No, you take it.

Still there lay a distance between the sisters and it struck her that the other women could see it and were making surmises about it. But for distraction from that awkward thought, there were antimacassars to lay the back of their heads against and the seats were of the softest leather. A superior foot-warming device—a canister with hot coals over which a carpet cover had been laid—was placed on the floor for their use. The women were barely settled when a conductor in a tarboosh told them respectfully that the dining carriage was open now. Matron Mitchie asked Sally, Would you be so kind as to fetch down my valise?

Untroubled by the gentle lurch of the ambling train, Sally got the scuffed leather thing down. Matron Mitchie took an envelope from it and turned to Carradine and Naomi.

Will you take those—be dears for poor old Matron!—and give them to the girls in the compartments? Meal tickets. Be warned and warn them. They do not cover beer and wine and certainly not whisky!

The stipulation implied the women would fall to whisky very easily.

Come, Sally, said Mitchie, after Sally had been handed her white meal card.

Sally followed Mitchie as she made her broad-bottomed way down the corridor of the train towards the dining car and bounced a hip off the walls on one side and then on the other. There is useful flesh, thought Sally.

They came into the dining room and found lamps held in lotus-like bulbs burning above each table. The tables themselves were set with brilliant, flashing cutlery and filigree-work tablecloths. The women who did the fine work earned very little, and here the grace of things sat balanced on want. And here too—as Lieutenant Maclean had said—all justice had to await the defeat of the enemy and mightn't even happen then.

The dining room windows seemed better placed for viewing. For a time—as they rolled beside the Nile—Sally could see feluccas as black shapes on the deep-blue night-time river. By lanterns in the bows and hung from masts, the faces of men moving along the deck were vivid for an instant then gone. Members of the same humanity she shared in and carriers of the same kind of blood. Yet their lives were unreachable to her. What did they say to their wives? What did they say to their children? And what was said in return? That was travel, she supposed. A dance across surfaces to see the face of everything and learn the meaning of very little.

The other girls arrived in the dining carriage. Naomi was with them and seemed to look at everything as from a great distance.

Come on, Slattery, Mitchie yelled, pointing to the two vacant seats at her table and at the table across the corridor. Come on, Carradine, sit with a poor woman, won't you? Empress Naomi, join us. Freud the diva, sit at that one with Leonora. Ah, Nettice, welcome.

So they settled as ordered.

Now, your father-in-law, said Mitchie, skewering Carradine with a brown eye. He's some great man, isn't he?

He is the attorney-general. And the deputy prime minister.

Carradine absorbed without apparent shock the news that Mitchie was aware of her marriage and willing to be forthright about it.

And your husband? Does he have political intentions?

He hasn't said it yet. I think he finds the military ones hard enough to keep up with at the moment. Poor chap, he's not thought of as strict enough by his colonel. But that's his method, you see. To appeal to people's good natures.

Well, said Mitchie, beaming. He certainly managed to appeal to yours, Nurse Carradine. Everyone seems content to ignore your marriage for now. A ministry letter said that single women were to be recruited, but it's not the law or anything. If asked, I'll pretend ignorance.

Carradine grew uncomfortable.

I'm sorry, said Mitchie then. I understand this should have been discussed privately.

In a kind of reparation she let nurses ask her where she was from. Melbourne, she told them. But where were you born? they asked her. She was born in Tasmania, she told them, a dairy farmer's daughter.

At first her mother seemed very severe—a Scots woman. But that was because there was a little too much fun in her father—he loved a horse, any horse on which there was a rider wearing silks. But there are worse vices, and then he died of meningitis and that settled things and her mother could be easier about things.

She turned to Honora. Now, with a name like Slattery you'd know about horses, since all the good papists are horse-crazy and gamblers? Isn't that so?

The words might in another's mouth be malice but it was somehow clear they weren't that here. Sure, said Honora, as if in imitation of her Irish parents, if you don't gamble on horses, you're denied the Christian sacraments. Too much drink is merely venial. Anything else, including talking to Protestants, is a mortal sin that'll send you straight to the pit without appeal.

The train seemed to have left the main channel of the great river. Sally saw Naomi squint out of the window and try to decipher some diagonal of desert they were crossing. Sometimes the whole apparatus would—with a huge groan of steel and snort of steam—haul up at a tiny desert or oasis station, and in dim light Egyptian effendis and their wives would get down or would board, on business beyond Sally's knowing. A dark and silent scatter of flat-roofed buildings sat behind the kerosene lanterns of the station. Sally saw one stationmaster escort a well-dressed Egyptian couple off the platform and into the mystery of the town. But sometimes the mystery was that there was no town behind the station at all.

When Matron Mitchie excused herself and vanished from the dining car, going either to the lavatory or for a snort from the whisky flask she was rumored to carry in her big valise, Honora started up on the question of whether Mitchie had ever been married.

Could she be a widow? Or did her husband do a flit?

Men often do with the best of women, said Nettice with conviction. They don't know when they're well-off and go looking for harpies.

Sally said she had always assumed that matrons were above the married state.

Honora argued Mitchie'd got too much sauce in her not to have led men on.

Well, said Naomi, exchanging a sliding instant's glance with her sister, I think she's wise enough to know being married's not the greatest state open to a girl.

What about you and that Captain Hoyle? asked Honora like a challenge.

There was a silence since it was somehow not exactly normal to ask a woman with an air of such austerity as Naomi a question about men.

Naomi said, If sharing a gharry means an intention to marry a fellow, I'd be married to half the Australian Imperial Force.

When the engine stopped nowhere and they sat still, the voices of the women in the dining car and their talk when they returned to their compartments seemed shrill. With a great gulp of air another train would pass—carrying English troops in one direction or the other—and you could see soldiers' faces close as they smoked and laughed at each other or lay with their heads back. It was the business of the army not only to fight wars but to shift the soldiers in Alexandria to Cairo and those in Cairo to Alexandria—and then for extra pleasure of authority to do it again.

The Alexandria Misr Station into which they came in the dark of three o'clock had a great dome, and the forecourt was like a Greek rather than an Egyptian palace—all to honor Alexander the Great. A few peddlers were around them even at this hour, selling replicas of Pompey's Column. Tommies in kepis—ready to outface heat wherever they were sent—sat on their kitbags or leaned against walls. They puffed smoke from blank faces and made tired comment from the corner of mouths.

Into a glass-windowed transport office Mitchie went to speak to a harried-looking officer and an NCO. The man she made her demand for transport to threw up his hands as if he had expected Mitchie to be the ultimate trial and here she was. The Australian orderlies marched up in less than military exactness—led by the tall surgeon Fellowes who was not yet comfortable with drill. The party was trailed by Lieutenant Hookes. All nurses looked at Leonora, who was assumed to be infatuated for life with Fellowes. They had learned from Leonora he was an ear, nose, and throat expert of little militia experience. Sally had seen some more militarily vain medical officers who even rode mounted in front of their precise-stepping men.

At last Captain Fellowes handed Mitchie out through the door, and it was clear they had won the transport argument. Mitchie invited her women to follow her two by two out of the main door and past the Greek columns to where trucks were backing and grinding in chilly air. Orderlies held the women's elbows as they ascended the steps to the back. The trucks drove them through night streets full of high-walled villas and tall blocks of flats, all quieter than Cairo. They spun a small way along the Corniche whose fame they were as yet ignorant of. The sea lay to their right with the water maintaining a kind of deep purple, lit only by the moon and the lights of the Corniche.

Then they swung onto an electrically lit mole crowded with ships both civilian and military. The trucks rolled as far as towers of boxed supplies and crowds of men smoking or slouched by stacked rifles—and opposing automobiles honking for leeway—would permit them. Mitchie's platoon of nurses got down onto the wharves. The orderlies from the trucks ahead came to carry their bags and portmanteaux and even their valises.

Some two hundred paces along the harbor pier the *Archimedes* came up like an apparition. E73—as naval notation had it. By the lights burning along the pier its wide bulwarks towered and its huge

crosses were deep scarlet. British soldiers were guarding the gangway.
The ship was not to be boarded until seven ack-emma, one of them
said. Meanwhile there was a waiting room.

That's impossible, young fellow, said Mitchie. My girls must be fit
and rested by breakfast time.

Be a good fellow, said Fellowes. There's a brick!

The young man—hating having been called "good fellow"—went
off to confer with superiors. Fellowes shook his head and openly
laughed at the military ridiculousness of it all. Leonora raised a gleaming face—whitened abnormally by the lights on the wharf. For she
and they all somehow loved it that Fellowes was still a young civilian
surgeon and was far from converted to war's protocols.

The soldier came back with a stiff, permissive, even herding gesture of his arm. So they went aboard—onto decks they knew, down
corridors they knew, into the cabins they were familiar with.

The *Archimedes* II

That first night on *Archimedes*—when it lay on the level surface of the East Harbor—in the cabin she shared with Carradine, Honora, and Naomi, the unconscious Sally came to a sleeping awareness that there was no separation between her dreams and those of the other three women, and that just as she shared the cabin's air she also shared its phantasms.

The dawn entered and hurt her eyes. She awoke in the upper bunk and adjusted to the trembling of metal bulwarks, the throaty howl of a steamer beyond the porthole, and the musk of the women—a peppery, flowers-on-the-turn smell with the honest overlay of clotted talcum. She saw Naomi at the porthole, peering out. At least one ship was passing and perhaps two or three were edging about and getting ready for the ocean. Each seemed to engross her sister. Then Naomi turned. Still in her bunk, Sally gazed back at her. Our mother's lean face, she thought.

Have you seen anyone you know? Sally whispered.

No, it's impossible, Naomi said quietly. It's just that the men line the decks of the ships and they're so excited. Can't wait to be in battle. It's contagious too. Come on deck with me.

Sally secretly assessed whether they were far enough away from home for it to be safe. Far enough away from the memory of complicity.

All right, she said.

They dressed stealthily while the other girls still slept and left the cabin and went up the companionway to the promenade. On the East Harbor, seaward side of the deck, an intoxication came on the northeast breeze from the decks of the transports. Men were drunk with possibility—the approach of the revelation, the core of meaning. The world had become simple for them. You could nearly feel it simplifying itself.

Their anchor raged upwards and they passed the Pharos lighthouse at midmorning into a vacant sea the transports had already committed themselves to. It was a sea a person wanted to watch at length, the deep blue of what was called spring in Europe—and Alexandria was halfways Europe. Nothing like the Pacific off New South Wales she had scanned from the *Currawong*. Its vivid and dark blue scared the watcher with depths that could eat you alive. Whereas this—this invited you and admitted light deep down inside it and seemed willing to let you plumb it. But no time to stand long on the deck of *Archimedes* and ponder that invitation.

Dr. Hookes began the day after a plain breakfast with a talk on splints directed at the nurses who sat on one side of the lounge and the more numerous orderlies who sat on the other. From his report, it seemed the bush town where he practiced was rich in fractures. The Liston splint was just the ticket for very dangerous fractured femur wounds which were to be expected in battle. Some orderlies smirked and nudged as Hookes expatiated on cock-up splints which forced the hand upright in cases of wrist fracture.

Then an older officer came into the salon—the colonel of the ship, in fact; a slightly dreamy-looking Englishman. He wore the same uniform as the rest. He had been converted to Australian-ness by immigration or secondment. He talked about the treatment of bullet wounds in the South African war. It required patience, hydrogen peroxide, and tweezers to extract uniform threads which had entered the flesh in company with the bullet. Do not forget, said the colonel, that the bullet is not a sterile instrument—it has been loaded by an almost certainly filthy hand, perhaps by a disease-ridden one. When it strikes the victim, it introduces dirt from the exposed part of the struck body and fibers from uniforms and thus—microorganisms!

The colonel went on to the question of morphine dosage. Sally observed Naomi. Her chin was undauntedly raised. The colonel's prescribed dosage for abdominal wounds seemed niggardly. The highest he sanctioned was a quarter grain for abdominal and thoracic wounds. But, he said, regularly and mercifully repeated as necessary. Everyone made notes in pads with pencils sharpened by penknives they carried in deep pockets in their skirts. Bullet wounds had not been spoken of before today when—supposedly—they were all on the lip of the cauldron.

The afternoon was taken up with crepe bandage preparation— running it through boiling water and eusol, hanging it out on rods to dry, winding it up. Cotton bandage was stored ready—soft and pure enough for the wounds of heroes—or so it was hoped, though there had been impurities reported in bandages and dressings opened in Egypt. But, as they still thought, they were about to treat the strong and not the weak—young men of good constitution purified by battle.

A dusk lecture was delivered by Captain Fellowes on sepsis and gas gangrene. He had seen it develop from wounds inflicted in the rough streets of Melbourne while an intern in an emergency ward.

With all this absorbed they were by now flattened by exhaustion. A little energy was left to climb the stairs to observe the half-moon above the sea. Others visited the lounge where Freud sang "Little Sir Echo" at the insistence of nurses and medical officers. The word was running around the ship. The troops were already landed in the Dardanelles. What-for for the poor damned Turks! Sally heard Lieutenant Hookes say.

Still—that evening and night and the next day—no one knew for certain where they were bound on their course across this Mediterranean Sea. The sun was on what they called the starboard beam both in its rising and then—rather astern on the port—in its setting. This meant a northwest direction.

At making up the cots fixed in their floor sockets the orderlies proved—it seemed to many—willfully clumsy. A handsome young medical corps sergeant was observed going around exhorting them towards a better performance. Forward, a former library had been set up with tiered bunks for walking wounded. Cabins forward on the promenade deck were to be reserved for recuperating or lightly wounded officers. Below—on a deck once used for second-class travelers—the pattern was repeated to accommodate humbler ranks. Mitchie warned the women they might not always be able to tell the difference between officer and man.

They wore their aprons and made hundreds of beds while the orderlies scrubbed steel doors and bulkheads—a job with which they seemed strangely more content than with bed-making since it left their pride in place and was clearly proper work for men. Only the nurses were permitted to scrub the floors and walls of the operating theatre and any stray surface therein bold enough to present itself. On Sally's count four doctors and a pharmacist were aboard, and if at dinner that night Dr. Hookes seemed wan and distracted, it was said to be because he might be called on to leave the wards and take on the role of surgeon. But one wondered why when the wounded might be a mere handful.

The women were given time to watch small Greek islands float past and to squint towards the coast of Greece, sadly over their horizon. There were a few orderlies on deck. One of them—the sergeant with the lean, darkling, and refined features who had harangued the other orderlies on their lack of competence with bed linen—said hello briskly and identified a mountainous ridged creature ahead. Its name was Lemnos. The sergeant's manner was that of someone who had been here before. And his uniform and the sort of khaki puttees that distinguished the ordinary soldier was also a relief from too much polished leather, too many moustaches and neat leggings. His name was Ian Kiernan.

He gathered a crowd of the nurses to consider Lemnos and instructed them without too much sign of wanting to be thought clever.

When Hephaestus was kicked out of heaven by his father, Zeus, said the sergeant, he had settled on Lemnos and fathered a bandit tribe with the nymph Cabiro. Hephaestus's forge was there, on that island. Then, when the women of Lemnos were abandoned by their husbands for Thracian women, they killed every remaining Lemnos man in vengeance—which seemed a bit unfair to the virtuous. The Argonauts, landing there, found only women left and created with them a race known as the Minyans whose king, Euneos, was Jason's son.

If the women were in charge, why wasn't it a queen? asked Freud softly and not expecting an answer.

Good point, Nurse, Kiernan admitted. If I ever get back to Melbourne Uni I'll ask Professor Challenor that one.

On the starboard abeam, he then told them, could be seen a hazy outline of Imbros associated with Thetis, the mother of famed Achilles.

Some of the orderlies were said to be men dropped from the infantry for incompetence with rifles and bayonets and even for unruliness. But Kiernan resembled a man who was precisely where he wanted to be. Still, he was wary with what by their standard passed as scholarship. He was aware of the taboo which until now had existed between the orderly and the nurse, between the carriers of water and stretchers—the hoisters of supplies and porters of nurses' bags—and the daughters of succor who had the theoretic power to command his labor, just as he had the unacknowledged but genuine power to harry them.

On that third evening they could see the sky in the east lit by a storm. Everyone rushed to deck on the rumor that there was what could be called "thunder." The word failed this clamor up ahead. The lights in the sky would dim and then fill it again like the pulse of that Greek's forge Kiernan had already summoned up. That wasn't Lemnos though. That was the Dardanelles, the peninsula of Gallipoli. Those are the Turkish guns. Krupp guns from Germany but manned by Turks, Kiernan asserted, who was on deck with all the others. The

Germans have seduced the Turks to their side, he told them. And now—here we are!

The *Archimedes* had dropped its speed the closer it got to the illuminations from the heights ashore. It edged its way in towards the fury at perhaps seven knots. All around were its new companions—transports and cruisers and destroyers with their guns leveled at the eastern heights but silent. One other hospital ship was there on the starboard and displayed its crosses. And everywhere smaller ships, as if waiting for daylight, and barges running errands between ships and the shore. Sally wondered how all this—the campaign seen there and set up ahead of them so hugely as to fill a half of the sky—had started without her knowing. When had it begun? How could something so colossal have been kept a secret as they had rolled along in trucks under the lights of the Corniche? She had thought from school that battles were the business of a single day. Hadn't it been so at Waterloo? But this clearly was a battle with some days' history behind it, and operating by night as well. It worked many shifts. Like a factory.

They landed about the time we left port, said an orderly with a cigarette at the railing. I know that. They must be giving the Turks what-for.

It could not be guessed from the deck of the creeping *Archimedes* who was giving who what-for. Matron Mitchie appeared amongst them as if likely to issue an order.

She turned to the scene ashore. Cadences of cannon light and quivering flares demanded all the available attention.

My dear God, said Mitchie. Do they go at it twenty-four hours a day?

Five minutes on deck, girls, she called above the massive metal roar of the unleashed anchor cable. By your watches. Then to rest. You understand we can expect some labor to come?

A spout of water rose beyond an anchored transport. Some of Mr. Krupp's manufacture had that ship, then, in its intentions. That fact was something that stretched the mind.

Look there, said Carradine. Men.

By the glimmer of flares, the beach ahead—about two miles off—could be seen and even looked as if it might be an illuminated fair. A place for Jason and the Argonauts to meet those Lemnos women. There were men on it though—mere dots but plentiful and busy.

Carradine and Sally and their small, dry-featured, reticent senior, Sister Nettice, showed here an even more heightened spirit of obedience. They expected a little sleep before the patients turned up. But at the companionway, Sally saw a pale Naomi in her pinafore standing as a triage nurse with Dr. Hookes and amongst orderlies—the men who would deliver the damaged to the doctor and her for assessment. Naomi's face showed that resolute nature which had murdered their mother. She would not get sleep. She had to stand and wait. Whereas they would be awakened to duty according to what Naomi and Hookes received.

They went down to their cabins beyond the hospital deck. Half an hour ago it would have seemed ridiculous to go to rest with Mr. Krupp as a sleeping companion. Now—even knowing Naomi must stay wakeful—it seemed the simplest sense. In any case, by the early hours of the morning they were all awoken by the hammering of an orderly and told to stand by at their nursing stations. The large hospital deck was divided into imaginary wards with whose dimensions they were familiar now, and Mitchie told them to take a lie-down on the cots meant for the wounded. Some lights were switched off to reduce the glare from the white bulkheads. Thus, in half light and with the noise of the barrage lessening, no one slept. At three in the morning a stillness had set in. The Krupp cannon rested. Naomi had seen the shore darken and return to its mythology. Night became absolute.

At that hour a minesweeper came up beside the *Archimedes* with wounded men on its decks. Matron Mitchie descended with the loud news that there would be patients now. The nurses stood a little more rigidly at their stations in the vast hospital than before. Tightness had also entered the demeanor of orderlies. They were like maids and porters in a great hotel awaiting the coming of guests. At central tables here and there lay untouched their hydrogen peroxide, their scissors, hypodermics and needles, thermometers and blood-pressure cuffs, cotton wool and gauze, dressings and bandages.

Initially, the harmed arriving on the hospital deck was a scatter of men who could move by their own power. They had come aboard up the lowered stairs. They were cheerful and rowdy and almost in a mood for celebration. As they entered the hospital they seemed restrained by a fear of appearing too willing to escape the shore. Most of these had labels pinned on their shirts or jackets marked "3." Mitchie told the nurses to put on their rubberized gloves.

The first of all the wounded Sally saw was a dark-haired, lanky young man whose face had gone yellow. He seemed confused. The young ward doctor they barely knew allocated him a cot and inspected the clotted mess of bandages at his arm. It would prove, Sally would ever remember, that his elbow had been shot away—a tourniquet was tied high on his hanging arm. The doctor ordered a quarter grain of morphine. Slattery went with hypodermic and needle to draw it up in the nurses' station. A half-dozen nurses had the time to aid or stand by each patient and in this case to witness the dampening and tender removal of the filthy bandages and the peroxide soaking and drawing out of the packed bloody gauze with tweezers. Someone ashore had put the gauze there. Someone careful amongst the lights and fire. As the dressings came off, it was clear that the brachial nerve was borne away and the humerus and the bones of the lower arm shattered. The young man snuffled and muttered, vomited, then swallowed his drowsy pain. An orderly supported the upper arm and there made his own pleading noise as Slattery and Sally attended to the swabbing of the bloodied and palsied forearm near the mess—until Dr. Hookes came along and punctured their solemnity by declaring that the man would need surgery to see what could be salvaged. Even so—Sally knew—the arm would dangle a lifetime. His hand would be forever a senseless withered fist. Orderlies put him back on a stretcher and hauled him off to the theatres forward.

Sally and some of the nurse witnesses were drawn off to attend to the second case, a man whose jacket hung over his shoulders and whose chest was swathed. Orderlies gave him a cigarette and settled him down as Slattery and Sally came to him. "Shrapnel chest and shoulders," someone had scribbled on his label. Sally was not sure what shrapnel was.

Now a number of men on stretchers were arriving down the main stairwell bearing filthy scribbled labels marked "1" and "2." Mitchie and the ward doctor inspected each and directed nurses to them. The colonel and Captain Fellowes and the *Archimedes*'s third surgeon came stalking for candidates for their operating tables and discussed the need of this man and that with the ward doctor and Mitchie.

To Sally and Honora's station was carried a craggy-looking young man whose features seemed to draw in on themselves. Under an opened uniform jacket—put on him as if to shield him from nighttime cold—the upper body was bare and his wound in bandages. The orderlies moved him with genial roughness onto a hospital cot. The stench of soured and recent blood, the exhalation of the wound and of excrement and of his fouled remnants of uniform puzzled Sally. It was as if he had been campaigning a year and not a few days. But there was no doubt of the rights his wound gave him. His "1" label had "thoracic" scribbled on it and a morphine dosage in dim pencil. Also— upstairs on deck—Naomi had attached to his bandages a red card to signify the urgency his wound stood for and had scribbled "lower right anterior of the chest with likely pulmonary involvement and exit." The bandages below his open uniform jacket were dark and saturated. He was unearthly silent and calm and his mind seemed to meditate on this wound which should have killed him by now except that it might have skimmed major organs.

Matron Mitchie went amongst the nurses not yet engaged, telling them there would be twenty-three stretcher cases in all. The finite number was a motivation and a comfort. Sally heard Carradine and Leo Casement reasoning with a man with a bloodied head wound who talked like crazy but in a rapid, unknown tongue. His chatter competed with orderlies' shouts and dominated the deck and ended with a slur as Carradine stanched his rattle of discourse with a morphine injection.

Similarly Honora arrived back from the dressings room with a hypodermic—a quarter grain. With this boy to command the entirety of her brain, Sally thought for an instant only, and with a little spark of memory and relief, that morphine had nearly lost its history here. It no longer stood for theft or guilt. A small patch of the arm must be cleansed with an alcohol swab and the stuff got into the body of this weather-beaten young thoracic case who had not received any mercy since he was bandaged on the beach. The lifting onto a barge, the lifting off—how had he lived through that?

The orderly assigned to Sally and Honora was a fellow of perhaps thirty-five years with eyes that might have been stunned or else sullen. His name was Wilson. He lifted and adjusted the young body's posture, dragged away the man's foul jacket and let it drop to the floor while Honora and Sally soaked the areas near the wound with hydrogen peroxide to dilute the sticky adhesions of dressing to wound. With the man eased sideways and then on his back and sideways again by their helpmeet orderly, by cutting the bandages they found both wounds: sockets of raw meat front and back with the bullet having made its exit five ribs up—the seventh thoracic vertebra as she must write on his chart—and about two inches from the spine.

Sally and Honora looked at each other since they shared a strange hesitation—not that the wound was beyond their comprehension or even beyond their expectation. It was the inadequacy of their functions and small medical rites in front of damage as authoritative as this. The orderly held the boy with gentle force, and Honora cleansed the flesh and the lips of first one wound and then went around the cot to cleanse the exit, while Sally probed with forceps for impurities and fibers. The patient took to shuddering all at once and the orderly—thinking it his duty to restrain him—pressed down on the man's shoulders. The pallor of the face turned to deep, cyanosed blue. This was the face of the human creature drowning in his own blood. Sally needed a trocar from the central table and by an apparent chance Matron Mitchie was by her shoulder with such an implement.

Mitchie commanded the orderly to let the man lie on his back. Then she drove the wide-bore trocar needle into the man's right chest cavity while ordering Sally to fetch rubber tubing and a kidney bowl—both of which someone of surpassing wisdom had placed on the equipment trolley in the ward's midst. Mitchie murmured good girl when Sally, perhaps instantly—because it was all an instant, immune from the fall of seconds—arrived back with them. Blood began to flow into the kidney bowl Honora grasped. Then it overflowed. Let it. It stopped, then flowed again over Honora's gloved hands. It was hopeless now. The soldier convulsed at an awful length of seconds, and that ended it. Mitchie nodded to Sally and Honora. Can't be helped, she said. Clean yourselves up, ladies.

They ran to do it. They said nothing as they shed gloves and scrubbed in a basin at a nearby table. Orderlies were to replace these once used. But as a first sign of plans breaking apart, a basin of bloodied water stood unremoved on the table beside their basin.

The ward doctor pointed them to a further patient in their section of the vast barn of white space. They stepped amongst discarded and sullied bandages and scraps of uniform waiting on the deck and reached their new case, his jaw bound up. He must have been forty years when judged from his forehead and eyes, and his eyes were awfully calm. An eighth of a grain to begin with. After the easing off of bandages, bone fragments showed in the mess of the wound. The bullet must still be in there somewhere—netted by bone. What was he doing on that beach and fighting for the heights at his age? It seemed willful idiocy for him to be here—a determination to get away from something such as family or else undignified or uncertain work somewhere.

Captain Fellowes walked by, surgically coated, and inspected the long, explosive mess Sally had revealed and was swabbing, and looked for the degree of tooth and mandible loss and claimed him for surgery. Fellowes must believe that this mayhem could be fixed with screws and wire under anesthetics and with surgical tools passed to him by brave Staff Nurse Freud.

So what have we done for the wounded? Sally had a second to assess. But Mitchie directed them on. Sally was—in a sense—ready. She was bolstered by hearing Honora say to a patient, Look at me. Come. Look. Can you see me, my fine fellow? It sounded as if she were talking to someone concussed in a football match. He looked at her as if he recognized her, she said later, but realized she wasn't the woman he expected to see and closed his eyes—done with the world of women. He was a man with a stomach wound who by some pointless mercy had not hemorrhaged to this moment. Crying for water he too was taken away to the theatre. Apart from him, the groans were less rowdy than the shrill suggestions of matron and doctor. This was strange and certainly a mystery.

Their orderly traveled around the ward with them wearing the same unreadable face as before. He looked world-worn but accustomed to labor, to lifting loads and digging hard soil. A young officer lay before them, his stomach swathed and wearing a soiled number 1 label from ashore and a red one Naomi had probably put on him. He was writhing and trembling, but with a sort of good-mannered lack of excess. Quarter grain, Mitchie instructed them, as he had not had any morphine—it seemed—since the shore. By the blood at his back, Sally saw another through-and-through wound. But when the dressing was rinsed off she saw a cavity created by something larger than a bullet—a shard of shrapnel, say—and edging from it an unexpected snake of the stomach lining named omentum, yellow amidst blood, lacy and frayed, hanging out of the slashed gut. While not letting go entirely of his surprisingly gentle hold on the baby lieutenant, the orderly Wilson turned his head aside and vomited on the deck and it seemed as if he might let go and clean it before someone of higher rank abused him for the mess. No, said Sally, leave it, Mr. Wilson.

He was older than she was and deserved the title.

Two beds away, Matron Mitchie called for orderlies to take the thoracic patient to the morgue. Where was the space for mourning in this air of blood and acrid wounds and unwashed men? Sally, Honora, and Wilson applied a Liston splint then to a man with a broken leg who had been knocked back into his trench by a glancing leg wound and who for some reason apologized to them for the ridiculous head-over-turkey act that had landed him here.

That was the lot for now. But the old rifles the Kaiser was said to have off-loaded onto the Turks had obviously not been entirely lacking in effect on the flesh of the legions of the good. At the end of the ward, nurses washed their hands at the basins refilled with water and disinfectant. They went to their mess, where a steward had placed tea and much buttered bread.

Great nurses us, eh, Sally? said Honora without seeming to grieve or ask for apology or consolation. We were busy, she continued, but we didn't do much good.

She stood at the porthole through which morning had selectively begun to pastel her face.

Sally felt her own less expansive soul preparing to be inconsolable, but then there was a yell from a staff nurse in the door. A minesweeper was alongside with decks covered by stretcher cases.

In a few minutes—it seemed no more—all the cots on the hospital deck were filled. Men carried in were laid in their stretchers on metal floors. Orderlies were looking for pantries or small offices in which to lay down the men. The neat divisions of responsibility blurred under this torrent of the harmed. Only those who were used to dealing with confusion—those who could see through the turbulence because of having come, like Honora, from turbulent families—could have decided where to begin. And Mitchie herself and Sister Nettice too—who moved and spoke without panic—resolved bewilderment by calmly directing the traffic of stretchers.

The ship began to tremble to renewed thunders outside. Large guns were firing by land and sea. These furies may or may not have been directed at them. But Sally became used to that steel shiver. It was the barely noticed pulse behind what she now did. She seemed after an hour to have been feeling that tremor all her life.

And every time Sister Nettice or Matron saw a man weep fiercely for an inability to utter pain, morphine was ordered.

Where are you from, Sister? a pale older man with a chest wound demanded, looking up above his bandages for an announcement of the place name that might save him. There were more of such older men than she would have thought. Men who had known labor and had been aged and hollowed by it. Again her sister on the deck—the unseen Naomi—had chosen a red card of urgency to be pinned on him. Knowing by now that men were solaced by this plain geography game, Sally told him. The idea was this, so it seemed: while I am from one quiet shire and you from another, no harm will approach us. Those who discussed locations could not die. But she knew now there was no dealing with the thoracic wound. The victim and the nurses must accommodate themselves to it. It would accommodate no one.

I'm from Moonta from the mines there, he announced. I'm one of the lucky ones, he persisted with his blue lips barely flapping with breath amidst the graying pallor of a sun-leathered face. Just as well. God knew, see, that I've got a wife and three kids.

Even Wilson had to admit he was from somewhere named Indooroopilly, the name sounding so fantastic that some decided to laugh. Wherever he was from, he was a good fellow. He nodded with her as the place names were told. She heard all the Enoggeras and Coonabarabrans, the Bungendores and Bunburys. Her own tongue stuck to the roof of her mouth and was released only to utter one plain sentence.

You must get better then, she said.

Bathing with gauze the skull wound of a youth deeply unconscious and finding it full of grit, its edges of flesh brittle and darkening, she saw the inner membrane torn away, the dura, the pericranium—she beheld the naked brain. It astonished her and gave her too much pause. She had taken up scissors to cut away necrotic flesh when the colonel descended in his gown and claimed the boy.

The wheezer with three children was gone. He had lost his hold on conversation, and it didn't matter anymore in his patch of Aegean where Moonta or the Macleay might be.

Sally knew something of the imperfections of men but those on this vast white deck continued to behave with a saintly forbearance. There were a few peevish cries from them of Nurse! Nurse! When you went to the caller, you might see panic in the face but were more likely to hear something almost fatuous. Very commonly the stupid thing said was that the patient had let his mates down by getting clipped, winged, hit, bowled base over turkey (as they put it even in their last etiquette of language).

Where did this sanctity come from? They couldn't have had it before? Not the men who rampaged through Cairo upsetting stalls in the souk and yelling curses at the gyppos and doing bad imitations of British officers' barked commands.

There was time for the nurses to take a meal in the mess, and all surprise was covered by gossip and stories and guesses. Naomi—down from the deck—sat looking so reflective and pale that Sally went to her and asked her how it all was up there. Naomi put a hand to her forehead and held it out interrogatively. She said, Sometimes there are so many at once it seems Hookes is just guessing at men's conditions. And other times he's so slow. I'm having to do half the work and I can't always assess them properly . . . bad light, the general mess of their uniform and clothes . . . The orderlies are confused and have been putting the wrong tags on cases. It's too much. Too much for the ship and the orderlies and Hookes. And for me. I've never been tested . . .

Sally kissed the crown of her head but then walked off as if by instinct—just to save Naomi from lapsing into dismay.

Carradine said that in the past few hours she had been put in the walking wounded officers' ward. When she heard the others talk about the unlikely lack of screams and pleadings on the men's deck, she said some of these officers are utter cowering and whimpering failures.

I'd cower, said Naomi from her place at the table with a sudden energy of conviction. I'd whimper.

Sally—with a mug of tea but no appetite on the other side of the table—frowned at this uncommon outburst and found herself reaching a hand across and patting Naomi's just as if they were girls without a history. As they were now. It was the now—and not memory—that had cornered all the power over them.

I bet they were the ones, said Carradine, who cut a dash in Mena camp and in the bar at Shepheard's. I bet they were heroes in the bar of the Parisiana.

Everyone was silent awhile. The men were wild in Egypt, Naomi said at last. But they are holy here. They're like monks, dying. If it wasn't so piteous it would be outright beautiful. Their wounds are the devil but their toughness is God.

An awed Honora suggested, Have you thought they might be better at this than they are at living contented in houses?

After lunch, Carradine later reported, Mitchie visited the officers' walking wounded quarters and asked them—good fellows that they were—to treat her nurses with respect. They were not chambermaids nor private soldiers.

Carradine later told the others this—and that an Australian colonel, a broad-faced, good-looking but portly man, was in the corridor on crutches listening to her speech and now entered the room. His accent might be British but he had the sort of complexion you could get only under the Australian sun.

Good for you, Matron, he said. Go for the bleeders!

So by evening Carradine told the mess that some of the officers were decent people, and many walked who should have been on crutches.

At some ill-defined hour they returned to their stations. Outside—for inscrutable reasons—shelling had paused. Dressings needed changing again. Wounds irrigated. Pulses taken. Recurrent morphine doses given. To Sally the swabbing and dressing was more like a preoccupying mercy to herself rather than the soldier. By these exercises she kept saneness amidst the stench and the weighty tang of blood. The customary nature of these small ceremonies of nursing kept her eyes from taking in the broader scope of injury from bulkhead to bulkhead.

On a cot before them now lay a man whose wound once unbandaged showed a face that was half steak, and no eyes. The lack of features made his age impossible to guess. He had a young chest though—it was naked. Even mercy was bewildered here. In a fresh surgical gown Captain Fellowes appeared and let out a little professional groan that declared this degree of harm beyond his powers. Wilson held the man's head by the intact side and Honora cleaned his face. The murderous streak in Sally emerged here. This man should be given three grains of morphine to save him from the improbability of what had befallen him.

He lived on. Others died with a sigh or strenuous gurgle and were carried away by orderlies, their places taken by others from above decks. All pinafores were bloodstained and there was no time to change. Mitchie moved down this deck herself in stained apron, and her air of purpose told you that this was all usual—this havoc could be reduced to order in the end.

Good girls! she called out in a busy but undistracted voice. The chief noise other than the shiver and now and then complaint of the ship's steel walls came from orderlies holding the handles of stretchers. They demanded room for their present burden of man and searched angrily for places to drop it. In that time they shouted and raged with questions and profane advice. They too had not thought they would be engaged in such events or would see their ship transformed so suddenly. And their knowledge of things had also been expanded beyond the reasonable. You knew therefore that some dropped the wounded too hard or at unlucky angles in which splintered bone might cut open arteries, or a shell fragment plugging veins or arteries be shifted by some minor nudge that let the dammed-up blood flow.

One man—younger than Sally—wept as she and Honora tended him because he had seen his brother killed. But unexpectedly he howled for the agony of his wound. Whatever chemicals of shock protected some men from pain had not flowed in this boy. Honora stayed on her knees pulling muck from the flesh beneath his ribs.

What is your name? Honora asked.

Peter, said the boy. And Edgar, my brother. How will I write?

Sally went to the trolley to collect the quarter grain his grief and pain entitled him to, and there was none. Then in the dressings room she found a rubber-capped solution bottle with dregs left and many used needles scattered about it. She came back with a hypodermic containing an eighth—she had felt bound to leave the dregs of the dregs for other men. Once he was soothed Honora drew the calipers from the wound.

At some hour all peroxide, all iodine too were gone. Orderlies came round with bread and "bully" beef and pannikins of tea for those wounded who could eat.

Good girls, good girls, said Mitchie passing amongst them.

Sally went on cleaning the flinching wounds and dragged the muck of the Dardanelles and the uniform out of holes in jaws and legs or from places close to the heart or from the neck—on the pretext of saving men for a disfigured life or even afterlife. With morphine gone, the distress of the injured was getting louder. The amputees—legs and arms lost ashore or in the theatres of the *Archimedes*—were some of them observant of the scene around and seemed ready to give bright-eyed if feverish assessments on the skills of the workers. When Sally and other nurses had eased the stumps clear and swabbed the sutures they saw some of these wounds had rubber drains emerging and others were stitched up fully to keep their inner processes secret. Therein lay a controversy of surgical procedure.

Hookes—it was said—was going by launch to surrounding transports and a British hospital ship begging for morphine. He came back
with some too. It was to be rationed.

An Indian in a turban—wounded in the side—told her what an
honor it was to be nursed by a memsahib.

From a further barge nudging alongside came walking men—
jaunty—with their shattered or punctured upper bodies. She believed
she could predict how they would behave—she felt she had encountered them a hundred times before, as if her memory and history was
completely what had happened in one night and a day and was now
set to recur forever without pause or surprise. New stretchers now.
Where? Where? the orderlies howled.

Earlier, the brain. And now the heart. They were working with Dr.
Hookes, down from the deck. When at his orders Sally eased the surgical dressing away from a right breast with forceps, they all saw for a
few seconds the wondrous upper outline of the heart. Air sucked into
that revealing cavity and releasing itself with a terrible low whistling.
They pushed on the wound with pads and Hookes left to inspect other
arrivals, writing this one off.

Later—dazed—some women were washing themselves at communal tubs near their cabins. They had stripped to their shifts, but
the smell of blood had penetrated even as far as skin. Without false
modesty they undressed and swabbed all the taints from their breasts
and bellies. Naomi appeared, her eyes stark ovals. Though newly
washed, Sally herself went to her and they embraced with a fierce-
ness impossible to imagine somewhere normal—in some place where
shared crimes counted. It has taken horror, Sally thought, to make us
sisters.

I was so bad at it, said Naomi, beginning to sob. I was so bad at it.

They got lethal wounds ashore you know, said Sally, soothing the
back of her sister's head. And not by you.

None of this is at an end, said Naomi.

Half-naked across the floor—and leaning bare shouldered against

the wall—Carradine was also weeping. The fact that her husband was
ashore, and today, gave her the sense that no one there could live.

We've all killed men today and yesterday, Sally confided to her sister. The orderlies killed men. Surgeons killed men—you can be sure.
We were all out of our depth. But the ship's full now.

Going on duty to the hospital deck again, Sally intercepted Mitchie
who was passing and made a pleading she did not even know she
would make until an instant before.

Don't put my sister on triage again. It's really distressed her.

Mitchie leveled her eyes at her. How astounding that she should
not have slept at all yet still have the means to extend a hand and say,
Well, she has nothing to reproach herself for.

And then Mitchie said, Would you do it? By *would*, I mean, are you
halfway trained?

Terror filled Sally. Look, said Mitchie, triage at a Sydney hospital is
not like triage here. You must be willing to take a sane attitude. Can
you?

She nodded.

Take the colored cards and go now.

Mitchie told Naomi some saving lie and left her below to work with
Carradine amongst the walking wounded. On a bright and crowded
morning deck gusted by an offshore breeze there were orderlies but no
doctor. Hookes had now been conscripted below. A barge lay beside
and cradles were being lowered to it. For the moment Sally was alone
with colored cards in her hands and a sense of rawest and clumsi-
est knowledge. As well as all else there were detonations from ashore
again, and shells aimed at ships around. This fire impressed a person
more here in the open and made sure that you understood you were
part of their business.

The lean sergeant named Kiernan who had a knowledge of Greek islands was there and raised his head a margin to greet her and allow her
his brotherhood. Out on the bright sea yet another barge—on which
Englishmen in pith helmets swayed on their feet in the bows—was

edging across her vision. There were barges at all places—attached to the sides of ships like piglets on sows. They were at troopships which had just delivered more armed men to great Moloch ashore. It was obvious that this was not the way things were meant to happen. In what Sally had read, the disasters of empires took centuries to ripen. Here it had all matured in days.

A new Turkish barrage of shells arrived, howling, and displaced the Aegean's surface water into fountains whose spray—Sally was sure—reached her face on the main deck. The great missiles bracketed a British cruiser a bare four hundred yards off and the detonations conveyed their power through the water. A few seconds later, she heard an orderly say in the hollow quiet—in the hope the whisper would reach powers beyond the *Archimedes*—I wish that bloody cruiser would move.

And, grateful for its luck, it did begin by inches to turn its bows and seek a new location to test out the Turkish gunners all over again. But then she could see that a launch and its tow—a barge full of damaged men—had become separated, the cable that connected them cut by a piece of shell. The swamped and torn-apart barge was sinking. Men floated face down or seemed to be waving sodden bandages like a flag signal. Oh Christ, said orderlies. Oh Jesus, oh Mother of God. For what of abdominals and thoracics and amputees in *that* stinging water? Where was mercy there? Other barges and the launch whose line to the sunken vessel had been cut began to nose about the area and sailors began to drag at the floating wounded with boat-hooks, throwing out lifebuoys and leaning over the bulwarks, extending both hands to those who still had the power to reach.

On the *Archimedes*'s deck, men from an intact barge were now being winched up in cradles four at a time to make their own demands. The first crate carrying a cot case drew level with her and was dragged down onto the deck by men under Kiernan's orders. The soldier had a head wound and bore the normal filthy number 1. When his stretcher was lifted out of the cradle, his gaze was wild and unknowing. He would never remember his rise up the flanks of the *Archimedes*. He might never remember anything. Sally attached the red card to him. The color game!

Put him forward near the theatres, she told the orderlies, not that she knew if there was room forward. She wondered if she would want to give each of them a mothering red until the reds ran out and the anesthetics and morphine. She felt the panic Naomi had on the bad-lit deck last night, all alone in authority over the shades of life and death that were so hard to tell from each other.

Wounds smelled. But she worked hard and without too much doubt. The cases arrived in numbers and she felt competent at numbers.

There were four cradles at work on the stretcher cases. With a part of her vision she could see orderlies signaling to the winch men on the upper deck to ease off on the handles and then they were swinging her candidates for triage on the deck, one every few instants, it seemed. Stretchers were accumulating. She speeded up. A quick reading of the label applied by the casualty clearing station doctor and a mere touch of the pulse, that was all. Kiernan—moving in to apply a blue tag to a boy of perhaps sixteen years who was bare-chested except for bandages—murmured, We can do only what we can do, Nurse.

Later she thought there could not be a more obvious thing to say, but it seemed utterly novel to her then—a new first principle mined by Kiernan's cleverness. A spate of walking English—Tommies in their quaint music-hall pith helmets—all seemed to say, Hello, Nurse, as they were asked to settle themselves in the shade along the open deck. One of them had it in him to bow, but in a kind of cockney mockery that was all right by her.

At an hour of the day she could not have named—there was not even time to consult the watch her parents had given her—the cot cases had suddenly been all taken down. The variously afflicted walkers sitting in patient exhaustion by the railing now came forward. Shell splinters in arm or leg or shoulder, bullets in soft tissue or peripheral bone. Orderlies had however been serving them pannikins of tea—the grand sustainer, a remedy itself and promise of further remedy. One man with his mid-face wrapped in bandages said in brittle, feverish humor, Nose shot off by some bludging Turk, Nurse. Wasn't my best feature anyhow!

He too had been lucky by fractions of inches in his distance from some propellant or other.

She dealt then with the men from the barge. Slattery told her that below on the crowded, enormous hospital deck, they had hauled Dr. Hookes off to the theatre and he'd looked like someone summoned to the gallows.

Through opened portholes the sun struck this man and that as if bent on dazzling them to their graves. But there was a different thunder now. It was the sound of the anchor chain rising. Everyone seemed to pause, the nurses at their hectic stations and the wounded in their anguish.

Half the nurses went back to work in the night reverberating with the *Archimedes*'s deep-set engines. To see who slept first, they drew numbers from a soldier's slouch hat Mitchie brought round. The fortunate—Sally included—fell into bunks so oblivious they were confused as to where they were when aroused the next dawn. Before rest they took turns at the basins and perhaps for the one time in their lives hitched their nightdresses in common for a brisk cleansing between the legs.

By morning the morgue was overcrowded. Men were committed to the sea. And at their tea break there was a sort of hissing girlish mutter amongst some—a particular sniping expression had come to several faces. One of them was Honora's. Honora—it would need to be said—had not slept for more than forty hours and had become mean and in-the-know and au fait. Something bitter and catty was arising—all the more because they were smashed with tiredness. Freud entered with her dark, large eyes rimmed with exhaustion after hours as theatre nurse. She looked pale and stayed by the door as if she were waiting for a welcome from one of her sisters to bring her completely into the mess.

Are you still under the influence of the chloroform fumes, Karla? Honora asked with a squinting intent before Karla could find a seat. Freud shook her head and looked at the coven of knowing women at the table.

No. Sorry, she said. Just distracted.

She yawned.

Singing any songs lately? asked Honora.

Where did that edge she had now come from? Her eyes were suddenly ablaze with ill feeling. Beside Honora, Leonora Casement stood up with tear-streaked eyes and left the mess. The tears were an assertion particular to her and nothing to do with the hours of peculiar nursing labor they had all been involved in.

What's this all about? asked Freud, though she could not choke back the yawn that overcame her.

I believe you're singing to the surgeons.

What? That's ridiculous.

Honora blazed. In falsetto she sang, "Oh, darkies, how my heart grows weary . . ."

Are you barking for yourself? asked Freud with a new iciness, or are you someone else's watchdog?

Captain Fellowes likes it a lot, I believe, and has told people so. He is suddenly song struck. I'd keep it up if I were you. You might net him yet.

And then it all developed.

Freud: Tell me what you're saying.

Honora: You choose what to make of it.

Freud: I want to know, Honora.

Honora: You can have any man. They all sit at your feet. Leo has the one who's fixed as the pole star. And you're trying to unfix it.

To hell with you, Freud told her.

She had a fine rage, Sally thought. Her stark eyes showed she was no average opponent. Do you know where I've been the last two days?

Same place as all of us, said Honora. Except you've been serenading blokes blown to pieces.

What if I were asked to sing, to calm the patient?

Naomi stood up all at once. She was rigid and intent.

Bloody well stop it! she yelled.

It was not typical. Sally had never heard from her such a roar and even for the others it had total authority. Freud and Honora were brought to a stop by this fury.

Don't you remember? There are men hemorrhaging—internal and external—while you squeal at each other. *There are men hemorrhaging, for dear God's sake!*

Honora's high feelings were all at once punctured. The anger she had accumulated on Leo's behalf seemed to drain from her, and the chance of tears of regret or repentance arose. Freud took her own dark-faced, unappeased place at the table.

If only you knew about me, Freud told Honora.

But Honora looked like a person who has just woken up to the fact she's betrayed herself. She was willing now to let Freud be whatever she chose. She could not concede it, of course. That wasn't her nature.

Sally slept two hours in the early morning and—wide awake then—put on a fresh white blouse and skirt and shoes without stockings and went on deck. It was a brilliant, kindly, salmon dawn. It did not seem to deny any of its children its even blessing, and there was no other ship and no spine of land in view. The rest of the world had made such a claim for so long that it was hard at a level beyond reason to work out where it'd all gone to. A man at the railing—tall, in loose uniform—stood upright as a courtesy to the new presence. He was smoking a Turkish cigarette. At home they had changed enemy names. But—as far as she knew—Turkish cigarettes were still Turkish.

Now—seeing it was a nurse—he yielded up the railing, even though there was no one else there to compete for its entire length. He was getting ready to walk off.

Sergeant Kiernan, she said.

That's right, Nurse. Caught smoking. Don't tell my parents.

He had dark hair, wind raked and so a little unmilitary. And his gaze was direct, as if there was still a lot of civilian in him. He had even, long features, no Irish or Scottish freckles. It was the sort of face people described as "honest" when they meant it didn't quite manage to be handsome.

So, she said, Alexandria then? Someone said Malta, though, because Alexandria's full.

No, Alex, he nodded.

He turned only his head to scan the deck. He knew that at the official level he was not supposed to fraternize with nurses. But the scales that measured infraction were missing for the moment.

He said, I don't like to call an ancient place like that by a short name, "Alex." Almost an insult. Such an old, old city. It deserves its title.

She admitted she was fussy herself about using short forms. I hate it when they call a surgical operation an "op," she said. And the Mediterranean is much too deep and wide to be the "Med."

I'd say it was, he agreed. Your name is Durance, Nurse, isn't it?

He crushed out his cigarette but placed its remains in his jacket pocket. So he hadn't repented of it yet. Also—she was sure—he was embarrassed to toss it into the fabled Mediterranean.

I think that's a pretty fine name, he said. I mean, if you put an "en" in front of it, you have one of the most flattering of words.

He saw at once that "flattering" was going too far for her tastes.

Well, if not flattering, he admitted, then at least sturdy.

She smiled. It was, after all, a soother of a word. En-durance. This wasn't the first time the obvious point had been made, of course. Old Dr. Maddox was just one who'd noted it. A few teachers had played on it too when she didn't understand mathematics or got the order of the coastal rivers of New South Wales wrong.

I doubt I want to carry a motto for a name, she confessed. It's better to have something people can just take or leave.

Like Kiernan, he said and smiled. Common Irish name. Slides right past people. Australia's full of Kiernans. Hordes in America too. I mean the family is Irish. But my grandfather became a Friend—I mean a capital *F* Friend—when he saw the work the Quakers were doing in the west of Ireland.

She could not comment. There were no Quakers in the Macleay.

I have taken to filthy tobacco, he said, only since Egypt. I intend to renounce it though. I have, thank God, stayed teetotal. When I've been most tempted there hasn't been anything around except surgical alcohol—which isn't a good place to start. But that has sometimes been a near thing. I was amazed. No brandy on the *Archimedes*. Not this trip. They should rectify that for the next trip. I saw a few fellows who needed it.

Then he turned his face back to the sea and made up his mind to go silent. He clearly thought he might have traveled too far in conversation.

Just to keep things going—as she wanted to—she herself played the geography game. He had mentioned the University of Melbourne earlier. Was he from that city? she asked.

Like all people from Melbourne, he rushed to say he was. Melbourne, he affirmed. South Yarra. A city boy. No hardihood at all. You can tell the hardy people. I bet you're from the bush. The land doesn't always sustain people but it does teach all its children to have a certain robust air.

That's city talk, she told him. There's no nobility in milking cows. And they would pretty soon complain, the farmers and their wives, if they thought they'd be listened to. It's the lack of a complaints department that makes people look hard. And it ages people as well. South Yarra. Is that nice? Broad streets? Trees?

Copper beeches, he said. And the river near where we live.

We have a river too. But it floods.

And so it does test you, after all.

It makes us take the cattle uphill. It makes some people sit on their roofs, and sometimes it drowns people. And so they fail the test you're raving about, Sergeant. *En-durance!*

Struth, he said like a non-Quaker. You know how to wing a man.

She laughed. That sounds like another girl altogether, she thought. So she decided to go easier.

Now, where did you learn about *these* places? I mean these around here.

School, he said.

Well, she told him, I left at the end of my third year of the high school. I learned a tiny piece of French. *Plume de ma tante.* And the angles on the square of the hypotenuse. That was about the lot. So where did you get all your knowledge?

All my knowledge? There's no *all* about it. There could be more, if I hadn't been such a clown when I was thirteen, fourteen. A wildness came out in me. My father blamed an uncle who was a drunk. However, there was a Classics master, wonderful fellow, splendid cricketer, all boys adored him—you've heard the story. He taught me to read Latin and Greek. And, you know, I fought him but loved it at the same time. Greek I was lazy at, but I relished knowing the alphabet, and it worked pretty well as a code for messages I wrote to other subversive boys. So I was much taken with the Greek world. And here we are in it. But I never thought it would contain what is on this ship.

Then university? she asked.

I'll admit to that, as long as you don't make much of it when there are all these doctors aboard. They've graduated, some from Guy's Hospital or Trinity or Edinburgh. High-school scholarship isn't a lot of use here. It's my honor to be a carrier of water—boiled if I can manage it—and a bearer of stretchers and linen.

No, you have leadership, Sergeant. You should be an officer.

I would never be an officer, he said, shaking his head. I have some convictions that prevent that.

He took a glance at the strengthening light and consulted his watch and excused himself. But he had somehow returned her to a settled state with the sort of palaver and primness that had characterized Lieutenant Maclean at the pyramids.

Did the *Archimedes*'s crowded decks and floors and corridors render it a ship of groans on the approach to Egypt? The supplies were teased out and young soldiers swallowed complaint in their peculiar way. And much had been learned—enough for despair and enough for improvement.

Near Alexandria the *Archimedes* emerged from a haze above limpid water and saw the East Harbor far off with the old fortress at its root to endow it with a remnant of historic authority. Across the harbor the fabled city looked bleary. Briefly on deck Sally felt none of the stir of arrival and none of the usual urgency to get ashore and see wonders by daylight. The great white mansions and hotels did not look connected to earth.

The lesser wounded were marshaled on the shaded starboard deck where it was cool to the point of chilliness. Some with blankets around their shoulders were at the rails. Others sat, sipping tea from enamel mugs, seeming sicker and paler and barely more pleased with arrival than she was. Of course they had had their shock as well. They had lost the wholeness of their bodies. Bacteria were working in their wounds and keeping them in suspense.

She went below to the wards again. Near the main stairs Naomi worked at washing a soldier, and the others about to come off duty were variously busy. The squall about Karla Freud's enchanting of surgeons was over and everyone—even Leonora—had chosen to write it off to the surprise of events and exhaustion. Honora seemed to have forgotten her own venom.

Sally could tell by looking at Naomi there had been a change that might last a time. She had not in a lifetime looked fraught but now had a peculiar, harried frown on her face. With that there, Sally could no longer envy her. The first night's triage had swept away all her smoothness and her air of knowing. Had she ever seen a rifle wound at Royal Prince Alfred? It was unlikely.

Nurses washed men and re-dressed wounds for the departure. There was something left in them that wanted nurses in hospitals ashore to marvel at what had been achieved at sea.

When it was reported ambulances were on the wharf, Mitchie was sent on deck to manage traffic and took Sally with her. The lights on the wharf burned biliously in the hazed night. As the two women appeared on deck, some walking cases rushed the gangway and—once down on the wharf—moved between trucks and ambulances like men looking for taxis.

No more of that, Mitchie announced. Other walkers, smoking by bulkheads and waiting for stretcher-case friends to be unloaded, disapproved of the stampeders with dark utterances of *Bloody awful way to act!*

The red-ticketed appeared—mute on their stretchers—and were put in cradles and winched down. The sight of them being loaded into ambulances was so pleasing to Sally that she felt a form of joy. We have managed to deliver them—that was her jubilant thought. Every man descending by winch or stairs now consoled and invigorated her.

Mitchie made a decision that Freud—no longer needed in the theatre—should be fetched and sent ashore to see that the loading occurred in correct order. There were no doctors to do it, for they were still working in the wards. Sally watched Freud's back and veil descend the gangway and then saw her enlist the aid of a young officer. Together they made trucks and ambulances wheel and edge beneath the sickly light and turn for the city. They struggled by quarter inches past vehicles arriving and choking the route to the city's military hospitals. Some military policeman gifted in initiative took a stand and held the returning vehicles for now and let the waiting ones escape. If he did nothing else for the business of war and brotherhood, thought Sally, he had done enough.

When the last stretcher had been lowered, Sally went below to feel and hear and smell the echoing deck. She fetched a bucket of carbolic and joined the nurses scrubbing surfaces. Blankets were folded and sheets soiled with blood and excrement collected for an intense boiling somewhere. The meaty smell of wounds still competed here with the sharpness of carbolic.

Making Friends

They were oblivious in their cabin—profoundly unaware of their own breath—when a polite but not-to-be-denied knocking on the door awoke them. Half-conscious in her upper bunk, Sally saw night-gowned Honora answer it. Because events had in a sense concussed her, Sally could not have safely named the time or the day or the place. It was Mitchie at the door and fully dressed. She had a telegram for Carradine. While Mitchie waited on with narrowed eyes in the doorway, Honora roused Carradine from her bunk.

The news soon broke in all the cabins, of course. Carradine's husband was a casualty. He was in Alexandria—brought by one of the transports—and located somewhere named the British Fifteenth General Hospital. All the women rose and dressed quickly, fussing over Carradine. Girls with aghast eyes came in from other cabins. Carradine was flustered—given that "casualty" could mean so many things. But they were all solidly with her. Leonora kissed her cheek. The meanness of a few days back—if any had lingered at all—had been utterly borne away by Carradine's stricken eyes and the fact that somewhere ashore was a wound whose owner they knew.

Mitchie had a truck for them. At the commandeered hotel and now British General Hospital near the old fortress, a clerk told Carradine, Mitchie, and three other nurses who had escorted Carradine from the truck that this was indeed the Fifteenth General Hospital and Lieutenant Carradine was on the list. But he could in fact be in any one of four or five places—convents and Greek mansions—overflow branches of this one.

Carradine stood by in her gray uniform with her face gray as well. Under Mitchie's intense gaze, the man decided to write out the addresses of the other hospitals. Mitchie took the list in her hand and waved it like a guarantee. They returned to the truck. As she settled herself on the hard bench opposite Carradine, Mitchie said, You must realize, dear girl, that this cable is signed not by some flunky, but a British brigadier. This would mean to me that your husband is being attended to at the most exalted level. They do not want to let down his distinguished father. That should be a matter of some hope.

They drove southeast, away from the sea, along a European-style boulevard towards a great parkland where an ornate building with old-fashioned curlicues and flourishes—a place now absorbed by military necessity—declared itself by an engraved legend over the main gate to be the Australian Hospital for Women. They got down and went inside the gate and up the path to search. The gardens were full of untended walking wounded smoking and chatting and contrasting their histories. Once inside, the women introduced themselves to British orderlies at desks. As Mitchie negotiated, the women spotted an occasional British nurse whose eyes glided across theirs and they felt comforted that the same bewilderment which had earlier afflicted them was here as well.

There was no Lieutenant Carradine in this place. They traveled eastwards now, past the ancient city. No interest in the meaning of ruined columns and tumbled stone was roused in them. As the road swung back to the coast and glitter of sea, their driver pulled up at what had been a French convent—Les Soeurs du Sacré Coeur. Beyond the gate, they saw that marquees had been set up in the garden and men on stretchers had accumulated amongst the shrubs. Mitchie and Carradine and the others entered the office of the former convent and the clerk identified Lieutenant Carradine's name. Are you all going up there? he asked, not having the authority to stop a matron.

Outside the office, Mitchie suggested only she and Carradine should go on upstairs to conclude the search. The rest should wait down here in the smell of new paint. Young nurses rushed by on their way into the garden or from the garden into the house. The women left behind felt odd and superfluous and lost for somewhere to stand.

They would find out that for Mitchie and Carradine it concluded thus: Carradine found her husband on the wide upper balcony above the garden, lying in clean linen but with a stained dressing on his head. A young doctor was leaning over him inspecting his eyes and pulling a lower eyelid down. This is my husband, Carradine told him.

Aug, said Lieutenant Carradine at the sight of her. *Aag gaut nair.*

They would all—when they eventually visited him—hear him speak in these terms. Oh be quiet, Eric, she said, falling down on her knees beside his bed and kissing his chin. But he would not. His brain had been roused and sent on the wrong tangent and he refused to cease speaking in tongues.

It's normal, the young medical officer told her, as if he'd seen this phenomenon through a long clinical life. It's normal for head wounds.

Yes, it is, said Mitchie at Carradine's shoulder.

Daug ack raga, said Lieutenant Carradine and began to weep.

No, said Carradine. No. Don't cry.

Mitchie went and at Carradine's urging let the other women come in one at a time. When Sally's turn came, the lieutenant was sleeping uneasily and with a face utterly pale. He pleaded once in his sleep. *Au rog,* he said.

None of them stayed long. Nothing could be said. They left Carradine there with her husband.

There were other nurses who lived splendidly at the Beau Rivage Hotel. But the *Archimedes* remained the home in port of Mitchie's women. They were meant to do their routine work and have their siestas and go ashore to take a cab and see those things they'd flitted by in their seach for Lieutenant Carradine—the Caesarium, which

Cleopatra was said to have built out of love, and Pompey's Pillar and all the rest. Nurse Carradine had other urgencies. Mitchie was stuck between not mentioning Carradine's marriage to those in power while getting her privileges because her husband was wounded and uttering gibberish. Somehow—during the previous night—the permission had arrived for Carradine to *special* her husband—to devote herself to his care. She wanted them to visit him, she said, and speak to him so that his brain reaccustomed itself to normal talk. She packed a bag and rushed with Mitchie to take an ambulance to the Sacré Coeur.

From the mess table, where oatmeal and tea and peacetime crockery steamed amidst dishes of boiled eggs and French-style rolls of a kind no baker in Australia made, four of them—Naomi, Nettice, Freud, and Sally—descended the gangway. That day the air was suddenly clear and pleasantly cool, and the city defined itself in sharper lines beyond the mole. With the help of a British military policeman they found a taxi, and told the driver their destination. It was the Sacré Coeur. For they felt they must accede to Carradine's call to speak to her confused husband before they did anything else.

They got there and entered the garden where the marquees did not now seem quite the sight of confusion they had been yesterday. In the lobby they saw Mitchie introducing herself to an exhausted-looking and restive matron. Mitchie declared that one of her nurses was here specialing a relative, a Lieutenant Carradine, whose father was known throughout the Empire as a notable statesman of the Commonwealth.

The Commonwealth? asked the matron. Do you have Cromwell down there in Australia or something?

Mitchie let it go—it was just a kind of frankness minus eight hours' sleep. They were familiar, said Mitchie, with the arrival of a mass of wounded men, and had been through the same thing themselves on the *Archimedes* hospital ship. They didn't want to take her time. They knew where Lieutenant Carradine was. What if she took Staff Nurse Carradine up there and introduced her to the ward sister. All the paperwork, she said, had already been handed in at the office.

The four nurses waited like applicants for a job inside the door.
They felt superfluous and tried to make themselves small and—but
for Carradine—thought of leaving.

Matron, said an English nurse coming up and addressing the British matron. She wore no red cape. General Archibald has arrived.

A group of officers, one of whom wore the red tabs appropriate to a
general—his uniform and those of his entourage without stain and their
leathers from Sam Browne to boots unscathed by the fracas across the
Mediterranean—entered the hospital and the British matron nodded to
them and led them up the steps. General Archibald was—as they would
discover—a legend in British neurology, and on his way by request of
the Foreign Office to inspect Lieutenant Carradine's head wound.

In his wake—discreetly—followed Mitchie and Carradine.

It came to Sally's turn to visit Lieutenant and Staff Nurse Carradine
on the balcony. It happened that though he slept, his dressings were
temporarily off and the ripe wound discharged pus. Carradine sensed
Sally's shadow and turned and with a small raise of her gloved left
fingers indicated the hole in her husband's—or as the British matron
possibly thought, her brother's—head.

It was a very dirty wound, said Carradine in a low voice. But Sir
Geoffrey Archibald says he will talk and walk again.

The foulness of the wound cast its doubt over the blithe opinion of
Sir Archibald.

Help me dress it, will you? There are gloves on the trolley.

Sally fetched and donned the gloves and rejoined Carradine and
her husband. She lifted the head a little from the pillow as Carradine
began to swaddle it in fresh bandages. A young man in a halter of bandages and one arm in a sling emerged from the door to the veranda.
Over his shoulders he wore a lightweight officer's jacket with one pip
on it and "Australia" on the shoulders. He had a precocious moustache, grown before the rest of the face had achieved the seniority to
justify it. He looked feverish as so many did.

Miss Durance? he asked in familiar accent. I found out by accident you were here.

She faced him and said hello and asked how he was.

Have to say I felt a bit chirpier a year back, said the young man.

His eyes looked as if they were rimmed with soot. He told her, I regret to say . . . you might have heard . . . Captain Ellis Hoyle took a knock on the second day. Did you know? I'd hate to be the bearer . . .

She kept her hold on the back of Lieutenant Carradine's head. Carradine kept briskly winding the bandage.

I didn't know, Sally said. But my sister . . .

He was clear-headed to the finish, you know. He gave me something he wanted you to keep.

He reached into his pocket and produced a silver watch.

It has his name, you see, on the back.

He had the look of a man who was already looking forward to a rest after this task was done. It was painful to tell him it wasn't.

Oh, she said. But it isn't me—I'm sorry. It's my sister who knew Captain Hoyle. She's somewhere in this building. If you're tired I'll hand it on to her.

A shadow came over his face. He lowered his eyes. Look . . . kind of you. But he asked me to do it and I reckon I should.

He seemed to consult himself again on this proposition.

Yes, he concluded. That seems to be the fair thing.

And he nodded and drifted through into the ward, looking for a corridor to take him to Naomi.

Carradine murmured, Poor Hoyle. Half of them gone in a few days! You know—the teatime group. The Sphinx group. Maclean's dead too. The lieutenant.

Sally went on supporting Eric Carradine's neck. A child is dead, she thought. None of Maclean's earnest boyish theorems would ever be tested. She considered yielding to tears on his behalf. But there was nowhere to put them. Both her hands were full of Eric Carradine.

Carradine finished the dressing and pinned it and Sally gently lowered the head. Lieutenant Carradine woke and said, *Aag. Bewl.* Carradine hushed him and touched his cheek. He gave one bleat and sank asleep again.

Carradine said, Did Maclean . . . ?

No, honestly. But Maclean was a boy. He hadn't worked out what he knew. That makes it sadder.

Carradine nodded. Sally collected herself. Carradine said, I didn't know Naomi was so . . . you know . . . so keen on Hoyle.

Sally didn't either.

A sly one, said Carradine. We're joining some of the other girls at five, for tea at the Beau Rivage. Will you be in it?

Sally was there—but not Naomi. Officers came up and offered to take them to dinners. Some of the nurses consented. There was something too Maclean-ish about these men, and Sally made her excuses. Freud took up an invitation from a major and did not insist he take others with him for her protection. She was her own protector—that was the air she gave off.

As if to amuse them Freud said, Not to raise our little quarrel again. But you might be interested to know I *was* nearly stuck with a surgeon. I was about to marry a surgeon from Melbourne. Bornstein—you can look him up. My whole family was in an ecstasy apart from me. Thank God for the war, that's what I thought. No more listening to my aunties' Yiddish lamenting. "A girl who can spurn such good fortune . . ."

So, might she be really telling them, I do not intend to get easily tangled with any surgeon again, or with stray majors taking me to dinner?

Now they were going back—without Carradine—on a sea that had chosen to be rough and under a steel-gray canopy of cloud. These deeps no longer beckoned either to heroes of history or to boys from the bush or anywhere else. Sally was on deck because Naomi had asked her to meet up there in a squall when even the orderlies had given up the effort of keeping their fags alight and gone below. Naomi must have had to struggle with the door onto the deck, yet was all at once silently there. Her hair was blowing out from under her cap. She had not been at the tea party at the Beau Rivage. Everyone knew she had chosen not to be there because of the Ellis Hoyle news.

So, I have Ellis's watch, Naomi announced into the wind. I believe, she continued, the young fellow offered it to you first.

Yes, said Sally.

Naomi's lips began to work like an older woman's—accommodating such an intimate and unlikely gift from the dead.

I don't have any idea, said Naomi, why he'd want me to have it. There are even nods and winks. He's dead. He's killed. And yet girls say things like, You two were sly, weren't you? As if he was still here and sticking around as a quiet mover. And if poor old Ellis and I *were* sly and were secretly set for each other, then they know I must be pretty upset. They get solemn and creep around me. Which I can't stand.

Sally reached out to put a hand on Naomi's shoulder. Naomi looked her full in the face in return but all the airiness of an innate seniority had gone from her. She asked, Why would he do it? Send me a watch? And a watch with a gold chain on it too. All that stands for. And . . . poor man . . . who am I to say no to it anyhow? But we weren't . . . we just weren't . . . And that's flat.

Maybe men aren't clear in the head when they're shot, Sally offered.

Naomi set her eyes on the middle air. She said, A machine-gunner killed him and the others, I hear, but the watch is running on. Not a dent.

This was a strangeness that weighed on her.

Don't read too much into it, eh, Sally urged her. He just thought of it. A gift for a friend. That's all. It's not as if it weighs a ton. And you can put it in your kit and forget it. Or send it to his parents.

Where are they? Naomi asked petulantly. I don't know.

We can find out when we're next in Alexandria. There'd be military records.

He talked to me no more than he did to Honora, murmured Naomi. He might've decided he wanted to be closer. But I didn't choose he should.

When you're a dying being, God knows what will come to your mind. And what seemed little beforehand might all at once seem large. Anyhow, don't you think the poor fellow's entitled to send you his effects? The dying have their rights . . .

Naomi did not believe it and put her long splayed hand to the side of her face as a kind of denial.

Then if you don't want it, Sally said in a half-annoyed way, why don't you toss it over the side? Give it a burial at sea?

You know I couldn't do that.

Sally imagined the ticking mechanism tumbling over itself in the famous water. They both stared at the uneven, blank waves. But it was clear to Sally that what seemed easy to her was a mountain to Naomi.

Again, the Business

There was a tentative feeling in the nurses' mess, a different air than on the first journey. The women had no reason to think that on Gallipoli, off the Dardanelles, the Hellespont, and all the other names that hung over the geography of the murders and manglings, the abattoirs had closed down for a second. It was normal hospital shifts and bed-making with unspotted linen while the orderlies scrubbed and Leonora watched Captain Fellowes walk slowly through—casually inspecting—as much calculation in her face as longing. Leo was too strong-minded or practical a girl to pine.

Now there was more of the necessary things—where on the first journey two Primus stoves had been placed in the sterilizing room, there were now eight of them. Autoclaves were promised. Orderlies were hauling boxes of a new local anesthetic drug named Novocain into the storage forward. "Novo" seemed to bespeak newness. Maybe it had power to change the whole equation when they anchored and the barges and sweepers came alongside.

As on the second afternoon, when they neared the peninsula, the doctors stood in an earnest conference at the forward part of the hospital deck. They had a new ward doctor and were proposing to use Lieutenant Dr. Hookes as a surgeon again if that were necessary. Freud—despite and because of her singing of tunes from "I Won't Be An Actor No More" to "Little Tommy Murphy"—had a strict mind when it came to the surgical theatre and would continue there.

Captain Fellowes was to be looked to as a man unaltered by that first chaotic journey. He and Mitchie approached Sally while she was on an errand to the pan room and she saw calm assessment in his eyes.

I would like you, he said, to be my anesthetist on this trip. Nurse Carradine did it for a time last journey. Have you ever administered anesthetics?

She said she had. But in Macleay District there was no center of the anesthetic arts. She doubted it weighed in the scales of ability. It secretly occurred to her that she and her sister did know how to bring oblivion.

Fellowes told her, I have a copy of Peel's volume, "On Anesthesia." I shall send an orderly to you with it. I suggest you go to the nurses' salon and have a look at its major recommendations which are at the close of each chapter.

She read Peel in the salon. In her accustomed but half-forgotten country hospital—anesthetizing for old Maddox—she had been following simple rules using a simple mask and an ether droplet dispenser. It had all been innocent of the range of chloroform and ether and chloroform dispensers and machines and masks she saw in Peel. The Yankauer mask was very like the one she had used when Dr. Maddox—to give him credit—removed a timber-feller's leg so neatly. It was at the time presumed by her to be the sole species of anesthetics mask on earth.

But there existed as well an entire zoology. The Schimmelbusch, the Vajnas. The Hewitt airway. The Boxwood wedge. The fanciful de Caux's inhaler, which was apparently not within the expense range of the Macleay District.

Fellowes and Dr. Hookes passed the door of the nurses' lounge to go to their own salon forward. Fellowes was working with a pencil and paper and paused to allow Hookes to look at a diagram before they moved on. Hookes's complexion was blotchy with sunburn. His hair was erratically brushed and his little russet moustache looked spiky. From the medical officers' lounge they could still easily be heard, Fellowes saying resonantly against the muted hum of the *Archimedes*'s engines, Look, Ginger, it has to be done. My God, the main danger lies ashore. Not at your hands here.

Hookes's reply couldn't be heard in detail. But what he said had the tone of a pleading. She thought, Like Naomi he hasn't got over the first night.

But you're needed, Ginger, simple as that. These ships have not been staffed according to the reality of things . . .

They were arguing about his transformation into a surgeon. Dr. Hookes's should be a man who—whatever his competence—could forget his own bush clumsiness in the same way she was trying to forget hers. He should consider all this a medical education. Doctors, she thought, were generally good with these adjustments of the mind.

From Hookes came something indistinct but still with the intonation of pleading. Fellowes sighed hugely. Then no more was heard. It was as if the two men had settled themselves in chairs to read newspaper reports about battles elsewhere. Hookes's anxiety hung in the air and reflected Sally's own.

There was, however, only so much study that was useful. Mind gorged with obscure considerations and chances, she visited her cabin to drop Peel on her bedside table and climbed again to the deck. There were other women there letting the saffron kindliness of these late hours above the ocean soothe them. She saw a group further along the deck. Freud was there, and Naomi, Leo and Honora and Sister Nettice. They seemed utterly restored to harmony. Women did not carry grievances here as long as on land. Sins massive on the earth were venial at sea and even more venial on this sea which had led them to *that* place.

Just now—weighed down by what she had absorbed of Dr. Peel—Sally chose to spend a few seconds on her own. She noticed that on the forward deck the orderlies were being instructed in bandaging and splinting. They and the *Archimedes* were protected by a law which all nations were said to accede to. But how firmly? Sometimes the threat

of those modern wonders and undersea beasts—the idea of the torpedoes—stung the imagination and made a person think of climbing to
the highest deck and casting a penetrating gaze across the seas.

At last she approached the others.

Here she is then, said Honora, slapping the rail beside her as if the
space there had been reserved by them. Is it true you've been asked to
do anesthetics?

Freud asked in self-satire, Will you sing to the patients?

They would already be suffering enough, said Sally. She saw her
sister smile at the witticism and was delighted. They kept an eye out
for Kiernan's lean presence. He was their favorite. Trustworthy in conversation. Our professor, Honora called him.

Kiernan did emerge from some task below.

Tell us all that's happened here since the last time we came this
way, Honora demanded. Any new shenanigans with gods?

Only with men, he said.

Honora Slattery narrowed her vivid eyes. For who would have
thought the Turks could do that much damage?

Our men are merely men, Kiernan asserted.

I'd have never known that, Honora told him with a sniff.

Kiernan conceded them the laugh they all had at his expense. No,
what I mean is, it's important for newspaper editors and generals that
we believe *we* have special gifts. We blessed Antipodeans. Worth ten
of anything else. But by all accounts the Turks aren't aware of it.

You sound pleased about that, Freud accused him and frowned.

No. I'm not pleased at all. It would be unspeakable to be pleased.
But one worries about shells, said Kiernan. How individual virtues
can stand up to them. I would be happy if it were all over. I would be
happy had it never started.

That sounds almost disloyal to me, said little Nettice, bunching
her features in conviction. In spite of all, that sounds disloyal, she
persisted.

It sounds something like the truth to me though, said Naomi, who was determined not to let such silliness reign. But territorially, Sergeant? We must be doing well in terms of territory.

Freud half closed her eyes to remember the news reports. There have been attacks from the toe of the peninsula, she announced. French and British. All still in process. The Australians in the west . . .

And everywhere the Indians, said Kiernan, who must wonder how they find themselves here.

For the very same reason we do, surely, suggested Nettice. It's either yes to the Empire or it's no to it.

She clearly suspected Quakers.

The second dusk after they left Alexandria, the Turkish guns were heard from a dark spine ahead. The *Archimedes* edged in towards Cape Helles where—with equal convenience—the Australians and New Zealanders, the Indians and British and French could all be welcomed to the ship. Before reporting to the theatre, Sally climbed to the deck in the last light. From the direction of the beach she heard a bugle call—apparently on Gallipoli the bugle did not lead men to battle but was blown to warn ships when wounded were on their way. Some little way off, destroyers were worrying and jerking about the sea in a motion bespeaking threat and fear. A minesweeper with a sailor in the bows—signaling by lantern swing—edged in to the *Archimedes*'s flank.

The anchor cable was let clatter, chaining them to their captain's choice of this acre of sea. Sally went below and washed and robed and stood in one of the small cabins set up with an operating table and with a bench for Freud's instruments, newly arrived on a tray and covered with a towel. Sally inspected her own equipment at a small table beyond the head of the operating surface. Well, said Freud. Freud and two orderlies in white coats and with a scout nurse—a young woman whom Sally did not know—arrived and maintained their restless posts in their surgeonless theatre.

Freud said to them all, It takes a little time before they come in.

Sally heard the barges bump alongside and winches paying out under the power of stuttering motors as the surgeons waited in the wards to choose their first candidates. Hookes would be there, Sally knew, maybe needing a choice forced on him.

Freud gave her long-lipped smile and gestured to the tray of covered instruments.

This is how I met my fiancé, she confided to the room. Even the orderlies. Your fiancé? asked Sally. The surgeon?

Yes. I was handing him a retractor. Not something simple and pure like a scalpel or a lancet. After all, they call that journal *The Lancet*. No one would ever call a journal *The Retractor*. A retractor's the turnip of surgical instruments. Anyhow, for him and for me it was a case of "eyes across the retractor."

Other women would be reticent about mocking such events—the weight of engagement. And of breaking it.

The hollow ship was ringing with the shouts of healthy men delivering the maimed. At last Fellowes accompanied a case carried in—the man yelping like a dog. Head wound—that was why. As with Lieutenant Carradine, the loss of the hold on language but not on the impulse to make one. Orderlies either side of him held swabs to the skull. The journey from barge to deck or from deck to ward must have somehow moved bone and brought on this frenzy. Orderlies dumped him—in his shirt and bandages—from the stretcher onto the theatre table. They held him down and called for reinforcements to help them restrain him in his demented state. Big enough to hold a bull out to pee, she heard an orderly wheeze. Quick, Nurse, said Fellowes. One of the dressings fell away and Sally saw through blood the occipital lobe and the cerebellum. The square-headed, sturdy boy looked up at Sally with the eyes of a demented animal and though two orderlies managed to hold his arms, their strength might not last. Sally felt that her movements were heinously slow but took up the anesthetics dispensing bottle and the mask and poured chloroform on the pad without letting any of it too close to his thrashing face. Near enough, however, for the fumes to dope him down and to numb that frantic brain and render him drowsy. The chloroform filled the theatre with its sweet, heavy fumes as she clamped the pad inside the mask. Fellowes—beside her—spoke urgently to an orderly. Hold him. And to Sally, Mask down now. Mask down.

She forgot dosages as she dripped further chloroform onto the mask which, for the first seconds of its tenure, needed all the force of her left arm to keep it in place. Then the patient made a bleat like a child and was under and the orderlies drew back panting, before leaving for more stretcher work. Sally flicked open the young man's left eyelid. The pupil was appropriately dilated and she felt grateful to the numbing chemicals.

Now she placed the airway device in between his teeth. They were a bush kid's teeth, with some gone and some fixed with fresh amalgam—for he had been to the army dentist in Egypt. His respiration was ragged. But what was to be expected? She moved to one side of the body to let in Fellowes and Freud and placed the cuff of the blood-pressure device on his arm, pumping it up. She saw a low diastolic and then felt his pulse, which was thready and leaking along the artery. She reached for a thermometer but Fellowes said briskly, Don't bother. For what if he somehow woke and filled the theatre with chaos before she could get more chloroform on the mask. Fellowes did his work. Retractors were involved, the unglamorous tools Freud had mocked. And the rest of the armory, which Fellowes nominated calmly and Freud passed to him. Sally took notice only of pulse, which maintained itself at its present unsatisfactory level.

The blood pressure had fallen, she saw. She called out the figures. Ninety over fifty. Her dread was the two figures meeting. Fellowes cried to the surgical orderlies, Elevate the table six inches. They got six-inch blocks from the corner and one lifted the end of the table. Gently, cried Fellowes and there was despair at their lack of skill in his voice. You could not get men to stay in the theatres and wards and become proficient at one thing. They thought it feminine work. They would prefer to lump the wounded or supplies around the ship. She wondered about her amenable old ally—Wilson—from the last trip.

For he had not seemed humiliated to work with women. These fellows finally propped the blocks under the end of the operating table to stop the blood fleeing the abused brain. The scrub nurse received bone fragments in a bowl, Fellowes saying, I want some of that back, Nurse.

He would in part rebuild the skull with suitable pieces. He asked for blood pressure again. It was not a good tale—the number for the heart under pressure falling to meet the measure for the heart at rest was a lethal union occurring one instant before the final heart fibrillation.

It happened. A tremor through the body. Oh damn, said Fellowes softly. And no adrenaline on board. Take him away.

Somewhere was an ammonia-refrigerated place where such men went. There he would be stored for an Egyptian burial amongst the other children of shock and hemorrhage—until it filled and the sea again became an option.

No sense of failure delayed things in the theatre. Orderlies washed down the surface of the table with soap and water and briskly dried it off. There was at once another boy. He had a shattered femur wound and was brought straight to her with a splint of dowel stick tied with rags from thigh to foot. He could smell the fumes and obviously feared anesthesia. Sally put the mask down and could hear him beneath it bravely counting numbers. When the putrid bandages were gone, there proved to be two wounds, one made by a bullet, the other by the upper end of the fractured bone showing itself jaggedly through the bloody hole it had made an instant after the bullet struck. After probing the wounds, Fellowes ordered the upper leg lifted and dragged by an orderly and the scout nurse. A traction splint was strapped on, and this man-boy was now destined to walk crookedly for a lifetime.

Amputations occurred at times on the *Archimedes*—in spite of the rocking of the sea—and when an overhopeful surgeon ashore had cut the limb off below the knee of another man brought onboard, the sutures were cut and the stench of the wound competed with the chloroform. A new and graver amputation must be done above the knee.

With the big strap tourniquet around the thigh, Fellowes's lancet went cutting decisively through fascia—*vastus lateralis* and hamstring and quadriceps. A good flap left. And the wound irrigated and sutured up around a rubber pipe. And then the bandaging. Here was a surgeon! Imagine had it been Dr. Maddox, with his confident cack-handedness.

The Turkish guns exchanged their metal with the warships off-shore, and the shudders of the *Archimedes* were something those on board dealt with without a thought. Fellowes would raise whatever instrument he held when a shell seemed near and start again once the jolt conveyed through the water to the *Archimedes* ended.

The timeless session in the theatre ended. Noon had eaten all time, and what was left was devoured by midnight. They were to have three hours' sleep. At subsequent meals—when they were taken—there was no conversation of any length. Salt was pointed to. Worcestershire sauce lay untouched. They could have been an order of silent nuns.

They slept for a full afternoon before a ship's steward—a man left over from the days of peace when the *Archimedes* took sane people to sane places   knocked on the cabin door and told them he had left a tray of tea for them. The bugles had sounded ashore. More barges on their way. More sweepers.

Nearly eight hundred men were on the *Archimedes* when the anchor was again raised—another battalion of men treated brutishly by metal but better accommodated now on new cots crowded in. This time more were dysentery and typhoid cases and so a hasty readjustment had to be made to the ship to create a contagious ward. It was a short run this time, a matter of four or five hours. From the ship they saw arid mountains in the sun—the harbor of Mudros on that island of Lemnos whose myths Kiernan had explained but which Sally had for-gotten. Tales of man-murdering women and the furnaces of gods had become thin and tame, even here. Military tents filled the valley be-tween the two great heads of the port. Hospital tents had begun to colonize the headlands as well. The camp's roads were marked out in brown earth by prim, white-painted stones. The olive and orange orchards grew inland—on hills—and meadows beyond the coastline were green. The hills looked enduring and real—whereas the camp looked like a giant and hasty misconception. A new order was to land the urgent cases here. Egypt for the walking wounded, the stable, the uninfected wounds. Lemnos for the rest.

That day in the harbor of Mudros, the women—their bloodied clothes being washed in a huge boiler by a Greek crewman—were served soup with some genuine beef in it. Sally watched her sister's head bent to the plate and its earnest concentration evoked a pulse of love in her. A conversation in the corridor nonetheless arrested their attention before they had finished eating. They could hear Captain Fellowes's voice and that of Lieutenant Hookes in a conversation Sally thought she had heard the beginning of some days back.

Fellowes: My good chap . . .

Hookes: No, it won't do. I've never dealt with anything like I am asked to deal with here. In the bad light and all the shudders and the mess of the wound, I cut a femoral. That's bad enough. But the nurses knew I had.

He repeated it. Do you understand, I cut a *femoral*? Drop me off here, for God's sake, where I can work in a ward.

Fellowes: Are you worried about the nurses seeing, or the mistake? A doctor is always a peril to people, dear Ginger. As well as a rescuer. How many have you saved in the past few days? Ask yourself that.

Hookes: I told you, I can't do it anymore. I'm tuckered out, can't raise a sweat. I don't care if they shoot me. Either let me go ashore here or I'm going ashore in Alex. I'll get a job, any job, in the hospitals there. Don't stand in my way, Fellowes. You're too kind for that.

Fellowes: I won't consent. The colonel won't.

Hookes: Then you will find I'll hang myself like Barcroft Boake.

Fellowes: Barcroft Boake?

Hookes: The stockman poet. He hanged himself with his own whip. And he hadn't done anyone the same damage I have.

There were tears in Lieutenant Hookes's voice. None of the soup eaters despised him. Something in them roared for escape too.

Fellowes: What can I say? The colonel wants three theatres working.

Hookes: Even if one of them is useless? Even if it's murder?

Fellowes: I've had men die on the table too.

Hookes: I promise you I'll finish myself before you can make me go again. I'm being made to do more than I'm qualified for.

Naomi looked around the table at those who shared it with her and whispered—not to them but as if to the atmosphere of authority that imbued the ship—her own pleading that he should be let go.

The two men moved on down the corridor, Fellowes murmuring now but both unconscious that their debate had been public.

Yes, said Honora. Let the poor beggar go. Some doctors wouldn't even feel any guilt. But he does.

She declared like a sudden discovery, We can get a new surgeon in Alex.

In Alexandria, said Sally—in honor of Kiernan.

Hookes became so distressed that Fellowes moved him from his cabin to the walking-wounded officers' ward in what had been some sort of elegant salon of the *Archimedes*. A young orderly was put by his bed in case he might wake and need restraining. His years as a country doctor were negated for now—doctors always being respected in the bush if halfway jovial and if they benefited even the handful of patients sufficient to get the word of their ability around the town and the region. Parks were named to honor them. Wards named in hospitals. Was that earnest future now washed away for Hookes?

Nettice was the sister on duty in here. She was a woman who rarely uttered orders. She directed tasks with a nod. She seemed to believe till proven wrong that if she could see a need for action then so could a nurse. Looking sour (that had to be admitted) she ran her ward by inclinings of the head. How old was she, this little prune? Twenty-seven? Forty-seven?

It was more like a normal hospital in this ward, Sally thought during a shift here. In the first place, it was a visible and contained ward. Here were lesser wounds already dressed and looking redressable. Morphine not called for as much as it had been in the early frenzy of overcrowding amidships and aft. Some young men lay drugged and palely still or turned slightly bewildered faces to her. Others sat on the sides of their cots in remains of Cairo-tailored uniforms they had once worn in Egypt's fleshpots. They smoked Turkish cigarettes and chatted. Many were chirpy—aware they had been plucked out of the furnace, though they would not say so. There were bullet wounds of the hand here that had subtly borne away tissue and fragmented bone. As surely as if they had been shot in the heart they could never again use a weapon. There was a blind lieutenant with bandaged pads over his eyes of whom they said, Watch that one, Sister. He's a larrikin.

The young man so labeled cocked an ear at Nettice's approach. Here we are, boys, watch it. The ogress cometh.

Beyond this part-cheerful ward lay the locked doorway to what used to be the ship's library. The typhoid ward. The women who nursed those cases were required to take antiseptic baths before returning to the messes or cabins or other wards.

When the *Archimedes* began hooting its way into the East Harbour of Alexandria again—amidst all the other hooting and protesting ships, the noise woke Dr. Hookes—Sally saw him stir and moved to him. He looked up at her, and his lower face formed a rictus. Will there be tears now? she wondered.

How are you feeling, sir? she asked him.

Which is it? Which of the Durance ones?

He swallowed with that audible dryness and began to weep very softly. I'm glad you're here. Because the first time, when they all came aboard in a rush, remember, I was on deck too. I could tell how frightened you were too.

My sister, she told him. It was my sister with you. I would have been frightened though if I'd been there.

He tried to stare hard enough to verify that this was a different Durance, but his eyes slewed about.

You would have been, yes.

He began to weep again. It was time for more of the valerian that had been prescribed. With the smallest movements of hands and eyes, she motioned the grubby orderly to be vigilant while she fetched it.

Naomi arrived to relieve her at her shift's end—since it might be some hours before these officers were taken ashore. Pinned to Naomi's white breast was not the normal nurse's watch but the gold-plated watch of Ellis Hoyle. They managed to say little to each other.

All right then?

Yes, you go and have dinner.

Ellis Hoyle's watch was no larger than the one their parents had bought Naomi. But in a sense it was huger than any other timepiece. Should it be mentioned? Sally asked nothing about it. But she knew all her sister's walls of reserve had been shaken down. Naomi sat within ruined battlements. Her safety was gone—the safety of the polished country girl who chose the city. There was a risk she might join Lieutenant Hookes in his mania. Because she believed she shared with him a kind of clumsiness.

Sister Talk

When the Durance sisters chose to, without saying anything they each had the gift to warn the other of people who might approach. In a palm court full of officers, any who might come within a certain distance would suddenly see they were absorbed in each other and feel the authority of their aloofness. The fact was clear that they weren't here to meet people, or to expand a circle of acquaintance, or to satisfy the inquiries of any young man—neither of one likely to be sent to Gallipoli as reinforcement nor of one slated to ride into the Sinai to face the Turks. When they first made their way in their approved uniforms—boomerang badge at their breasts and their nation's name at their shoulders—from the ship to the place down the hill where the gharries waited for fares, they had already taken on something of that preventive air almost without thinking about it.

The palm court at the Metropole was a bazaar of officers—if that was what a girl wanted. There were even some in kilts—and an occasional Frenchman carrying his pillbox hat under his arm. And there were few other nurses to satisfy the surmises of these fellows. So it was just as well that they were not gifted with airs of acceptance. Their airs of rejection were of a high order.

The surprising thing was, though, that—within this ring of immunity they made so easily for themselves—Sally had no idea what to say. It had been Naomi's concept to have tea and a talk. Sally did not know if her sister had brought her here as a duty because sisters should sometimes meet up and have tea. The only men Naomi looked at, meanwhile, were the musicians in dinner suits and tarbooshes who filled the court with music as undistracting as the play of a fountain. Naomi waited for the tune to end—a Strauss waltz kind of tune—as if it would be impolite not to give it a chance to curlicue itself away.

And then she turned her face as the players let their instruments drop from their chins and eased their posture for a second or two. You look tired, Sal, she said.

Sally could have said the same. But it wasn't a competition. One more good night's sleep, she promised, and I'll be right.

Some officers have invited all of us from the *Archimedes* out to a café, you know. I forget the name of the place. But the cars are coming for us at eight.

I think I'll stay on board, said Sally, and have the stew.

On the other hand, said Naomi, it's a distraction. And if I'm willing to be distracted then you should be too.

Yes, all right. But do you think going out to cafés will help us the next time a crowd comes on board?

Maybe not. But that's not its job. Its job is to make us feel that for now everything's A-one. Just for an hour or two. I don't mind being distracted, I've decided. You're the one of sterner stuff, Sal. You're like Papa. You're the one to reckon with.

They ordered their tea from earnest young waiters in crisp jackets and jalabiyas. It arrived very quickly. Sally found it strange that though there was nothing like this—the trolleys with cakes and the waiters with their murmuring politeness or the musicians in tarbooshes—anywhere in their history before the war, she and Naomi behaved as if this was their lot and they were as used to it as to the *Archimedes*. And cars at eight to take nurses to "dinner"—not tea, but "dinner," tea here being this serious afternoon ritual. To "dinner" along the Corniche, and a stroll along the Mediterranean to finish things off—to see if anyone in uniform was worth talking to. The coming evening and its foreignness were the silken hours, and for enjoying them young men were willing to then be shipped to Gallipoli and give up their brains and limbs and hearts. And yet Sally could still not see how she could be enhanced by these hours.

I reckon I'll stick with the stew, she reiterated.

Fair enough.

The band had taken on its formal posture again and had begun playing something that sounded Scottish and drippy—the-only-lassie-for-me sort of stuff.

You were in the theatre this trip? reiterated Naomi. Giving anesthetics?

Our first patient died of shock, Sally admitted. But that didn't stop Fellowes and Freud getting on with things. It's peculiar what you'll accept as normal. But that red-headed lieutenant—Hookes—he can't take it on.

I don't think the poor fellow should be despised for that.

Though it's a pretty basic thing, to cut the femoral.

Well, the wounds are quite a mess, aren't they? They're not like an illustration in a book.

They both took a spoonful of cake.

I wanted to let you know, said Naomi then, I'm back to my normal self. The first night was what you'd call a jolt.

We were all jolted, Sally told her.

Yes, none of us are quite the same. But it isn't a jaunt anymore, is it? I mean, you go for a ride to the pyramids with a soldier and end up carrying around his watch for the rest of your life.

You don't have to carry it round, said Sally. Where is it now, anyhow?

It's in my bag. I keep it wound up for some reason. I think if I'd known him well, I would have found it easier to get rid of it. I'm sorry to carry on like this. I don't normally carry on. You know that story about the man whose clock becomes like his heart . . .

Edgar Allan Poe? And the body under the floorboards?

That's right. The body . . . I think he isn't dead if I keep the thing going. Dad's book, wasn't it? That watch-on-the-dead-body story?

Yes, Adam Lindsay Gordon and Poe. They were his two. And the Bible for show.

Not bad taste, Naomi decided. When you think about it. He wanted to keep us out of the milking shed, remember. He'd employ people he couldn't afford, just to get the milking done and keep us out of the shed. I'd see some of the Sorleys and Coulthards coming in to milk for him and I'd look away.

Naomi had her gray gloves off and her right hand reached across the table to take Sally's wrist. I planned to have this afternoon tea to ask you something. It sounds strange. But I've got an idea you'll understand exactly what I mean.

Sally's body tensed while waiting for some unguessed-at demand.

Will you be my friend? And don't say that of course you will be, you're my sister. That's not the issue. Will you be my *friend*?

They both knew it was something they hadn't thought of asking before this—and would not have without the *Archimedes*.

Understanding what Naomi had done, taken the morphine into her hands and along with it the burden of bringing their mother to that mortal quietness, Sally had not been able to say such simple things herself. To utter thanks to Naomi—so Sally thought—would have brought the heavens crashing down. What Naomi asked was something humbler than gratitude.

I know very well, said Naomi, that I shouldn't have dumped you at the farm. I don't know why I wanted so badly to get away. Why can a person hate a place where every love and every kindness has been shown to her? It's a great flaw of character.

No, said Sally. Or else I've got the same flaw.

Anyhow, you stayed there. I didn't give you a choice. Tell me to sling my hook if you want. Because it's easier to sound wise now— after the manner of the *Archimedes*. The *Archimedes* is like a telescope that makes you see far-off things in their right proportion. But I was a pretender to do that to you. I knew it, and I couldn't—or didn't—stop myself. That gives you plenty of grounds not to be my friend.

They listened to the teatime music for a while. Sweet scrapings. It was not momentous to them and mimicked conversation.

What I want, Naomi ventured further, if you'll be good enough, is that we talk like friends. You don't have to like me as much as Freud or Honora. But if we talked somewhere along those lines . . . That if we had to share a cabin, it wouldn't be a hopeless cause. If we could talk woman to woman. I would love that. I hope you'd be able to imagine it.

Sally wondered if it could be done. Between such great love and great dread, something simple and little and comfortable as friendship. But she was not ready for the largest subject of all.

She said, For one thing, I was cranky about the clearing-off thing you did. But I was proud too. To have this swish sister. And you were the pretty one.

Don't be ridiculous. *You*. All the girls say so.

Well, are we going to argue about that? And I don't see the men in this room having too many arguments over it. But I ought to warn you. I'm a cold cow. I have a cold heart.

The same with me, said Naomi with an excitement—as if they were comparing birthmarks. Friendship isn't easy with people like us. Ellis Hoyle misread me by some means. Our cold hearts are what we inherited. That's not to blame Mama and Papa.

Sally shook her head. I wouldn't like to blame them, she agreed.

Naomi still had her hand. Sally studied this meeting of flesh.

I can't bubble away with conversation, that's the problem.

Yes, said Naomi. I envy the gift to do it.

So do I, said Sally.

But if we could find friendship beyond that. If we could talk. About things held close. Secrets, even.

Is she preparing, Sally wondered, for the subject of subjects?

The cake trolley had come and they both took one more French pastry off it—winged capsules of cream.

I've told you about Ellis and his damned watch, said Naomi with a sort of pride. I have told you things I could not have said a year back.

Yes, said Sally. Now her hand, having been the limp object of affection, grasped Naomi's as the band played "Rose of Tralee" and at a nearby table four officers of the Scots Guards were overtaken by gales of laughter at some folly of an absent colleague.

The women of the *Archimedes* visited Sacré Coeur to see Carradine and her husband. His wound was healing, but he was not yet ready for shipping to an English hospital. Apart from the wards full of long-term patients such as Lieutenant Carradine, they always found the place in partial chaos. In the lush, palmy gardens of the Beau Rivage, where the orchestra of Egyptians played sweet English ballads and lullabies and unexacting twiddly-dee pieces as tea was served, they would sometimes encounter an Australian or British girl who—utterly outnumbered by orderlies—worked alone or with one companion on these echoing troopships on which young men sang jolly songs on the way towards the great heap of debris, of rock and barrenness named Gallipoli, and swallowed down their dread. On the way back . . . well, they knew what was what by then.

Black Ship

The authorities now insisted that they spend two full days in the splendor of the Beau Rivage. Sally and Honora shared a room, since the friendship she had pledged her sister didn't need to be slavish. They were told that in their absence the *Archimedes* would be refitted in some way, but "in some way" was not defined. By pure luck Sally and Honora were given a room appropriate for officers and with a balcony above the sea. Since it was early summer, the air was clear as the sun rose behind this piece of strand and revealed itself gigantically by breakfast time far down the coast. An embarrassment of recreations were at their command—they could ride along the coast on light horse mounts. They could attend picnics in the Botanic Gardens or accompany a British education officer on a tour of the antiquities from which their bush ignorance would come back amended. There were bathing parties they could join with swimming costumes provided by the Red Cross. And then the afternoon *thé dansant*—to which they were so used now and so worldly at.

It was at the end of an excursion to the Temple of Poseidon and Pompey's Pillar that an officer approached them and asked, was it true they were from the *Archimedes*? In that case, what did they think of the *Archimedes* going black?

Black? they asked.

Becoming a troop carrier, I mean—traveling blacked-out.

He could tell they knew nothing and could barely understand him. Not to worry, he said. I believe it's only temporary.

When they returned to the Eastern Harbour and the *Archimedes,* they saw Egyptian workers were hanging from the sides painting out all trace of red crosses. Approaching the ship along the mole they could also see its lower doors were cast wide open. Through these doors provisions were generally lumped aboard, but now it was mules and horses that were being led by bridles. Soldiers ascended the gangway with rifles and kit. Men with rifles on their backs already looked down from the railings and possessed the ship the nurses had thought of as theirs.

As they drank tea in their mess with jackets off to release the musk of the morning's scurry through ancient places, Sergeant Kiernan himself arrived and said the colonel wanted to see them in their lounge. They went there straightaway. As they entered, the colonel seemed to nod to them individually. Fellowes and a new surgeon to replace Hookes stood there too—and near them Mitchie and another newer matron with set, uninterpretable features.

They all found seats and the colonel told them that for military necessity the authorities had decided to make the *Archimedes* a black ship pro tem. It was his recommendation that the nurses should choose to be left ashore until the higher authorities decided to transform it back to its true calling.

Nettice asked a question bearing on the point. Wasn't it true that nurses traveled on black ships?

Not in great numbers, he said. Perhaps one or two per ship. Very much volunteers.

Captain Fellowes wanted to speak and sought the colonel's nod.

You are entitled to leave the ship, he told them when he got it. The colonel cannot say so—but it seems to me an act of recklessness to chop and change the nature of a ship like this. For this journey we will replace you with competent orderlies. I heard a staff officer say that surely *they*—whoever that is—did not contemplate that you would sail for this journey, in any case. We'll wait then and see what happens next to the ship.

When the colonel and the other surgeons left the room the nurses rose—militarily adept now—to honor their military ranks. Then Mitchie told them to resume seats.

Well, it's all lunacy as usual, she declared like a reassurance. There's the risk of submarines—you see—on a black ship.

That's so, confirmed the other matron as if they might doubt Mitchie's word. *That* ought to be taken into account.

The enlightened above us, Mitchie declared, intend that the ship go to the Dardanelles black and that we see these horses and mules and men off. Then the *Archimedes* will transform itself back to white and take on patients and go to Mudros and thence to Alex. Of course it is a folly and you must not let yourself be subject to it.

But are you going? Honora asked her.

Our situation is different, claimed Mitchie. They need us to guide the orderlies who—I am pleased to announce—fear us. But it is different with the rest of you.

But of course it was at once apparent—by eyes lowered to avoid the force of her argument as by exchanged looks with the same force—that they were all to go.

They waited all day. The loading of these men and ponies and mules of the Inniskilling Fusiliers ammunition train finished and then the soldiers sat on deck talking and smoking and contradicting each other in an accent sharp as an ax. They gave off a sort of discontent—the growls and mockeries of men who had just been worked hard and could foresee harder still. This unexpected form of soldier—all rifle and webbing—came hobnailing it through the main deck of the hospital. One of them turned on seeing nurses and—instead of the applause or the brotherliness of shouted greeting when soldiers on other ships passed the *Archimedes*—hooted with harsh delight.

Here come the fooking chorus girls!

Kiernan, however, tailed the soldiers and drove them along and told them that they were guests—this wasn't *their* ship. They told him to get—as they said it—fooked. And their rawness did own the *Archimedes* for now. Even so, the soldiery was relocated by their considerate officers and sergeant majors to places where it would be harder for them entirely to take away the purpose of the ship. Towards dusk the *Archimedes* pulled away from its mooring with a few blows of its whistle. Even the *Currawong* used to leave the Macleay with more ceremony.

Dr. Fellowes passed along the hospital deck, which was now restored to quiet. Ponies all over the cargo deck, he said. They'd built stalls and loaded them last night. How well would dung sit with medical supplies? Nurses went below and saw the mule lines and fed some sugar to the rows of ponies. They saw wagons and shoulder-high green boxes of munitions mysteriously numbered for war's purpose. Young grooms in khaki shirts looked at the nurses with a blunt hunger unknown in the world of the town and the street.

On the promenade deck, Sergeant Kiernan and some orderlies were tying ropes from the inboard handrails to the ship's railings to keep the men of the munitions train off the starboard promenade. The work with roping-off was done and the orderlies leaned back against the walls smoking or making their narrow cigarettes, seeing nothing in the haze.

You're a fine fellow, Honora called to Kiernan, nearly as a tease.

Leo said beneath her breath once they had passed on, A man of beliefs. A Quaker.

Holy mother, said Honora. I can imagine a girl or two quaking for him.

Sally would remember this dusk—cramped in by haze—as having an air of uncertainty in which the *Archimedes* itself seemed to take part. She would think later that the day was like one in which a horse who could smell a cliff ahead, and had a purpose to avoid it, did not trust its rider to achieve the same level of wisdom.

Two destroyers appeared on either side of the ship. Surely this scale of naval seriousness wasn't devoted to them. Was it a chance meeting at sea by vessels with the same landfall?

Sally heard Irishmen doing physical jerks on the afterdeck and an NCO telling them to put some elbow grease into whatever exercise he demanded of them. It was not a comfortable sharing that existed here. The nurses felt yarded in to their cabins and their salon lounge that night. The Irish soldiers loudly occupied the bunks on the hospital decks. All the ports were battened down to enclose any chance beam of light from inside. The nature of sleep seemed to Sally different from the usual. It meant—for a beginning—that when she woke she did not know whether it was day or night unless her watch inscribed TO DEAREST SALLY ON YOUR GREAT DAY, 23 SEPTEMBER 1911 was consulted.

Next morning the women stirred—ill-humored—from the enclosed humidity of dreams.

Oh God, said Freud, as if she'd turned up in a world less satisfactory than yesterday's.

Honora slipped warm as a loaf of bread from her lower bunk and began whispering her mysterious prayers fast. They needed to open the ports now to verify the day. Air which had lain all night on the ocean swept in. They dressed in their white ward uniforms and went up on deck to diagnose the morning. It was growing bright out there, and the sea breeze fell away to let in a torrid offshore wind from the nastiest core of Egypt. It penetrated their nursing veils and lightly flapped the red borders of their capes.

Honora asked, Could you really believe that down there below, in that great water somewhere, there is a steely tube of men who would do us harm? I could believe in a lot of things. But I can't believe in that. The tube of steel with men inside.

They sat in the lounge reading and playing euchre. Tomorrow—after the soldiers' last night aboard—they would be busy cleaning and readying the hospital deck. Restless by nine o'clock, they went up on deck. Naomi remarked that the destroyers had vanished. That—she hoped—had no sinister naval meaning.

The *Archimedes* Gone

During the nurses' visit to the promenade, the ship swayed in a way a person would not call alarming but that they were unused to. Some of the orderlies on deck stumbled and took their cigarettes from their mouths and looked at each other with a question. They did not return their fags to their lips until the balance of the ship had been regained.

My heaven, Honora told them, we're swerving.

It's to throw the fellows in your tube off, Honora, Freud asserted, narrowing her large eyes and sharing the joke with the glaring horizon.

They could see Lemnos—by now reduced from myth to the level of any other dreary island. The hot breath of land was left behind. The air had sharpened and there was that true sea again—that sea into which today the light dived and split apart and met again at some visible point far down—a gem of light beneath, hard to take your eyes off. It imbued Sally with a welcome if temporary joy.

They remained on deck that morning and Captain Fellowes—no surgery to perform—appeared looking grave and in the full authority of his uniform. He said, Ladies! But his nod—or so they liked to think—was directed at Leonora.

These Irishmen never stop saluting me, he said of the interlopers. I'm not used to that from orderlies. And have never had it from nurses.

They all laughed along a little creakily. He was almost too perfect a creature to exchange banter with. He tipped his cap and moved forward.

Oh well, said young Leonora then. She seemed happy with the exchange—if you could call it that. She nodded to them and went below.

Freud raised the old question. So do you think they've done it? You must understand what I mean. Fellowes and Leo?

There seemed no malice in the question. She appeared scientifically interested.

No, said Nettice. Nor should you ask.

Freud declared, Doctors are the men who know how to manage these things. Without damage to the girl, I mean.

What of the moral damage? asked Nettice dryly.

No one had asked Freud, Do you know these things from experience? But they presumed she did and gave her credit for her urbanity and the possibility of her glamorous sins.

Well, said Honora, moral damage or not, done it or not, she's crazed for the man!

And why shouldn't they have gone further? Naomi said as a sudden late challenge.

Oh, Mother of God, murmured Honora. Even the Methodists are voting for jig-a-jig.

Honora and Freud and Nettice and the Durance sisters decided amongst themselves to shift subjects by going to view the sea from the uppermost deck. They ascended a stairway or companionway and stood exposed totally to the sky with mysterious equipment and winches and piping for company amidst vibrating cowlings and heavy painted grilles. The two great funnels dominated, but the Egyptian painters had been here too and their red crosses were submerged behind a layer of white. The water seemed greener and vaster still. They all at once saw their future approach them like a fish—coming straight at them. You could faintly hear it thrash the water.

Look how straight it is, said Honora in a kind of doltish admiration.

There was a profound thud of impact and a shattering and steely explosion which, had they not been young women, would have knocked them off their legs.

Life belts, said Honora almost lightly then. Their life belts were in their cabins. Come on, she said.

They flowed down the stairs. On the main deck forward they could for a moment see the soldiers leaning over the bows and looking for enlightenment on what had happened to the *Archimedes*'s flanks. Below—running through the hospital decks nearly empty of soldiers—they reached their quarters and their life belts and calmly put them on. Sally felt an abstract and intense curiosity on what was to happen next and they all seemed averse to any rush. They walked in good order back to the companionway that would take them to the deck. On the way Naomi approached Sally and disapproved of the way her belt was tied. A double loop, I think, she said as she adjusted the belt with strange cheeriness.

When they got up to the deck again they found it was already slightly angled sideways and forwards. It didn't seem likely to Sally that the threat would become more severe than that. Forward there was a melee of ship's officers and sailors and soldiers who seemed to have the same conviction that the *Archimedes* had become unstable only in a minor way. An officer said on a foghorn, Please, ladies—forward. Thank you. Plenty of time. Plenty of time.

Mitchie stood back and ushered her women along the deck. In passing her, Sally could sense at once that water—now that it had become a serious issue—frightened Mitchie. She was palely and only by a margin in command of herself. Kiernan and his orderlies bearing stretchers were making their way urgently towards the melee. By their rush they introduced a new level of concern in the soldiers they pushed through. A hatchway had exploded up forward where the torpedo had struck. Men had been wounded by fragments of steel. Mitchie saw the bearers pass and caught up with her women and faced them.

Quick, she said. Two nurses. We must attend to those fellows.

There was a ship's officer with a beard like that worn by the King of England who said, No, they'll be attended to. You must take boat number two forward.

Mitchie called for Karla Freud and Nettice and bustled past the man. Sally struggled to follow.

Mitchie turned and screamed at her, Get back! This was in all the hours they'd been at sea the first time Mitchie had become a fury. Someone was blowing a trumpet in a way that was not triumphant, and then the captain let the ship's siren sound endlessly. Sergeant Kiernan was back, and he and the officer who looked like George V began hurrying women along the downward-leaning deck, where suddenly you had to walk by shortening a leg and reaching with another.

Honora stretched out her hand in panic. Hold my hand, Sally. Hold your friend's hand, for God's sake.

Naomi, Sally called, and Naomi called back. Here, here, behind you! We should take off our veils. Nurses made a neat pile of their veils against the bulkhead. They still seemed sure of what Sally had begun to doubt—that they would simply collect them again when the small emergency ended.

Mitchie and Freud and Nettice had been driven back by orderlies to join them. Two dead, said Karla Freud, and the others are on stretchers with tourniquets.

We ought to take off our skirts, yelled Nettice. She immediately and functionally did it herself. The others began to obey by dropping their skirts until they were all in drawers. That would have amused the Fusiliers had there been time for hilarity and perhaps had the deck been level. A lifeboat was being cranked down from the upper deck and swung way out. It was unreachable because the ship was listing and at the same time inclined by the bows. But there were men with boat hooks to haul it closer. Sally held Honora around the waist.

Honora muttered, Sea bathing. I never understood the charm of the thing.

Are you saying you can't swim? asked Sally.

In my book it's not a natural thing to do, said Honora in defense.

The noise from the unwounded soldiers surging from the bows and climbing up the deck towards the stern was like the hubbub of a football crowd and seemed almost as innocent. But that was now joined by the sound of braying mules and screaming ponies. For far below them some brave man had opened the double door on the livestock hold and offered them a hope of escape.

They're trying to make them jump into the sea—all those horses, said Freud, looking at Sally starkly. Mitchie herself had taken off her skirts and showed her plump, bloomered thighs amongst the shuffling girls. But then she broke off and went forward against the tide to direct orderlies with half a dozen stretchers. She looked helplessly at the deck where stretchers might be laid. But it was taking on an angle which—as yet not decisive—would become comic pretty soon. Two of the wounded were howling.

Ladies, said the George V officer, whose men had secured the swaying boat to the fixed starboard railing by its down ropes and who had opened the removable railing to allow easy boarding. Come aboard quickly. No false bravery or hanging back now. Up you step!

Four sailors were already aboard the boat to act as oarsmen. Their oars were held vertical. Nurses stepped over the gunwale to board the lifeboat with a display of reluctance—just to show the others they were not panicked. Last—determined to speed things up—Mitchie edged Naomi ahead of her and stepped off the ship and into the boat, where the upraised hands of her women helped her down.

Sally, called Mitchie, aware that Sally was still on deck.

I'll be in this one, called Sally. Already a second boat was being cranked down from the upper deck. The Fusiliers still maintained decent order. Officers arranged them in ranks now, as they watched the boats further aft descending to receive them. The nurses' second boat was lashed to the railing at a steep angle some might consider perilous. The officer gently but with an increased urgency pushed the women aboard. Sally traversed the tilting boat and took a seat on the seaward side. At her angle she could see—in Mitchie's boat lower than this one—her sister's face frowning up.

Sally's boat filled up with women whose upper bodies were bulked out with life preservers. Sally held Honora's hands, which were blue with fright. A few soldiers came aboard—almost apologetic. Peril had civilized them. The rope that attached the boat to the railing was let go and they swung wildly into the air with a joint female scream that lacked any composure. And so the *Archimedes*'s daughters dangled over the sea and were lowered away an inch at a time.

Other boats were descending further aft—but so slowly. Sally saw the ranks breaking up at the officers' permission. Resignation and calm were no longer the day's order. And the swinging out of boats seemed to present technical difficulties and was not occurring fast enough. The rake of the far side of the ship must be presenting awful difficulties for boat lowering. So men were now permitted to seek their individual rescues. Soldiers milling at the railings seemed to speculate on what the canting of the ship might mean. Then they climbed the rails to come splashing down into the sea all around the boats. Sailors hurled rafts from both the bows and aft.

Sally's boat—descending by its hawsers—now picked up too much downward speed. Looking over the gunwales she saw that because of the growing steepness of the deck her sister's boat had swung in part below hers and had stuck in place, dipping unevenly. A mere instant later it dropped hectically and splashed into the sea. The ship was nose down and Sally saw that her boat would slam the stern of her sister's and Mitchie's unless it could be detached from its hawsers and rowed clear. Still attached to the *Archimedes* by its thick cables, the boat below them—with her sister in it—now turned crazily beam on and crosswise.

She looked up and cried to the sailors at the winches, Stop!

But her lifeboat smashed into the midsection and across the thwarts of Naomi's. It wildly jolted Sally and Honora, and they could hear the screams of those below them.

This was the place where Sally's memory changed or died. The thud of the one boat atop another numbed the brain. Sally and Honora were thrown by the impact head and shoulders first into the water and their hands separated on their individual arcs. Time ceased. Only the nurses' watches—till choked by saltwater—kept it. But the time of the heart and brain vanished now in the minuteless, hourless, choking sea. They flew through an atmosphere of lusty but impotent shouts from men and were unhearing then in green water where she went so much deeper than was justifiable for someone wearing a life belt. She had a memory that this was the way of water in the muddy Macleay too. This was why—unlike other farm children—she had never liked to drop from tree branches into it. Rising by painful inches rather than as a cork, she squandered all the air in her lungs. In her aching want of breath, she wondered remotely—though without intimate concern for anything but air—about Honora. But breaking into air and light she rejoiced to see her friend bobbing in her dun life jacket with its collar pushed up high around her ears. Sally could hear Honora utter a gasp that was halfway to a scream—like a picnicking girl ducked in the surf by a lout. She was slick-haired but she seemed to Sally a breathing promise that this might be an adventure after all.

Sally? Honora shouted, wanting identification. She gave the impression she really wanted to have all this explained to her. We're fine now, said Sally.

Wine-dark sea, be fucked! yelled Honora. Kiernan had told her that Homer called the Mediterranean that.

Suddenly Sally could not contemplate the fretfulness of losing Honora and knew she must lead. Stay close! Sally called like a woman with a plan. All around, nurses in life belts were thrashing with unnecessary zeal—as if they had lost any water skills they had once possessed. In front of Sally—as she spun—was the blank steel flank of the *Archimedes*, and forward the upper rim of a part-submerged hole, which the green sea was entering like a tide invading a grotto. Its upper shredded contours were visible—complicated by explosion. Its irregularities were known only to God but otherwise were savage and unreadable. She saw the two lifeboats—one atop the other crosswise—and sensed they were about to sink. Naomi agreed, for she could be seen lowering

Matron Mitchie into the water. Mitchie displayed all blood from the waist down. It shocked Sally like nakedness. Mitchie's mouth gaped, and she did not seem to know her circumstances. But Naomi had soon skidded into the sea beside her. Ah yes, Sally remembered. Naomi was the family swimmer. Jumping from Sherwood bridge or tree forks into an opaque gray-green mixture of topsoil and escarpment grit from up as far as Armidale.

Sally saw the midships doorway open and tilted a few feet above the water. Protesting horses were jumping, their hooves stuttering on the last plates of steel beforehand. There were men in there, screaming at them to go and lashing their hindquarters. Mules fell gracelessly on their flanks as the *Archimedes*'s own leaning flank loomed above them. Two nurses and some orderlies walked down the canting ship's stairs a step or two and launched themselves. Still looking out at the sea from the rail Nettice could be seen—squinting like a woman trying to recognize a face at a tea party. How had Nettice missed the lifeboats? By choice or accident? Already Sally and Honora and the remnants and population of their own shattered boat were sliding astern of the *Archimedes* and could see a little of the great rump of the ship rising by degrees. They could at once see men dropping from the lower port side closest to the shadowy surface of the water as well as others—by choice it seemed and with the howl of their lives—throwing themselves from the upmost, portside railing. They slid down the ship's sides. Why did they choose that? What did the rivets do to their flesh? But men were queuing for the fright and abrasions of it.

The thing will drag us under, called Honora. The bloody thing!

Sally saw Naomi swim one-armed—a true surf Amazon indeed—dragging Mitchie by the collar of her life jacket. The water was full of claims to mercy. There was a soldier with a bandaged arm dragging another whose face had no flesh. Mitchie and Naomi were not any longer in the nursing and tending business, however.

Some boats seemed to get away easier than hers and Sally saw two of them rounding the low but visible bows. The high tail of the

Archimedes was exposed—its screw turning and turning in air and still driven by unknowing engines.

Rafts everywhere! Sally yelled to her sister. Black, rubber—square-thwarted and unsafe-looking things with maybe a sailor aboard or a few Inniskilling men. A soldier was kneeling on one near them and dragging a boy soldier aboard. Soon it would be loaded to sinking point.

It isn't as cold as it could be, is it? Honora asked hopefully. Like a girl in a bathing party again.

Cold or warm, Sally had not taken account. It seemed up to the massive sea to decide what it was. It had absolute rights to impose its temperature.

Other lightly populated rafts were revealed by the rhythm of the sea but with no guarantee they would stay that way should you take the trouble to approach them. One came close, though, with a soldier sitting atop. Sally saw Naomi haul herself to it and supporting Mitchie with the vigor of a woman making a claim. She linked her free arm through the loop of rope on the raft's side. Sally forgot Honora and swam up behind her sister but remembered then to turn. Honora was like many others—making a mimic of swimming and chopping the water with exaggerated liftings and plunges of her arms. But she was worthy of encouragement. Naomi attached the dazed or perhaps comatose Mitchie by both arms to a rope loop. Then she herself sprang aboard. She was so lissome. It was a gallant emergence into the air and an exhortation to strength in others, the way she levered herself from shoulder deep up and aboard without any help from the soldiers, who were distracted entirely by their own needs. Mitchie lay still in the water. Her black hair was plastered to her blue-white face and her smashed lower body made dark clouds of blood around her in the ocean. Oh, said Mitchie and became aware of Sally's arrival at the raft and of Naomi's attention from above.

Oh, don't heave me, she pleaded. Let me drift.

No morphine for her. Yet she said plaintively, Oh, and, Don't heave me, when she was entitled to her screams. Her wounds were full of saltwater and her bones might be splintered in unknown ways.

Sally hooked her own arm into a rope and dragged Honora the last
yard to share it with her. Naomi hauled Mitchie up. From below, Sally
hugged her and—with little leverage in this water—lifted her by the
waist and then the buttocks. Honora too—turned by the security of
the rope loop from a panicked girl back into a hoister—gave one arm
to the effort. But the chief lift came from Naomi, who was full of frantic energy. Argh! cried Mitchie loudly and ceaselessly as she emerged
from the water and Naomi laid her face-up in the raft. From Sally's
place at the rope loops Mitchie could no longer be seen. She could be
heard plaintively saying, What a thing to happen to a woman! What a
thing!

Naomi negotiated with the soldier the use of his belt and was applying it—as far as Sally could tell from this angle—as a tourniquet
on one of Mitchie's thighs. More raucous cries came from Mitchie.
Mitchie's wounds justified at least that much sound.

Sally remained in the water for she was uncertain if she possessed
the athleticism needed to get aboard. Honora stayed with her—both
arms hooked through the rope. She seemed now almost at ease with
the power of water which lay around and so massively underneath her.
More men were struggling up to hang from the exactly angled side of
the raft and its other vacant loops. There were unseen men hanging
on the far side too. Two or three lifted themselves onto the raft. Yet it
still felt balanced. The men aboard and those in the water called to
each other in their raw accents. Their words seemed the remnants
of sounds from old battles. Don't push, said Honora to one oblivious
youth wallowing up. She had regained her former self.

Since she had recovered the breath for it, Sally half turned her
body towards the ship. Once she saw it she could not take her eyes
from it. Its stern was rising from the water. There were still soldiers
milling around its canting decks and the stern railing. They tried to
keep their footing and were reluctant to leave the steel plates that had
pledged a solid foothold to them. Poor Rosanna Nettice must be lost
amongst the splashes and threshings between the raft and the *Archi-*

medes. The mast and funnel rose higher all the time and with more authority than they had had when the ship was solid. They reached up at a sharp angle and this looked more like a boast of power than a submission.

Honora too was watching.

That mast will thrash them, she screamed. For it looked as if the masthead would come down like a huge log as the ship heeled. The door from which the mules and horses had left was nearly under. Yet still one pony seemed to lower his head and scrape through. She could hear screaming like humans from the animals who had not jumped for fear or lack of time—a massed animal shriek of blocked escape. Men still on the ship were now reduced to jumping from the stern or sliding down its curves. She saw two land in the churning propeller which cut them to sections and threw their blood about in a terrible mist so instant you could doubt it had happened. She began to weep silently. This was a thing that stretched imagination and defiled at the last second what she thought of as the kindnesses of the *Archimedes*. Far down in a half-flooded deck where stokers drowned, the engines still churned and the unwitting screws spun in air.

Quick, said the older soldier from the raft. He leaned over the side with a canoe paddle which must have been part of the raft equipment—it would turn out the other one had been lost. This was a useless implement anyhow. But he was like a man awoken.

You in the water there—paddle, paddle!

Paddle yourself, yelled Honora. He was at one blunt end of the raft frenziedly plying the thing. Like a homing compass the raft swung nonetheless head-on to the *Archimedes*. Huge metal shrieks and thumps could be heard within the ship and the unearthly lament of mules and ponies went on. There was a blast within the skin that sent itself through the water and buffeted Sally's spine and tried to wash her under the raft. The *Archimedes* used this great sound as a pretext to jerk its stern as high into the air as it could reach. More thunders and great iron scrapings and crashes came from within. Mother of

Christ, said a soldier hanging in the water. The boilers are breaking loose. Brace yourselves.

But the *Archimedes* had found its desired angle of glide and now entered the water fast and smoothly. It left steam and a mist of coal in the air. The wave, called the sergeant with the paddle. Hold on.

The raft dipped by one of its corners, then conceded itself towards the ship's suction. The vanished ship sought to drag them away by the legs. But there was a wave, high enough to be called surf, a strong swell at a beach. Sally held Honora by one arm. The wave did not break. They rose on it and a beam of wood broke down on the raft and bruised her shoulder but then swept away quickly. It lowered and pitched them and moved on with a tolerable smoothness to meet the floating faces of the *Archimedes*'s other orphans further out.

Now that the *Archimedes* had orphaned them, there was a hubbub of conversation across the face of the water, echoing as in a cathedral, spiked here and there by howls of grief or fear or pain and desperate yells of insistent advice. Many voices rose in heated expressions of opinion. It seemed perhaps a thousand spoke at once. So many in the water? So much life thrown out of the *Archimedes* and fretfully determined to deal with the sea. A mule swam by with its glazed eye fixed on Sally. It found no succor there and blundered on. An Irish sergeant swam up with his chevrons showing below the armpit of the life preserver. He was a large, sandy-haired fellow with a sunny unpreparedness to let harm befall him and was hauling another man. He found one of the raft's loops with his free hand. Thank Christ, he said as he attached himself to the rope. The soldier he held on to with a meaty fist had a spike of steel protruding from his face below his forehead. A man beside Honora said, Let him go up on top, Sarge. Your man there's in a bad way.

The feared Inniskilling Fusiliers. Feared by the nurses, anyhow—perhaps without necessity. For now the sea had taken all the male boast out of them. So the sergeant rose up into the raft and pulled the boy with the lump of steel for a face after him and—Sally supposed—laid the young man beside Mitchie. Nurse, the sergeant said, acknowledging Naomi like a gent. They saw an upright lifeboat nearby and Sally envied it its substance. But it was a target now for many swimmers who were dragged aboard until its leeboard was so narrow that the yearning of those who grabbed its sides tipped it over and hurled all in it back into the sea. Those now in the water gamely set themselves to get it the right way up again. They would by great heaving from sailors and nurses and soldiers manage it at last, and climb back in. But fewer chose to do that. Some had been stunned by the capsize. Some— whacked on the head by the gunwales—were floating away.

From here advice could only be shouted. The amiable sergeant yelled to the population of the raft not to make the same mistake. There was after all a notice about capacity on the small rubber bulwarks and they had reached it. See there now, said the sergeant—who was their self-chosen captain—in his glottal voice. We can't take on so many we go under. False mercy, you see. Defeats the purpose. We can change places later perhaps and those in the water have spells up here.

Honora—hanging by her rope—began to pray. Hail Mary, full of grace, the Lord is with thee.

The sergeant said, Keep at it, girl. That and a passing steamer will get us to dry land.

She sounded as businesslike with her religion as with her sewing long ago. Do you know contrition, Sal? she asked. We should make our acts of contrition. O my God, I am heartily sorry . . .

And who's heartily sorry the *Archimedes* sank? asked Sally with a waterlogged fury she could not herself explain.

A horse with bulging eyes came swimming up, the sort they might use to pull cannon. It floundered and wallowed—floundering being two-thirds of what it did. Holding on to its mane and trailing and riding it in so far as it would let her was that little prune of a woman Rosanna Nettice. Her drenched face—when Sally could see and judge it—was set. It no longer looked an indefinite thing as it had in Egypt and in the *Archimedes*'s wards. Nettice half-rode, half-clung to the mane with small, unrelenting hands. She seemed not to notice them, and Slattery yelled, Hey, Nettice! Stick to it like a plaster! And in fact Nettice looked more suited to the horse than they were to the raft. Her blue lips were tight but she seemed in charge of the terror-stricken beast. It was revealed by the horse's plunging that she wore on her lower body a pair of soldier's drawers. She looked as though she would ride illimitably past even though they were calling to her—except that the horse could not overtake the drift of the raft. The animal galloped and weltered but had no traction. The splashes created a sort of surf as it tried to renew its capacity to go forward by plunging harder. It was an honest horse for a hill but now began to scream and sink. The sound was horrifying and pitched Nettice into the water. She wore no life preserver and seemed all the more a mere fragment.

Come, Nettice, yelled Sally. And Nettice swam quite functionally to the edge of the raft to be gathered in one-armed and attached to the rope that already held Slattery and her. Now there were eight people in the raft and sometimes a dozen hangers-on suspended in sea.

Are you hurt? Sally asked Nettice. But Nettice needed to wait for breath.

I got sucked down, she said, her lips beginning to shiver a little. I was very deep and gone. I was very deep.

She paused for the breath she had not yet fully got back after her long fall through the layers of the sea.

I was beyond what you could believe I could ever come up from. The horse was down there. It came up underneath me. It tangled its mane in my hand. It got beneath me and brought me up here to you. It was an instrument of God.

Some yards off, the horse was laboring and still protesting.

Save it, poor beast! called Nettice. It labored away and turned to give them one last flash of a panicked, unexpectant eye. Its neck sank and the nostrils tried to hold their place above the sea. It reached a point—fifty yards away or more—where its hindquarters began to drag it down backwards. So it went under, whinnying until choked off.

It was God's will for you, Nettice, said Slattery crazily.

But Nettice howled for the loss of her pony. The suck of water was now what Sally heard above all. The hollow cries of others seemed to disperse somewhat as all the parties to the *Archimedes*'s disaster drifted further apart.

An unmeasured time passed in the water. Naomi was hushed, and reassured Mitchie still, and Honora chattered from an instinct that while she was full of talk she could not be consumed by the sea. The boy with the shrapnel spike cried out once and again. But those things were to be expected. What was not expected was that a soldier or sailor secure on the loops of rope would let go as if he had seen a better prospect nearby. The sergeant yelled after them but they were no longer regimental enough for him to stop them.

Where are all the destroyers and troopships and such? Sally heard Naomi ask. We see them all the time when things are normal.

The sergeant said, It may be they're too frightened to come near. The U-boat, you understand.

No one tried to paddle with that little plank. Where would they paddle to? They were on a sea lane, were they not? They were on a sea that was all sea lane.

Patience, said Mitchie so clearly. Do we have water on this float, Nurse Durance?

No, Matron, Naomi admitted.

Mitchie should be raging with uncontained, overflowing pain.

Well, said Mitchie, one wouldn't expect . . .

Naomi leaned over the side of the raft. She whispered to Sally. You come up here and I'll go down there.

Not yet, said Sally. I'm happy, she lied.

She chose not to be up there with Mitchie's great damage and be powerless before it. Honora—offered the same—said, Don't know if I could manage it without showing the world my fat arse.

The sergeant laughed but without prurience. The other soldier with the younger boy, the original occupants, were utterly silent.

After a further interval, Naomi leaned over the side and confided to her sister that Mitchie's pelvis was intact. The upper thighs though— hopeless. Compound fractures both. I've got a soldier's belt on one and some of my blouse on the other.

Sally leaned her forehead against the raft's black rubber flank while Naomi began to lift Nettice, who was vulnerable for lack of a pre-server. Nettice was light to lift and of surprising agility. The sergeant did not help but not out of ill will. After so much presence and command he had gone suddenly silent. The high intoxication of his reaching the raft waned in him. He lost his powers of command as awful surprise and cold entered him.

When Nettice disappeared aboard Sally thought it grew suddenly cold in the water. Ridiculous to think such a thing. But you could believe the little woman—in rising to the deck of the raft—had shed off upon them the iciness of the depth she'd been to. In the surf back home, all you did was cry to your sister or to young Macallister, Getting cold! Going in! Into the golden strand where the sun was warm honey on quivering shoulders. She'd half-imagined till now that she had the same choice here. But now she knew by a reflection of her own coldness in Honora's blue lips that she didn't. One of the soldiers along the loops of ropes began to sing raggedly.

> *Hail, Queen of heaven, the ocean star,*
> *Guide of the wanderer here below . . .*

Through lack of memory or life force he ceased.

Thank Christ, yelled someone from the far side of the raft. Don't need that papist shite!

For the Inniskilling Fusiliers, it was known, were from a divided Ireland—though the sea was willing to accommodate them all equally.

She could not separate herself from the cold. It seemed determined to *be* her. The idea of being incarnate cold put her in a panic she was hard-pressed to manage. She felt cheated that—with all it was cracked up to be—the Mediterranean could prove so bitter in the early or midsummer. Best not to say a word about it, though the useless words about the shivers pressed against her lower lip like a sneeze. Nor did she think that climbing aboard would help. She believed it would exhaust her more than give her warmth.

Are we all here then? called Naomi. She made a graceful reconnaissance over the side. No doubt over all four sides. She was the authority. Yes, Naomi could be heard, checking the unseen side of the raft. Five handsome soldiers and a sailor this side. Are we holding on? Are we downhearted, boys?

That was the stupid thing the troops always called: Are we downhearted? As their troop ships took them off to get minced.

Two of them at least replied. We're still having a committee meeting on the downhearted business, Nurse.

Ragged half-witticisms.

You've got the tay going there, have you, Miss? And, What time's the shuffleboard start?

A copper tank—a cube of about a yard each way—came cruising unevenly along. Two men held on by some sort of railing soldered to two of its sides. It seemed likely to roll at any encouragement but was kept steady by its two passengers' life jackets.

Holding one of its handles was Sergeant Kiernan and, grabbing the other, an orderly whom Sally had seen but whose name she did not know. They were twinned. Each relied on the other to keep their cube steady.

Honora called to him. She seemed pleased to be able to make her complaint in person. This is nothing like what you told us, Sergeant Kiernan. All that Greek god claptrap. Never this cold at Clifton Gardens!

Kiernan was actually smiling! Keep angry with me, Nurse, he suggested. Angry people have a lot of staying power.

He made the water more habitable. A sort of hope floated up with him and raised the temperature for the moment.

He asked who was aboard and Naomi told him. Two wounded men. And Sister Nettice. And our three soldiers here.

Naomi—not quite in Sally's line of sight from her position in the water—was doing a census for Kiernan. Apparently she inspected the young man with a steel fragment now.

This young fellow . . . he's dead, I'm afraid.

The man's sergeant roused himself, combating the decree. Are you right sure of that, Miss? he asked, sounding half hostile.

Feel the pulse, Naomi suggested. There is none.

Oh, Jamie, said the sergeant, doing his own assessment. Oh, Jamie.

Ease him down then, said Kiernan. That's my suggestion.

Yes, said Naomi. I'll take his life preserver first.

"He will swallow up death in victory," intoned the sergeant in a grievous voice, "and the Lord God will wipe away tears . . ." He's my fookin' nephew.

What would you like me to do then? asked Naomi.

Let him go, said the sergeant with resignation. Let him go.

They could feel the jolting of Naomi and perhaps the sergeant dealing with the body. Naomi persuaded him to help her turn it over the rubber gunnels. A young body—but the face erased by a wedge of steel deck. Naomi and the sergeant operated on the reverent principle that he should not be simply dumped. Soldiers who knew him and who hung from the raft helped his descent into the sea. There for a number of consolatory seconds he floated, upright, face down, arms out. He waited until a decent space developed between him and the raft to raise his lower body and float in the posture of death. Then he gave up the surface and fell from sight. There was more discussion between Naomi and Kiernan. The ice now forming in Sally's brain prevented her from grasping what was said. A delirious boy from further down the side of the raft was lifted aboard and Kiernan and his orderly abandoned their copper cube and took his place on the ropes.

Chafe him a bit, Miss, one of his friends called. He hit his head when we jumped.

They could feel rather than see Naomi rubbing the boy's upper body as Mitchie, in shock, murmured half musically, "Wrap me up with my stockwhip and blanket, and bury me deep down below . . ."

Naomi was so busy and so much in command. She leaned over the squat rubber bulwark and said, Sally, we'll change places *now*.

Sally desired it above all. But, No, she said, furious. Honora should go!

Come on now, said Naomi, with a commanding testiness. This isn't a game of tea parties.

I'm here for good, said Honora, with stark blue-green eyes and clinging to her loop of rope. It was *her* pony or even her parent.

Honora, Sally insisted. And so Honora was hauled aboard and chafed. But the rubberized sides of the raft now threatened by a squeak to fold it up like a closed book, and so Naomi slid into the water, her bare feet pointed to make the entry as accommodating as it could be to everyone around the craft. There was no gasp from her, no sense of the shock of the sea.

So, are all you chaps awake? she asked after shaking the water from her hair. Their wakefulness had become her business.

Around the raft there were strange and weary cries. Yes, Nurse. Yes, Nurse. They sounded so much like a ward that they evoked the idea in Sally of the steel plates of the *Archimedes* and its decks crowded with cots. There was in their voice the expectation of orderlies arriving with trays of cocoa.

To Sally, her sister seemed above nature. Naomi conversed with Kiernan in tongues Sally could no longer grasp. They made their way around the raft to investigate the state of its passengers. On the raft, Matron Mitchie began singing again—this time in a finer contralto:

> *They don't plant potatoes, nor barley, or wheat*
> *But there's gangs of them diggin' for gold in the street . . .*
> *But for all that I found there I'd much rather be . . .*

Once she had made the mountains run down to the sea, a few soldiers gave her a raggedy cheer.

Oh, God, she groaned artlessly.

Kiernan—floating free of the raft—frowned as he surveyed Sally. He reached out with the sort of force allowed only here and lifted her into closer connection with the rope loop. Now, don't daydream, Nurse Durance. The current would love to take daydreamers. You should be atop, you know.

He turned in the water to see if Naomi was in reach to consult. There was no doubt at all that Naomi must be party to decisions. And it was not many seconds later that—as if to confirm Kiernan's adage about daydreaming—a soldier simply let go of the side of the raft. He floated away a little with his head back and his face skywards. What are you doing? she heard Naomi call to him.

I'm just . . . he called. See!

He half raised a finger to the sky. That other one . . .

No! Back here! Naomi called. But not even she had the strength to retrieve him.

Indeed, there were other rafts but removed now by hundreds of yards from them. An upright boat could be seen—but too far away. Another—upside down—was further removed still.

There is no other one than this one, called Kiernan. Come back!

No, the other one, he called out in cheery exhaustion.

Come back now, Ernie, one of his fellow soldiers called. But the current cooperated with the man's intention. He spun in the water. His face grew smaller and it had a mutinous serenity on it. He laid his head back and his naked feet rose. He adopted the posture of resignation to the waters.

Some wisdom prevented even the overactive Kiernan from trying to fetch him. Dear God, Naomi said. It's starting, is it?

She cried loudly, We're all staying *here*. There is no other boat for us. Just this one.

No one answered directly except that some communal discontent at her edict came out in groans. They speculated about the chances of something warmer and more mothering.

In the raft Mitchie berserkly said, I don't know where I've been, but I'm pleased to be home again.

A large gray ship appeared and was seen first by Honora. In the north, she called out. Yes. The north.

Leaning back a little way and her flesh blazing with ice, she could see the ship revealed by a swell. The men shouted and shrilled and whistled, and she bayed too. But it was set on finding its way to deliver more battalions to that terrible shore. Too busy delivering the dead to find the living.

Bastards! yelled one of the Ulster men.

Language, called Kiernan as if the rules here weren't different.

Go to hell, roared the Ulsterman back. When I'm dictated to by a fookin' colonial . . .

But he suddenly ran out of steam.

May I point out, called Kiernan, that it's your crowd who want us here, beating our heads against the Turks. We are doing your Empire a favor.

There was another communal outcry from men on and attached to the raft.

Nettice leaned over the side and confided to Naomi, I'm finished now. I lost too much air. I went too deep.

She slid like a dolphin and was in the water, but Naomi gathered her in with a long arm and attached one of Nettice's small blue hands to the rope. Nettice slumped there with a disappointed weariness.

Sally wondered why others were not so incarnately cold as she was. They complained in terms she knew were understandable. They spoke of the false current. They cursed a passing ship. But no one spoke of cold. Naomi was in the water but superior to it. Certainly she had lost all her authority on the *Archimedes*. Triage had chastened her. Ellis

Hoyle's watch was an albatross. Yet now she had not only resumed control but done it in a particular way—by becoming the jolliest girl and the best camping companion. Sally was pleased for it since it was the accustomed arrangement which she welcomed at the moment. It was a grateful wonder. It was a light shining through ice.

There was another gray ship appearing up north and from the populace of the raft more waving and shouting and hooting and whistling in which Sally took part, but only by reflex.

Nurse Slattery, called Kiernan from the water, is there a box there, on board? One end of the raft or the other?

A box? There *is* a box, said Slattery. A young man has his head on it. Move him a little to the side. That's right. So you want it, Mr. Kiernan?

Open it up, said Kiernan.

Honora said it was locked. Kiernan asked who had a knife.

Slattery inquired of the now mute sergeant if he had a knife. It seemed he produced something appropriate. Unskilled metal sounds were heard of Slattery working at the box. Fingers hopeless, she admitted. Then, Dear God, she cried. Broke the blade.

Keep working on it, said Kiernan. You see, there might be a flare.

Sally could hear Slattery battering at the box with the broken blade. She grunted, God, if you ever loved a poor girl, help me open this damned thing.

It amazed her by opening. A papist miracle of which none of the Ulstermen around and on the raft were heard objecting. Well, said Slattery, a jug of water here. Just right for Matron Mitchie.

I'll have a sip of that too, said the sergeant aboard with a clotted voice.

In hearing that plea Sally discovered her own thirst. Dryness and ice. She was a cold desert no living water could redeem. She was not surprised to see her mother floating at her side where Honora had been. Life is sweet, said her mother but with the famed Durance frown which raised the chance that death was sweet too. Sally felt with a strange loathing pride what she had achieved—the lethal hoard of morphine gathered in as honest girls gather in . . . what? Linen, blackberries, peaches? Time to put her money down on the chance death was sweet. Time to discover the infinite space of what she had done. The space lay beneath her and could be explored without limit.

A bandage and this stick thing, said Honora, further reporting the contents of the box.

The flare, said Kiernan. Hang on to it and keep it dry.

But there's nothing dry here, said Slattery.

Kiernan redefined the objective. Well, don't let it get too sodden. And pass it to me when another ship appears. It can give you phosphorus burns so don't let it off yourself.

I wouldn't know how to, Slattery reflected. She sounded a bit amazed that she had neglected this section of her education.

Go aboard when the time comes, Naomi advised him. Else you'll drop it in the sea.

Sally saw another soldier slip away and no one but she seemed to take notice or be able to afford to. She could see him floating—she believed—towards Egypt.

Does anyone here have a red handkerchief? Naomi called.

Aboard, Honora repeated the request. Then she seemed to go about rifling pockets. We've got gray, she announced.

Use that too! said Kiernan.

For he and Naomi spoke and thought with one mind.

We're as good as rescued, Naomi told everyone.

Men dangling on the sides of the craft were calling for their sip of the water. Naomi handed it over the far side of the raft. It had gone to only a few men when someone—according to the yells and reproofs of men—dropped it so that it half sank before it could be retrieved, already useless and tainted with salt. There were groans and curses all around the raft. The treasure was gone. That was the conclusive disaster. And the light was growing conclusive too, the sun getting low. In dark—it came to Sally—no one can stop me going to explore. Her forgiving mother said, We'll slip off alone. Sally looked forward to it, rejoicing. The pain of her hooked arm and the ice at her heart would be relieved.

She could not see more than the upper structure of one of them but it happened the sea was all at once full of ships. Two large shapes—Honora reported—and a smaller, faster one. The flare, called Kiernan, and Slattery passed it over the side like a baton without it being lost in the sea. Sally saw Kiernan—frowning like a prodigy of care—pull some string from it and hold it as high as he could. It blazed brighter than suns in his hand. He waved it while Slattery dared to stand in the raft and wave the gray handkerchief. One of the larger ships veered towards Kiernan's light and Honora's cloth. Around the raft ran a sudden, hoarse conversation.

They bloody seen us, cried the sergeant. They've got some gobshite there that isn't total blind. Seen us! Seen us!

But after small hesitancy it turned broadside on, then stern on. Renouncing them.

No excuse to let go, cried Naomi at once. Everyone stay. He's lowering boats.

A British naval launch—the smallest of the three vessels—presented itself and swept past them making a wave. They could hear the reverberations of its braked engine as it sat by a distant overturned boat to which some still clung. From the raft they could see people lifted and laid down or allowed to limp on its deck. A brisk pennant flapped above them from the mast. Then—instead of to them—it turned to another unseen raft to take its living aboard. The deck seemed to bristle with the rescued as it came onwards to their raft.

Hold on, called a fine, casual, polished voice through a loud-hailer. Hold on there. The French will get you. We have signaled them and they replied.

Their powers of reason were dimmed, but the people of the raft could see that it was so, and the launch was so crowded that its stern dipped. Sally felt a murderous hatred for those who were already on board. The raft swung in the launch's wake, and they beheld a launch and cutter being lowered as promised from a dusk-lit naval shape. A destroyer—someone said. As the raft swirled in the vortex made by the ship's displacement of water, they could see the tricolor on the high mast.

Boats were being lowered from a suddenly apparent second French destroyer too. Substantial rescue was about to occur.

The French destroyer held on its deck and within its bulwarks dozens upon dozens of the *Archimedes*'s children. After being lifted up to the deck each of them had been wrapped in a blanket by sailors with pom-poms on their hats like in a play. The thoroughly dry, thick texture of the blanket was a mercy so vast that Sally—laid on the deck beside Nettice—thought the men's foreign names should be taken by some-one so that they could be the recipients of regular thanks. Matelots. They were rubbing men's bodies but were inhibited as yet from rub-bing the bodies of nurses. Nettice shivered, eyes closed—encased in her blanket, beside Sally—on the tender surface of steel reminiscent of the *Archimedes*'s lost bulk.

Below a hung sail was separated off part of a sailors' mess as a women's ward. They were each lifted onto tables and now their life jackets were cut away with their blouses and remnants of clothing. The water had made the women neuters. Sally was washed with wine-tinted hot water and was given a towel to manage her own drying. She just about could. Then a French orderly helped to dress her in the undershirt of a tall sailor. In an officer's cabin—Honora already asleep in the officer's bunk—Sally was given a palliasse on the floor. The hot breath of the ship's engines entered through a vent somewhere.

She quaked with remembered and not yet dispelled terror, and found herself concerned above all with her mind. She tested it and thought she found it a stranger's mind. Her own having dissolved in the sea, she had picked up someone else's drifting and bobbing mind. She saw herself now not as a continuous thing. She was no more than a mute core—or a pole on which rings of a particular nature could be

placed. Each ring was a successive self—that was it. Her self was utterly new and needed to be learned all over. The childhood ring of self
was not connected or continuous with the morphine-stealing one. Nor
did the morphine-stealing one share any fragment with the Pyramid
gawker. And now she was utterly new again, she found herself alarmed
to be so. The latest hard little hoop—being taken out of the water—
could just as easily be lifted off and replaced by another as accidental,
whose description was: drowned in the Mediterranean. Since she was
so tenuous, she might still swerve at any second from her rescued
state and into oblivion. There was no such grand connector as destiny
at work in her and never had been. Such a thin skin existed between
parallel states and chances that they could leak or bleed or be welded
into one another.

An officer with a molded beard came along, bowed to her and
tenderly called her Mademoiselle. A blanketed, streak-haired Naomi
appeared in the doorway. Her half-demented certainty and her zest
astounded her sister. She held up Ellis Hoyle's watch which must have
been attached beneath her life jacket to her blouse. She looked joyful
and still in command in a way that sidestepped the command of the
French officers. The sea's finished it, she explained. It's seized it up.
It's just an empty case now.

With her half-mad and all-commanding sister above her, she felt it
safe to fall into sleep and did without further thought.

She awoke to a bright evening world and sailors carrying her on a
stretcher through places full of glaring electric light. On deck a launch
hung in the air and she was loaded on when it was level with the deck.
She had an impression they were in a harbor—Mudros, she decided.
On Lemnos. From the deck of the descending launch she could see
Naomi—a blanket on her shoulders—walking the destroyer's rail and
looking seraphic. No eye had ever been clearer or readier for this place
than hers. The Argonauts landed blind compared to Naomi.

Bitter Lemnos

Sally and others were carried down a cramped laneway that smelled of earth and urine and into a large tent. Naomi passed Sally's stretcher on foot and scouted ahead. She felt canvas brush her elbow as she was brought into a tent and placed on a cot. Here she fell asleep and—after not one dream—woke in gloom lit by a hurricane lamp hanging from the central pole.

She heard a significant voice and struggled to identify who it was by the dim lamp and an early morning glimmer of light through the canvas. Carradine bent down to pull back her blanket. A band was playing in the distance, orderlies shouting—for its own sake, it seemed—and a few blowflies buzzed in the tent.

Look, said Carradine. The blanket says "RF" and then down here *République Française*. A bit of the old *parlez-vous*, eh?

Sally reached up and took her by the elbows. She found them solid and present. She gazed into Carradine's face.

I was hoping you were all safe, said Carradine.

But we left you with your husband, Sally protested. You're with him, not me.

Ah, said Carradine. Well, that's a tale for later.

That awful hole in his head . . .

He's well. He speaks well. He's fit to get elected to parliament like his father.

Sally let Carradine loosen the sailor's shirt she still wore and wash her shoulders and her breasts, and then her belly and genitals and rump and legs. All of it was the sweetest friction.

You've washed the others? she asked with feverish democratic concern.

Oh, yes, said Carradine. They're all clean. And fit to talk to.

Oh, said Sally. But Eric?

Carradine said in her nurse's whisper, The doctor in England—at Sudbury Hospital—said I was holding up his recovery. The terrible thing is that he's probably right. Eric's depended on me so much. But he cried when I was sent off here. He cries easily, then gets angry and afterwards never stops apologizing. It's the nature of the wound. He gets periods of delirium when he thinks the world's out to get him. I've seen more men weep in the head-injury ward in the last four months than I've seen in my whole life before.

The feel of the towel remained exquisite. Had such a fabric existed before the torpedo?

The problem, Sally assured Carradine, is that men are not strong. It was men who drifted away from our raft. Whereas Mitchie . . .

Carradine nodded—assenting to the proposition that Mitchie had endured.

Well, she's had surgery but I haven't heard any more . . . Most of the time I work as a dresser. I have a fine tent. Or if it's possible to have a fine tent here, mine is. And everything I need—and two orderlies who treat me with contempt, the buggers.

There were suddenly tears on Carradine's face. My God, she said, I'm as bad as the fellows at Sudbury.

She rose. Another nurse had finished bathing Honora, who had barely stopped talking in a hushed voice.

Carradine! hissed Honora, Carradine being the icing on survival's cake.

Honora was sitting up. Sally saw an apparition of Freud stirring and settling in a sailor's shirt on a camp cot across the tent.

Sally drowsed further now and was awakened by her sister's lips on her cheek. Naomi was in her long sailor's shirt and shivering beneath the blanket around her shoulders.

Imagine what it would have been like for Papa, she said. If we hadn't been lucky. We wouldn't have lasted the night. The night would have done for us.

I think you would have lasted, Sally insisted.

She heard a sudden wind blow grit against the side of the tent. An officer and a matron entered with an orderly. The officer was a man of middling years who held himself with that certainty peculiar to a particular kind of surgeon. He had not made any notable noise in entering, yet the women roused themselves and looked up, wan faced, and Sally swung her legs to the dirt floor and sat.

Ladies, he said, Colonel Spanner here. Welcome to Lemnos. May I present my congratulations on your survival.

Their survival, however, did not make him smile. Something in his greeting made Honora turn a mad, mocking face in Sally's direction. Nettice frowned from the far side of the tent with that vehemence with which she had yesterday risen out of the ocean on the pony. There was something improper in his dominance of them—with them prostrate or lolling.

Are there any problems then? he asked. Concussion, abrasions, contusions, lesions of any kind?

The women all chorused their No's and felt foolish because they sounded like a class of schoolgirls. The colonel—responding like a headmaster—asked, were they sure? The matron said there was no mention on their charts of anything beyond exposure. So the colonel turned to the orderly. Private, you are my witness that they have vouchsafed no information indicative of trauma.

Yes, sir, said the orderly and smirked.

So, said the colonel like a jolly uncle but one who could not hereafter be blamed, no grounds for a long delay in returning to work then.

Carradine stood there with narrowed eyes.

Orderly, will you see that the women are issued some clothing? Chemise, blouse, skirt, or pants . . . Yes, and shoes and Wellington boots.

Doctor, said Naomi suddenly, with a sort of impetus. There were more than twenty nurses on the *Archimedes*.

Yes, said the colonel. Six of them are missing. Please accept my condolences.

Naomi—the one nurse standing—declared, How dare they put soldiers and military equipment on our ship! And apart from the painted-over red crosses, men were visible on deck, exercising when they should have been below, hiding. It gave the U-boat its reason to sink us. I would ask you on behalf of all of us here to protest to the military command.

These are arguable points, said the colonel, but moot. Damage done now, wouldn't you say? And don't you normally address officers as "Sir"?

If we had a military status then we would, said Naomi with her eyes full on him.

Ah, said the colonel. A barrack-room lawyer here. You should feel free to write your own letter of complaint, if you choose. But may I say this is a small matter in a landscape of huge matters. Perhaps best forgotten in light of your deliverance.

The English matron read the names of the missing. Egan, Weir, Stanmore, Keato, Delamare, Fenwick. They were Sally's acquaintances, but belonged to other cabins and another clique. All these lost women had sat generally at the other table of the two in the mess. So they had stuck together in the water—just as her clique had—and been unfortunate together. Someone in the tent began to grieve and her frank tears could be heard. Freud mourned Keato as a fellow Melbourne girl. Sally felt her kinship with them too. She felt nine-tenths saturated by the Mediterranean and that she might carry its weight around in her for good.

And our matron? Honora asked.

Since the question has been asked, I can tell you that Matron Mitchie has undergone an above-the-knee amputation. The second leg remains, for the moment. That is it, then.

He nodded to the matron and orderly. They left. Carradine was left gazing at the women in the tent with her mouth set.

Is he really in charge here? Honora asked her.

Carradine conceded he was.

The orderly put his head in again.

Nurse, he said as a command, and Carradine—after a pause that counted for minor rebellion—followed him out.

Holy Virgin, said Honora. Do you think that colonel creature has a wife?

Dr. Fellowes isn't gone, Nettice assured them. I saw him on the deck of the *Tirailleur*, the destroyer.

Sally saw tears on Freud's face and felt them pushing at her eyes— a little of her saturation rising. Those pitiable girls who had yelled fear and encouragement to each other in the ocean, and it had smothered them. They had howled and the water took its opportunity.

And Leonora, Freud contributed. Leonora's not gone. They're fated to last, she and Fellowes. They live on outside all complications.

In her conviction she looked dark and pretty and a little bit cracked. There was silence then, and a surge of wind and a scatter of small gravel and the sound of rain asserting itself.

They died in our place, Rosanna Nettice argued while sitting like the rest in a shirt that had belonged to French sailors. She did not unclench her brow. They were the tithe, weren't they? God knew that with me he had taken too much and sent the horse to take me up again.

That was her map of what had happened, so they would not argue with her. Reveille ran with an instant's delay from bugle to bugle and headland to headland and across the intervening lowlands of the harbor. It insisted even the dying hear it—and the women who were not as yet utterly convinced they had escaped drowning.

Other nurses arrived. They carried clothes with them—veils, blouses, shirts, and pullovers hostile to gender, some plain gray skirts, army pants, army boots. Wonderful Lemnos creatures—so assured of the air and so convinced of their own breath. They offered to show the *Archimedes* women where the water pump was and pointed out a washing bucket and enamel basins which were stacked by the side of the tent. They had also found for them those forgotten instruments of dignity named toothbrushes. They complained under their breath. The colonel preferred the work of orderlies, they said. He thought nurses an imposition. He was a regular soldier from India. The Australians had asked for a Medical Corps surgeon to run this hospital and the British army had taken the opportunity to dump the colonel into the job. He had brought a matron-in-chief who sided with him, and their Australian matron knuckled under to the two of them. Hence the colonel had a lot of time for both these women. But the staff nurses were supposed to be mute laborers. The man was a passable surgeon but behaved as if soldiers suffered dysentery out of willfulness.

A number of the other women who had been on the *Archimedes* met them in the mess tent and swapped their tales of redemption. Voraciously they ate fresh-baked bread and great cans of blackberry jam—the plainest food and the most soothing. Flies were thick around the condiments. Asked by Sally, would the rescued women have to go on duty that day, the experienced nurses of Lemnos laughed. Take it easy, you were only sunk a day ago, one said. It was an eon of a day though. It was long as one of the divine days from the start of Genesis.

And now they went in twos to visit Matron Mitchie. Sally made the pilgrimage with Naomi at her side. There were two cots in the tent where Mitchie lay with another matron—an English woman suffering pneumonia. Mitchie had color in her face. A little semicircular tent lay over what was left of her leg.

I was a dancer once, she told the Durance sisters as soon as she saw them. It was not any attempt at a joke. There was a glimmer of fever in her eye but not of delirium.

When I danced with the surgeon-in-chief at the hospital ball, people would stand by in a circle watching. I know you don't believe me.

Both the sisters assured her they did.

A tide of pain ran over her face, and her mouth gaped like that of a woman twenty years older—a pleading, gummy mouth. So, said Mitchie when it passed, it is with a certain sadness . . . But poor women drowned, younger than me.

One could not doubt Mitchie's grasp on the world. It seemed firmer than Sally's.

They are mistaken, said Mitchie, if they think I will be hereafter content in a sedan chair.

She held up her hand.

You have met the officer commanding? I know you have. How I hate to leave you in his hands. But I am due my injection in half an hour. I have become quite the opium fiend. You'll find me in the dens of Little Collins Street when you get home.

Her pain filled the tent and they felt forced in the end to retreat before it—to give it the room it vastly needed.

Orderlies delivered their meals in the mess. Beef and biscuit at night. Some of the men appointed to the job did not care to deliver that joyless tack with grace. They wiped their noses between placing enamel plates in front of the women. They did it because they had not been told they must not.

As Sally finished a letter to their father, Naomi asked whether she was up to an evening walk. They walked along paths marked with white-painted stones, emerged from the shadows of the Canadian hospital on the cliff and saw a lovely bluish light in a sky crowded by great fists of headlands on the low foreshores of the harbor. Vessels lay at anchor in the lazy mauve water of Mudros. In silhouette they were washed clear of any military purpose. They seemed to be there to lend perspective in the great bowl of stone and pasture and sky and sea.

In terms of their friendship, it still had the color of novelty. They chatted about the state of their gang: Nettice's mute face but her forehead locked into an unrelenting frown. She might simply need glasses, suggested Sally. Freud, said Naomi, looked as though she'd seen everything. As if nothing surprised her. Yet she seemed very surprised underneath. Honora? Leo? Well, with those two you got what you expected or at least you hoped you did. They were more knowable than Freud was.

Who would look after poor Mitchie in old age? Hadn't she mentioned a brother in Tasmania? Mitchie—they agreed—would make a very rebellious invalid.

Naomi then said something unlikely. I have had no periods. Not since April.

This was friendship then. This was the sort of thing friends gave ear to.

And, said Naomi, I haven't accommodated any man. So it's not a pregnancy.

Sally's face reddened at this sort of unusual conversation. But Naomi reflected her own bewilderment. She too had missed what she had been trained to call her "time," for three or four months. Had others? She had seen no sign of the curse of Eve in any of them—no bloodied cloths or toweling hurriedly unpinned from belts beneath nightshirts to be dropped in the soaking bucket.

It's called amenorrhea, Naomi informed her. Another thing, I don't daydream about men at all. I'm indifferent to them except as patients. Has that happened to you?

Sally gathered herself. *Daydream about men?* She must get used to the pace of this new friendship and even to the concept that Naomi had once daydreamed about men, however indifferent she was to them now.

Sally said, I'm still waiting for June's and it's already nearly August.

Poor girl, said Naomi softly. Were you worried?

I thought I might ask Mitchie . . . But then . . .

Things will return to normal. The triage and the damned wounds. And now, the *Archimedes* going down. That won't help.

She took Sally's hand. Sally could feel her own sweat-slicked palm against Naomi's dry one. So, nothing to worry about, you see. We'll lose Mitchie to Alexandria, and Fellowes and Kiernan have been sent to the stationary hospital across the headland. So we don't have as many allies as usual. So be it. Things will return to normal.

But Sally could not imagine how they would. To confirm that opinion they heard from the whitewashed stone cemetery below the crash of rifle fire and the lonely bugle striving to honor someone whose body had been committed to the earth. She began to grasp her sister's hand with more of a will now. Her fingers were no longer slack. The bugle had brought their walk to a stop. They stepped off the road to make way for three ambulances grinding their way up from the harbor.

"Hysterical women," said Naomi when the ambulances had passed. That's what they say when ships sink or trains go off the line. Hysterical women.

She adopted a gruff voice. "The women were hysterical." I've seen it—Mrs. Carberry when the wagon her kids were playing in crushed her son's head. But children are a special case, aren't they? The point is, we *weren't* hysterical, were we? In the water? A little bit strange now. But men are strange too. Going silent. Drifting off. That's another mystery. Our periods are gone and our duty to be hysterical has gone too. They'll never be able to print the story of the *Archimedes* because we weren't hysterical enough.

I'm tired, Sally confessed. The exhaustion felt unanswerable.

We say it's "the curse." But when it goes missing we feel a bit lost.

Sally had the sudden confidence to laugh.

After three days their survival became somehow boring to them. They were sick of the burden of the gratitude they were told by all the other nurses they must harbor. Mitchie was the comfort of their days. Her conversational flurries were thinner than normal—interrupted by the encompassing sharpness of her pain. They discussed the nature of her wounds with her day nurse—an English girl as sweet-tempered as the supreme matron was sullen and tyrannous. What drained from the amputation? they wanted to know. The usual, said the English girl. Blood and serous fluid. The wounds on the other, compound-fractured leg showed no sign either of sepsis, but were even harder to attend to.

They were rostered to begin duty on the fourth day and were al-located by the junior matron—their much-dominated and dominating countrywoman—to work in the dysentery wards. One of these was located in a long hut down an alleyway from their own tents, and there was an overflow brigaded tent—what normal people would call a marquee. Nurses called it the "circus tent." Dysentery was said to be cruel on Gallipoli these days—as lethal as machine guns. The *Archimedes* women advanced to these wards through a miasma of excremental stink and air spotted with blowflies. The sharp-boned faces of soldiers—flesh retracted around their eye sockets—waited for them inside both the hut and tent, where flies clamored more thickly and where their first impression was of heroic mismanagement. Other harried nurses in white aprons and skirts hurried to answer shamed and urgent cries and helped men hobble towards outside pit latrines, or rushed up with basins of disinfectant to replace linen, or wash a stained rubber mattress while a withered young man waited on a chair for his fouled bed to be remade. Bare-legged men in shirts and shorts—some hopeless cases swathed like babies in clouts—displayed their faces a second but turned them away in a kind of self-reproof for their loss of control before women.

An orderly sergeant set the women of the *Archimedes* to scrub out the place. They were directed brusquely to a supply tent down the alleyway and came back to the wards with brushes and buckets of ammonia-fortified water. They thus held in their hands the simplest and bluntest instruments of their trade. In fact, they had lost that trade. The idea seemed to be that they must by scrubbing earn their way from an all-fours position to become again upright nurses. They began to cut the stench with their plied brushes and were grateful as the ammonia claimed their nostrils while they blew their breath upwards through clenched teeth to gust flies from their cheeks and eyes.

The floor of the hut done, they went to the circus tent. There were no beds here, no wounds, yet it was hellish—the air dense and feverish and possessed by flies. Men lay on the floor on mattresses and were even more crowded in. Sally could smell the fetor of their breath as she scrubbed the boards between the patients. An ambulance arrived outside, and orderlies were numerous, carrying men in and finding space for them.

Get out of the fuckin' way, the orderly sergeant screamed at Sally. Where was the kindly and urbane Kiernan? Sent to another hospital, it was said. She stood to make way and considered what had been said but could not devise anything. She saw orderlies lower men onto mattresses already fouled with excrement.

Are there no fresh mattress covers? called Naomi, suddenly rising.

What did you say? asked the orderly sergeant from the mid of the three poles of the tent.

I wondered, were there fresh mattress covers.

The man's eyes engorged. He pointed a sort of NCO's baton or crop at her. That is not your flaming concern!

Do you speak to your wife that way? asked Naomi.

Bloody shut up, Nurse, one of the stretcher bearers murmured. It almost sounded like well-meant advice.

You can't speak to nurses that way, Naomi insisted—fixed on the sergeant and his poor man's imitation of an officer's riding crop.

Yes, you go and complain, you stupid cow, he told her. It's been bloody tried before.

Some bearers seemed to laugh, and the faces of the upright, accustomed Lemnos nurses remained tight and their eyes sought upper reaches of canvas. One of them, however, called to her sisters on their knees, They're not all as bad as this one.

The sergeant laughed at that—the easy laugh of a man with official permission or indifference backing him. Naomi's reply to the sergeant was the best one that could be chosen for now. She kept her narrowed gaze on him and dropped to her knees, still gazing full-on.

Then she set to scarifying the floor again.

Sally saw a man rise from his palliasse and rush out shuffling with that dysentery urgency. He had been a soldier but now was a flue—a man in flux, paying away his stinking animal substance.

At the end of the shift, carrying basins and a jug, the nurses drew their water ration from the pump, and it seemed an inferior quantity for the task of redeeming themselves and their clothes from the foulness of the day. In the mess tent and at the nurses' stations at the end of the ward there were at least large water-filter jars brought in by ship. From these they could drink unpolluted water.

There are said to be more bedpans on the depot ship in the harbor, Carradine told them at mealtime. But the colonel feels no rush to get them ashore. He's got this cracked belief that it's better for the man with dysentery to have a bit of a walk. It teaches him self-control. Besides, it punishes him in case he's scrimshanking.

Scrimshanking?

Malingering. His beliefs belong to other wars. The wars in Africa and India that Kipling writes about.

He can't be serious, the women protested. Doesn't he know about bacteria?

They were on their knees all the next day in the typhoid ward. It was run less primitively—the absence of uncontrolled voiding of the bowels helped that. The ward doctor seemed more visible. Though of a colorless character, he cast at least a mild influence on the orderlies to take a less cutting air. Thus when a scrubbing *Archimedes* woman was in their way they emitted merely small hostile hisses. It was their ward though—the hisses stood for their title to it. There was a spirited nurse who spoke at a more than hushed volume and ignored them. There were even orderlies whose manner was inoffensive if not apologetic. It was generally older men who said, Excuse me, Nurse, as they delivered infectious cases to the beds.

The men with typhoid were apparently under suspicion of scrim-shanking too. Sally saw the colonel enter attended by the ward doctor, the matron-in-chief, and a sergeant-major. They stood by to honor this high-ranked crackpot who seemed to think the blowflies represented a test of character. The ward sister inclined her head but repressed a bow.

Don't rise, he instructed the scrubbing women airily.

As he and his orderly stopped near her, Sally could smell—even penetrating the wholesale fug of the place—the strong, masculine odor of polish from the boots of the colonel and his sergeant-major. As the medical grandee and his aides gazed across the typhoid ward, the ward doctor ventured a suggestion.

Sir, I don't believe the creosol is working well in the latrines. The Canadians are recommending chlorinated lime and the New Zealand-ers blue oil.

Colonel Spanner was at least indulgent as he put a hand on the ward doctor's shoulder. Let them recommend away, he suggested. Let them go at it as they will. Creosol is the official British army prescrip-tion and thus the Australian.

Sir, said the doctor gamely, the very proliferation of these flies . . .

Well, yawned the colonel, it's summer. Of course there's a prolif-eration of flies.

He chuckled then. Those Canadians, he said. Only just off the prairie and full of ideas about chlorinated lime . . .

He gargled some further, forgiving laughter for the raw Canadians, slapped his leg with his swagger stick, and led his party out.

Sally heard the ward doctor tell himself, There're a bloody sight fewer flies at the Canadian hospital.

An arrival of two hundred men from a transport lifted the *Archime-des* women off their feet. They were allowed to disinfect their hands and put on their veils and begin work in the general wards. There

had been an August offensive on Gallipoli, and now the orderlies unloaded the ambulances. Sally was sent to be Carradine's aide. She
was equipped with shears to cut away the stinking and lousy uniforms
from those who wore them. She remembered the first time she had
done this on the *Archimedes* and how fouled she believed everything
was after only days of the campaign. But that was nothing to how men
and uniforms were now. Her next work was to wave away flies from
bloodied bandages and naked wounds. The air vibrated with ecstatic
insects delayed only by questions of choice. One-handed she provided
surgical scissors and the angled forceps needed to extract the gauze
which packed the wound. Then the irrigation hypodermics, the new
gauze and dressing and bandages.

As Carradine worked on the facial dressing of a young man with a
tag which declared his wound serious, Sally labored with blunt scissors, cutting away his serge jacket. Australia—so proud of its wool—
had devoted too much and too densely to this young man's uniform.

To see the blackened wound in his mandible as the dressing and
gauze was eased away was to see a monstrous man—as Sally imagined
him in the future—living solitary in some hut of bark and burlap on
the edge of a town and lacking the features to reclaim his life.

Oh dear, said Carradine.

She took up a swab doused with hydrogen peroxide. The young
ogre groaned as his face burned with disinfectant.

It's good, Carradine whispered to him. It occurred to Sally that a
nurse was the seductress—telling her lies to coax back those whose
minds licked at death.

Within the ambit of Lemnos floated a boat with four putrefying dead
soldiers and three dead nurses in it. One of the nurses—identified
by her watch—was the girl named Keato. All the *Archimedes* women
were given an hour to descend the hill and stand in the neat cemetery
for the commitment of Keato and the other two women—known only
to God—to the earth. In the half-forgotten life before this, a nurse

might die of pneumonia or peritonitis, and her parents put on her grave a shattered column for a cruelly uncompleted life. But Keato's funeral was from this new and unprecedented order of existence and thus of death.

How the men and women buried today must have celebrated at finding their lifeboat. Had they needed to right it—and then congratulated themselves on achieving this and climbed aboard its hollow promise? To perish in an excess of air, Sally believed, was worse than to drown in water.

Nonetheless, the solemnities of the padre and the trumpeter did release the pressure of grief. After it was done, Sally was pleased to go back up to the tents from this field of putrefaction of young flesh—from this ground which lacked aged souls—to counsel the bewilderment of the lost young spirits.

In the night—under the black canvas—Sally was awakened by a hand eagerly exploring her stomach. She screamed at the outrage. She thought of one of those terrifying, sneering, venom-dripping, slash-mouthed orderlies. All the other girls rose up. Half of Freud's face was seen as she lit the hurricane lamp which hung from the pole. Light was shed. It caught a furious rodent scurrying across the earth floor. A patch of ground was rubbled and into the rubble black fur disappeared.

Oh God, cried Freud. Remember? We were warned. Moles.

Sally covered her eyes. I was scared it was an orderly, she confessed.

Maybe the colonel, suggested Freud to make them laugh. They all gagged with mad hilarity.

I vote we leave the lamp on, Honora said.

I vote with you, said Rosanna Nettice with her weightiness. A considered vote.

A hailstorm came over the island on that same night of the mole. Its edged ice slashed the tent canvas. In the morning Naomi solemnly repaired the hole with sticking plaster inside and out. They would stir at night now and see by the lowered flame of the hurricane lantern small dark shapes scurrying or hear them shuffling rubble on the earthen floor and being busy with their nightly animal duties.

A scatter of mail always lay on a card table by the inside door of the mess tent. Sometimes a parcel dutifully sewn in cloth. The parcels created tremors and cries of joy. People ran to get scissors to undo the stitching. The Durance sisters never looked at this table. In their own minds they had passed through a veil into country that the normal postal arrangements could not reach. Oh, they could write out to others. But others, they presumed, could not write in.

So one morning they needed to be told by some other women that there were parcels for them on the table. When people rushed to put them in their hands, the Durances frowned at each other. Their parcels had been addressed to the Australian Army Nursing Service, Mena House, Egypt, and then sent on to Alexandria, where they had acquired a label on which someone had written, ON THE ARCHIMEDES— ON LEMNOS IF LIVING.

Naomi assessed her parcel and read the writing on its sewn cloth wrapping. Sally took out her penknife from her pocket and began to cut at the fabric of hers. Inside lay a rough wooden box. It looked homemade. She could see her father running it up from grocery boxes. She could as good as hear the scrape of his saw. Inside that box lay so many good things that other nurses gasped with wonder. Condensed milk, delicious in tea. Jugged ox tongue—which they had stated a taste for early in their girlhoods. Their mother had been an expert bottler and pickler of all the earth's fruits—whether vegetable or animal—but it had been some years before her death that she had given up the effort. The girls themselves had failed to pick up the skill. So their father must have been given the tongue by a neighbor, as well as the other preserves of fruit and jam and the cloth-wrapped fruitcake. The two of them placed the jars and packages side by side and smiled at each other and at the other nurses smiling back.

Inside each package was an envelope. Naomi opened hers while Sally was still showing off her delicacies. Naomi's lips pursed as she opened the envelope—she seemed ready for dubious tidings. Sally at last opened her own. It had a number of pages and began with "My dearest girls" in her father's hand. It was dated 30 April 1915. Naomi and Sally compared their mail. The two letters were identical. And so they each read in silence while the other women drifted away to talk and drink tea.

My dearest girls,

I have made two copies of this letter and put one in each of your hampers since others tell me that not all things reach their intended destinations in the area you are in. This letter carries your father's love. To be honest with you both I miss you a great amount. It has been heavy rain this week. How often Easter is like that! I thought we were for it with a flood again—you know. So I got the cattle into the upper paddock. They're not happy since the grass is ranker there but not much. Not like pasture the other side of the Great Divide but you would think it was like that to see them mooning and sulking. Anyway, I thought we'd be sitting on the roof pretty soon. But the level of water fell then and some good upriver mud has landed on our lower paddock. Jolly good is what I say. Delivered by nature.

But the main issue—I have very large news to tell you both and my hope is that you will be pleased at it. For I think it first-rate though I understand your feelings for your dear late mother which are as strong as mine still remain. Mrs. Sorley and I have got married by Presbyterian rites. I know we are Methodist but she is firm Presbyterian. No harm done—or so I thought. You girls know her well enough. The widow Enid Sorley. And her husband was killed earlier than his time in that timber-felling accident, poor fellow. Mrs. Sorley helped me put together this hamper which I hope you find pretty A1 and a reminder of your home in the bush. Enid

Sorley pickled and bottled the tongue which I know you both used to like and we packed it in amongst the cans so it wouldn't break too easy.

So now with Mrs. Sorley to look after me I feel a lot flasher than I used to. As for my girls—I pray you are well and in powerful form. I am proud as I read the papers that you are looking after our heroic young fellows. It came through that the Andrews' son just died of typhoid in Egypt. Such a big fellow, you wouldn't believe it.

It is your father here then who hopes you are well and happy and that the news is all jake by you. Mrs. Sorley has written you a letter too. I should say Mrs. Durance but am still getting used to the change. So I still say Mrs. Sorley all the time.

With all my fond love,
Your father

Once she had finished reading, Sally looked up. Naomi's eyes were on her. The murderous children honest with each other now. And their lesser crime—the abandonment of the father. Leaving a vacuum into which Mrs. Sorley had rushed. That reflection made them both hesitate in irrational anger. Naomi raised her eyebrows. It couldn't be avoided.

So, she said, Mrs. Sorley has become our stepmother. The old man says that in yours?

Sally nodded. She knew there was another letter enclosed behind her father's and whose it would be, but did not want yet to read it. She heard Naomi murmur, If I were a better daughter I'd be entitled to say, she didn't waste much time.

Sally said, I feel exactly like that.

But it was two years and nine months, after all, since their mother was gone. An argument could be made that such a delay was just about close enough to the approved-of three years' mourning not to matter to a reasonable observer.

The envelopes each turned to now were addressed to Misses Naomi and Sally Durance.

Dear Miss Sally and Miss Naomi,

I feel I must call you by formal names because this news will be a shock to you one way or another. I cannot say it more plainly than that your father and I have chosen each other in the eyes of God and I will be to him as good a helpmeet as in my power. I thought a lot about whether you would like to hear this news from me in that distant place where you are and knowing your fondness for your mother who was such a dear woman the whole district loved her. But now that I have had to get the courage to write this letter I hope that you can accept me not as a new mother—which I would dearly love to be considered—but at least as a new friend. It might be happy for you to know that my two sons are helping Mr. Durance a lot though one has just turned seventeen and has his eyes on the army which makes me anxious of course. I cannot think of what else to say but that I beg kind thoughts from you both since I have plenty of them for you and pray for your welfare daily since I know that Egypt is a place of diseases. I hope you like what is in this parcel. I put it together with your father not to be some sort of a softener but as what it is—a sincere gift. I send you all my affection and best wishes.

Enid Durance, formerly Sorley

Enid Durance! Sally thought and was resistant to the title. Her two big boys, said Naomi when Sally had finished reading. I imagine now she'll combine her farm with ours. Quite a fancy piece of land it will make. And she—being younger than the old man—well, she'll get it. And her "two big boys" too, I suppose.

Do we want any of it? asked Sally.

No. We left it behind, didn't we?

Damn her though, said Sally. Damn her for writing a nice letter.

The new situation put their mother a degree further from them now. She was growing dimmer and less plaintive out there in the space where the dead floated and wavered in memory. Yet she had the capacity always to come back to them sharper than a knife's edge and keener than the apparent world.

In the meantime they couldn't say too much that was snide against the Presbyterian seductress—honest and unfussed and philosophic as she'd proven to be. The size of the campaign—and the scale of stupidity at whose altar the colonel was but one regional bishop—had shown them the size of the world's sins. Mrs. Sorley seemed minor in that regard. She was crowded out by the sequence of amazing, cruel things, by that compounded element in which time and horror occupied the same line and time's arrow was horror's arrow too. And all else in life was hazy as infancy.

Naomi said suddenly, You could have cooked him all the meals in the world *and* stayed at home and still he would probably have married her!

The thought of her father and Mrs. Sorley lying together in the bed where they had finished their mother was best not to be entertained.

Well, it is done now, Naomi said.

The Violation on Lemnos

Freud had her stylish and knowing air that was above mere fashion. She could also elegantly pass on the sort of gossip about Melbourne in 1914 which passed for knowledge with most of them. Melbourne was so despised in New South Wales and Sydney that contempt sent its way by Sydneysiders was itself a sort of awe—a kind of applause and a suspicion of undue sophistication. And Freud seemed to stand for the Melbournianism which people from elsewhere condemned but envied.

When they found her in the mess at dawn, however, all that was gone. She sat hunched with a blanket across her shoulders. Leo and Sally came in together from their night duty and paused when they saw her.

Are you tired? asked Leo.

Leo was a member of the blessed for whom sleep remedied all fret. Freud raised a tear-muddied face. A blue-black brow and blood-engorged eye and bloodied and swollen lip were obvious. Sally and Leo swooped in with consolation—hugging and assuring her and asking her what had happened. But she howled and they couldn't get her to say anything. Other women arrived—Naomi too. Freud still answered no inquiry. It was Naomi who went to get brandy for her and who made her drink it. Freud choked on it and then vomited on the floor. At this manifestation they realized there were too many of them offering too much help. Some stepped back and hovered by the tent flap and others cleaned the mess with towels and fetched a bucket of water and ammonia. Freud gasped and composed herself, turning inward as Leo tended to her lip with a swab, saying, Sorry, Freud, whenever Freud flinched. Naomi bent towards Freud's blanketed shoulder and Freud reached her hand across her body and—shivering with grief—took Naomi's wrist.

It was to the few nearest that she confided she'd been attacked. She'd been attacked not only in the face but afterwards by penetration. It could not have been a patient. The man was strong and angry in the predawn—it had happened after she left her ward and while it was still dark. She had been punched and had fallen. From behind, her blouse was dragged up and her undergarments down. She was penetrated violently while the man talked and hissed. Yes, an Australian.

One of the orderlies then, it was decided amongst the women on the basis that Freud had said he was healthy and his body had a strong odor but not that of the Dardanelles. At the memory of his smell she was ill again.

How the news of her having suffered this ultimate ordeal got around was not known. Naomi and the others who heard Freud speak swore it was too important and unhinging a matter to pass on. But the details emerged like smoke from a flame and entered the air under the force of their viciousness. It was obvious straight off that if the colonel so beloved of orderlies should declare Freud was lying—or that if the orderly's crime were lessened or dismissed by him—then Freud would be brought to madness.

Naomi, Honora, and Sally went to speak first to their too-timid Australian matron. They found her in the shadow of the postoperative ward. They were pleased to see that this was not a matter on which she had to call on the colonel to approve her sense of outrage. She said it couldn't be tolerated for a second. She wanted to interview Freud. En masse—in probably too many sisterly numbers—they accompanied Freud to the matron's tent. She balked at the idea of going inside, so Naomi offered to accompany her. Naomi was somehow up to her gravity.

They decided they needed to call as the first male ally the ward doctor—the doctor who had shown himself more than a cipher when he spoke low to the colonel about chlorinated lime. After a while those not on duty and still waiting outside the matron's tent saw the ward doctor arrive, glum-faced, for the obligatory inspection. This would be the worst aspect of it, Sally believed—that so soon after being mishandled and possessed by the form of man, the victim must face a magistrate of the body who inspected with a purely clinical interest the same flesh that had been attacked with raw, savage force.

When he emerged he would not answer any questions. The details—I'm afraid—are for the colonel, he told them.

They were frazzled by the idea that the colonel was the sole possible punisher of the crime.

Naomi escorted the shattered Freud back to their tent and sat by her camp cot grasping her right hand. Provosts arrived at eight o'clock. An officer and a sergeant major. Freud was sleeping—the doctor had given her barbital. But the officer told Naomi that she must be awoken. Like the ward doctor they were not unkind. If there was a small tinge of hostility, it seemed to Naomi to be related to embarrassment. This was an alleged crime of the kind they thought they'd left behind on the streets of cities.

They stood back from the cot. Naomi was permitted to rouse Freud. Karla, she whispered. These gentlemen . . .

The gentlemen moved in. The officer dragged a stool into place and sat at a distance from Freud's thunderous dark eyes. They seemed—the clear one, the bloodshot—engorged with imminent tears. But Freud refused to let them flow in front of these men. She would await a private hour.

The officer asked her, would she know the man who attacked her if she saw him again?

Yes, she said after a wary consideration. Yes, she could tell him again.

By some light from the ward she glimpsed aspects of him as he first hit her. Then—at the end—he stood over her for a second and she turned her shoulders and saw him. The rest of the time, nothing but earth.

When they asked if she could tell them about him, Naomi hoped Freud would keep silent. What if Freud surrendered these toxic details and nothing was done? Or the man was proclaimed not to exist on Lemnos? The risks seemed gigantic at that second.

He was young, said Freud. She rushed to get it over. Maybe as young as eighteen. He had a broad face. What people call moon-faced. He had not washed lately.

She half-gagged on this remembered odor.

His hair seemed to be fair, she concluded.

The officer made notes and then looked up wanly at her.

Aren't you pleased? she asked frantically. Aren't you pleased I saw all that in the light there was? His damned animal face.

And you had not agreed to meet him?

Freud's face showed the purest contempt combined with a fear of powerlessness. What do you think? she asked with a dangerous insistence.

All right, said the military police officer. Please . . . Did he say anything to you?

He said, "The blokes said!"

"The blokes said?"

"The blokes said. The blokes said. The blokes . . ."

The officer looked at his sergeant major.

A funny thing to say.

Yet you could see he believed—given its oddity—that it was the truth.

The provosts left. Naomi led her—still stupefied with sedative—to the mess tent and they drank tea. Here the colonel found her. He paused beside the flap and said, Knock! Knock! with a rusty air of geniality. Naomi got to her feet but Freud still sat. In her world all rank had been canceled.

Just to say, Staff Nurse Freud, that I have read the report and am appalled. Appalled. That one of my men should . . . "The blokes said." Sure of that, are we?

Freud did not answer.

I'll give him "The blokes said"! Now, my dear, you enjoy your tea and I'll . . .

He shunted one of his arms to indicate firm punishment. When he had gone, Freud lowered her head on her hands and drowsed for two hours. At the tea table that night there was a fraudulent cheeriness as Freud sat at Naomi's side. In the midst of it Captain Fellowes arrived from the other hospital. But, like everyone else, he was at a loss when it came to what service he might perform. At last he and Leonora went out for an evening stroll. This would have been in the past a subject for Honora's irony. But now no comedy could be borne. All the available breath needed to be spent on comfort for Freud and the hope of punishment.

In their tent later Naomi came and stood by Sally's bed. Sally was reading for comfort and distraction a remarkable book—*Of Human Bondage* by Somerset Maugham. If in her colonial innocence she thought of his name as "Morg-ham," the book still spoke to her and told her things she did not know she knew. It gave her the illusion of opening doors which the outrage on Karla Freud had slapped shut. It was also a new book and smelled wonderfully of glue and pages. Someone had brought it from England and somehow left it in the small library in the mess. She was hungry for its distractions and for the variousness and sameness of humans it proved. It was an education she could resume after a day of frightful shock.

On the scale of pure information, she had learned from Maugham things about the Anglican Church she had never known. She had learned something of living in Heidelberg, which made her think of the Germans as sharing the one soul of humanity. That there were German girls on whom the character Philip could "feast his eyes" was a revelation a person had to deal with. In this book—just published and whose buyer might have died in one of the wards or been shipped off wounded to Egypt or Malta—the author put his voyager, Philip, in the heart of German families. The subversion of that was somehow to be relished. She took a portion of delight in that the other nurses presumed she was reading some English romance. Whereas she read risky sentences such as, "Men are so stupid in England. They only think of the face. The French who are a nation of lovers know how important the figure is."

And how did that relate to Freud? Which had the attacker wanted to punish in Freud's case—the face or the figure? Did men divide up women in this way? If they did, it made the brutality more understandable.

And now Naomi was there. Getting down on a knee, she murmured to Sally, If Freud is like us, no periods, I mean . . . Well, at least no risk of pregnancy.

A pregnancy would be unspeakable. They could not want to understand what it would be like to bear such a child, waiting for the monster's face to emerge. Would you love and hate it at once? Would you send it to an orphanage? Would you murder it at birth?

So nature has some wisdom, asserted Naomi. Then she kissed Sally and went.

Next morning the supreme matron—the colonel's consort in spirit—entered the tent. She trod on ground grown cold overnight and on the rubble left by moles. She spoke to Freud, who was dressing determinedly and wanted to work. Clearly the matron was offering her a choice of wards. Post-operative, Freud decided. No, she said, she did not want to mope about, but a new ward was advisable because it was in the dysentery wards she had been seen and speculated on and become prey.

They ate their poor, cheerless breakfast of hardtack and—though condensed milk sweetened the tea—then went to their duty. Freud inherited the post-operative, the young men as dazed as she was, and the gravity of what was done to her matched by the gravity of what had been done to them. Here, they were reduced to an awful humility by anesthesia and their wounds. Here, pale, blue-lipped boys were dependent and someone's children. The holiness of man could be again believed in.

The following day was cold, but there was a distraction of a kind. A car grinding up the hill pulled to a stop outside the nurses' mess tent. After car doors were heard being slammed shut, a male voice called, Anyone in?

Sally—*Of Human Bondage* in her hands—was one of the dozen or so who were in the tent. The inquiry was so genial and so markedly different from the snarls of orderlies that a number of voices called, Yes. Two Australian officers in their slouch hats entered. One was on crutches. He moved easily and had the reddish, pleasant, broad face of a future publican or auctioneer—or at least a town worthy. The other was leaner and taller and watchfully shy. He looked to Sally like someone remembered from a vastly distant time. They were both well tailored. They shamed those nurses from the *Archimedes* who, despite the kindness of their sisters, were still wearing little better than army shirts and pants or else drab skirts—the sackcloth of their survival.

Both visitors were from the rest camp of Lemnos, and a closer look at their uniforms showed them to be not quite as flash as at first blush.

The shorter one declared, We heard you were here. Our battery is over there in the rest camp. We had a visit from a certain Sergeant Kiernan, who said he had heard you young ladies have a hard time of it here. Rather upset about it, actually. So we thought we'd come over with a small box of things.

They had heard of the attack on Freud, of course. But they would not say that.

Just hang around a tick, said the lanky officer. He went out of the tent and as he ducked his head to go out, Sally remembered him. Lionel Dankworth, who'd been keen on Honora.

Well, said the genial, huskier man left behind. He rubbed his hands as if the day was actually colder than it was. This tent is a bit draughty, isn't it?

Except when it is stifling, Naomi conceded.

Did you do yourself an injury? Sally asked him.

The old femur, he said. A bit of a knock, but a clean break. I'm hoping to go back when the boys do.

Sally and Naomi exchanged glances. Femurs took longer than that.

The tall gunnery officer was back, toting a bully-beef box. But when he put it down on the table by the giant enamel teapot there were better things than bully beef in it. He said, A little contribution.

The stockier man asked if he could take a chair. He did it with his stiff leg stuck out in front of him. He recited the contents of the hamper. Canned asparagus, he said. Canned salmon. Then there is some cocoa, he declared. Chocolate—it goes a bit white when it's been in a ship's hold in the tropics. Never mind. Oh, and some biscuits— macaroons, not hardtack. Marmalade too.

Lieutenant Dankworth, said Naomi. We met in Egypt. Honora's here, but sleeping. Off-duty. I could go . . .

No, said Lionel Dankworth, let the poor girl sleep for now.

He seemed frightened of the reunion—or at least of it being public.

The women pulled the cans and packages from the box and squinted at the labels like scholars trying to read hieroglyphics. Nettice spoke.

There is a young officer who is blinded. He's a jeweler, you see. Rather down. Since the supply in the ward has run out, if you've no objections I might take him some of this cocoa.

Why not? asked the tall man. If the others don't mind.

The shorter man with the femur injury gave the sort of smile over which no shadow had ever fallen. And yet he had been on Gallipoli and been part shattered there.

Sally inspected Nettice. It was strange that she would mention one soldier in that way.

Look, said the officers, we should introduce ourselves.

The lanky one said his name was Dankworth—as Naomi had already said. The man with the femur injury was Lieutenant Robbie Shaw.

Shaw lowered his voice. We heard one of our girls was having a bad time here.

They told him Freud was on duty. At her own insistence.

We don't like that sort of thing happening to Australian girls, the lanky one grumbled. If there is anyone you'd like us to talk to . . .

It was the normal male proposition—we can take your enemies aside and box their ears for you. That would fix everything.

She wouldn't want you to do anything just now, Naomi told them. They have promised to find the man.

You just let us know if they mess about, Lieutenant Shaw advised.

In the meantime, said Dankworth, there's a depot ship full of tea and frozen lamb and other delicacies in the harbor. Comfort from home. The laziness of quartermasters and other people meant the goods on board just sat there. They had the other day grabbed a fistful of quartermaster's invoices and filled them out and gone on board and collected the goods that they'd brought here.

So this isn't the end of it, Robbie Shaw promised.

Lieutenant Dankworth surveyed the mess. He referred to Naomi's face and then his eyes moved to Sally's. You young women are sisters, I seem to remember?

Yes, Sally admitted.

The two men seemed to welcome the idea, as if it were some sort of souvenir of home. On their way out, Dankworth paused by the tent flap. Remember that we are willing to protect you, he growled with his eyes lowered. But the shield he offered them was not the right one for the time.

Honora was outraged they had not woken her to meet Dankworth, but she was half pretending—she seemed invigorated to know he was on the island. Soon they'd be promenading the foreshores together, and that would restore something that had been lost here.

It was raining when the military police officer and his sergeant came to the mess tent to collect Freud. Nurses had till now been muttering about how well she seemed to be taking things. Nursing—Sally knew—was a great if temporary distraction from all memory. The two provosts shone like deliverance in their slicked waterproofs. The Australian matron also appeared in an overcoat and was a fellow authority. The provost officer asked Freud to come with them, and the matron said Naomi could come too.

When Naomi and Freud set out with the military policeman and the matron, they were themselves bulky in khaki overcoats and as good as disguised under sou'westers. Their gum boots robbed them of all grace as they tripped through puddles to the hut down the hill which served as a police station. Naomi was later spare with details about what had happened there. Freud could not be asked for fear of what the question would bring on in her. The man imprisoned and identified by Freud as the rapist was an eighteen- or nineteen-year-old who was wide-faced and fair-haired—an orderly from the medical wards and the circus tent. Freud was asked to swear that this was the criminal. She gathered herself and—as Naomi recounted it to Sally later—it was already apparent that she *could* swear. But the forces working on Freud for denying it were potent. The provosts and others would be pleased if she did refuse to point to the attacker.

The young man brought in front of her was blushing. Freud snorted at this—as if it were a plea of innocence.

Did you say something? the officer asked.

That's him, Freud answered. She looked at the boy full-on. He would not look at her. At the moment of identification the boy's mouth hung in a way which almost made Naomi pity him. He's not clever, she thought. He's a muscular child. Those who recruited him carry their barbarous portion of the blame. But suddenly Freud needed to be restrained by Naomi and the matron from attacking him. She managed only to spit at his face. After a second—held by the arms—she went peacefully. There was no answer for what this blundering kid had taken. The young man was charged in front of her with rape and marched away hatless. Afterwards Naomi and the matron guided Freud back to the tent and suggested they would need to call the doctor again with his benevolent sedatives. No, said Freud—upright in their hands. Whatever he gives me, I still have to wake up in the end.

She wanted to go on duty with Naomi, so Naomi was promoted to post-operative. Dysentery was declining anyhow as autumn came to the Gallipoli Peninsula and to Lemnos. The medical wards were not as full, as the armies on the peninsula dug deeply rather than raged forward. Freud worked with a neutral and measured air. She took temperatures and blood pressures and encouraged young men to wake from chloroform. She had the power now to call on orderlies to help her move patients onto their sides. They obeyed her with their own neutrality or with a strangely shy sullenness. Naomi heard one man who worked with them— an orderly who must have been near forty years of age—bend forwards and tell Freud he was sorry and that he hoped she understood they weren't all like that, et cetera. Freud said nothing to him.

The entire nurses' mess felt a certain solace to know the evildoer had now been arrested—and identified as barely more than a child and not a very clever child. They could not help feeling it reduced the scale of menace which had hung over them. Now—more than in the interim—it became clear to them that they had been frightened of someone satanically astute and not to be appeased. They were relieved by the anticlimax of an arrest to which one plain face belonged.

Dankworth had been back to stroll down the headland with Honora—that was a token of the normal. But the women as a group acted in Freud's company with the false breeziness appropriate to a fatal condition. Her fatal condition was that the trial of the rapist was still ahead of her and he might get exonerated.

• • •

Lieutenant Robbie Shaw and his newly promoted friend Captain Lionel Dankworth did help ease the weight of such questions by calling at the mess again one evening. They found a small group of nurses ready to go on night duty—Sally, Naomi, Honora, Nettice, Leonora. There are thermal baths on the other side of the island, Shaw told them. We're going to try to get a car on Sunday to take us over there. Would you like to go?

These two had a wonderful air of unstoppability about them. They walked on the island on their own terms. And behind their joking, their casual watchfulness, and their unspoken sense of affront at what had been done to Freud, Sally could tell that they were by their very instincts assessing and weighing the women as men customarily did. Is my wife here? they asked themselves. Is she amongst these gravel-dwellers with their mixed clothing and their harrowed looks?

Speaking of the coming excursion, Robbie Shaw said, Why not invite the girl who had the problem too? It'll be good for her.

Ah, said Dankworth—sidestepping that noxious subject. That girl Carradine, is she here? We have a truckload of bedpans outside.

They went outside and there was the improbable truckload. As they carried canisters of tea and tins of fruitcake indoors under Shaw's rowdy orders, Naomi went urgently to find the right orderly to get the bedpans unloaded. It seemed to her that these two young men of no great gifts were angels of efficacy on an island whose masters sought to forbid every gesture of cleverness and grace.

Naomi told the men that there would be at least eight women free to make the journey.

Will you be one of them? I mean, the ones who come? asked Shaw confidentially—and out of Dankworth's hearing.

It depends. I would like an outing. If Freud comes, then I'll go too.

He lowered his voice. Lionel likes the brunette with the eyes. And all the impudence. Could you get her to come?

I doubt she could be stopped.

It was agreed amongst the women that if anyone should have a holiday from the general hospital—assuming she could be persuaded—it must be Freud. And so Naomi must—of course—go too. Apart from that, names would be drawn from a hat.

That night in the darkened wards Sally moved amongst fevered amputees, those whose wounded arms lay in cock-up splints and legs in long splints. Taking temperatures and pulses, she was a meek inspector of frantic dreams and listened for pain and anguish in those whose sleep was shallow. She saw the English matron loom out of darkness. Her torchlight skimmed the beds and bounced off her white bosom.

Sister Nettice? the matron asked Sally. Nettice was somewhere in this darkness and still to be found. The matron's torchlight went probing into corners. It brushed over faces in repose and eyes starkly awake.

Accompany me, Nurse, said the matron. Sally walked in her wake and they moved down the chicanes formed by army cots and came on something extraordinary. The torch beam discovered Nettice standing by a cot. Sitting on the floor in blue hospital pyjamas was a young man whose eyes were still bandaged but who cocked his head inquiringly towards the light. Nettice had been only partially successful in putting a distance between herself and the patient. The matron-in-chief hissed at Nettice and asked what she had in her hand. Nettice slowly produced something from the folds of her lumpy skirts. It was—Sally recognized—one of the chocolate slabs Shaw and Dankworth had brought them from the depot ship.

The matron gave the appearance of understanding this scene—at least in her own terms. Nonetheless, she breathily called on God to shed light on what was happening here. The young officer—a little smear of chocolate on his left cheek, a childlike and forgivable smudge—turned and began haltingly to feel the edges of his mattress. Unaccustomed to his dark within the dark, he levered himself slowly up. He intended to stand upright in Nettice's defense. Nettice, how-

ever, reached out with authority and put her hand on his shoulder—
exerting pressure so that he sat down on his cot.

What's the problem, Rosanna? he asked.

I was taking some time, Matron, said Nettice—low but without
apology—to give Lieutenant Byers some chocolate. In my estimation,
it does him good and lets him know he still has a name and a future.

"Let him know?" Of course he has a name.

He had forgotten it with the blow to his face. I have had to school
him in it and now he knows it again. But his memory must be fortified.

Must it be fortified with chocolate and on the floor? I would imagine not.

Nettice's face was set. It would not change to mollify the matron.
It refused to take on any trace of shame or contrition or justification.
Nettice said reasonably, It's so big here with voices coming and going.
He would have forgotten who he was without me telling him. And a
bit of chocolate.

Come, said the matron. We can't go on hissing and whispering
here. Come to my office.

Matron, Lieutenant Byers called out in a voice firm and loud
enough for the daylight, if you are suggesting that there was anything
untoward . . .

He stood again, as if with the intention to follow the matron and
Nettice.

Here, said Sally, taking one of his shoulders and then the other.
Nettice will handle it. Don't worry.

She helped him sit once more on the side of his bed, a slight figure
in his large drill pyjamas—the uniform of those lost in that confused
space between soldierhood and the lesser life arising from the scale of
the harm done them.

I've got her into trouble with the ogre, said Lieutenant Byers. Are
women ogres or ogresses? Poor little Rosie.

She'll just get a talking-to. We're all used to talkings-to. Don't worry.

A hiccough of sorrow came from him. She patted his shoulder.

It's nothing at all, she said. That woman disapproves of people breathing.

He shook his head. Rosanna's right, you know. Living here is like living in a factory.

Oh, will you get some sleep? asked or commanded a voice from across the room.

Sorry, mate, Byers called lowly. Sorry, all. No sweat. Can't keep my eyes open a minute longer.

He gave Sally a little stutter of laughter.

That Sunday forenoon the two omnipotent artillery officers arrived in a car and a truck and with a young Greek guide to take them to the promised baths.

Listen, said Robbie Shaw, limping around the car, I hear different reports of these hot springs. But let's give it a go, anyhow. By the way, this young bloke's called Demetrios.

Four of them—Sally, Naomi, Honora, and Freud, who Naomi had somehow persuaded to come along—were able to sit in the car. Dankworth drove, with Honora in the middle of the front and Shaw with his legs stuck out as the window-side passenger. The truck—driven by one of the artillerymen—followed with the other women.

But Nettice was not there. Nettice had been suspended, which, in this windy island on a headland of gravel and with no place of entertainment but the mess, was a severe test of the soul. She was forbidden to enter the wards or speak to Lieutenant Byers. She amused herself by playing Patience with a dog-eared pack. She gave Sally a daily note for delivery to Byers. She seemed to look calmly on the possibility of further discipline.

Now the expeditionary path took her off-duty sisters jolting north away from the sea—from the place of ships and hutments and encampments—and upwards amidst fields in which green pasture grew. Scrawny cattle and plump goats availed themselves of this. On the hills, the lines of olive trees seethed in a brisk wind. Here, without warning, the colonel's Lemnos gave way to Sergeant Kiernan's. The gods *were* here, Sally thought, though she could not have named them. A long white wall contained a patch of hillside in which there stood a white Greek chapel and its gravestones. In the backseat of the car, Naomi pointed it out to Freud, who took polite interest. But the dazzle of Greek white walls wasn't enough to soothe her. Most of her could not be reached by light.

They threaded between hills and exclaimed to see wildflowers on hillsides and speculate what they were. In a village of white walls and houses, Demetrios and Dankworth had a loud discussion on directions before continuing on and passing an ancient amphitheatre beyond. Before Christ? shouted Dankworth. Demetrios nodded his head emphatically. Far before Christos. Greco-Roman, he said.

The road began to wind, and the truck stopped to allow Carradine to be sick. They all got out for the occasion and picked wildflowers and looked down the long ribs of the island towards the brilliant sea. Sally demanded that Carradine take a seat in the car, and she joined the girls on the benches at the back of the truck where the wind blew their veils horizontal. Rising up a hill now, they saw the sudden apparition of mountains beyond a whitecapped sea. For that instant they were utterly released from earth and absorbed by the company of those mountains across the water and their remnant snow. The car stopped, and at Dankworth's order Demetrios came back to the truck and pointed at the mountains for the benefit of the nurses aboard. *Thrakya*, he said, and ultimately the word "Thrace" was suggested and Demetrios agreed. Then earth dragged them back again and down a stony hill and into another glittering white village, where clothes blew on lines like regatta flags.

The road beyond the town ended above a bay. They gathered their bags and their bathing costumes—borrowed from the Canadians—and accompanied Dankworth and Shaw down a pathway over which sheltering trees cast shade. So they came to a long white building with a tiled roof and a disused-looking open-air café to one side of it. The bathing party milled inside while Demetrios bought tickets from an old man in a glass booth and—in a heavy atmosphere of sulphur from the baths—feverishly distributed them while pointing to the doors for men and women. Shaw apologized for the smell. I believe, he said, it's not your normal baths. Demetrios told me it's about smearing on mud. Some Greek saint used to do it and it cured his gammy leg or some such. I suppose it all adds up to an experience, anyhow.

An elderly woman in a scarf, with gentle, hooded eyes, smiled at the women and—holding a stack of aged but clean towels—led them into the women's baths. They were half blinded by the miasma of hot sulphur. The foreyard of the baths seemed to be dominated not by a water pool but by two pools of gently stewing mud. The old lady mimed rubbing the mud on her body and—when the women looked mystified—smeared some on her arm and then traversed the room to a small pool above which was placed a tap and its handle. She turned on the tap and rinsed her mud-streaked arm under steaming mineral water. Then she left—satisfied that all was now clear.

There was a debate about whether they should ignore the chance of this sacred mud bath. But Carradine said that, having been brought so far by the courteous officers, a few of them ought at least to have a go. A further conference developed on the damage the sulphurous mud might do to the bathing costumes they'd borrowed from the Canadians. But Naomi pointed out that they could rinse the mud out in the surf below. Freud settled it. Still in her shift—not having changed into a bathing costume at all—she stepped forward to one of the mud pools and got to her knees. Testing it for temperature, she then lowered both her hands into the viscid muck and scooped it up and daubed it across her cheeks and forehead. Slipping off the strings of her shift, she loaded it on her shoulders and—when the bodice of the shift sank to her waist and hips—plastered her breasts. She worked fixedly. There was no cure in what she was doing.

Naomi understood at once this attempt at self-obliteration. She ran up, pulled Karla Freud upright, and held her by the shoulders, receiving broad smears of mud on her own costume. She helped Freud away and across the room to the water pool and sat her down by the tap and washed her thoroughly with a towel. Naomi left the face till last. She murmured reassurances all the time. She was telling Freud, You mustn't blot yourself out. *He* is the one to be blotted out.

As a sort of duty the other women coated a few of their extremities with the mud so that they could report to the men that they had done it.

They could hear that next door Dankworth and Shaw were asking each other raucous questions and answering with barks of laughter. A mud fight had obviously developed. Since the women felt they should not leave their room until the men left theirs, Carradine had time to tell them that there had been such an improvement in her husband that he'd been to London with a theatre party. They had worn their proper uniforms. And then Sally found herself announcing as a marvel that she and Naomi had a stepmother.

He was just waiting for his daughters to get out of the way, suggested Leonora.

She's a strict Presbyterian, Sally explained. She's made our old man a Presbyterian as well.

But that won't kill him, said Carradine.

I can't imagine anyone being willing to marry my old man, said Honora. Now that he's old and bitter. Just as well my poor mother's still alive.

They were relieved in the end to clean themselves off and change and climb the few steps out of the baths. Dankworth and Shaw emerged ruddy. Somehow they had had a wonderful time in the fog of sulphur. What a place to bring you! said Shaw. You can get mud anywhere you like. But we brought you all this way as if it's a treat!

This is holy mud, Demetrios reminded him.

The women exaggerated the delight of the experience. In the outdoor café, a dense coffee was served with pastry full of honey, and cakes with fruit at their center and their dough teased out into strands. All this revived the day. The chatter became hectic, and Freud—holding Naomi's hand across the table—took trouble to keep up with it and occasionally contributed a smile. But she did not seem certain about whether it belonged at the particular point she bestowed it.

Sally saw Shaw wince as he unwisely crossed his legs. She leaned towards him.

How long were you there? On Gallipoli?

Three months or so. Hard work, positioning the guns.

Was it terrible? she dared to ask him.

Well, he said, it was hard achieving elevation for the guns. They allowed only thirty percent elevation. And we just had to try to haul them up the ravines to level ground. That was the worst of it.

He was determined to make it a problem of terrain. He wished to abstract from the blood. She did not dare push him any further on the matter.

Did you happen to know a man named Captain Hoyle? Naomi asked—still holding Freud's wrist across the table.

Shaw's eyes tried to measure how much grief the name might carry for her.

No, she said, he's not a relative. Nor anything else. But I went riding to the pyramids with him once.

Captain Hoyle fell on the first day, he said. Just after we landed.

It shocked me at the time—he left his watch to me. I didn't know what that meant. I knew him socially but that was all. The watch puzzled me and upset me at the time.

As she spoke she stroked Freud's wrist.

Shaw had become solemn. Solemnity didn't sit easily on him.

Instantaneous, I promise you, he said. There was a lot of "instantaneous" that first day.

They sang all the way back to Mudros. They were exhilarated—even Freud—by wildflowers, the reaches of the Aegean, the mountains of Thrace. And the holy, sulphurous mud was forever part of their comic repertoire. On the final ascent to the hospital Sally saw distantly the military stockade and men shuffling across a reach of gravel to collect a meal of what she hoped was bitter bread.

On Monday morning the colonel and both matrons came to fetch Freud from her place at the mess table. The colonel said he wished to invite her to what he called in their hearing "a parley" in his office. Naomi—given the lopsidedness of numbers between the authorities and Freud, the single victim—had risen, expecting an invitation. But the matron-in-chief said with a confident measure of scorn that Staff Nurse Durance could sit again. Sally's suspicion was that in some way they were taking Freud onto their own ground to make her prey again.

Only those still there in the mess tent at eleven o'clock that morning saw Freud come back with a mute face and utterly dry eyes. Sally was not there. According to the chanciness of rosters she had been placed on day duty. So it was to only a few of her fellows that Freud announced they had posted her to Alexandria. But there has to be a trial, one of the nurses said. Freud's face knotted and melted then into some ageless and unredacted mask of rage.

There will be no trial, she told them. They were *all* in agreement on that. They say the boy was too easily persuaded by his mates. So he's been sent—you won't believe it—to Gallipoli. And it's considered good enough for me to be sent to Alexandria. The orderlies return to their ways, and the monster and I are removed.

She reflected on the inequity. Her face was almost abstracted.

We could win on Gallipoli, and men would still be brutes. And there would still be stupidity.

The news—as it spread—demented the others too. They shook their heads but their outrage was too huge and subtle to be stated. When Naomi offered to walk with her through the wards, Freud said she was forbidden the wards. But imagine the wounded over there on the land being dragged down the ravines by my monster. And falling into his hands.

So it came down to near-useless gestures and words—such as Honora telling her not to forget a rug since the cold season was coming and they all knew it could be chilly in Alexandria. Yet she and everyone else understood well that climate could not alter things for Freud. Naomi and others went to help her pack. A truck arrived for her, its engine vibrating with impatience. An unsteady Freud was helped up into the cabin. Naomi and the others could not lend enough hands to lift her portmanteau and her hatbox into the rear of the vehicle.

One last idea struck Naomi then. Mitchie is in Alexandria, she called.

But the truck had circled and was on its way, and she did not know if Freud had heard.

Nor was this the only departure that day. Nettice had by now been moved to the post-operative ward in lieu of Freud. Here, amputees and other dazed survivors of surgery from a newly arrived convoy lay in a hut amidst groans and murmurs. The matron-in-chief was flanked by two orderlies when she found Nettice there and announced that she was to be sent to a rest compound until she had recovered from her mania.

The "rest compound" was—in this case—the evasive name for the mental hospital below Turks Head. Other nurses saw Nettice refuse to go, but it was pointed out to her that the orderlies could take her straitjacketed if she chose. The Durances were sleeping at the time. It was not until an orderly clanged a series of shell casings to signal time for the night-duty nurses and orderlies to leave their beds that they and others discovered what had happened. It gave Sally that sickening sense of the authorities creating their own world, working by their baleful rules and excluding all other versions. This awareness made other nurses feel a disqualification from protest and an unfitness for struggle before the powers at play on Turks Head. The local regimens seemed more potent than the prerogatives operating in the known but remoter universe beyond the island.

Sally sensed that her own feelings of outrage—like all those of the cowed women—were secondary in their depth to Naomi's.

But at breakfast Leo told them no visits were permitted to the rest compound. Nettice was as unreachable as Freud.

The sisters slept deeply after their morning failure. Defeat and fiasco, loss and stalemate acted on them like a drug. Yet when Sally was awakened by the evening bell, she saw Naomi across the room washed and half-dressed and still wearing an air of purpose. Sally observed her and hurried to keep pace with her for fear of what she might do when she was ready to go out. They left the tent together, and the now relentless autumn wind blew them across Turks Head and down its slope.

British hospital, Naomi declared.

They came to the British general hospital and found at last the nurses' mess. As they knocked on the pole at the tent flap the dusk meal was in progress. Asked in, they could see at once that it was a place of far kindlier climate than theirs. Someone had had enough spirit and license to paste pictures of the English countryside on the walls. Everyone seemed properly dressed in white pinafores. The record of a soprano singing folk songs turned on a table-top Victrola. The women were talking over the music with a liveliness—thought Sally—which bespoke their greater confidence in the world. A young woman noticed them standing at the entry and rose and said, Hello there, Kangaroos, come and have some tea.

How can you tell we're Australians? asked Naomi.

Those great gawky overcoats, said the nurse.

She made her friends move up and found them chairs at the table. They all exchanged names. The one who had welcomed them in was Angela. She had young, glittering, impressive eyes. She had not yet had the goodwill pummeled out of her. She introduced them to two other Englishwomen there. These are the poor girls who were sunk on their ship, Angela explained in wonder, as if the sinking had been an achievement of theirs.

Poor things! one of the girls said. It's really too bad you have to wear those old clothes. We should take up a collection for you.

Please, said Naomi, don't go to the trouble. We're dressed the way the colonel chooses we should be dressed.

That can't be true, said Angela soothingly.

No, we are meant to be degraded, Naomi insisted.

The three English nurses frowned at each other. Sally felt a duty to show them her sister did not overstate the case.

It's true, sad to say, Sally confirmed.

Naomi said, One of our friends has been put in the rest compound for no particular reason than being sweet on a blind officer. You British nurses look after the rest compound. We'd like to send a message of cheer to our friend.

Oh, said Angela, you must talk to Bea over there. She's rostered in the compound. Angela lowered her voice and confided not in Naomi and Sally alone but in her three friends as well. Bea got in hot water herself for getting too friendly with one of our boys here. You see someone with a terrible wound who looks like your brother or your cousin or a boy you used to know . . . It's easy to get a bit infatuated with them. But you know that.

Naomi and Sally both studied the girl who had been pointed out. She was very pretty, with ringlets. She was the sort of girl who would have one of them hanging down her forehead—in defiance of the strictures about keeping hair enclosed. She looked childlike. But no one could be a trained nurse here and be an utter child.

Nonetheless, said Angela, I can't imagine someone being actually *binned* and diagnosed as mental just because she liked the soldier. Come, we'll see Bea.

She got up and led the Durance sisters across the room. The sisters stood off a bit as Angela spoke to Bea and indicated them. Bea scraped back her chair and got up. The four of them moved into the corner by the Victrola. Bea had a less posh accent than Angela. It was Yorkshire or some such. But she was—Sally thought—by far the prettiest mental nurse a person was likely to meet. Yes, she said, she was the day nurse in the women's compound. She knew Nettice—there weren't many patients in there. Just nurses who'd gone a bit unsettled. There's a guard with a rifle by the gate but that was to protect the women patients from the males' mental compound because the behavior from those men was not to be predicted. A boy will think he's at home and go off wandering down to his local pub.

Some of the fellows were so awfully upset by the thunder of the other night, she said. Jabbering mad from Gallipoli and Cape Helles to begin with. There is one of yours who hid under his bed, poor kid—a boy of about sixteen or seventeen. Whoever let him into the army should be shot.

But Nettice, said Naomi, what sort of company does she have?

There are only four of them. One is a girl who got a big crush on another woman and one is a girl who doesn't speak at all. The one who doesn't talk sits there until she pees herself. I do the changing, of course—we couldn't allow one of those orderlies. And then another girl who can't stop speaking. These two are both pitiful cases and will be sent back to Alexandria, or else home. The sooner the better too. We don't have any mentalist here worthy of the name.

But Nettice? said Naomi again.

Obviously sane as you and me. And a great help.

It's too much, said Naomi, rendered reasonable by the geniality of the English nurses, to ask you to let us visit. But if we gave you letters for her—letters to cheer her, I mean . . .

Bea laughed. It was a lyrical laugh. I'm in enough trouble myself, she said.

But she had not said no. It was because she had an excess of good nature—a tendency not without danger on Lemnos.

Maybe just one, she conceded.

She and Angela provided the pencil and some British Red Cross notepaper.

You write first, Naomi said to Sally, offering her the pencil.

For Lord's sake, said Bea, don't mention me.

Sally wrote,

Dear Nettice,

I hope you know we are all thinking of you and we will send you some comforts if we can. It goes without saying you should not be in this position. Our minds are set on finding an answer to your situation. It must be hard to get by in the compound. Lt. Byers is well and says that he looks forward to seeing you again. So do we all.

Your loving friend,

Sally Durance

Sally passed the pencil to her sister who took it up with energy and wrote in a conspiratorial, certain, fast hand.

Just keep it brief, said Bea, brushing aside one of her ringlets.

Naomi produced from the pocket of her coarse dress a little slab of chocolate.

Is it too much to ask that you give her this too?

Bea laughed in disbelief. But she said, In for a penny, in for a pound. Don't worry. I slip them all a few extras myself.

They could believe in this beautiful innocent who tended the supposedly mad.

Sally would stop on her rounds and talk to Lieutenant Byers, who had been moved from the general medical ward to a more sparsely populated tent. It was as if he had incurred isolation too. Her conversations with Byers needed to be discreet. There was an embargo on talking to men unless it was to ask them symptomatic questions or order them to lift an arm or a leg or open a mouth. The rules had been reiterated after the Nettice matter. After a time, the wounded themselves became parties to the discipline of the wards rather than land nurses in trouble. But Byers wanted to know everything about Nettice.

They've taken her off duty, said Sally. She's having a good rest. She's needed a good rest since the ship.

She said a horse brought her back to the surface.

Yes, it's true. A pony. I saw it.

Thank God for ponies is what I say. Wonderful creatures! Rosie is a real brick.

I'd say so.

Yes, he said. She believes in a divinity that shapes us. And she doesn't worry about my background in the least, you know. My father sent me to a school for Presbyterians but we were Jewish—changed our name from Myers. The other kids could tell—I don't know how. But the young have a high degree of discrimination in some things. Is it safe to talk?

Indeed the matrons were not in sight so she said it was.

I'll tell you something about city people who declare their belief in God too easily, he said. They're not like Nettice, to start with. Their morality is really a kind of fussiness. Maybe jewelers attract these sorts of people. People who depend on their name and profession to avoid paying their bills. How many gold rings and brooches bought on deposit from Byers and Sons, and we're still chasing up the full payment. And the problem is that if my father took a writ and summoned them to petty sessions, they'd say, Don't go to Byers's place. Why pay the avaricious Jew? So there it is. I'm Jewish as Paddy's pigs—as a comedian once said. And Rosie doesn't mind. I'm blind, too, and Rosie doesn't mind that either.

She heard him give a sudden snort of grief. These humiliations of his childhood—and his father's humiliations—seemed closer and less bearable to him than the damage to his eyes.

Well, he said, I won't be worried that way anymore. The "Son" in Byers and Sons isn't accurate now. I won't be making much jewelry hereafter.

In the dark she often found a chance to talk with Byers. The more frequent her visits the more his concern for Nettice emerged.

You say she is resting? he asked one night. Where is she resting? Is she ill?

Perhaps a little influenza, said Sally. She'll be back soon.

You're not hiding something? Nothing's happened?

No, said Sally. An energetic liar.

Sally knew that Nettice had become her sister's mania as she had become Byers's. She had let herself grow dour and hardened. But Naomi had become a fury. Her eyes darted as she looked about her for the right gestures to help rebalance the earth. Through a further visit to the good-natured English nurses' mess, Naomi began to work at poor Bea to take her in to see Nettice. Sally could tell Bea's general goodwill would be no protection against her sister's tigerish resolve. Naomi planned to go down to the rest compound with Bea as a junior nurse getting an education.

Naomi recounted to her sister her persuading of Bea.

You can say, Naomi had argued, that I told you I was rostered on to the compound. You had no reason to suspect it wasn't true. And I'll only stay a while, I promise. But she has to know she's not been given up.

Poor, susceptible Bea took Naomi one morning, therefore, through the outer wire. She greeted guards whose faces lit to see her and who unlocked the gate which led down a raceway contained by barbed wire on either side. The male patients' wards were beyond the wire to the south, said Bea, but the violent ones were behind the wire to the north. They progressed between these two. After two hundred yards, they came to the small compound for women. The outlook from this part of the headland, Naomi thought, was not very curative. It was blocked off from the harbor and from at least the notion of escape by a rock outcrop.

Bea's task—after she said good-morning to the sentry on the gate and asserted airily that this morning she had brought along an apprentice—was first to relieve the night nurse. Naomi was to watch from the tent flap as Bea went in. The night nurse proved to be a Canadian. She was writing case notes at a little table and seemed tired enough not to pay much attention to Naomi as she rose and brushed past. She went to wake up her orderly, who had been on call and who rested in a small watch house in the corner of the compound. Peering into the dim tent Naomi saw first a region with a few soft chairs and a table with magazines. There was a rough bookcase with maybe a dozen titles. On top of it lay a pack of cards and boxes containing draughts and other games. Bea—scanning the notes—mentioned to Naomi that two orderlies she called her "boys" would be along soon with a bucket of porridge and another of water and some loaves of bread. Her reference to them was nearly affectionate. This was a place where it was possible for orderlies to work with women in a manner that was not poison. Bea then left the little table and the notes and cried good-morning to the stirring patients. Her cheery voice would itself be a kind of poultice on the day.

Advancing behind Bea, Naomi saw Nettice sitting on a tousled bed beside a woman who chattered or—more accurately—spoke in tongues.

Bea said, Nettice has become her friend and is very handy to me. Keeps the poor girl less excited. And then the Sapphist is very good, too, trying to get poor Lily talking. Between us we're a well-rounded crew.

Nettice reserved her most clenched and characteristic frown for the sight of Naomi. She rose upright in her shift but kept one hand on the chatterer's wrist. While Naomi embraced her with two arms, Nettice had only one free hand for the task. Naomi was surprised to find there was almost something grudging in this welcome and in the pressure of Nettice's one hand on her back. Nettice explained to her murmuring fellow patient that she was going to sit with her friend for a while. Naomi and barefooted Nettice went and sat together in the soft chairs at the recreational end of the tent.

What are you doing here, Durance? Nettice asked first of all. You could get yourself in the deepest trouble.

We thought it was important to let you know that you have not been forgotten or anything like it. They want us to forget you, but we refuse.

I already knew that, said Nettice plainly. I knew you were all my good friends. But I didn't want you to put yourself in such danger as this.

It's right I should be the one to visit you, said Naomi.

Nettice—as if implying she might as well ask questions while she had Naomi there—wanted to know how Lieutenant Byers was and whether he knew where she was.

Naomi reported they hadn't told him more than she'd been suspended. But he asks after you endlessly, said Naomi.

Does he ask after me endlessly? asked Nettice. It's not something you should say casually unless it's really happening.

Given the trouble Naomi had taken to be here, it appeared Nettice had only a middling respect for her visit and now seemed to suspect her of deception.

Well, it is the absolute truth, Naomi insisted.

I deserve to be here you know, Nettice confessed. I had in a way gone a little mad, you have to understand. I can't think what got into me.

But you don't deserve to be in an asylum, for God's sake.

The punishment is appropriate, said Nettice with a certainty Naomi hated. It was *my* lunacy. It's certainly not Lieutenant Byers's fault.

It is all someone else's fault, insisted Naomi. Maybe not all, but whatever you did were minor crimes. If we are ratty and berserk, they have made us that way. We didn't invite a battalion of troops onboard the *Archimedes*. We didn't invent the brainlessness of the colonel and the slavishness of the matrons. Some would say that my being here was criminal. But I say that *your* being here is the crime.

Anyhow, she argued, you can see I have some nursing to do here day and night. So I am not empty of all purpose. If a person were to mention God, he could say that God sent me here for the sake of the mute and the babbling. We have one each of those.

Naomi should have been pleased to find Nettice so sturdy and very nearly content. And yet there was still a certain disappointment too.

In any case, Nettice conceded, please give Lieutenant Byers my warmest respects. You needn't tell him—because he already knows—that I might have mistaken friendship and our mutual chattiness for something of a profounder nature.

Are you certain it wasn't more serious than that? He appears to hope it was.

It is true that if you've been rescued by a pony from the bottom of the sea, you get ideas about yourself. Delusions, you know. They evaporate when you're somewhere like this. As for him, tell him I won't tolerate any palaver about him being at all to blame. If he starts hogging blame, it is actually selfishness on his part.

Bea's "boys" could be heard exchanging greetings with the guard and came just then through the door with their buckets. Naomi got up and kissed Nettice good-bye. Then she went to embrace the generous Bea, who had been making beds and was now talking to the thin mute girl.

You're the kindest girl in the world, Naomi told her. And I've taken advantage of you.

After another doubtful look and wave in Nettice's direction, Naomi left the tent. The sentry opened the gate wide for her. At the main gate at the end of the raceway she began the ascent up Turks Head. She kept to the verge—a pathway by the white-painted stones—to make room for ambulances and supply trucks and the wagons of timber driven by Greeks. She assessed the morning and found she felt a modest sense of triumph to have broken into Nettice's place of detention. Coming down the road as she rose was a party of people for whom even the trucks and wagons themselves pulled to the side to make clearway. A British matron in a red cape and an older man in a tailored uniform, red tabs, and gleaming boots were attended by two young aides. She stopped out of a reflex respect to let them pass in the certainty of their own authority. She moved on and only the matron glanced briefly in her direction.

That evening—when Naomi was woken by the clanging of a bell—

the matron-in-chief was waiting at the door of the officers' ward. She strode up as Naomi approached and without introduction asked what she had been doing in the rest compound. A British matron accompanying the deputy inspector had seen her leave the place and—knowing that only her own nurses were employed there—had been mystified. And—indeed—was further affronted by her surly lack of respect towards the passing brigadier general. The mention of surliness nonplussed Naomi. She had not taken any surliness she was aware of into the encounter. Had the British matron accompanying the general misread her? Or had events imbued her with that quality? The matron-in-chief now told her that she—Durance—had been at the center of all disorder since she had arrived on Lemnos. She had been grievance incarnate, the matron intoned.

I cannot see you have any future in the nursing service. You are suspended from all duty, and I do not trust you with my patients.

Aren't you getting short of nurses? Naomi asked with a layer of genuine concern that momentarily submerged her rage and contempt.

But there was no arguing with that austere woman who spoke for the colonel and was wedded to his berserk medical creeds.

The idea of being on Turks Head, and of having no purpose to fulfill, seemed to Naomi to be a fair definition of hell. She took her sentence dry-eyed. If they wanted to see tears they'd have a long wait. Ditto repentance. There was a temptation to go and lose herself amongst the villagers on the Thracian side of Lemnos. There the landscape and the light had seemed richer.

You'll have to take the news of Nettice to Lieutenant Byers, she told her sister.

When Sally at last saw Byers, he insisted—of course—on saying that he was the one who put Nettice there. That was understandable. But Sally felt it as an unnecessary self-indulgence.

Yes, we're all to blame, she told him fiercely. Except the stupid generals who sent you to be blinded, and the enemy who obliged them.

And those who dreamed up a terrible, oppressing place like this. They are obviously all innocent and you and I are utterly to blame.

Byers said, How do you expect me to feel though? Blameless? But, yes, to put her in the compound is a mongrel act.

My one hope, said Naomi to her sister at breakfast the next morning, is that they will ship me back to Alexandria in disgrace. Can you imagine that when I nursed in Sydney I saw myself as a future matron? But I am afraid I am spoiled goods now.

And she must endure meaningless days—all without the comforts of tending others that Nettice enjoyed. She tried to read as energetically as her sister but found her attention frayed. She was permitted to take exercise on Turks Head and favored the cliffs facing south. Her pride did not allow her to call on other women for company. She felt a long erosion of her spirit, could even sense the risk of madness.

Two days later, however—when she was dreaming of the *Archimedes* and of her failure to drown with it—an Australian medical inspector named Colonel Leatherhead arrived on Lemnos. In retrospect it seemed to all of them that Leatherhead's appearance had the nature of an angelic visitation from the Bible. He placed himself between the world of shadows where they dwelt and a world of possible light. But none of that was clear at first. He was not built on angelic proportions. He was round faced and round bodied and his hips were wider than his shoulders. There was the possibility in his face that in a second it might slide in either direction—mercy or condemnation.

He appeared in time for morning tea in the sisters' mess, introduced himself and spoke plainly to the nurses. He had been sent to report on the conditions they worked under. Again, he did not depict himself as some grand spirit of rescue. But he said that certain conditions had been reported by complainants. Mitchie, they thought. Even disabled, she would have chivied—and told her story to—surgeons who possessed military eminence.

He nonetheless managed to give them a suspicion that their behavior would be as strictly scrutinized as anyone else's. For a while he did nothing except to move about the wards and make an occasional note. Naomi, however, found that so many of her superiors had their attention fixed on Leatherhead that her movements were not strictly supervised. She used her days to walk down to the peddlers and buy cigarettes and chocolate for the patients or to visit the graveyard and study the tragic names on crosses.

Leatherhead's presence did not in the first few days suppress the clique of abusive orderlies who—after behaving better in the shadow of the assault on Freud—had now got back to their habitual braying of commands at nurses. In the meantime, portly little Leatherhead seemed to concentrate on making notes on the theatres and wards and on the dressing and irrigation of wounds. With ward doctors he debated the use of sodium peroxide and asked whether Dakin's solution might not be better. He came to the nurses' mess for an evening meal and held one of the girls' enamel dishfuls of bully beef and rice and found—as far as you could tell—the meal neither tasteful nor distasteful.

The colonel talked away unabashed whenever he was with Leatherhead. He was proud to have the excellence of the place observed by an inspector from Alexandria.

Without seeming urgency, Leatherhead had the women one by one to his temporary office in an annex off a hut where a number of medical officers had their desks. Naomi secretly had some hopes for her turn with Leatherhead. But she was nervous of how he would read her. Would he write her off as hectic or sullen? But Leatherhead was in no hurry to relieve her limbo with a summons.

It was her sister who was called to visit him first. Sally found him as precise as he had so far appeared. He had an ink blotter which he regularly applied to what he wrote. He was not a man to take the lazy way out of letting ink evaporate. His copious papers were not strewn. He had his own typewriter for transforming them into official reports. Sally felt certain in his presence that his chief concern was to expose her flaws. But the questions were not aggressive. Place of origin. Place of training. Places and length of civil nursing. Yes, I see you were on the *Archimedes*. So of course you lost all your clothing, your uniforms, your nursing kit . . .

Yes.

And that was why you were provided with this makeshift wardrobe?

She explained that they had started off with a French navy shirt and blanket.

And those rough dresses, he declared, look like they've been bought secondhand from the Greeks. That aside, there have been complaints about orderlies and their treatment of nurses. What has your experience been?

We are not treated politely, said Sally. She felt a rush of released fury.

He told her please to be more precise.

And so she devoted herself to their history. The orderlies began by treating the nurses as full-time drudges and skivvies. They were commanded by orderlies to clean excrement and carry waste buckets and bedpans. To lug buckets of tissue and used dressings and amputated limbs to the furnace. None of this they were unwilling to do. But it was all they were asked to do, and they were abused by orderlies for how it was done. They were not admitted to the operating theatres except to scrub them. And sometimes called by names not normally applied to nurses. They are not all bad—the men. But the good ones seemed silenced.

By their fellow orderlies?

Sally decided to risk her entire opinion.

I see it as permitted by the colonel, she said.

He didn't seem appalled. His head was down and he wrote with his neat fountain pen in an even, infallible hand. His bowed scalp was covered with bristly tan hair. Then he looked up.

Were any of you touched violently or improperly?

Not me. Nurse Freud . . . you must know about her.

Leatherhead leaned forward at this—like a man about to be engaged in gossip.

Did you know, however, that the young man who attacked her is dead?

I'd not heard that.

It is important for you women to know that there was a price exacted. A double price in his case. He was carrying a wounded major on his shoulders to a field ambulance when he was shot dead. His captain recommended him for the Military Medal. But obviously it could not be granted in such a case.

Even then Sally wondered how it was that the dry, non-disclosing Leatherhead had let this story out. To some it would seem gossip. But to the nurses it served as a vindication. She would conclude that he had done it so that they would somehow see the issue as settled. She did wonder if clever Leatherhead had merely fabricated the tale—his inventive way to put the matter to rest. But that would have been a touch of a storyteller rather than of a dry functionary.

He suddenly brought the interview to an end. He thanked her. She rose and was leaving. But he stood up as if impelled by etiquette and intercepted her before she reached the door.

So you did not think Staff Nurse Nettice unstable in her mind?

I think her mind is fixed on the *Archimedes*. The way the minds of some of the men are fixed at the moment they were wounded. But she is as sane as anyone else.

His dismissal of her came through turning his back and returning to his notes. His manners, his moves, his questions, his measured gossip were all so jerky and unnatural. Yet it had been a genuine cure to be questioned by him in every particular of the tribulation she shared with the others.

When she came off duty that evening she was astonished by the apparition of Nettice sitting on her own cot. Nettice looked up with her traditional frown fully in place. She said flatly, So you see, I am out.

Sally rushed over to envelop her. But Nettice showed no appetite for celebratory hugs at all.

Lieutenant Byers will be so relieved to see you. And happy as well.

Nettice said, He won't quite be able to *see* me, will he?

Sally grew suddenly furious at Nettice's sophistry. For God's sake, Nettice.

All right then, said Nettice. I *can* imagine the poor boy will feel some solace now I'm back.

You sound almost as if you're unhappy to get out of that place.

On balance I'm very happy.

You take it very easy. But did you know Naomi has been suspended for visiting you?

Nettice pondered this. I knew it was a risky business, she conceded. You will have to understand, though, that I'm not lacking in gratitude. I am just too stunned yet to fall on my knees in appreciation.

Yes, said Sally. Forgive me.

For she understood that state of soul precisely. Nettice made a better effort at sharing the enthusiasm of the others when Carradine came in. Naomi returned from one of her shopping expeditions, and the sight of her broke down Nettice's reserve and sent her into a strange mixture of tears and hacking laughter. Would you believe it? she asked. I'm out!

Naomi said in wonder, This is the work of Colonel Leatherhead.

Carradine had a smart idea. I'll go and fetch Lieutenant Byers and bring him for a constitutional. And you can see him by the mess tent here.

Nettice was now all at once anxious for that meeting to happen, and it was organized. She waited in the wind with Sally and Naomi on either side of her and saw Lieutenant Byers come walking forth on Carradine's arm in his hospital pyjamas and with an army jacket over his shoulders since the evenings were turning so cold. Even with Carradine to guide him, he tested for obstructions and swept the gravel in front of him with a white stick.

Sam, called Nettice in a thin voice.

Rosie? he said with his head cocked. Darned sorry to get you into trouble.

There is no more trouble now.

He shook his head. For there was the untellable trouble of his blindness. But then he inhaled a deep breath and managed a wide, generous smile.

A triumph for justice, he said. Not a common thing in armies.

The women chose to find this heartily amusing and gave themselves up to more laughter than was perhaps justified.

Uniforms arrived from the depot ship to relieve them from the harsh oddments of coarse cloth. There was a rumor sweeping the stationary hospital that Colonel Spanner had left that morning on a ship for Alexandria. The arrival of a new chief medical officer, a Scots surgeon from Adelaide—a former civilian used to treating other civilians with at least some civility—occurred with equal suddenness. The Australian matron broke the news to them—as if they might be aggrieved at it—that they were required to wear the capes ordained by their military authorities. The near-forgotten and halfway elegant gray overcoats with boomerang-shaped "Australia" on their shoulders were also provided, and a neat array of shoes almost too refined for the mud and gravel of Turks Head.

Sheep from Salonika had been landed. On some nights fresh mutton replaced the bully beef on their tin plates.

Orderlies—former tyrants amongst them—now carried out waste buckets and limbs and bloodied bandages to their points of disposal. No "Bloody dumb cows!" anymore. This was the wonder the Leatherhead visitation had produced. He had switched the poles of the earth—or at least of that planet named Mudros. Because of her experience with Captain Fellowes aboard the *Archimedes,* Sally was asked to administer anesthesia in some shrapnel cases amongst the newly arrived from Gallipoli. She observed the vital signs as metal was removed from wounds or as limbs were taken off by amputation saws and wrapped in linen and carried out to join the heap of arms and legs awaiting prompt incineration. Honora worked as theatre nurse. Leo worked as a scout, preparing and presenting the appropriate packs of instruments and the swabs, keeping count of them, and even supervising sterilization carried out by orderlies.

The matron-in-chief who had been Colonel Spanner's chatelaine survived for ten days before her temporary assignment to their stationary hospital similarly ended and she was sent elsewhere. Everyone felt that the hospital had been renewed.

There had been a sad revival of the wound of Lieutenant Robbie Shaw, however, the officer who with Dankworth had taken the women across the island for a mudbath. Sally had discovered that open-handed, sociable Lieutenant Shaw lay in the officers' medical ward with a fever and a distracting pain in his all-but-healed femur wound. Doctors and the matron conferred over his exposed hip, and the redness and swelling which bespoke sepsis.

I wish they'd open the flaming thing up, he told Sally. It's just a bit of temporary flare-up in there. They can get it out like a core from a boil.

The ward doctor called a surgeon. By now Robbie Shaw's pulse was racing and he had begun to rave with pain and a fever. An eighth of a grain of morphine was injected every four hours. The wound had cracked along the suture lines and foul matter seeped from within. He was taken to surgery and—with the wound opened up—had some inches of rotten bone cut out of the shaft of his upper thigh. Sally visited him in the post-operative ward and found him depressed and whimsical.

I'll spend the rest of my life walking like a bloke riding an invisible bike.

But pain regularly distracted him from the issue of his future gait.

Honora developed a pronounced melancholy as notable as her usual elation when Captain Dankworth was sent back to Gallipoli with his artillery battery. He visited his accomplice Shaw before leaving. Sally heard Shaw tell Lionel Dankworth, Well, this buggers me for the artillery.

He was correct about his chances of more campaigning. It was mysterious that he would want it. But it seemed to be an unfeigned desire. No idea of a future profession could console him for not being capable of further gunnery.

The potent rumor arose almost as soon as the women had their new clothes on. There was to be a ship of wounded back to Australia. It took only hours before an embellishment came forth. Some of them were to travel on it. Their Australian matron—now chastened to an amenable tone by the rigors of explaining herself to Leatherhead— soon confirmed that. She read out the names a few mornings later. To show there was no full justice to be found on earth, the list included those with a reputation for giving trouble. Carradine was to make the journey—punishment for the shortcoming of being married. When she raised the matter that her wounded husband was in England, the matron suggested she leave the celibate nursing service and present herself as a Red Cross volunteer. Then, if necessary, she could pay her way back to the Northern Hemisphere and her husband's bedside. There was no final absolution for Naomi's rebellions of word and commission. Nettice, for her irregular ward demeanor, was to go too. And some non-offending others. But not Sally. A strange flush of relief ran through her when her name was not read. If she was sent back to Australia, she doubted she could escape again.

I hope I can make my way without you, she told Naomi. And this was not for form's sake. Naomi seemed quite even-tempered about it all, neither pleased nor displeased.

Who would have thought I'd be the first back to Kempsey? I'll have to break in our stepmother for you.

Sally became aware—the closer the departure came—that her dependence on her sister had been near absolute from the day the *Archimedes* sank. Naomi had stood between her and harshness. Without Naomi, she would need to become her own defender and asserter of her own dignity. But it was clear that there was no argument against these shipment orders—no matter how fretful Carradine might be at the idea of putting a world between her and her husband. It was fortunate that Carradine came from a family of means. She could possibly be back in Britain and by her husband's bedside within three months of arriving in Australia.

The unspoken but deep, sly idea of torpedoes lay as a shadow over the nurses chosen.

Homewards with Doubts

In easterly slanted rain, candidates for the process called repatriation were loaded on launches and barges and taken out to a troopship. On crutches now and with a healing wound was Robbie Shaw and—guided along the foreshores by orderlies—Sam Byers. As they boarded, a black ship from Gallipoli disgorged its sick and wounded onto the pier. A great recycle of soldiers' flesh was in progress.

On the wharf, the Durance sisters were permitted to stand aside and transact their own leave-taking. They shared an umbrella and wore their gray overcoats, newly provided through Colonel Leatherhead's marvelous intrusion into their lives.

How long will there be hospitals on Lemnos? Naomi asked as a form of speculation.

There'll be no end to them, since there is no end to Gallipoli, Sally declared, utterly convinced. For an end to it could not be foretold for this year or the next.

If you are stuck here, said Naomi, then I must do my best to get back. I don't care if they make me carry buckets of diarrhea for entire shifts. Because you are my sister. And you have been the same person throughout. Steady. No, don't dare protest. You have been calm and brave and solid. And better able to govern yourself than others have been.

What about your own courage? What about you breaking in to see Nettice?

They were acts of pure ratbaggery. Done out of hopeless anger.

Sally wondered what a person could do when being praised so wildly for calmness and valor. And by your sister! It felt close to being wrongly accused of theft or treachery. She was persuading herself not to say so when she saw Sergeant Kiernan in the line of men waiting for the launches. He was overcoated and carrying a kitbag on one shoulder and the normal duffel bag. He saw them and came over.

You are both about to escape? I'm so pleased.

No, said Naomi. I'm the only one going. I'm not escaping. I've been thrown out.

You can describe me in the same terms, Kiernan told them. He looked at the gray bulk of the troopship standing offshore in the gale— and then up the long road to Turks Head—as if weighing all that was about to be lost.

I felt powerless, he said. I knew what was happening to you where you were. All I could do was tell the officers at the rest center and write to my father. He's a friend of the alienist Dr. Springthorpe who is treating men in Egypt and has a lot of influence. So he wrote in turn to Springthorpe—enclosing my letter. The counsels of impotence. But I hope it did some good.

When he turned his eyes back to the Durance sisters, there was none of the normal humor in his face.

Laws against fraternization, he confessed, were all the rage at our general hospital. And I was cowardly enough to obey them.

You couldn't have done anything, said Naomi.

I must go back to my fellows, said Kiernan. It will be easier to speak on board, Miss Durance.

He turned to Sally. I do hope we meet again. Though not on this dismal island.

So you're cured of all those mythologies?

There was a stutter of laughter from him. Yes, they can keep the whole lousy lot of them. I'm sticking to modern history. It seems to be an absorbing enough study to me.

Sally watched her sister's launch depart the shore. Despite the dimness of the day she also saw it arrive at the bottom of the ship's stairway and at last the tall figure of Naomi ascending. Sally had once thought of a ship as fortressed against all elements except internal fire. Now she saw it as a flimsy tube—or an egg awaiting the hammer. When Naomi had vanished into the ship she turned away from the bay and climbed the hill to be ready for the ambulances now beginning to roll along the pier. We'll all grow old in our work, she decided. She felt aged already beneath the low, malicious clouds.

In her three-berth cabin on deck two Naomi received by way of a steward a letter from Lieutenant Shaw, whose femur wound was sending him home too. "A bit down at the moment," he confessed. "But there has to be something I can do in the military sense. If you see me, I'll be the one who walks at an angle of 45 degrees—unless the ship is at 45 degrees, in which case I'll be leveled out completely."

She hoped Shaw wouldn't plague her. That thought was unworthy—for his kindness on Lemnos he deserved to be humored. But she needed a certain solitude to absorb what had befallen her and to contemplate her Australian future. Her vanity when she first presented herself at Victoria Barracks had been to think she would return home with legible success on her brow. Now she was to return as one of the rejected. She was weighed a failure. *That* would show on her brow. Her father and his new wife might not see it. Yet—knowing it was there—she would cramp in all she did.

Cheers rose from other and incoming troopships as the nurses showed themselves at the railings to take a last view of that isle whose hard edges were veiled by rain. Naomi did not go up there to see her sister's island shrink away in veils of dimness and downpour. She stayed below to sleep as soon as the ship began to move. But once stirring and turning on her bunk she promised herself that should the ship sink during its weavings across the rough surface of the Mediterranean, she would let herself fall straight to the base of the ocean without waking.

She heard no more from Robbie Shaw the next day and spent her time reading *Punch* in the lounge. At dawn the next morning they approached the coast of Egypt. But the waves breaking along the Corniche, the apartment buildings which looked like confections of icing sugar, the buildings dreamed up by an architect who had then taken decoration a step too far, the lighthouse where Pharos had once stood, one of those wonders of the world which children were required to number and write down—the whole fabulous city—was a scene she now lacked the means to relish. The Qaitbay citadel they used to see from the docking *Archimedes* was today like a fortress from a flick or a novel. The British flag above its turreted central tower suggested war was a simple thing—achieved by musketry from battlements aimed at some unwashed tribe.

Nettice was comforted that her troopship had so easily quartered the Mediterranean. She had been busy, in any case—using a steward who attended to their cabin to carry messages to Lieutenant Byers in his quarters one deck up.

They were rested in nurses' quarters at a British hospital in Alexandria until their train was ready the following morning. At that ornate railway station in Cairo—through which Mitchie had long ago led her untried charges to board the Alexandria train—they set out for Port Suez.

Out of the windows Naomi found camels and their owners on the roads they passed and green crops tended by unaltered, strong, black-clad, bent women so much more unchanged than the world at large. The sky above Suez grew murky and yielded a gray evening—like a scowl from the Red Sea Moses had parted. She saw—as their train rolled into the port—British army and navy officers sitting at tables under the porticos of the Grand Pier Hotel, men still engaged in a rearwards sort of way with the war Naomi and the others were now departing. The sight made her feel excluded from life rather than fortunate in it.

The train came right to the wharf. Orderlies bustled in to help them with their bags. A cluster of wheelchair cases began to form on the station. The amputees on crutches—their trouser legs bravely pinned up to about knee height—tried not to collide with rushing orderlies. Smoking casually, those who missed an arm walked with a balanced air that claimed they had always wanted to sport an empty sleeve.

Their ship looked—according to Carradine's habitual assessment of vessels—around sixteen thousand tons. It possessed what people called "good lines" and was named the *Demeter*. The great doors of the lower deck—more or less at dock level, the same doors which on the *Archimedes* had been opened to admit horses and gun carriages— stood agape.

Those chirpy on this grim Egyptian afternoon cried, Make way, boys! as they stood back to yield the nurses the gangplank. Their wounds were not visible—were covered by their uniforms—and some of them were possessed by the happiness of valid homecoming. But not all. Some were dreading it like she was.

From the deck, she saw below on the pier a contingent of blinded officers—each with a stick held edgily and unfamiliarly in his hand— advancing towards the lower doors in a line. The first had his free hand on the shoulder of an orderly and the second his hand on the shoulder of the first. And so on. She had never seen the blinded so arrayed or in such a force. She noticed Lieutenant Byers in the midst of the column. He looked lost in the mass.

The nurses were now the first to be let below. The steward who led them told them that their cabins were A1. Walking further forward in the ship the women saw what could easily be imagined as peacetime salons and libraries and smoking rooms. And the promenade deck they had been ushered across felt just that—a deck for promenades and not for heaping the wounded. Nettice praised the ship endlessly and kept some of her applause for the spacious ports in their cabin. Naomi suspected that it was Byers's presence onboard that brought out this applause in her.

At dinner—seated with the captain and his third officer—they began with an entree of fish in a near-vacant dining room. The captain was a Scot and of a certainty, a gaze, a solidity that would not easily yield to any projectile thrown by an enemy. Other nurses they had not yet met arrived in the dining room in their long gray dresses and jackets. Some looked to be women as old as Mitchie and were puffed from climbing the gangplank and companionways. They were all from the great barn of a hospital in Cairo known as Luna Park and from a hospital at Ismaïlia. It turned out that at least two of them—having lost a brother each—were being sent home to console their parents.

The matron of the *Demeter* spoke at the end of dinner. By then they'd had some miraculous beef and roast potatoes and pudding with custard. The matron was broad-shouldered—she looked like a country girl grown up—and had an eczema outbreak on her cheeks. She enumerated the range of work they would need to do according to a light, six-hour-a-day roster. The demands of the eight-week journey home would tend to be medical rather than surgical. So there were the two small medical wards—for officers and men—and a contagious ward. There was also a small mental ward. Most of the patients here were depressed or suffering delusions harmless except to themselves. Forward and on a lower deck lay the living quarters for some fifty syphilitics. Smile on them, issue their medicines, and then leave them to the orderlies. In the meantime, the majority of the men—in stable condition—would occupy the normal cabins and bunk spaces.

Nettice's face bloomed and the knot which had fixed her features in place seemed suddenly to release itself.

Naomi's job some days was to take blinded or lamed men for a turn on deck. Nettice thought it was against the spirit of the matron's lenient instructions that she should always accompany Lieutenant Byers—she found other ways of meeting him during the day. Naomi was therefore in the company of Sam Byers amidst a now-vivid-blue Red Sea when she saw Sergeant Kiernan in overall control of a string of orderlies guiding blinded men on a spin around the promenade. He stepped aside from the procession a moment to speak to her and Byers.

Sir, he said to Byers, I hope you're well.

Who is this? asked Byers with his head cocked in a way which had now become habitual to him. Kiernan introduced himself. He wondered whether the lieutenant would allow him to have a word with Naomi.

Byers laughed. Pardon me, he said, but I was never used to such courtesy from my platoon.

So Kiernan turned to Naomi, calling her Sister Durance. He said he had undertaken to produce a newspaper for the ship. Could she write something about the sinking of the *Archimedes* for him? He said he would publish it after they'd left the Cape and got into safer waters.

Her very blood revolted at the idea. To put the thing down in ink would be a form of self-exposure and would profane the drowned. She told Kiernan she was sorry but she could not do it.

Oh, go on, Nurse, said Byers. It should be recorded by somebody. I have been at Rosie Nettice to set something down but she won't consent.

Naomi challenged Kiernan. Why don't you write it?

I think it will have greater authority coming from a woman. And I remember that you were very conscious throughout. I might have approached Matron Mitchie but I doubt she remembers much. But if you like, I could write it and say how thoroughly brave you were and that you deserve the Military Medal.

That idea appalled Naomi. She felt rage towards him, that he would play such mean games when it came to the *Archimedes*.

I beg you not to do that, she told him. You will never be my friend if you do.

Yes, he said, chastened. That was a stupid joke. I'm sorry.

There was much wire netting on the *Demeter*, and as the ship reached the end of the Gulf of Aden the nurses—if stifled by heat in their cabins—were permitted to sleep under distractingly brilliant night skies in a wired-off area at the stern of the promenade deck. They made their way there each evening carrying their palliasses and pillows. Beyond a canvas curtain they disrobed to their slips. There was some conversation here before women trailed off into sleep.

Drowsy Carradine told Naomi she had met Lieutenant Shaw while he was undergoing a strenuous massage of his upper leg and hip in the room off the officers' medical ward. He had promised them a stroll around the deck but he wanted to get his leg fit so he did not hold them up. Though she wished him a normal gait, Naomi was pleased to be free of social duties. The literary ones were enough for the moment. Kiernan's request for an account of the *Archimedes* had unexpectedly started in her a compulsion to set down the whole business in ink without exaggeration or vainglory. It was an imperative that came from within her—not from Kiernan. She still had time and space for dutiful strolling with blinded or lamed soldiers. But not yet for Shaw's bush whimsy and flirtatious chat.

Two days' sail from the equator—when both the starboard and port decks seemed open to the withering sun, and the tar in the deck became liquid—Naomi went into the officers' library. Here nurses were permitted amongst all those writing letters home and reading bound volumes of *Punch*, and it was here she continued her account.

"The Sinking of the *Archimedes*," she wrote after she'd chosen a desk.

Whether nurses or doctors or orderlies, we had all come to think of the Archimedes *as our full-time home. It was also our post of duty from the first time a barge from the beach at Gallipoli came alongside with wounded men on its decks. Some of the men on the* Demeter *might even have been nursed on the* Archimedes *at one stage or another. We were not to know that our ship—which seemed as solid as a town or as a hospital in a city—would soon be taken from us. But not before it had brought many damaged men to Alexandria and to the harbor of Mudros.*

What a delight it all at once was to write of this—even in the plainest terms. But the horses and their terror. How could that be conveyed? And the boyish apathy of those who slipped away and yielded themselves up? And Nettice—the layers of ocean through which she sank and rose. The horror of men hitting the propellers—as if they preferred to be obliterated quickly by the mechanical instead of slowly by the weight of water. Could all this be put down?

As she went on, Kiernan drifted into her imagination, grabbing on to his copper cube. He had been a full partner in her command of the raft. She remembered having been loud and high-handed. For the torpedo had strangely restored her authority when it took down the *Archimedes*. (That was something not to be included in the account.) The *Archimedes* had taught her about her weakness and yet educated her in the nature of the woman she was.

As she was writing, too, the idea of Kiernan having been admirable—of his proving he'd probably be admirable anywhere he was put—took hold of her imagination. The word itself seemed lodged in her brain for the two days she was engaged on the task. When she later saw him on duty, he seemed to her to be placed in the midst of people with a special distinctness other figures lacked. This sharpness of outline was not a form of infatuation but rather a new version of seeing things. It was more akin to identifying a prophet.

The captain recommended that they be at the railing to see the coast of South Africa and the approach to Cape Town.

Naomi and Carradine caught a grimy little train to town. The city was comparable to towns they had known in girlhood—with the strangeness, though, of African women in their swathes of wildly colored cloth selling flowers and fruit from baskets on the footpaths. Black children harried Naomi for money, shouting, Australia! Rich Australia. Give us some.

They were treated with reverence by shop girls as they browsed in Cape Town's emporiums.

A climbing party met up on the quay the next morning with robust young women who were members of the Cape Town mountaineering club. Naomi was a member of the group and suffered a phase of guilt. Given she'd felt obliged to walk the deck with Shaw for more than an hour last evening, she had deliberately chosen an outing Shaw certainly could not embark on. From the middle of the barely woken city—occupied only by black street sweepers—they caught a train which took them around the base of the mountain. The party walked upwards through scrubland and wildflowers, at the end of which great rock platforms presented themselves. Nurses and soldiers were helped upwards by young black men who climbed ahead and reached a hand down with unpredictable strength. They were not permitted to eat or swim with whites, but were essential for scaling a mountain. From massive platforms of rock along the way the local mountaineers pointed out Simonstown and—out to sea—Robben Island, where lepers were kept. At the summit of great, split-apart boulders from which grew wildflowers and shrubs, they looked down at the city and bay and could identify the *Demeter*—rendered minute by distance. They were exhilarated and distracted to happiness by the utterly physical demands of getting here.

Guilt made her seek out Shaw in the officers' lounge that evening. She talked about the climb as if she had done it for its own sake—for its enlivening enthusiasm. She was pleased to see that his face as yet was the face of Shaw the Joker and not of Shaw the Tragic Lover.

He said, Lucky girl. Of course, I can fall off the donkey with the greatest of ease but I haven't mastered Table Mountain yet. Spent all morning with massage and exercise. And it pays off, you know.

She found she liked the ease of his company. He never said anything that would make a person sit up and see the world afresh. He therefore gave her a rest from her own unchosen gravity of soul.

He said, It's not as if I'm less a man. A man's whole life can't rise or fall by a few inches of bone 'this way or that. I'll be able to ride a horse as good as ever if I balance out the stirrups. And my old man has a motor anyhow. But it's true a stock and station agent ought to be able to ride. You wouldn't want to take a motor over some of the tracks up there. Anyhow, I'm well set. And I reckon we should change the subject. We're getting morbid.

It was to his credit that he thought these modest detours into discussing his condition were morbid. But there was another thing besides the unwillingness to look distress in the face, and that was the inability to see it in the first place.

Look, you don't have to hang around talking to me. Like a duty to the sick and the lame.

No, please. You are a good and kindly friend and despite the wound and all the rest—despite all that—you seem to live in the sun. So you'll always attract friends. It's not a duty for me.

Anyhow, he said, leaning forward and keeping a half-inch or so greater closeness than was preferable, I was off on a jaunt while you were climbing mountains.

He and others had been taken to Cecil Rhodes's home and seen the grand library with Rhodes's bust and his last words, "So little done, so much to do," and then his bedroom full of lives of Napoleon. Robbie Shaw said he couldn't get over those words.

I've never heard a better argument for leading an easy life, he told Naomi. I mean, he ran round Africa like a demented being—diamonds here, gold there, land somewhere else. And still . . . he was disappointed.

This—she could sense—was like an argument for a pleasant life in a Queensland town and children running in the garden. He did not understand that a person had to possess a gift for contentment to take up what he was offering.

From the decks outside, they could hear the sounds of the *Demeter* unmooring. No announcement of sailing time had been made earlier. It departed of its own will. There was a rush to the deck now. Robbie Shaw insisted on taking part.

Some nights the nurses dined in their mess. But they were frequently invited to the dining room where Robbie Shaw remained one of the officers who paid them special attention in the Lemnos way. And always that glint—directed at Naomi—that suggested some shared and indefinable secret. At one of the chief tables sat Padre Harris with crosses on the lapels of his uniform. He was a harmless case Naomi had met when she worked in that small section of cabins set aside for the officers with mental concerns. There was a little cabin with a Primus stove in that part of the ship where nurses made tea and cocoa for themselves and the patients. Whenever she gave the Reverend Harris a cocoa he responded with the remotest politeness—one transmitted over a vast and disabling space. Or a display of etiquette remembered by the cells but not by the man. No doubt he had been shocked and became burdened by the men whose hands he'd held for a last "thine is the glory." His features—which were long and lean—seemed always in false repose. Parsons had a duty to adopt the smugness of possessing the truth on free will and sin and the mind of God. That look seemed long vanished from him.

There were two other padres on board to serve the Anglicans and Catholics. So Harris was not called upon for any duties and was allowed to take his time to find his way back to sureness and solid ground. In the meantime, he was likely to say extreme things suddenly. There was no small talk in him. One evening Naomi delivered him in the officers' salon his evening mixture of ethanol and laudanum. Other nurses were similarly dispensing pills and mixtures across the room. And after he had drained the mixture, he told her, Two of the boys from the venereal section have jumped overboard, you know. It's been kept quiet. But shame, you see. Shame killed them.

And then he returned again to his remote self.

Naomi did not know whether this was reliable news or not. At the first chance she asked Carradine whether any men from the syphilis ward had jumped overboard.

Not that I've heard, said Carradine. But then they wouldn't tell anyone, would they, in case the idea came to others.

The next evening Naomi approached the matron of the *Demeter* and asked the question—whispering it so that the infection did not rise into the air.

The matron inspected her and then looked at the ceiling. It was a confession in a gesture. Lowering her head she murmured, You must not tell anyone. You might start them off like lemmings.

Lieutenant Shaw seemed innocent of the information when he asked her to go for a stroll on deck. He wanted the exercise before the Roaring Forties set in. For when they did, unsteady men would need to take to their bunks. It was a brilliant morning of fierce sunlight when they met up. There was much promise of future violent seas in today's choppy ocean. The wired-off section where the women had slept on torrid nights had been dismantled. A small section of a lower deck—where the worst mental patients exercised—had been cooped in by wire to prevent the disturbed casting themselves over the side.

Her problem in walking with Robbie Shaw was that she had entered a stage of her existence in which she could imagine the company of men as endurable and more than endurable. Was this the beginning of delusion which would suck her down into drudgery and weariness? Was it the dawn of wisdom?

Walking on the promenade that morning with Shaw she sighted Padre Harris. He strolled in the fraternal care and company of the uniformed Catholic priest and Anglican minister. He was in the middle of the two. Since—as Naomi knew—his conversation was erratic and prophetic, it was understandable that they tended to talk across him. An impulse arose in Naomi to excuse herself from Shaw and run forward to advise them that—though self-harm was unimaginable in a clergyman—they were coming towards the point in the bows where the steel canted away to become the blade which cut the water. The priest and minister were so involved in some topic now that they moved towards each other behind the Reverend Harris's back. Whatever they discussed—the Nicene Creed or horse racing—they were distracted and barely ready for the fluid way their friend climbed the crossbars of the railings and stepped onto the polished wood at the top and let himself fall into the Indian Ocean more or less in the direction of the bows. The two padres threw themselves against the railings and shouted, and then one rushed up a companionway to the bridge. Shaw and Naomi and others who had seen it all also ran to the rail and gazed down.

One might have had a hope of turning back and retrieving him had it happened in the stern. The captain did of course turn the ship and stop the engines. Lookouts were posted and the decks became crowded with unofficial searchers—officers, nurses, and men. On the sea's brilliant surface a little white froth gave a mimicry of a floating head. Hence, many at various stages yelled, There! No, no. I thought . . .

The idea of suicide was now unleashed. And they all knew that according to the ruthlessness of physics the padre had been drawn straight under by the ship's motion and bludgeoned and hurled along by its hull and thrown into the sweep of propellers. The idea shook Naomi. She knew what propellers could do.

The ship continued to circle but everyone knew it was futile. Naomi consulted her watch.

I should take you down below, she told Robbie. I'm sorry, my shift's beginning.

Shaw said almost as a complaint, Do you think I'd do something like that if you left me up here?

No. I know you wouldn't.

But she insisted he come too. There was nothing he could do for Harris by staying on deck. And the chop was too pronounced for him to stay there alone.

Now a fatal trend was in place. Though two young men afflicted with syphilis had thrown themselves over the railing, it was Padre Harris's example in particular that confirmed the availability of such a release. Within an hour orderlies armed with rifles had been placed on sentry duty on the decks. Perhaps—as Nettice said with dry humor—to shoot anyone who thought of killing themselves. As for aft, it was believed that even a halfway-alert orderly could intercept a blinded soldier or a fellow with amputated legs or a man with a ruined face. But two guards were put there anyway.

In the evening the mood in the mental ward was solemn as Naomi handed out the pills which were meant to keep these men equal of soul. Eyes strayed towards a particular lieutenant colonel named Stanwell. He was a man who sat that night smoking on his own but who was not often seen there in the reading room. Like Harris he had been on dosages of ethanol, but even higher ones than those given to the unfortunate padre. Most of the time he could not sit upright or perform the functions of lighting a cigarette. Since there was concern that he might fall asleep while smoking and inciner- ate himself, his former batman had been assigned to sit in a chair in his cabin and mind him overnight. Naomi understood too that Lieutenant Colonel Stanwell had the respect of young officers—it was apparent in the concentrated concern they radiated towards him. It had a quality very different from the purely professional care Padre Harris's two fellow clergymen had extended to that unfortu- nate man.

Colonel Stanwell—with the same sudden and urgent and remote seriousness as Harris—had enough clarity to ask Naomi later that eve- ning, Did you know, Nurse, how many of my men could be mustered after Krythia? Ten percent of them. That's the number. Ten percent! Have you heard of such a percentage rate since Hannibal defeated the Romans at Cannae?

That is a very sad figure, Naomi agreed.

And real, he said. And real! Not invented.

But you are here and your family will soon see you, Naomi prom- ised him.

She settled pillows too. Nurses with nothing further to say punched pillows as if to drive the trouble from patients' heads.

Stanwell asked her, How did I dare lead men down streets in front of families? To speeches by mayors? How did I have the arrogance to do that? Mocking the wombs of mothers and the breasts of wives? Mocking them!

A hill and a ridge on Gallipoli were named after him and he had raised a battalion from the Victorian countryside.

That night a young man from Hobart—his chin had been severed in two by an ax of shrapnel—noting on paper that he possessed twin half-faces, threw himself over the stern into the wind and a sea running in long, foamy swells. It developed that the orderlies on guard there had strolled together around the deck to shelter and share a smoke with those amidships. They were just returning when they saw him on his perch above the sea. Then they saw him drop into the dark. The ship was stopped yet again. The difficult ocean was swept with lights. A boat was lowered to seek the boy in the area where he had thrown himself. But nothing was found. Guards were doubled and the shirking provosts deprived of a month's pay and given three days in the ship's cell. But the contagion was rampant.

At breakfast their matron now told the nurses to do their best to anticipate the suicidal impulse in men. Suddenly the women—who had been required on Lemnos to talk as little to men as could be managed—were to talk to them as cheerily and as long as was needed to thwart self-destructive daydreams. In the meantime, Naomi got her draft of "The Sinking of the *Archimedes*" done and polished.

The ones I felt sorriest for were those who gave up and slipped away when, had they waited two more hours, they would have been saved for a longer and fruitful life. So might the young man with the broken face, the one who recently threw himself off the ship. For, after all, the surgeons had still much to do and skills to do it and might have given him a decent life in the end.

She did not see these reflections as moral. She saw them as embodying the tragic—and in pretty plain and ordinary terms. She delivered the pages to Kiernan's office two decks down. Here—in congealed heat not penetrated by the colder air above—a clerk typed. But there was for the moment no Kiernan.

He met her on deck later. She was no longer with an officer but escorting a Western Australian boy suffering from the effects of a bullet through his lung. She listened to stories of a childhood she thought of as rougher by degrees than the one people lived on the Macleay. He had grown up in a hut set on a creek bed which flooded and drowned a sister and brother. Western Australia seemed another rung down in the scales of civilization than the place—narrow in mind and spacious in geography as it was—that had bred her. She advised her charge to sit and rest on a rudimentary bench riveted to the bulkhead. Kiernan passed her with a section of orderlies on their way to some duty. He paused, broke away, and spoke to her in a hurry.

I saw what you wrote, he told her. It's a parable exactly suiting the need. It will do more than sermons and better by far than a dozen sentries.

What of the accusations against generals?

Let them stand. The senior officers can make a fuss about them after I've published them.

She wanted to deny she was capable of anything as high-flown as a parable. Yet she was also suffused with literary vanity.

I shall be distributing it about the ship tomorrow, said Kiernan. The *Demeter Times*. I have to go. Forgive me.

Kiernan had infused a new soul in her. And now that she was in the soldiers' wards, it was Sergeant Kiernan who invited her on a promenade the following morning. Kiernan had fixity. In his presence the universe was still.

You said, she asked, or Sally said . . . you are a Quaker?

A Friend. As in "the Society of Friends." It's a matter of argument, you see, whether any Friend should wear a uniform. It's true we have always done our best work out of uniform.

She asked him why he had got himself into uniform then—and with stripes on his arm.

Oh, he admitted. Innocence. Vanity. Ignorance—I was not aware that there would be volunteer ambulances that weren't military. And I might have been caught up in my own way in that war fever. The whole of society was swept up, and I was part of society and wanted to belong in it. I got the simpleminded sense that this was a furnace we all had to be tempered in, the fierce and the peaceable alike. I *wanted* to be part of it.

I had exactly the same feeling, she said. Certainly, I wanted to get away. But as well as that, I felt the same as you.

Even then, we make up half of our motives. All of us. Just to cover the fact that at the time we moved by instinct. We impose the reasons for it afterwards. What will you do now? Nurse in Australia?

Perhaps. But I want to go back *there*.

Oh, we all want to go back, he said, and he laughed in his secretive manner. But I think we'll have plenty of time to organize that. No end is in sight.

I believe my file is marked so that I can never be made a senior staff nurse or anything grander than that—such as a sister. But I know I am going back.

Yes, he said. Do we want the sensational, you and I? To see how far humans will go in inflicting and enduring? I want to be with men who've had serious experience. If it were otherwise, I would have joined some hospital-visiting body before the war. I mean, the Friends *do* have such things.

But it is like a disease, she agreed. To want to tend deaths instead of births.

You don't really want to see deaths, he said with certainty. I'm your editor and I know.

In the rest of the voyage, those who did not wish to perish outnumbered those who did. This was combined with the new watchfulness of sentries to ensure that throwing yourself off the ship was now difficult. Soldiers on deck told Naomi in excitement that both the padres had read from her "Sinking of the *Archimedes*" in their sermons—though not anything on the folly of planners and generals. But on hanging on. Redemption being an hour away. So . . . a parable . . .

That Sunday afternoon a demented boy amputee swallowed caustic soda he'd found in an unlocked cupboard and died, scarlet-faced, gagging on emetics. And that was the last of it—the final act of avoidance of the home shore. His family would of course turn up at the dock in some Australian port—unless they lived too far out on remoter farms, insulated by bad tracks from any immediate crushing of hope. Their hopes would then be centered on the local railway station. They would be required in the end to swallow the bitter, tactful lie. Your son—weakened by wounds—perished of meningitis. Or pneumonia. Or jaundice.

A raging gale came on and kept men in bunks and distracted them with queasiness and the smell of vomit from concern for their testing homecomings. Naomi found herself immune from the disease. Her companion on the stormy decks was Sergeant Kiernan—the Quaker who wanted more of the war.

Antipodes

Was it to cut down on dockside grief that the *Demeter* slipped southwest of Perth—that rumored western city—and sighted the sharp lines of Cape Leeuwin in a clear morning rinsed by a furious west wind and then made for Albany? Only men of Western Australia would land there—in that hugest of whaling ports and at the small town beneath its bald foreshores. Albany's scatter of human dwellings offered a discounted homecoming, and one from which men would need to be transported to other places by railway. There did not seem to be enough people here to acclaim heroes and to utter a compacted roar of praise. The bands and families on platforms and the banquets offered by grateful shires seemed far off. A few officials came out on launches to meet the ship. Then the *Demeter*'s launches themselves began to be lowered to act as ferries.

So men who might have previously feared arrival on Australia's mainland found this one—the huge harbor and modest whaling town of Albany—far too plain. As barges came out with fresh produce, a rumor started amongst the men that a feast had been planned to honor them in that port. They wanted to taste it, Australian beef and roast potato and currant pudding and bottled beer and all the rest. Take us ashore too! they began chanting over the stern as they saw the western men handing their sticks and crutches ahead to sailors, then following them edgily and with a jolt onto the deck of the launch.

That night twenty men of sundry wounds and experience stole a launch which stood tethered to the side of the ship. These had the small joy of walking the Albany wharfs and of a brief search for drink and for women. They were applauded when brought back to the *Demeter* under a guard of the military police. But their renown was brief. Their story depressed men in the end. They had dreamed and half feared that the Australian earth would drag them in like a ferocious magnet. But there had been no passion in the neutral arms of Albany Harbour. A late-assembled brass band ashore was heard remotely as the *Demeter* slipped out in the morning. Immediately they were claimed by the ring of storm which ran around the world at that latitude. Lieutenant Shaw—declaring himself immune to seasickness—invited Naomi to walk the decks. He argued he was expert on his legs now. It was true that he used the imbalance of his legs deftly to deal with the pitches and yaws and rolls of the vessel. Both overcoated, he and Naomi allowed themselves to be blown along the deck and climbed to the wing of the bridge. Wind threatened to whip them off it like leaves as they watched the white collisions of the ship with the ocean. There was no ship's officer here on the exposed part of the bridge. Shaw turned to her to share his delight in the shifting pillars of spray. Flecks of it had settled on his face. Here—in the most private square yard of the ship—he was free to let that light of especial recognition shine unabated towards Naomi.

All right, he shouted, yelling because in this gale a yell was a whisper. I've shown enough cowardice and I ought to tell you straight. I feel a real pleasure in your company and I can see you are a first-rate soul of a woman. Me being the joker and you the rock. I reckon we could be world-beaters.

He let her contemplate that idea for a moment.

I mean to say, he continued, I read your item on the sinking of that ship and I thought it was of a pretty high order. It showed a stalwart soul. You are a clever woman too. If there are men who don't like clever women, I'm not one of them. And then you're beautiful as blazes—no small thing, that! Sets off all the other qualities in a most marvelous way. A *most* marvelous way!

The *Demeter* took a massive dip into the trough between waves. She nearly lost her footing and a real baptism of spray over the fore-peak wet their heads. They both laughed. It was exhilarating. It was a stimulus to Shaw.

I favor you greatly. That's the truth. I'm saying all of it in a bit of a panic, you see, because I know that with this wind behind us we'll be in Adelaide and all the rest in no time. So I don't want to postpone, even though this is an uncomfortable moment for both of us. Would you consider marrying me?

That ridiculous, wind-drenched shout of a question. She did stare fullface at him. Looking off to the side wouldn't work. Yet what surprised her was how much pleasure the offer in itself gave her. It was far greater pleasure than discomfort. He hadn't figured much in her inner and random imaginings, but she saw he was not repellent. The idea of sharing a table and bed with him, and all that, was not unpleasant. She could also tell he'd be ardent and that it would take a lot of coldness and meanness from her to make him think she was less than a decent woman. And there was the sudden and strangely attractive possibility of being defined. The concept of a ritual sealing, a lifelong promenade with no threat from Robbie Shaw and no foreseeable tempests. It appealed to her—the idea of a companion who had come through the Gallipoli slaughter with an even soul appealed to her. The doubt was whether she could live such a straightforward and resolved life.

People do say I have a future, he rushed to tell her, howling against the wind. I mean, in my area of Queensland.

Oh, she roared, I've got no doubt about that.

Then what do you say?

This is how it happens with women, she knew. Independent beings one second and transformed forever the next. Just by the improbability that someone would want them. Yes, it would be sweet to be held—though that couldn't happen up here. Not within the possible sight of captains and helmsmen.

It's too early, she shouted. I believe men are often early with these ideas. And often wrong. I don't mean *you're* wrong now . . .

He nodded. He took the point seriously. For Naomi the great question returned. There was no more honor in any man than there was in her father. There was no more fineness of soul in any woman than her mother. Yet there had been a discontent in her mother which could not be defined but could not be argued with. A particular, occasional sense of loss—of unease and genteel unrest—in her mother's face caused Naomi's blood to turn. In a quiet homestead, they had all crept around her mother. Yet Mrs. Durance should have been aware when she married of what her life would be—she was a cow-cocky's daughter getting married to a cow-cocky. She knew that love wouldn't save you from the butter churn or the chapped hands of winter milking. Eric Durance saved his daughters but not his wife from that toil. Mrs. Durance must have known it would never all be a stylish promenade on the mudflats of Sherwood.

Naomi was pleased she could not imagine a milk churn in Robbie Shaw's future, but that look in the eyes of married women often seemed to tell you there were equivalents to it.

You have to realize, she yelled, I'm going back—at least to Egypt.

What if they don't let you?

I'll find a way.

He laughed, and the laughter was stripped from his face by the wind that flattened his cheeks.

I'm going back too, he asserted. They won't stop me.

Come indoors, she shouted when he said something else she didn't hear. The gale was if anything wilder. The wind did not tolerate cavalier movement. But with her care he came down the ladder competently. They reached the double doors that led into the greater quiet of indoors. With a whipping sound the inner door closed and the tactful shudder of engines from deep below was now dominant. Shaw looked sheepish, as if he would not have said what he had if he'd been in a place for normal speech. He peered at her from beneath his gingery eyebrows with a gaze of conspiracy which she was sure had always helped suck in lovers.

She said, With our futures so unsettled . . . Well, what can I say?

I will get off in Sydney, he said. If you stay a day or so we can visit the sights. We can go sailing. Do you sail?

You must get home to your parents.

I can catch the coastal steamer to Brisbane. Faster than this old bucket.

Well, I have a stepmother at home who though a pleasant woman can't be bursting to see me, she admitted. I suppose . . .

Two days, he told her. Two days' leave in Sydney. Delightful. The Australia Hotel—a fine dining room, that one.

I'll stay at the Young Women's Temperance Hotel.

That sounds severe.

And I've nothing to wear except a uniform.

The same with me, he said.

All right, she said.

If a man went to the trouble of suggesting something as eternal as a marriage then you owed yourself a few days in a place away from masses of nurses and soldiers to study him.

In Port Adelaide—where the ship moored on a bright Australian spring day and the band was close and the wharf triumphantly decked with flags—Rosanna Nettice helped Lieutenant Byers down the gangway to the brass exuberance of "The British Grenadiers." Nettice herself was leaving the ship and had volunteered to join the staff of the Keswick Military Hospital. She left their company promising to write letters and shedding a few tears but with no apparently profound regret. She took Naomi apart for a special show of thanks—plainly uttered—but her objective to marry Byers overrode all other issues and affections. In her mind it was not for exchanging letters with them that the artillery pony had saved her. It was for Byers.

From the railing of the *Demeter*, Naomi saw a solidly dressed man and woman and a number of near-adult children greet their blinded son and brother. The mother began to weep on his shoulders despite the grin of reassurance that Byers wore. The father looked on from under his homburg and over his European-style, pointed moustache. He studied his blinded son with his trained jeweler's eyes. Naomi saw Byers turn to Nettice and introduce her to his family. Was he telling them the entire story? That Nettice would devote herself to Lieutenant Byers's battle with the seeing world? In any case, Naomi saw his mother extend her hand to Nettice and the father kiss her hand by way of courtly but uncertain thanks. But what were the clan dramas to be worked out? If the father had changed his name from Myers to Byers he was probably open to the concept of his son marrying a gentile. Nettice was conscious her friends were watching from above and as she moved away with the Byers family—a porter behind pushing his luggage and hers—she looked up. She had faced out the parents. Who—in fact—could set a test for Nettice that would defeat her purpose?

In Melbourne two mornings later, Naomi saw some of the men from the syphilis ward go down the gangway to a reunion with families who must not be told—with girlfriends who must not be caressed and wives who must not be penetrated. The homecoming wharves—where people met their variously damaged men, whose minds had been licked as with fire by the daydream of suicide—creaked with laughter and smiling which might yet prove friable. The overearnest band music was doomed to fail everyone as soon as the players stopped for breath. Carradine landed happy on her way to disqualify herself from further official duty by giving the authorities proof of marriage. And then to return as a self-funded volunteer to England.

On their one night in that city, Lieutenant Shaw took Naomi to dinner at the Windsor Hotel—once a temperance palace but now the "flashest pub in town." He insisted on a bottle of red wine and when it was decanted, he told her he thought it delightful on his palate—

though she secretly thought it was sour. Yet under its warm influence she told him about Mrs. Sorley—this woman she must visit in visiting her father.

Easier for me, he said. My family aren't complicated. My parents are just my parents. My sis and the brothers . . . quarrelsome beggars. But no grievances. It makes life easy. Quarrels get settled on the spot.

My sister and I, she confessed, are just learning to do that. And making some progress.

Good girl, he said. You'll need to be forgiving if you're married to me.

But nothing's been decided, she warned him. I don't know that you're a man for a long engagement, in any case. There's too much life in you. And there's no chance of it being a short one.

He shook his head. My God! Until now I've only met girls who are busting for marriage. I can't imagine myself *not* waiting for such a noble girl though. When *will* this war end—next year, 1917, 1921, 1925?

Noble, she snorted. That's you throwing a light on me. Like the Egyptian who used to stand under the chin of the Sphinx with a flare. But the flare burns out and the Sphinx stays the same.

Well, he said, the Sphinx part is right. You don't give a lot away.

She warned him she could not sponge on him because that assumed some degree of consent she hadn't given. He won the argument at dinner. For heaven's sake, he said, women never pay for dinner there. Don't show me up.

On Sydney Harbour—amidst ferries and pilot boats and launches— they enjoyed a sailing expedition with an associate of Shaw's father who owned a wonderful clinker-built yacht. His slight limp looked gallant in the lobby and created military fables about him amongst those who still believed that war's chief duty was to lightly mar the brave.

She found the kisses they exchanged that night before she left the Australia Hotel—and the next morning when his coastal ship left Darling Harbour—were the more arousing because she was kissing her possible partner for life. These might be the opening gestures of the solemnities and fevers of the flesh for both of them. She felt enlivened and her blood churned pleasantly. She found them less than ecstatic. Were they meant to be otherwise? Last night they had not delayed her in getting ready for bed nor very much in falling asleep. He had no part in dreams. In fact, if anyone ever featured, it was Kiernan—though not in *that* sense. But as a kindly quantity he spoke like a sage in a dream of sun-drenched spaces. He was not forgotten.

The End of Lemnos

On bitter Turks Head on Lemnos the gales became near continuous, and rain was honed to sleet and crystallized to snowfall during nights. It was easier to keep warm in the wards than in the women's tents. Now the moles stayed under the bitter ground. Come daylight, the women rushed across ice to their breakfasts—better breakfasts though than had been the case under the old regime.

Typhoid burned on in the infectious wards and pneumonia began to fill the medical wards. The wounds that arrived now often seemed to be bullet wounds to the head—from places where men had accidentally given away their presence at a low part of a parapet. Or else shell damage. It was apparent though—as the winter bit and ice formed on water buckets—that divisions were no longer going forth from their trenches looking for trouble at Anzac Beach and Cape Helles. Their gambits would have to be renewed at a more clement time.

Outside the mess tent the orderlies were unloading Christmas billy cans—stamped with a kangaroo and a boomerang and full of chocolate and minute puddings in cloth. A letter inside was addressed to "Dear Soldier of Australia." Ten days to Christmas, and intact men were landing on Lemnos each day in numbers suddenly too big for the rest camp. Sally and Slattery—shopping from peddlers—watched them march by. Their faces were gaunt and stained with weariness. The eyes seemed not yet aware that they had been brought back into the living world. There was too much continuance of geography between Gallipoli and here.

As they went past they could be smelled—not just filthy flesh but fermentations of the skin and uniform. They still carried the trench-fever lice. For the louse it was always summer in the clefts and crevices of the body. From these men a faint rumor arose. They're pulling soldiers out of Gallipoli, one of the senior nurses heard and passed it on. Don't mention a word of it to any Greek peddler around Mudros. As Sally had learned, the Greeks hated the Turks. But one of them might be on the Turkish payroll, people said.

As Christmas ribbons went up to decorate the YMCA hut at Mudros, the number of wounded diminished for one day—which might have been luck. Then it stayed the same the next day, and a third. The diminution in wounded and sick began to look like the result of some human cleverness.

Walking-wounded officers and orderlies and nurses were now openly strolling or riding down to the wharf to greet the morning arrivals who had been spirited off Gallipoli at night. But all conversations were almost in code. It was as if every sentence might be listened to by an unseen party and the ruse which would redeem the Gallipoli folly would be thwarted.

The air around the hospital was pensively triumphant. There had been that night-after-night escape better planned than anything else had been in all this calamity. Yet the last wounded were still there. And so were the many dead, or in the snowy cemetery below Turks Head—both places impossibly located for devout flower bearing or grave visitations by relatives.

Sally and Honora took a cup of tea each and drank it with Leo—that girl whose temperament had never betrayed her. But later in the morning—amidst shouts along pathways and whispered messages in wards—it became known that two last ships had come from the black peninsula. Honora and Sally—due to go to sleep after night duty—were amongst the rush of people who got to the pier where the very last of Gallipoli's harmed were being unloaded into motor ambulances.

By Christmas Naomi had returned from her brief Macleay Valley homecoming and had been working some weeks at the military hospital at Randwick—not far from her Aunt Jackie's place. She had dutifully visited her aunt and chattered tentatively with her about the new Mrs. Durance.

Randwick Hospital was an orderly place. Patients were admitted not in a calamitous flood but one at a time. The food was regular and of the wholesomely plain ilk. Hours of rest could be banked on. But restlessness plagued Naomi. The war had made a misfit of her.

Every two days she got a fervent letter from Lieutenant Shaw about his efforts to be returned to Egypt. He had written to the adjutant-general in Melbourne, had garnered reference letters from a bishop, a member of the Legislative Assembly of Queensland, a federal senator. She too had gathered letters to help her own cause of getting back— one of them from Matron Mitchie—now returned to Victoria—and another from the chief medical officer on the *Demeter*. It was not only the sedateness of nursing life she found hard. Above all and beyond reason she wanted to put a great mileage between her and home ground.

Why did she hate it? That beautiful place, that river brown with fertile mud, the sweet pastures of Sherwood? And the blue Kookaburra Ranges full of plentiful native cedar—a stalk of which had killed Mr. Sorley and gained the Durance girls a stepmother. Weighing her home element by element, she had seen few places more well-made by nature and more temperate in her journeys. She had no excuse in her stepmother. Mrs. Sorley—as she remained in Naomi's mind—was an enthusiast. As a result of Naomi informing her father and his wife of her arrival by *Currawong*, Naomi found the town mayor welcoming her to the landing dock in East Kempsey. He was attended by journalists and photographers from the Macleay *Argus*, and her proud father in his Friday suit and with his wife and her children. There was a procession of cars from the landing dock to the mayoral chambers. A ceremonial breakfast was held with Naomi in her gray uniform at the mayoral side. Naomi envied Kiernan who would not have to go through such ceremonies or be greeted by flatulent speeches. The mayor saw Mrs. Sorley along the table and called congratulations to her. But she said she could take no credit for this brave girl. Naomi was the product of the breast and influence of another woman. Unlike her mother, though, Mrs. Sorley seemed a woman in command and confident in the fruits of marriage. Her pride for her new husband's sake and her renouncing of any credit on her own part were both disarming.

From the mayor's speech it was apparent they had heard about "The Sinking of the *Archimedes*." She did not know how. She discovered then that it had been published in an Adelaide paper and copied by the *Sydney Morning Herald* before the *Demeter* itself had reached Sydney. Who was to blame for that? Shaw or Kiernan? Shaw, she decided. A ceremonious man like Kiernan would have sought permission.

She was asked to speak at the breakfast. You become another person when you see the faces turned and the ready ears. The keenness to be heard and an electric curiosity ran through the speaker and jumbled and altered her. She heard herself say that the men were "Christlike," that there was never a complaint, that it was her life's privilege to nurse their wounds. She did not mention the dysentery ward and its shitty mattresses and its atmosphere claimed by flies. At last the breakfast ended. Women presented themselves who said they had been to school with her. Some of them said they had children. Of course, one of them said, our little Clarrie was killed last September. Mum can't ever get over it.

The Durances were delivered home—down the hill from West Kempsey and over the bridge to Sherwood—in a car driven by the town clerk.

You do whatever you like, Mrs. Sorley whispered to her in the wide backseat. You rest if you wish to or go riding a horse. It was your home before it was mine.

Naomi kissed her and Mrs. Sorley beamed with pleasure. Naomi couldn't depend on Mrs. Sorley to drive her away from home. Her father asked with an edge of concern about Egypt and Lemnos.

I could have lost both daughters, he said.

She could tell he had taken the *Sydney Morning Herald* and the mayor to heart. But he had accommodated himself also to having bred a heroine.

As they ate roast lamb on the Sunday of her visit home and as her father applied himself with earnestness to his plate and Mrs. Sorley beamed at her, Naomi thought of her stepmother, You will weep at his graveside but you'll be there foursquare. You will live easily but earnestly with the grief.

She stayed on a week at the farm amidst the blackbutt walls of the bedroom she and Sally had shared. The creosote of the foundation posts—and some natural form of turpentine the timber foundations themselves imbued the soil with—still created the faint and familiar and forgotten odor of this place where she had been a sister to Sally and where she had abandoned her. And of course in which she now with mere justice did her duty under the added weight of her reported heroism. Despite all—love of father, kindness of stepmother—she merely observed the pieties of gratitude and of chatting with her half-brothers and -sister. And when awake at night she would be seized by the thought of her uneven-legged and eager captain. Sometimes she thought of admirable Kiernan. Kiernan had left the ship in Melbourne to go to his unimaginable Quaker family. There was pleasure and yet little desire of more than a general kind in her memory of either man.

Before she left—that morning at breakfast—she suddenly grabbed her father's chapped, leathery hands and kissed them. The sight of them reminded her that Eric Durance had hired labor to prevent his daughters' hands becoming leathery. When they saw her to the East

Kempsey dock and to the *Currawong* steamer, Mrs. Sorley embraced Naomi and whispered, You kissing his hands. It meant the whole world to him.

She was bent on using her eminence as a *Herald* correspondent to her benefit. She had not forgotten to include that cutting—admiringly published and just a little edited by some censor to take the blame for the *Archimedes*'s death from the army—amongst her documents. She presented all of it now to the senior matron who interviewed her in Sydney. She could see there was some hope. She blessed the bush impishness in Shaw that had possibly released her creation to the newspapers. She realized she had two things that could not be found in any nurse out of a civil hospital. She had experience of terrible wounds. And she had stayed afloat after being sunk.

So there was to be a further interview—she read that as progress. Now it was the senior matron and a very elderly colonel who told her he had been in Egypt but repatriated. You're not dealing with a doctor of any distinction in me, he told her frankly. My work is pure administration.

He studied her file and seemed impressed she had been a triage nurse. It was an asset she was willing to grab at that summer morning.

And your sister is nursing, I see.

Yes, Naomi asserted. She's on Lemnos in the stationary hospital there.

Sally could serve as another argument for a return.

I should warn you that your intractability which is noted here is of some concern. But my God—this was under Spanner. I see that Colonel Leatherhead believed there existed extenuating circumstances. Still, your acts of rebellion will not be tolerated in future. Do you understand?

Naomi assured him she did.

He turned to the matron. An Old Testament God, this Spanner chap.

She had an exhilarating expectation now. They would send her back. She would not need to share a continent with Mrs. Sorley.

There is a ship due to leave Melbourne in two weeks, the colonel told her. You will be notified with the details and issued with a travel warrant closer to the time.

Her impulse was to kiss his hand like some feudal woman. But that would have convinced him that she was unreliable.

Should I say congratulations? asked the senior matron.

From a form of politeness rather than passion, she had written to Robbie Shaw. News—that was all. No false feeling. And she heard from him in return.

Dearest Naomi,
There's some hope they're going to put me with a transport unit.
Organizing freight trains and so on. Better there than here. Would
like to say more but am between interviews. I think of you all the
time.

Your devoted friend (I know you don't want me to be called
more than that),

Robbie

BOOK II

Rare Pyramids

Sally near collided with Honora Slattery in the corridor of the Heliopolis Palace Hotel. Through double doors nearby they could hear the hubbub of conversation from the grand ballroom, where beds were laid out ten across the width of the room and in God-knew-how-many ranks—she hadn't had time to count. Above the ballroom floor were galleries, and these too were loaded with beds—so fully that their creaky floors and the ornate Moorish columns which attached them to the roof seemed too frail to take the weight.

The officers' lounge, midnight, Honora said. Come on, we've got to have a drink to get rid of this bloody year. Lionel Dankworth will be there.

Dankworth was wounded?

He had an ear shot off. His hearing's intact.

As narrated by Honora, it sounded less than threatening. She did not seem tormented by the quarter inch which dictated Dankworth had lost an ear rather than a head.

Mudros was gone and there seemed too much life at the Heliopolis for anyone to be wistful. The huge rooms pulsed with it—the strident outnumbered the shy and the convalescent the sick.

It turned out that Lionel Dankworth had been enchanted with Honora Slattery to the extent that he had accompanied her to mass in the chapel of the Heliopolis Palace. Catholics were like that, people said—ruthless with using love as a lever to shift people.

Sally knew that—unless it was for a purely ceremonial event—no one could inveigle her to church. God had left the earth by now and was hidden amidst stars. Good for him! A first-class choice, the way things were. Yet she also knew that even in her disappointment with the deity, behind her failure to believe any further, lay a soul designed for belief. Under different stars she could have been a dour votary. It was Honora who seemed designed for raucousness and fun and a kind of frank sensuality. The tension in Honora between jokiness and devotion seemed to hold Dankworth in wonderment. He'd never met it before.

There were the tents of a new camp beyond the town of Heliopolis and in the desert. The streets were full of new boys—reinforcements. They were as amazed by where they'd ended up as their forerunners had been a year ago. They caught the tram outside the Palace to go into the center of Cairo. There they would repeat—as if they were newly discovered and their own invention—the japes of those who were now too mangled for levity and whose sportive pulse had been quelled on Gallipoli.

There was little to make Sally go to town. One night Lionel Dankworth and another officer took Honora and her to dinner in the piazza on the Nile embankment outside Shepheard's—the hotel having now been elevated to the status of Allied headquarters. Dankworth's ear wound was barely visible and well healed. Honora's clear hope was that Sally and the other officer would *take*—as Lionel Dankworth and Honora had *taken*. Though she was not against the idea of infatuation and the life it might give to banal hours, she could not seem to achieve it when a specific man was presented.

As for the antiquities . . . well, the idea of looking again at the pyramids was painful when so many of the company she had visited them with were gone. It was a good time of year for it though, Lieutenant Dankworth said. You could get to the top of the pyramid of Cheops without any heat exhaustion and see forever in all directions in a clear atmosphere. So Honora and Lionel went—scooting diagonally across the length of Cairo and even visiting the army camp at Giza for drinks with some other Gallipoli chaps.

Time to toast 1916, said Honora—extending her invitation for New Year drinks. It has to be better than this because it couldn't be worse.

May we, or at least some of us, said Lionel—making his toast that night—punish John Turk in Palestine for anything he might have done to us in Gallipoli.

There was quite a crowd of men and nurses present. One of them had visited an aerodrome in Sinai and, seeing the airmen take off over the desert, had decided that was what he would dearly love to do. There were so many fellows applying, but the infantry and even the light horse lost their shine when compared to climbing into the air like that.

You see, he said, we've never had an eagle-eye view. Napoleon didn't. Imagine if Wellington at Waterloo is wondering what to do, how long to hold out before retreating, say, and Napoleon is pouring the Imperial Guards in and the future all depends on Blücher's Prussians turning up in time. Just imagine if Wellington had been able to say, "Lieutenant Fortescue, can you hop in your B.E. and go up four thousand feet and tell me if Marshal Blücher is on his way?" Now I'd say that's true power. An ordinary soldier with greater power to see—to get a grasp of things—than any general.

All right, said Lionel, but then you've got to come down. Remember that bloke Icarus?

The men were drinking whisky and ale, the women champagne and orange and—for those who had not essayed liquor yet—fruit juice with chipped ice. And a quiet voice speaking not of vast pictures of desert or sky-highs but of earthbound things asked, Excuse me, aren't you one of the Durance girls?

Sally had been talking to some of Lionel's friends and saw the face of a grown boy when she turned—the features in the suntanned face had a delicate neatness a mother and aunts would cherish. A choirboy face, people said, and also, in common wisdom, that they were the most dangerous.

Charlie Condon, said the young man. East Kempsey.

Your father was the solicitor? she asked.

Yes. That's it.

The Condons were part of the ruling class of the town in reputedly classless Australia. The gentry were the solicitors and the accountants and the bank managers whose children played together and whose wives spoke to each other. Yet this young man was shy about talking to her. She thought he did not look like a veteran. He lacked that dark pulse in the eyes.

Didn't you go away to Sydney to study? she asked.

He said he had.

One of the boarding schools, she surmised. Then . . . was it the law?

Heavens no, he said. A stab at law maybe. But other things interest me. By the way, you were a year ahead of me at school. To a bit of a kid, that's an age.

Thank you, she said and was willing to smile. You make me sound like a maiden aunt.

I'm so pleased I saw you. It's ridiculous, but we spend all our time looking for faces from home, our part of home. And I don't even like the place.

But we want to know, don't we? Like it or not.

What about you? Were you nursing there? In the Macleay, I mean.

Yes, she told him and then it recurred—that she'd nursed her mother to death. In his presence it was something she wanted to suppress—to the point of oblivion.

My sister left as soon as she could, she told him—as a matter of history and not grievance. She's back there right now, but she says she's coming back here. She's visiting my father at Sherwood. And my stepmother. You remember a Mrs. Sorley?

I remember a boy called Sorley, Condon admitted. I remember the widow, but only dimly. Wasn't her husband killed by a tree?

That's right.

Oh, he said, a famous Macleay tragedy. I always thought she looked pretty jolly for a widow. Not that I'm saying . . .

No, she said, I know you're not saying . . .

He developed an even smile. She had for some reason expected him to grin crooked and to show the devil beneath the pretty features.

A funny place, he told her confidentially. There are a lot of people in that valley who think they're the ant's pants—as if Kempsey and the Macleay were Paris or London or Moscow. And when you come back from Sydney everybody's trying to land you with their daughter—as if it's the only place you could possibly meet a girl. Crikey, I am being critical, aren't I? You must have brought out the moaner in me.

That unblooded look emerged in his face again. It was still a serious matter for him—his boyish rebellion against the Macleay River and its valley and its principal town.

He didn't give off that almost chemical mixture of fatalism and bloody remembrance and tired ruthlessness the survivors did. Some of the veterans were courtly and polite because it was a railing to cling to, and to save them from the pit. The new men were polite to and courtly towards women and the world because they thought they had a life to pursue and had not yet faced the force that so utterly overpowered politeness. It wasn't his fault—after all, he was a year younger than her. It was simply obvious.

They spoke for the rest of the evening—she broke away only when she saw Honora smiling in her direction and presuming that her conversation with Lieutenant Condon stood for some outburst of magnetism. It would be useless later saying that she had found it pleasant talking to him, since because of Honora's own infatuation with Lionel Dankworth—deformed ear and all—she was geared up to read intense attachment everywhere and even in the mildest friendliness.

At three o'clock in the morning everyone went up on to the roof. There was a resolve to stay up there and see the first light of the year come out of Sinai—it would happen about half-past five. It must be seen—went the proposition—because this would be the year of victory and peace. Sally decided not to share the experience. As the party took to the stairs, Sally called from below, Honora, I'm going now. Thank you, it was very pleasant.

That pale word again.

Charlie Condon was already on the lower steps. Coming, Charlie? asked Honora, who obviously knew him.

Just a tick, Miss Slattery, he called, raising an arm and an index finger up the stairs to beg indulgence. The others ascended.

Well, he said, it was a fine thing somehow. Meeting you again in such altered circumstances. Look, Miss Durance, you've been to Giza, haven't you? I bet you're a veteran of Giza?

I was there earlier this year. No, it's last year now.

Yes, well, it's all new to me. You can't believe it when you first see it, can you? You can't believe you're there, sharing the same air with it.

Yes, I think I felt *exactly* like that.

Now there's another one I want to see. It's up the river. Sakkara. The first pyramid of all—King Djoser. I wondered, would you do me the honor of visiting it with me? Not a huge distance. Hour or two on the truck. Or there's a bus. We could take a picnic.

For the first time since she had come to Egypt, she had been asked to go somewhere she wanted to go and in the smallest party possible. The chance of an excursion without being swamped by conversation— after so many continuous nights of such conversation—was welcome.

If you will excuse me, he said, I will go up to the roof garden. I'm new here. This year is likely to be my initiation in military matters.

Condon suggested they try the adventure of an Egyptian bus to Sakkara. It was a novel idea since everyone else she knew tried to cadge lifts in army trucks or ambulances or commandeer a car when on a jaunt. People had told him they could get a truck back to Cairo or even Heliopolis without difficulty that afternoon. Sakkara was on the south–north road from Aswan. To her it counted for little that soldiers might smirk at picking up an officer and a nurse from the side of the road.

Catching the tram from Heliopolis and the bus from the railway station seemed a genuine adventure. It bemused the bus-traveling effendis—the Egyptian gentlemen in heavy European suits and tarbooshes—and the shy fellahin, laborers and small farmers, Nile cow-cockies as Condon would say, who frowned and stared as if the universal order had been upset.

As she watched unaccustomed quarters of the city sweep by, she realized that her elated feeling that the world had altered was because she and Condon had for a few hours moved beyond military reach. They rolled out into the irrigated countryside and its strips of cultivation and she assessed that the day was like a warmer autumn day at home and the sky wide open and vast. Occasional trucks going northwards showed unwelcome glimpses of khaki.

It's a little mean of me, said Charlie as they sat and the bus engine whined and dragged them along at perhaps twenty miles an hour. I know all the travel guides at Sakkara try to make a living. But I think I'd rather not have a guide. I mean, some of them talk you blind and distract you when you see something marvelous and try to sell you rubbish.

He wanted to know—of course—whether this was agreeable to her. She said it was. He assured her he had a Murray guidebook with him—people preferred them over the German Baedeker guides—and somehow she knew that he had absorbed it conscientiously and would reliably tell her everything she needed to know at Sakkara.

As they traveled he confessed he'd been studying in a Sydney art school which emphasized sketching as the building block of all art, and whose motto was that it was better to sketch well for a lifetime than to paint badly for twenty years. He didn't like to bring out his pad when there were lots of people around. But the reason he liked sketching was not just that a sketchpad was so much more portable. It began to show you—as one of his teachers had argued—that light is everything. Color was a mere servant to light. Light is everything *to* everything, and *in* everything too. It was, of course, the first time she had heard a discourse on these matters. She was as impressed with this reflection as with the bus—which seemed in part Condon's own conception.

When they got off in the flat-roofed oasis town of Sakkara, a dozen men came up and mobbed them and tried to rent them donkeys and offer themselves as guides. Children milled and plucked garments and called Charlie "effendi" and "sir."

No guides, no guides, called Condon, right or wrong, just or unjust. No, no guides. Just ponies.

He went down the line of those available. He turned to Sally and said, These two look good, pointing to two beasts who looked to her little different from the other sinewy creatures. Their owner shook his head sadly as if his animals were too precious to him for lease. How many piastres? Condon began. Though new to the place, and inexperienced, he brought an air of casual worldliness to his transactions.

Sally and Condon—once atop the ponies—rode off. Children ran behind praising the bey (a term of praise above effendi) and lady for their horsemanship. This ferment of applause was the product of poverty, and she and Charlie had already committed the crime of depriving a local of a tour-guide fee. Yet they had all they wanted—Condon carried in his kitbag water, boiled eggs, and canned salmon, and some flatbread from a bakery stall in Cairo. Condon amiably telling them, *Imshi,* the tail of children faded beyond the edge of town. Their ponies scurried across gravel and left the last little irrigated green plot of Egyptian clover behind.

Very soon the pyramid began to rise in huge steps before them. It ascended to a blunt apex in the sky. She could sense and shared in Condon's zeal to walk along the remaining colonnade in front of the pyramid. They tied up their ponies to rings embedded in a low stone wall for the purpose. Then they got down and were alone. No Scots in kilts. No slouch hats. No British officers in tropic-weight tailored uniforms. No one. Small gusts of wind sounded enormous as they turned over pebbles in the great, silent dome of the day.

Condon was carrying a battery torch. They might be able to visit the burial chamber, he said, and see the frescoes. He let go of his knowledge easily. He seemed no pedant. This ancient tumulus involved an architect named Imhotep, he said, who used limestone for the first time in history here—in Djoser's stairway to heaven. Charlie Condon was more interested in the four-thousand-year-old cleverness of Imhotep—which had lasted—than in the power of Djoser, which was lost. This columned approach, he said, must have been crammed with people—image makers, butchers, money changers, wine sellers. For this was the great market of the necropolis of Memphis. One of the tombs was, in fact, said Condon, of Djoser's butcher.

Charlie Condon populated the place without effort—a man who wanted to see the total present in the light of the entire then. But they found the entrance to the burial chamber padlocked—a guide would have no doubt fetched a key to open it. As a further exercise of his stylishness as a traveler, he picked the lock with a penknife. Sally laughed—but in part for fear of the winding chambers he was so keen to enter with her.

Do you know where I learned to pick locks? he asked her as they entered darkness and he switched on the torch. Newington College. It's an excellent place to go if you want a criminal career.

There were vivid, graceful human figures painted on the walls, she saw as Condon's torchbeam lit the way down the first dark passage. Some of the painted shapes had their faces chipped away as if by chisel. Condon wondered was this the work of Christian iconoclasts? No, he decided. I believe they really got to work in Greece and Turkey. Here it could only be the Muslim iconoclasts. Mohammed had approved of his iconoclastic brethren but had asked them to spare a painting of Jesus and Mary.

Smelling the dim must of centuries, feeling the closeness of the walls, Sally was tempted to say ironically that she was pleased he had made that clear. They took turns into further passages and Condon marveled. Sally thought, however, that no one knew they were here beneath Imhotep's limestone. The passages, she suspected, had been designed to confuse those who entered. Charlie Condon—in sketcher's raptures—praised his ancient colleagues. We know they thought like us, he told her, because they drew like us. To her they seemed to draw very differently. But he was the expert. At last—to her great solace—he said they should go out again. He assured her he had the map worked out in his head but it might become confused if he took more turns. He half chided himself on the way out for not having brought a guide. But how could you tell which ones were good?

At last they reached the sunlight. We did excellently, he told her and shook his head. But this is an astounding trinity, when you think of it—the oldest remaining stone building. The most potent pharaoh of the Old Kingdom. And the oldest building of which we know the name of the architect.

To the side of the pyramid lay a lower, stepped building and Condon led her in there. It was not as disturbing as the long passages of the pyramid, and lit up a statue of Djoser. Someone had been at his nose with a chisel but the rest was so immediately human—including the tight, unhappy mouth and low forehead and braided hair.

They had absorbed and been absorbed sufficiently to need to seek a pause when they emerged again. Condon spent a little time reconnoitering for the stone floor of an early Coptic monastery, said to be near the pyramid, and complained that the man who'd discovered it had cleared out all sign of it and given or sold it to museums. So they found a fragment of wall which cast shade and sat on stones, Condon producing the food from his kitbag, Sally a tablecloth she had brought with her in her satchel. They sat on a stone surface and ate the fresh, appetizing flatbread.

They tell me, Charlie murmured, chewing, that you and Honora were on a ship that was sunk.

We were fortunate, she said. And it seems a very long time ago.

What is it all like? When everything starts. The other fellows don't even try to tell a person.

They can't tell you. It's like a new world where there aren't any words. As for me, I've only worked around the edges. But even I can't explain . . .

I was ready to come away in November 1914 and got scarlet fever—had a dreadful time talking doctors into letting me get here now, but of course a person thinks all the time, What is it really like? And even—what it's like when men die around you?

I can't remember screams, she said. By the time they got to us on the ships or the island, most of them were quieter than you would think they should be. Morphine might have helped. If they're our patients, we see them go—sometimes it's hemorrhage. But twenty paces away no one in the ward hears anything.

You must think my questions are absurd, he admitted.

No, she hurried to tell him. I would ask them myself if I were where you are. But don't forget pneumonia and typhoid and dysentery. They can bring a fellow low too.

Thank you for being so frank, he said, his head on the side. The men aren't as frank as that.

Well, it's true you seem to be a different person when these things happen. Not your daily self. You'll find that. I wasn't my ordinary self when the ship sank. I was another creature. And that creature finds it hard to explain things.

There *was* something fragile about him which made her remember the war shocked, the men of bad dreams and waking fears. Was it the fundamental delicacy of his face? His passion for the ancient sketching?

Suddenly he was on another tack. Have you ever looked at the black fellows? he asked.

What do you mean by *looked*? she asked.

Well, I mean, taken a chance to have a good gaze at their faces?

I don't think anyone does that, she admitted. I haven't. Gazing? People don't *gaze* at them. Sometimes it's politeness—they'd be embarrassed to be gazed at. And fair enough—some of it's fear too. Our fear. And, I mean, the blacks at home seem a pretty desperate lot, don't they? And that puts us off looking at them.

Well, I used to gaze at them when I was a kid. I got in trouble from grown-ups for it. I played with our abo laundry woman's kid in the yard in Rudder Street. I wasn't at my gazing stage then. Gazing came later. This building . . .

He nodded his head towards the pyramid.

They're older than this, you know. The Aborigines. You see it in the face. If I find the courage, I might go one day and negotiate man to man with one of them and try to sketch his face. They say at the art class it's easier to do if you go to the desert—one of the teachers has done it by train and camel. It's easier to gaze at them there than it is at home. But I'd like to gaze at them at home. Where they're not romantic figures. Where they're living in misery.

The mention of art teachers serious enough to penetrate the interior seemed to suggest to her that these were no fly-by-night art classes he attended. She asked him what school it was.

It's run by an artist, Eva Sodermann. She was worried when the war started she might get interned. But we all petitioned the government. Up to the time I left, it had worked. Anyhow, one of the men who comes there, who teaches with Eva, quite a jaunty sort of fellow—he studied in Paris. Even sold a few paintings to the Royal Academy in London. We used to look at him in awe. You know what he told us? All the paintings he did in Melbourne in the 1890s . . . no one bought them. Now they have. But he still has to earn his bread teaching. So . . . God help the rest of us.

I wish you'd brought your sketchbook with you though, she said.

Oh, he said, I'm no good at it in company. I won't mind showing off when I succeed. But on the way I need to fail and I like to do that bit privately.

But I wouldn't be critical, she assured him.

You should be critical, that's the point. There's no art even at my level unless people are critical. Art doesn't exist until someone says,

That's good. Or else until someone says, That's on the nose. I'm too proud to be on the nose in public. As an artist I'm still tentative, even if I talk as if I know what I'm doing. In fact, I was a law student taking a bit of a break to go to an art school. And I'll probably study law again if no one buys my work. Or at least if no one employs me as an art teacher.

I hope you come to trust me well enough, she said, that you'll feel free to sketch in my presence.

The even, too innocent smile again. That's a wonderful thing to say, he told her. When I rally the confidence, I'll sketch you. Even if I'm not one of those fellows who gets popularity by sketching their friends halfway well. But I'll study you unawares and do the sketch later. No sense in sketching someone who knows she's being sketched. It just encourages the subject to put on airs. I want humans in the moments they're unaware of their grace.

The compliment shot past her eyes and was gone—just as their sudden discomfort wanted it to be. The glare of early afternoon began to hurt the eyes. The sky was vacant of all screening devices, whether sand or cloud. They went and looked at the flat-roofed tombs around the pyramid and made a few investigations of their chambers. Less worried about being lost beneath the vanity of an old emperor, she saw more clearly why the frescoes were marvelous and why they might evoke a kinship between Condon and their makers.

British trucks coming up from Aswan could be expected to roll through Sakkara from three onwards. Charlie and Sally packed their satchels and fetched the ponies and left King Djoser for good.

The West Encountered

Easing back into the velvet and leather of First Class, Leo said, I pity the boys back there in Third with their wooden seats.

On a long train, the nurses occupied perhaps no more than two carriages—a living and breathing buffer between the officers' carriages forward and the harsher ones back there where the masses of infantry and gunners and sappers, stretcher bearers and orderlies rode. Everyone had been rushed away from the old port of Marseille—from the sight of offshore Château d'If with its Count of Monte Cristo associations and from the city's dominating cathedral, as well as from other more profane possibilities which could have created the problems of Australian discipline that Cairo had. Nearly all their ship from Egypt was—within an hour of landing—on a train bound for the more serious north of France. Heading north through unafflicted sections of France they gawked at their railway squares and church spires, at their *mairies* and hotels with the tricolor flying. The train pulled into sidelines to let other trains pass loaded with French soldiers—*poilus*—in their blue-gray uniforms. In the Rhône Valley—the rail running amidst ploughing farmers—nurses from farms exclaimed about the chocolate-colored soil that promised fertility. There were gray fortified medieval towers the farmers took for granted but which to girls from communities shallow in time riveted the eye and the imagination.

On the station at Arles, French girls gave crucifixes from large baskets—one for every passenger who would accept it. The wives of the town offered apples and oranges and wine at the carriage windows.

They sat in a siding for four hours near Avignon and saw beyond a bridge the heights of its papal palace and its skirt of humbler buildings obliquely visible across fields violet with dusk. At Lyons they queued with soldiers at the station's taps with the water jugs from their compartments and a wash basin loaned by the porter. Sally filled one of those decanter-like water bottles and stood up and looked straight into the face of Karla Freud.

I saw you, said Freud in a tight sort of voice. She carried a decanter too. It was exactly as if she was continuing an unhappy conversation begun on Lemnos. How are you?

Karla! cried Sally with a complicated joy. She put her decanter on the ground and hugged her.

Ah, said Freud, you missed me, did you?

Yes, of course we did, Sally claimed but already she felt guilt. It was a revelation: they had tried—in fact—to forget her.

I wouldn't have known you gave me a thought. No letters. No visits in Alexandria.

Freud was located far beyond complaint and blame though. The accusation was sad but absolute.

They didn't give us time, Sally told her. They sent us straight across to Heliopolis.

She knew she was equivocating.

Yes, and I suppose mail didn't occur to you. May I use the tap, if you don't mind? There's a bit of a queue behind.

Sally moved away and picked up her decanter. She waited for Freud to be finished. Honora and Leo appeared and also waited to talk to Freud. That was it, they couldn't help solemnly waiting. And solemnity was the wrong mode.

Freud finished filling her own decanter and walked to where they stood. Honora and then Leo kissed her on the cheek.

We had no idea where you were, Leonora claimed.

You must have really searched, said Freud. She let them stew a while. Then she said levelly, I know how it is. You thought rape was catching. I was as good as dead. Don't worry. I might do the same as you, *mutatis mutandis*. You didn't know what to say and I'd probably have resented anything you did say.

Sally said, You're absolutely right. We were a disgrace.

Naomi writes though, Freud told them. Naomi always has the right word. But anyhow, they put me in a British hospital in Alex. It was good. I could start from square one. So forget what I said.

But still—in the midst of all the milling around the tap—it astonished Sally that she had not thought to chase up Freud; that she had considered her at an end.

What I won't stand for, said Freud, is if you start any gossip about me here. I'll hate you for that all right.

What sort of girls do you think we are? asked Honora.

Well-meaning. So were the generals at Gallipoli.

Oh, I don't bloody well know what to say, Karla, Honora continued. But at least the fellow's dead . . .

That makes everything all right, doesn't it? asked Karla with an extraordinary and withering combination of forgiveness and irony. Look, I've got to take this back to the girls. But I might see you somewhere. Don't worry—I mean it. We're all stupid bitches on our day.

She raised and tapped the decanter. They went back to their carriage too since the engine was making head-of-steam noises.

After the train moved out again they awoke often—it was frequently sidelined and being static was what kept them awake most, with thoughts of their neglect of Freud. As morning came they looked out from the moving carriages across flat fields where old men dug. Bluebells and irises could be seen pocking the edges of copses and promising a vivid destination. Nearing Paris, though—they could even sight the Eiffel Tower—they veered away towards Versailles and looked at the vanishing promise of the great city. They assured each other they'd get there soon.

At some stage—while Sally slept—the men started to leave the train. She woke to see long lines of them shuffling onto double-decker buses—the first such contraptions she had ever seen. Were the men to be carried by bus straight to the front? After they had gone, the nurses and orderlies were asked to descend and climb on old-fashioned buses to be taken to a number of destinations they had been allotted. They were allocated to Rouen, but saw Freud climb on a separate bus, which someone said was bound for the British hospital in Wimereaux.

The fairly plain little villages they passed through—the doors of houses crowding to the edge of the narrow road—lacked the charm of the awakening fields. They were no longer, in any case, in a mood to be fanciful. They were willing to believe that the people who lived here were as plain as the people of Dungog or Deniliquin. Sally received small thrills of difference at the sight of a bakery in a square or of crossroads Virgins and crucified Christs in their little shrines. Even over there eastwards—on the way to the front—Christ and the Virgin obviously presented themselves village by village to the French soldiers as a small promise of protection and another scale to a man's armor. Nurses drowsed and shifted irritably by the misted windows of the bus.

After rolling through a half-rustic suburb of Rouen and glimpsing the dull river—the same Seine which ran through Paris—they entered some ornamental gates with a stone arch proclaiming in metal script *Champs de Cours de Rouen* and—on a sign beyond the gates—*Hippodrome de Rouen*. Their bus ground past a few stables on which soldier carpenters were working. They saw before them then a metropolis of huts and marquees, and were delivered to the open yard beside an assembly of these huts marked with signs and corps and divisional colors and a kangaroo and emu. Orderlies—already standing with clipboards in hand—met the bus and directed nurses to their tents down firm-surfaced roads lined with sandbagged walls to waist height. Birdwood Street, they might say, number seventeen. They would point to a veritable street—with a pole and a name on it, as in a township. All the streets were named after an Australian general, and one of them after the director of medical services. And in the midst of a vast racecourse—with the distantly glimpsed railings of the course and a brick wall marking the perimeter of the medical town—was the Australian general hospital.

As Honora, Sally, and Leo found their way down General Bridges Street, a number of men came out of a tent—their faces bandaged, their arms in slings—to watch them. They were Tommies. Honora waved her hand not occupied by a valise towards them with the ease of a spoken-for woman which Carradine had once shown. So they found their tent. To enter beneath the canvas did not feel at all like entering the canvas of Lemnos. The beds looked better. Each woman had a cupboard to hang her clothes. Pleasant orderlies brought their heavier luggage in and told them where their mess tent was. In the mess tent were apples and porridge—or a decent stew and fresh bread. So now—they decided—they were located in the kindly stream of a good supply system. They received the standard lecture on flirtation's limits. They were to use proper titles when speaking to matrons—not least because it shocked the British Red Cross volunteers if they didn't. They would notice that most of their patients were—for now—Tommies and Kilties and Taffies and Paddies.

After their meal they strolled back, restored, along the hospital roads and said hello to Frenchmen and Britons to calls of, "Wotcha, luv" and "*Quelles jolies Australiennes*" and so on.

Sally was sure they were all still thinking in part of Freud and their stupidity in her case. Yet they devoted themselves to issues such as whether the stove in their hut needed to be lit. Honora declared it was no colder than a mild winter's night at home. Then they slept.

When they awoke late that spring afternoon they gradually became aware that the patient capacity of this city of a hospital at Rouen racecourse was two thousand—and it was a hospital of beds, not just mattresses. As a sign of its seriousness there was a well-set-up dispensary from which in an orderly manner drugs were given out on doctors' prescriptions, as happened in the civil world. This too—as the establishment prepared itself for a war-ending spring slaughter—was a sign of good order. The conclusion the women slept under was that this French affair was a better-ordered war altogether than the hit-and-miss affair of Gallipoli.

When they rose they reported to the reception ward where men were brought on arrival at Rouen. The first ambulances to arrive were full of German wounded. Some came in by the rail spur which ended near the gates of the racetrack. Others arrived by motor ambulance—even by the barges which docked at the quay on the river. Sally was impressed that the more severely wounded Germans were carried in on stretchers which proved to have a blanket not only over the patient but underneath. Femur wounds were splinted and amputees draped over by protective canopies. Many of the supposed enemy wore only tatters of gray uniform and some of them entered the hospital tents on crutches. Others already wore smocks which were marked with the letters "POW." Many of them ridiculously retained their military caps—those with peaks for officers, and those without for men, and the little button of German colors in the center on the front. It was hard to believe in their culpability. Sally nonetheless could not help studying the faces of the enemy for signs of difference. She gave up the effort as the medical demands of moving bodies for washing and dressing took over. Flesh was flesh.

In the morning a matron called them together in the mess and—using a compliant British Tommy and one of his number of shrapnel wounds for illustration—demonstrated how to irrigate wounds with the newly appointed official disinfectant and method called Carrel-Dakin. A Frenchman—peppered by a bursting shell with extensive but non-fatal wounds—was also brought in on a stretcher for them to practice irrigation on. He lay without complaint throughout the demonstration smoking cigarettes provided by orderlies.

Their sleep that afternoon was broken by the cries of Australian carpenters and of German captives in "POW" smocks who worked as their offsiders. Language incomprehension added to the noise both made as they hammered and sawed in the evening light and tried to convert the stables for thoroughbred racehorses into wards.

The matron-in-chief now called the ward doctors and nurses together and addressed them. The spring and the summer and their battles were on the way and there was something those from Lemnos or Alexandria, Cairo or Heliopolis had not seen yet. There was gas. Yes, they would be taken on a tour of the gas wards.

This was a dimension of barbarity that had not existed on Gallipoli and had been undreamed of in the *Archimedes*. The nurses were required to take notes on the variety of gases, and all this felt to Sally like a forewarning that there was an even less contained savagery in France than there had been in Lemnos. An unease kept the palms of her hands wet as the matron enlarged on the array of afflictions contained under the general term.

A chemical gas recipe—said the matron—devised by this or that German gas officer is projected towards our poor fellows in a cloud from a line of cylinders. Or else shells full of a recipe are fired by batteries and land with a thud amongst them. We have our own chemical officers since the Germans forced us to retaliate in kind—they began the practice by firing grenades full of tear gas almost as soon as the war started.

The poison gases fell into four distinct groups, the matron instructed them. They were told to make notes, and Sally ended up with dismal columns she would never remember—"Acute Lung Irritants," "Lachrymators," "Sternutators," "Vesicants."

There were also superficial irritants such as tear gas—although those attacked by them might not consider them superficial but grounds for fleeing trenches. The acute irritants were capable not simply of irritating but of killing by pulmonary edema. Some were solids packed into an exploding shell. Microscopic particles of them could destroy men's lungs. There were also liquids or liquefied gases, such as chloropicrin, phosgene, and chlorine, and these were dispersed as sprays by cylinder on the right wind, or, increasingly, in a shell by a small explosive charge.

The malign inventiveness of it all made Sally think that she had entered a new continent of human bile.

They should approach these cases with confidence. Most of those who suffered lethal effects had already died closer to the front than this. Here the cases were chronic. They still needed oxygen and—in the case of lachrymatory gassing—care of the eyes. And even here, pulmonary edema could strike a man.

She was brisk—this matron. She had the hydra-headed vileness of gas under her management.

But there was something else they would not previously have seen on such a scale. They should follow the matron—out of the mess into the last lilac light. In the fine spring afternoon day nurses and orderlies who had had the patients' beds out in the sun were now moving them indoors. Nurses helped the blue-pyjamaed wounded on a last evening stroll. At the end of General Bridges Street there was a crossroad named in honor of a racehorse—Carbine Street. Here the matron-in-chief led the women into a long tent with a cardboard plaque on the door that read NYD. A few dozen of the German prisoners the British had caught in the shock of their first spring foray lay on beds or walked about arguing amongst themselves in German or sat rigid on chairs under the care of a number of orderlies. Some of those who at first looked tranquil on beds were—on a closer look—convulsed into shuddering balls. Some of those who walked about began pushing themselves against the tent wall and bulged it out in terror when an orderly approached.

The matron gathered her nurses about and spoke softly—a tour guide in a strange church.

On both sides of the line, said the matron, whether in clearing stations or general hospitals, lie men who show no wounds but who are

afflicted in some disabling way. Doctors believed this mental disablement was funk at first. At the other end of the scale there were even
alienists who claimed it had nothing at all to do with a man's mental
history. They argued that such was the absolute shock of the war—the
shock of high explosives or of being buried alive—that the invisible
disablement might befall any soldier, however brave. Unlike inmates
in many mental wards, these men never or rarely show violence.

She walked the nurses down the aisle under a guard of orderlies.
Sally knew that even in Egypt the term "shell shock" had escaped as if
from a burrow and run through the wards and was picked up by some
doctors and debated by others. Its relationship to cowardice—that
was the debate.

What is NYD on the door? asked Leo softly.

There is always doubt, said the matron. So it stands for "Not Yet
Diagnosed."

They were permitted to sleep longer that night and were awakened
later in the morning by an Australian orderly with a Scots accent. He
rang a bell and walked amongst the tents singing genially that his heart
was in the Highlands a-chasing the deer.

They die so quietly, said Leonora of the British and the Germans they
nursed. It's just like Lemnos that way.

If conscious, a man might announce his awareness of death in the
quietest tones—as if telling a friend that he was going to a shop on the
corner to buy tobacco. Some of them were more appallingly young than
in Egypt. Britain was scraping boyhood's barrel. Some were chatty—
telling their horrifying stories of the hours of being carried back out
of the trench system. Or else they had limped rearwards on shattered
limbs or with chest wounds against the tide of reinforcements and
supplies—ammunition boxes, cooking boilers, barbed wire—making
for the front trench. The worst of cases died at the regimental aid
posts or the forward dressing stations. If not there then at a casualty
clearing station.

But the wounds of those who reached Rouen were still full of murderous potential. One night in the ward labeled "C" and reserved for Germans Sally watched the heart rate of a young prisoner who had suffered a mere upper-arm flesh wound climb ferociously as his temperature rose in concert. She and Honora watched him gasp and were pleased to see early morning, when he could be sent to the theatre. Here, his arm was amputated. But the bacteria had beaten the surgeon's knife and entered his system. Or else, some meningeal infection had been provoked in his brain. The boy died not with the quiet Leo had remarked on, but raving. His corporal grasped his hand and gave answers to his hectic, fearful inquiries.

Because Rouen was so large—and authoritative in its bulk and marked streets—it struck Sally as a hospital where men were kept for their entire medical care. But the ward doctors had nurses mark the British and Canadians and Indians with a "1," "2," "3"—according to their readiness to return to the front (1), their likelihood to recover within three months (2), or their unreadiness for battle for at least six months—if ever (3). If marked 3, they would be taken by ambulance to the port of Rouen for shipment to England. The recovered—of course—went in the other direction. Back into the threshing machine.

Coming Back

A Melbourne late summer day. The desert that had killed Burke and Wills was breathing on the city. The air moved as fiercely as anything Naomi had known in Egypt. And in that furnace heat she saw from the deck of yet another sister—the *Alexander*—a thousand young reinforcements sitting on their kits on the blazing wharf where tar melted beneath their boots. They shouted to each other and endured the withering day. Maybe they thought, If we can't put up with a hot Melbourne afternoon, how will we put up with other places?

Across the wharf came a party of nurses in summer straw hats and the same lightweight gray Naomi wore. They were led at a sedate pace by their matron, who moved stiffly on a stick and bore in her other hand an unfurled parasol designed to fight the sun. This party was not delayed on the wharf at all, but—reporting to a sergeant-major at the gangway—immediately permitted to climb the gangway. They were slow. The younger legs of the nurses were inhibited by the awkward gait of their leader. Even though she was so lamed, this woman leaned on her walking stick with a flamboyance which falsely suggested it was an implement of gesture rather than something needed. Naomi saw then it was Matron Mitchie. A nurse behind her carried her satchel. On both feet—including the one that was prosthetic—she wore black shoes. She rose up in the fierce air, with the wind tearing at and buffeting the face veil which hung from her hat. Naomi concluded that

Mitchie had been sent to conduct these girls and to advise them on shipboard life. By that night she would be back to one of the military hospitals around Melbourne to continue practicing how to walk on a false limb.

My God, panted Mitchie. She stepped off the top of the gangplank and down a little into the shade of the deck. She waved her stick for the pure joy of arrival.

My God! she called. It appears to be Naomi Durance!

She handed her parasol to her assistant and embraced Naomi with one strong arm. The other women arriving on deck looked startled. It wasn't in the normal repertoire of matrons to caress.

Did you notice what an athlete I am these days? she asked. Not waiting for an answer, she introduced Naomi to her aide. A Nurse Pettigrew.

Poor girl, aren't you? Mitchie asked Pettigrew. Given an old wreck to look after. And having as well to carry her satchel.

Naomi said, You must be visiting someone aboard. Or seeing these girls settled?

No, I'm visiting you. And I'm visiting France and what it holds. I may visit England, land of my forebears, though they did not frequent distinguished parts of that kingdom. But, in a word, Mitchie and company are open again for business—and not without some little argument. Come, let's find the cabins for these girls before the officers get on board.

In the passageway inside—where the purser sat ready to tell them where their assigned cabins were—Mitchie whispered, It's brave of you to go back. After that hospital at Mudros Harbor in lovely Lemnos. Not to mention the little bath we had in Mare Nostrum.

I felt that I had nowhere else to go, said Naomi.

How peculiar, said Mitchie. My very feeling too. We've been spoiled for the usual regimen.

Naomi was aware of her good fortune in finding a benign aunt aboard a vessel in which she might have been a bewildered spirit.

She had already seen Sergeant Kiernan come aboard and had felt reinforced by that fact, even though they had barely spoken. But he was her seer. He was a quantity of shrewdness and wise counsel—a sort of essential store.

Robbie Shaw was not here. He would have dearly desired to be, but was still waiting—so he said—in all senses of the verb *to wait*. She had frequently let him know that she would not remain in Australia throughout his struggles to have military and medical boards ship him abroad again. Now she was proving it. Robbie wrote that he hung discontentedly around military offices in Brisbane where they had the hide to tell him, he said, that he had already done all that any man could be expected to. But he—having felt that attraction to horrifying circumstance too, to serving the giant mechanism—was not willing to be orphaned by it until the halt was called. What a peculiar thing it all was. This desire to find a home with the gods of sacrifice. She had assured him that she cherished his friendship and wished he could fulfill his ambition. She had once written that in her assessment he was a completer fellow than nearly any other man she had met. But though this was true, she said, she must also insist this did not mean they were suitable for one another.

Baying sergeants and the echoing, metallic thud of boots on corridors—which in more peaceful times had been carpeted and subject to less din—showed that now the ship was taking on its new warriors. She had heard the urgency of sergeants' commands before harrying soldiers along. It was all so anxiously reminiscent of the Inniskilling men entering the *Archimedes*. In the meantime Naomi welcomed three new women to the cabin she had occupied on her own along the coast to Melbourne. She felt little of whatever original itch she'd possessed to know shipmates. She knew they would think she was aloof. That was the price of being a Durance.

Through the opened ports she saw thunder clouds surging in, to the relief of the city. Everyone climbed on deck again and watched the cooling electricity of the rain torrents over Melbourne and the thunderheads dropping hail on the wharf like a good-bye gift.

At Fremantle the *Alexander* became part of a convoy. In the Indian Ocean—in that vastness which made a pond of the Mediterranean—it was rumored that German raiders were loose. All deck lights were doused and cabin lights hidden by curtains. No French destroyer with a supply of blankets could save them in this immensity.

With the troops on deck agog, the *Alexander* and the other transports entered Table Bay, Cape Town's harbor. Here it became known by rumor that they were bound direct for England or France. Naomi went to town twice on the squalid little train from the dock. The first was with Kiernan to travel to False Bay and drink tea and eat cake while watching the dazzling southern Atlantic.

The two of them exchanged tales of their homecoming. But Kiernan had not run into a wall of bogus congratulation. His father had been prayerful and rather depressed. He was developing that unjustified repute for disloyalty which afflicted all Quakers in wars. He was fighting off by every legal means a—to quote Kiernan—"compulsory offer" from the federal government to buy his engineering works for war production. He had been promised by public servants that his steel containers would be used purely for water storage. He was certain that they would also be used to store fluids of greater military intent.

I am afraid I complicated things, Kiernan confessed to Naomi, by pointing out that motor fuel was needed not only to run military trucks but also ambulances. In any case, it's becoming clear he could end up being considered a pariah. Yet he's a fine citizen when it comes to civil society. I won't boast of his exercises of charity, because it is the duty of all Friends to perform such things.

It struck her that this discourse was more substantial provender than Robbie Shaw offered.

Her only other journey ashore was to accompany Matron Mitchie to the emporiums of the city. Making her part-sideways, part-direct approach to the glass counters, she showed a taste for jewelry and face powder and bought some talcum. That evening, as on others, she asked Naomi into her cabin and—sitting in a shift—exposed her raw stump and the long, tough scar for Naomi to apply ointment to.

The hard tropic times and sleeping on deck began. By day the ships of the convoy pushed through a gelid ocean which made dense opposition to their bows and gave their sterns no encouraging push. From nearby cruisers they heard machine gun practice—a submarine drill which caused a surge of momentary panic in Naomi's chest. Moored off Freetown in saturated air they were not let ashore because of the fevers the place was so willing to pass. They watched from the railings the Africans on the coal bunkers below—singing as they loaded coal aboard in baskets. Everyone formed up on deck for the sea burial of a tubercular stoker.

Out to sea again, and further ceremony occurred when the convoy stopped briefly as three soldiers on neighboring transports received similar rites. Then—in one day off the Azores—the air grew cooler, and in a further few days cold. The ocean turned turquoise somewhere off Spain or Portugal—from both of whose shores the convoy took wide berth for fear of observation by enemy spies. It turned gray under the influence of a lingering winter off Biscay. Soon sleek, lithe, and darting destroyers met them and herded them into the Channel.

A spring fog both protected them from the submarines and prevented those young soldiers who were not immigrants to Australia but were born colonial from sighting the isle of their progenitors. When the ship found Southampton and fabled England, all seemed low sky, grim, gray derricks, long warehouses. Trucks took them to the railway station, past dour, unwelcoming terraces and boarding houses little better than tenements and comfortless pubs on corners. And so to a crowded and besooted railway station. Some of the young soldiers must have secretly asked themselves if this was what they had volunteered to die for.

The railway station—it had to be said—was also a coal dust–ridden wonder, august in its columns and great vault. The troops were bound for the training grounds of Salisbury Plain and the nurses for London. In Horseferry Road, Westminster, where the Australian military administration had its headquarters, they would have their future disclosed to them.

Cosmopolitans

From Rouen they could go for a day to the Paris they had been cheated of on the way north. Sally had written to Freud's hospital near Wimereaux and named the spring date on which the three of them would be under the main clock at the Gare d'Orsay—a clock which none of them had ever seen but which surely had to exist in all railway stations—at ten o'clock. If Freud could get a lift along the coast to Boulogne, she would find the train journey from there less long-winded than their journey from Rouen.

For their Paris leave they were issued with rail warrants and taken by ambulance to the great white railway station of Rouen-Rive-Droite, where the light through the artfully designed windows was uncertain as to whether to be dreary or display some pastel subtlety for their day out. By the time the train left, the day had decided to honor their journey with color and they were in a mood to let the countryside enchant them. They passed copses of elm trees and poplars which seemed to Sally to have been culled down from ancient forests into ornamental size. The dying ring-barked verticals of tall gums which marred Australian distances were utterly missing from the scene. In the villages women and children were drawing their water from the pumps at the end of streets while— puffing on a cigarette—a boy in sabots and aged about ten watched the train sweep by. An occasional grand house would stand in its own company of trees beyond ploughed fields. But no châteaux were jammed up against the railway line—coal grit was for ordinary people.

Then they approached the squalor and glimpses of grandeur in the city and rolled into the Gare d'Orsay—the grandest locomotive palace one could imagine, the most infused with style, a structure of French jollity to stand in counterpoint to all the solemn domes and columns of British-built railway stations from Tasmania to Egypt. They found on the concourse the great clock they had expected. Beneath it—tall and pale and a little undernourished-looking— stood Freud. Her appearance there—upright and singular and even with that vacancy on her face which belongs to those waiting for a train to arrive—seemed to round out the day with absolution. They rushed to her and she returned their kisses soberly but without any hesitation.

Where are we going? she asked—as if they were in charge.

They could cross the bridge to the Louvre and decided to do that first. The museum was full of soldiers of uncountable nationalities. A good argument for the ultimate rout of the enemy seemed established in this variety of uniforms of alternating dourness and flamboyance. The fancier the clobber—went Honora's opinion—the less fighting the bloke had done. They had time only for a few galleries—they told themselves they would be back and would devote a day entirely to the museum. Sally was unexpectedly startled by the figures in landscape (landscape for some reason being the lesser element for her) or figures alone. But she was inhibited—since meeting Condon—from ill-educated Oohs and Aahs, from saying something basic when something better should be said. She nonetheless found herself rehearsing—in case she met Charlie Condon soon—the names of artists. She liked David—he was easy to like—and Ingres's woman with the high-waisted gown. Somehow she understood that she would not have brought the same eye to them if it weren't for Condon and the brief but intense education on sketching and allied matters he'd given her at Sakkara.

When they emerged from the Louvre they found the day still bright with high, streaky clouds and—though it was chilly—they walked in the Tuileries Garden where trees were still bare. Their branches offered buds though, like promissory notes on a coming exuberance. Then—following the map Sally had bought—they hiked along the embankment of the river towards the island where the great cathedral was to be found. This too they had all seen represented in childhood compendia of the world—and then there was Quasimodo lurching and dominating their imaginations. Like the pyramids, the cathedral could be approached by ordinary steps taken by one's daily legs—the same legs with which one emerged from Kempsey's Barsby's Emporium and crossed Belgrave Street to Mottee's Tearooms. The cathedral bloomed with side chapels and before each one were ranks of burning candles. Honora lit one after another for what she called "my special intentions" and sank to her knees before the Virgin, moving her lips in beseeching God's favor for Lionel Dankworth, whose last letter was from Egypt but who might even now be in France. Another little flame for her family and one for the Allied cause. And a fourth. For Freud, she confided to Sally in a whisper. For the wrong we did her. She went on fitting small franc notes into the cash boxes attached to the racks of candles.

When Honora's votive candle foray ended, they climbed Quasimodo's tower where—looking down the reaches of the Seine—she covered her Paris amazement with a more earthy issue. She could see the hatted heads of men in the open-topped *pissoirs*, capable without embarrassment of lifting their hats to passing ladies.

The Eiffel Tower waited in its gardens for them and was reached by the Métro with its crowds of soldiers and older men in suits—all with lush Gallic moustaches—and worn-looking housekeepers, seamstresses, wives. Their weariness was unlikely to be dispelled even by a military triumph. Then, as they mounted the Métro steps—*there*, the tower beetling and dizzying but tethered by its four giant feet to four distinct plots of earth.

Back at the railway, they kissed Freud good-bye in the belief they had at least in part expiated their earlier crassness. She responded with a wary affection—not sure yet whether she wished to go back to full sisterhood. She found her train. Then they took theirs to Rouen, on a long-lasting spring evening.

As they ate chocolates and pastries, Leonora suddenly asked the others whether they thought there were malingerers amongst the NYD. On the table before them lay the litter of what Leonora called in her private-school way a beano—boxes which had held exuberant gâteaux and little fluted cups for the most improbable chocolates and the most fanciful confections. As Leonora raised the matter of NYD, Honora made a sucking, dubious sound through her back teeth as if uncertain that she wanted to discuss it.

Warwick thinks there are, Leo said. Not all. But a sizeable number. Malingerers.

Warwick was of course Captain Fellowes. Leo would be the sort of wife who would gladly take on her husband's opinions and not feel imposed upon by them. She was an excellent nurse, energetic and willing, skilled and kindly. But she thought that Captain Fellowes's ideas were worth a lifetime of assent.

Sally ran through the catalogue of cases she'd met. The young Scotsman who talked a great deal when not heavily sedated and who, as his dosage wore off, was likely to rush around the tent asking everyone where his mask was and—comic if it weren't tragic—looking for it under beds and chairs. He had been gassed himself—though the doctor said not badly. It seemed, though, that he had seen his fellows choking to death and thereafter even the smallest residual waft of chlorine or phosgene left behind in the trenches after a gas attack was enough to unhinge him.

So was this pretense? But to pretend for weeks on end to be out of your head with shock was itself a sort of madness anyhow.

Honora gave a small chocolate burp and echoed Sally's thought.

If any of them are fooling us, then we shouldn't be ashamed because it means this—they have fooled their way through three levels of doctors and officers, from the front line to the dressing station to the casualty clearing station and on to Rouen. That's what you would call a worthy performance.

I was on duty in there one day, Leo persisted, however, when I turned suddenly and saw this sly, half-smiling look on one of them. Just in the second before he went back to aphonia and shuddering away. It made me wonder.

It might just have been a variation in the condition, Sally suggested. Or it could have been a rictus.

You're very charitable, said Leo with some of her beloved's skepticism.

But, said Honora, even if they are pretending, something horrible made them give up their sense of honor and become pretenders.

Leo ploughed on in a way Sally now found overblown. Perhaps it was the binge of sugar and chocolate and cream that had made her uncommonly persistent.

That's easy to say. But they've abandoned their comrades, in that case. Warwick doesn't think they're deliberately shirking though. He believes it begins with the medical officers at the aid post. If the first doctor they meet is too sympathetic, it has a knock-on effect—they act it up for the next MO they meet at the dressing station and then for the next one at the casualty clearing station. So that by the time they've got back here, they're convinced they're a complete mess and act accordingly. Warwick says he would like to be a doctor at the regimental aid post, and tell most of them they were fine and give them some medicinal brandy and a good sleep and send them back.

But he's too badly needed at base, isn't he? asked Sally.

Yes, said Leonora. In a sense he would be wasted up there.

They assessed that. It was true—even if uttered with a touch more certainty than required. She continued, He's a man of kindness. He doesn't easily suspect people. But he's entitled to his skepticism.

As we are, said Honora with sudden sternness, to our conviction. I think it's clear there's such a thing as this shell shock. Most young men can't act for two bob. You can see right through them. The cases I've seen aren't acting.

Let's not argue over it, Sally urged them. It's been too good a day to end in a brawl. Besides, another few months of nursing, I think, and we'll *all* know for sure.

I wonder, will there be less of it when our Australian boys go into the line, said Honora in a whisper.

Warwick believes so, said dutiful Leo.

This was in many regards a spring of jaunty hopes. Wounded Englishmen strolling General Bridges Street knew what the boomerang-shaped badges on the nurses' go-to-town uniforms meant, and the Gallipoli "A" for Anzac at their shoulders as well. And English officers stopped them to say, We saw your chaps coming through Armentières to relieve our Twelfth Division. My heavens, they looked so robust and confident!

The influence was more in people's minds, though, than in military dispositions. Not even the greatest Australian patriots could argue that they had the tens of millions as America did to make an army so massive that it could by mere numbers tame the year and bring it to peace. Of course, the newer women in the mess believed that each Australian was worth a number of the others. But as Kiernan had said on the *Archimedes,* flesh was flesh.

What could not be argued with was the fact that to other armies the Australians *were* like the birds of the spring. They were a sign of things turning—of the greater and greater accumulation of armies whose soldiers would resolve it all before the trenches froze again. The Australians were the harbingers.

In that atmosphere of newness and hope, Captain Fellowes and Staff Nurse Leonora Casement sent out a cyclostyled invitation to all doctors and nurses of Number 3 Australian General Hospital Rouen to attend a party in the officers' mess to celebrate their engagement. It was considered they would not need to wait much beyond autumn to have their wedding. Speeches of praise for the couple were made by the colonel and matron. Leo's face shone with such authority that for an hour it was easy to believe the Western Front would accommodate itself to her nuptial timetable.

Now the first of the Australians began to arrive. One was a young officer who had been training in a quiet area they called "the nursery." But a shell had found him there and his entire head was—for the moment—bandaged. The wound beneath that was a test Sally and Honora were set. This scale of harm and outrage numbed and drove from her mind for days on end the memory of her mother and of all connivance with Naomi.

In the surgical ward—since it was considered his wound would need occasional trimming under anesthetic—the young man took in soup and tea through a tube inserted into his bandages. Other nutrients in sterile solution were infused through a vein in his arm. The ward doctor seemed pessimistic and had declared a face wound a prime site for sepsis. When they first exposed the raw meat of the man's face by removing the packing placed there at the casualty clearing station from which he'd come to Rouen, Sally and Honora found that one eighth of a grain of morphine did not save him agony. Stutters of complaint escaped from the bloodied hole in his face. His one eye seemed to shed tears. So the dose was raised to one quarter—which left him drowsy by the hour and was a good arrangement in Sally's estimation. When so relieved, he could dazedly attempt to speak, making words from the throat and not with his palate. The voice box was intact but many words were unformed for lack of lips. The name on his label when he'd first come in was Captain Alex Constable.

This young man—whose face was steak from his upper right eye socket to the corner of his lower mouth—uttered one day after his wound had been dressed the sound "A'her ease nur." He repeated it, quite politely but insistently. They eventually realized he wanted a pad of paper and it was all at once so obvious that he should have been given one—and a pencil—earlier. It was as if his lack of a face had somehow prejudiced everyone into thinking he couldn't write. Honora fetched a pencil and a notebook with AUSTRALIAN COMFORTS FUND on its cover. He held up a hand—long-fingered—and had it do a form of salaam in thanks. There was humor in his remaining eye, now left uncovered by the dressings. And so he set to writing a letter. The energy and fluency with which he wrote were astounding to Sally. When he was finished he tore out the pages he had written on and coughed—that was one form of expression thoroughly remaining to him. He folded the letter in four to fit the flimsy envelope they gave him, and handed it over for postage. He then wrote on a full, unfolded page, "Nurses, could you kindly send this missive to"—and there was an address—"Mrs. G. D. Constable, 'Congongula,' via Narromine, New South Wales." They said, Of course, and he nodded and began writing again. "Sorry to hold you young women up," said the page he ultimately handed to them.

> But I heard people saying I am the first Australian wounded in France. It is an annoying thing to hear. If you can find the means to do so, could you contradict this silliness at every turn? It is the one thing I cannot stand. To begin with, there were Australians in London in 1914 who enlisted in the British army. Their cases were written up in the Sydney Morning Herald. Some of them must have been wounded before now. Could you please tell people as kindly as you choose to cut out the rubbish?
>
> Yours,
> Alex Constable

Honora assured him she'd get the word out. She was not any surer than Sally as to why this concerned him. But his wound entitled him to consideration. He had no face. He might not live. At best, years of painful remedy awaited him. And the thing he claimed annoyed him was the rumor that he was the first Australian to be wounded on the Western Front.

A letter awaited Sally one evening when she got to the mess. It was from England.

16 May 1916

Dear Sally,
I am safely in England would you believe? Matron Mitchie—yes, Matron Mitchie—is here to demonstrate her toughness. Or is it stubbornness? Kiernan is here too—training at Wandsworth—and was our squire around the sights of this great city. It is interesting to us that though a Quaker and friend of man he enjoyed the Bloody Tower.

You'll be amused that when we turned up in London—at Paddington—the only rooms we got were at the Salvation Army Home for Fallen Women. Even Matron Mitchie! They'd covered the sign with Union Jacks. Thank God for the War Chest Club in Horseferry Road where we can meet up and have a bit of a meal. We have not been given our posting yet but hope to see you soon in France . . . Have you heard from Papa?

There was soon a letter from Charlie Condon as well. He too had arrived in France and had been at first delayed in Marseille with suspected typhus. But the symptoms had misled the British doctors and he had recovered in a few days. This gave him the chance, he told her, to visit the Musée des Beaux-Arts of Marseille—it was in a palace, and the seventeenth-century sketches there put the last remnants of his fever to total flight. "When you looked at them," he wrote, "you felt light as a breeze and you thought, I can produce a line like that."

He was, he said, about to find his way north.

And if not immediately required to spread myself on the altar of Mars, I shall seek out your location in Rouen and come to visit you. I enjoyed greatly our trip to Sakkara. Perhaps that was because you permitted me to talk so much. But I remember your interjections as demonstrating a wisdom which does great honor to the valley I was running away from.

The Chariot Descends

Matron Mitchie—refusing help—had taken the train to a hospital at Sidcup in Kent to have the bucket of her false leg redesigned to the final healing of her stump. She now returned and professed the adjustment to her prosthetic leg so satisfactory that very soon—so she claimed—she would be able to walk without that pronounced stiffness which gave away most amputees. Naomi did not understand how this would be achieved but did not argue.

Nor did she when Mitchie told her to pack up for a move. Mitchie had already packed under her own steam. She had not long tolerated the personal nurse Pettigrew. Not that Pettigrew was lacking in skill. But Mitchie was a woman who wanted to attend to things herself.

Are we all packing? asked Naomi.

No. You and me. We are off to improved digs. A bit of an undemocratic arrangement vis-à-vis the other girls. But they'll survive.

Descending the grim institutional stairs of the Home for Fallen Women an hour later, they found waiting for them an enormous white limousine trimmed with black—a Vitesse Phaeton no less surprising than if Elijah's chariot had descended on this bleak street. Naomi's dun uniform and gray hat were a welcome option when faced with such a vehicle. She would otherwise have had to find something up to the style of the thing—for which she had neither the resources nor the gift.

A middle-aged chauffeur in a uniform of cap and jacket and leggings stopped and opened the back door to admit them. He introduced himself as Carling. Once amidst the splendor of upholstery, they were driven through the center of London and across Hyde Park and its exercising cavalry and baby-walking nannies to the Dorchester Hotel, where they were allotted rooms they had no time yet to see. Instead, they left their baggage and returned straight to the enormous car. Then the great vehicle found its way into Mayfair, whose astonishing townhouses seemed as gratuitous and wonderful to Naomi as buildings on a different planet designed to house a different race.

Well, said Mitchie to her, now we're ready for socializing in London.

As the Phaeton slowed, Mitchie told her, The people we're meeting here are the clever Lady Tarlton and her total donkey of a husband, Viscount Tarlton. He was governor-general of Australia for a time until the prime minister got fed up with him. That's all fine with you, I assume? I've kept it as a surprise.

The house they arrived before was tall and painted a jovial cream color. The driver helped them out and they rose up the steps to be met by—what else?—a doorman in livery. He made a hand gesture that they should enter the great circular lobby which rose to a brilliant dome trimmed with gold-leaf moldings. Naomi thought it must be a stage set. It was surely not for occupation by people.

A servant who looked more like some masquerading duke in morning suit took their entrée cards and pointed them towards the large room beyond the lobby. At the double doors into the room stood another servant in morning suit next to a most beautiful, upright, muslin-draped, and well-bosomed woman wearing her brown hair informally ribboned at the back and—unlike any of the other women who were arriving, including Mitchie and Naomi—with no gloves on her hands. A slim, slightly shorter man with a ginger moustache stood on the other side of this woman. He was dressed in a suit which so exactly fitted him that it was like an outer skin. His face was handsome in a boyish way but his eyes were vacant. The morning-suited servant—having got their names in whispers from Mitchie and Naomi—muttered to the gentleman and the smiling, splendid woman that these newcomers were Miss Marion Mitchie and Miss Naomi Durance.

Oh, cried the woman with the not-quite-perfectly-done hair. I don't need an introduction to Marion. I know Marion. You remember her, Bobby? From Melbourne?

Oh yes, said Lord Tarlton, who didn't remember Mitchie at all.

His wife kissed Matron Mitchie on the cheek with a sisterly intensity.

My champion in the wilderness! said Lady Tarlton. Do go in, Marion, with your friend. Have whatever you like, and I'll come along in a moment to have a good confab.

Lord Tarlton put a hand into Naomi's gloved one and muttered, Delighted! in a voice of great indifference. Lady Tarlton shook it with more earnest energy. I do so admire you for being here in embattled Britain, she said.

In a room full of men and women who were chiefly middle-aged and looked important—some of the men proving it by wearing the red tabs indicating they were generals—a waiter with a tray came to ask them what they would care to drink. Matron Mitchie nominated dry sherry and so did Naomi—though purely for lack of something else credible. No one came to talk to them so they went to a deep-set window and Mitchie gratefully took a seat in a gilt-backed chair placed there. The honking in the room was like that of poultry who knew a thing or two. Naturally enough Naomi asked Mitchie how it was that a woman from her world had met someone so preposterous as to bear a name like Lady—or, as she was announced, Viscountess—Tarlton.

Well, Mitchie explained, Lady Tarlton asked me to help her set up a nursing service in the bush—for women, you understand. She'd traveled in the bush with her husband when he was governor-general and living proof any fool can do the job, and while he looked at horses and girls, she looked at the way real women lived and gave birth on the farms further out. She also tried to go up into the tropics to see what was happening there. But the prime minister told her it would cost too much for a naval ship to take her. Really, he was just trying to hurt her husband. Mind you, she's disapproved of. People call her "spirited." And you know what they imply by that? Immorality, that's what.

Mitchie snorted at that trick of words.

And did you set up this scheme of nurses in the bush?

She set it up. She gave her own money for it. Oh yes, she might seem a long way removed from your ordinary shearer's or selector's wife. But you'll see she has this sympathy. It's in her nature.

Naomi dropped her voice. And is it in Lord Tarlton's nature?

She wanted to hear a mischievous answer and got one.

Very little you could put a reasonable name to is in his nature.

Within herself, Naomi was dizzied at this conversation. I am talking, she realized—or at least being spoken to—like a worldly woman in a play. She was warily delighted with it but would have been happy to be free from the stiffness and furtiveness this house imposed on her and go back to Paddington.

Mitchie said, They don't really live together as husband and wife, and it's just as well, since Tarlton doesn't deserve her. Look at her! See the loose hair? The ribbons? Posh people don't like that at all. Some of the Melbourne snobs didn't like it either. They said she was "untamed." As for him, I've got to admit he was in Gallipoli for a while. But he's the sort of man who always comes through, or—more likely— gets out in time. Probably by being sacked.

Mitchie shook her head to clear it of Lord Tarlton. She sipped her sherry a while. Now, the point is, she said then, Lady Tarlton has visited every rich Australian in London. And likewise the English who have Australian connections and are making a slap-up fortune from Australian copper and iron and so on. With the blessing of that chap over there—recognize him, the slightly portly fellow? Fisher, our former prime minister. The very chap Tarlton annoyed. He's here out of respect for Lady Tarlton. No other reason.

Naomi glanced. So I am also looking at prime ministers as if they were mere bank managers. Mr. Fisher was certainly portly, though his face bespoke good intentions.

She wants to create an Australian voluntary hospital in France, Mitchie continued. The military people hate her for the idea—maybe they're frightened she'll do a better job than them. But she is very powerful and they have to take her seriously, and even give her nurses from the army nursing services.

You don't mean us? asked Naomi.

If you like. She wants me to be matron of her hospital, and I can offer a post to you, Naomi—a means to get away from all the army stuffiness.

I promised I'd join my sister.

I know Sally. She'd understand. Look, I'm not pretending it won't be hard. You'll be helping to run the place, as well as nursing. And there'll be a lot of paperwork for us to do. We'll be working with Red Cross volunteers who might come and go for all I know. Do you think you might like to work with me on such a scheme?

A rosy feeling of both deliverance and promise swept through Naomi. And Sally would be within reach. France was not immense.

In fewer than two weeks, said Mitchie, you and I would be off to Boulogne with Lady Tarlton to find a site that might serve for the hospital. When I say *the* hospital, I should tell you that she would not have her name formally attached to the nurses in the bush, and she intends in the same spirit to call her hospital not Lady Tarlton's but simply the Australian Voluntary Hospital.

Barely knowing it was happening, Naomi began to weep softly.

Oh, my dear, said Matron Mitchie. Is that grief?

It's that you trust me.

Oh yes? asked Mitchie. I give you an impossible job and you shed tears of gratitude. See what you think in six months!

The portly, tall man with the long, benevolent face and the soft eyes—that is, the man who was once prime minister of the Commonwealth—had begun to look over and now excused himself from men and women around him and advanced on them. Naomi could barely grasp what he was saying. Mitchie displayed her easy worldliness by calling him "High Commissioner," because he'd given up his life in Australian politics to take up that role in London—not bad work for an old coal-miner, as Mitchie would later remark. He talked of their dedication and how Australia honored them. He uttered the normal hope about the war ending with any luck by the autumn of this year of Our Lord 1916. He even quoted generals—British and French—who had assured him of it. Across the room, people were beginning to leave the reception, and when nearly all had done so, the high commissioner shook their hands and went too. Lady Tarlton—smiling and tall with her hair having further escaped her ribbon—approached them from across the room.

Charlie Condon turned up overcoated one chilly morning at the Rouen racecourse to see Sally. When he took his slouch hat off, she could see how carefully he had combed his brown hair during the journey. His eyes still had the same enthusiasm as they had shown in Sakkara, his nose was flared as if he were anxious to breathe in the encounters he was about to experience, and the V of his well-shaven jaw ended in a bulb of chin which shone with what she thought of as boyish inquiry.

He had set out early from a rest area near Amiens and found a truck that was coming to Rouen, and had been on the road for five hours—even though he had needed to travel barely sixty miles. He would need to leave by three o'clock—when a truck would come to get him again.

His arrival at the door of the nurses' mess was the sort of thing that got fatuous talk going, but by good fortune she did not need to swap shifts and go to the matron for permission to rearrange the roster. She had, in fact, just finished the night shift in the surgical ward which contained Captain Constable. Charlie Condon's eyes glittered in the doorway of the hut which had now been put in place by Australian carpenters and German prisoners to accommodate the nurses at meal-times and during recreation.

After she'd got him some tea, they were able to go into Rouen—there were always trucks and cars and ambulances going there. They squeezed into the front seat of an ambulance and walked from the dock—where it was going—to the cathedral square. About the cathedral, Charlie Condon had—as Sally knew beforehand he would—absorbed a great deal. Would his continual enthusiasm ever become tedious? It was not yet. Knowledge was for joy with Charlie and not for showing off. There were newly famous paintings by an artist named Monet, he said. Done some years back, but the world was just starting to catch up with them. About twenty paintings of the great cathedral, he said, the façade and towers in all hours and every degree of light.

She liked the majesty of that phrase: "every degree of light."

What gives me hope, said Charlie, is that's what we have back home. Light, light, and more light. Light to burn. Light to waste. But you've heard me go on about all that.

He had no idea of the scale to which everything was news to her. He told her of the stained glass seven hundred years old which had a unique turquoise that modern glassmakers couldn't reproduce. She sensed that the fact there were such things made the world liveable for him.

He listed Rouen's relics which had brought in pilgrims from all over Europe. And they weren't all pious pilgrims. It was because they were sinners that they went on pilgrimage and hoped that the sight of the body parts of saints would save them from their crimes. Of course now, he said, it seemed there was no end to body parts of saints and sinners strewn across France and Flanders.

After a few hours a cathedral wanes in interest—something infinite gluts the finite taste. He took her to lunch. It was an auberge called La Couronne which claimed to be the oldest in France—a gabled house, with balconies and leadlight windows and a certain droop to it from the long-running work of gravity. The landlord seemed to expect them. Charlie confessed he had sent a telegram to make a reservation. All without knowing whether he might be eating on his own. The scale of that act of daring impressed her.

Later, she found that the sauce for the duck they ate was made from blood. Because she was a farmer's daughter, the concept did not repel her. They drank Bordeaux wine—though her hayseed palate took no special delight in it except in its worldliness. But the subsequent feeling of lightness combined with the idea of the telegram and with turquoise glass and the ageless recipes contained in this old house all made an entrancing hour.

What are they like? he asked then. They were eating an apple tart with fresh cream. It was improbably laced with a brandy named Calvados. The fellows you nurse?

He still had that unrequited curiosity about it all.

There's the new element, Charlie, she told him. There's gas. We're shipping a lot of men with gas damage back to Blighty. Which means they're almost certainly finished as soldiers—and maybe as men. So you must always keep your mask handy. The foul stuff seems to be everywhere up there.

They sent us through a training field full of gas with our masks on. It isn't the most comfortable experience.

Captain Constable occupied the center and forefront of her imagination. She wouldn't mention him to Charlie, for there was a fear of infecting him with this reported ill fortune.

Are the Germans shelling you where you are?

No, said Charlie, the shelling's pretty mild. Sometimes one comes over. It almost seems an accident. There's a story that can't be true— but it goes that the Germans have made a deal with us that if we don't shell Steenbecque, they won't shell Hazebrouck. Anyhow, that's how it's working at the moment. But when we're considered fit for blooding, off we'll go to somewhere less cozy.

She sipped wine as a sort of necessary tribute to the day.

Charlie talked about a farm family he and other officers had been billeted with for a while in a small house near Steenbecque. The family had been sullen at first. It had been roughly treated early in the war by German officers and then fairly contemptuously by some British ones from a highfalutin regiment. But Charlie helped with chopping wood and even with milking the family cow—doesn't hurt to do one cow, he said—and the French family warmed and were astonished. The farmer's wife asked him how he could actually be an officer and chop wood?

They walked the streets afterwards and Charlie was willing to look in the windows of boutiques—what in Australia they delighted in calling "frock salons." Charlie was not uninterested in fabric and in the lines of garments. After all, he explained, it was just an extension of his interests. In Rouen it drew no remark at all to go looking at fabrics on the arm—for she had taken his arm—of a man. It seemed to be considered that a woman was fortunate still to have an ambulatory soldier to promenade with on a quiet afternoon.

At two or so Charlie said that he meant to see where Joan of Arc had been burned. She had seen it before—in town with Honora and Leo.

But you must have been there before? he asked. No, she said.

They progressed down the cramped medieval streets to a little square—a church stood there and a monument with fleur-de-lis engraved—topped by a cross to mark the place Joan had died.

Imagine how scared she was, said Charlie.

None of them had thought of that on her earlier visit. They'd marveled at her gameness—a French foreshadowing of Ned Kelly. She was a creature from a valiant tale rather than a girl *really* tethered and planted in the midst of a burning terror. But Sally could all at once now feel panic in the air.

He was scanning the eaves of the old houses of the square—as if there was some prayer and cry of fear wedged up there. His jawline was straight and his neck scraped and red in places from an earnest razor.

Simply her and the fire, he murmured. And her conscience and her terror.

He turned his face to Sally and laughed then—the memory of their pleasant day retethered him to air that was tranquil and did not blaze. He consulted his watch. My God, his truck was due at the racecourse in half an hour. They looked around for a motor taxi but saw only the occasional private auto and farmer's dray. They raced back to the cathedral, where a British ambulance driver—in town on some unstated duty—got them back to the hippodrome. There the two of them stood in the gravel road before the administration buildings. They were both uneasy—they were further embarked on friendship than they quite knew what to do with. His truck rolled up and saved them from their bewilderment. She wondered if he would try a kiss before he boarded it and could see he considered it but found that perhaps the day had been too randomly built by him—too plump with jumbled incident—to justify it.

He'd sent a telegram to the auberge! The idea seemed flamboyant beyond the limits of anything she'd known. People sent telegrams for deaths and weddings and urgent unexpected arrivals. He'd sent a telegram for a table.

From the time of their visit to the Tarlton townhouse, Matron Mitchie and Naomi had rooms provided for them at the Dorchester. Although Naomi's was appropriately more modest than that of Matron Mitchie, it still astonished her with its sumptuousness and—by contrast with Lemnos—its vast bed. She had not slept in a room and on her own for close on two years. Yet the luxurious solitude made her edgy. As payment for this high living, Mitchie set her to work immediately, devising a roster for a hospital of two hundred wounded—to begin with anyhow, said Mitchie. So Naomi planned a schedule for phantom nurses not yet recruited from the army nursing service or from the Red Cross volunteers or from civilian hospitals. Forty trained nurses were needed just for the two shifts of twelve hours and the one day's rest a week initially planned. Nearly as many women would be needed by night as by day since inquiry showed convoys often arrived then.

Occasionally the grand Vitesse Phaeton collected Michie and Naomi and took them to the dazzling house in Mayfair, where Naomi attended to the filing of requisition forms and receipts for all that could be needed for a genuine hospital. The requisition forms represented what Lady Tarlton was asking the army to provide. But the receipts represented what she had bought with her own money or that of the unspecified rich Anglo-Australians whom she held in the palm of her hand. Naomi filed as well letters on hospital rations—right down to the level of salt and mustard and thrice-weekly oatmeal—which Lady Tarlton had exchanged with members of her London Committee. Amongst Lady Tarlton's personal purchases were autoclaves, arm and leg splints, bedsteads, and two first-class theatre tables. She had elicited from a medical supply company an X-ray machine. The requisitions addressed to the army were for disinfectants, antiseptics, dressings, sutures, surgical instruments, and all that the army should—in good conscience—provide its wounded. One letter assured her that once the voluntary hospital was established in the Boulogne region—where advice from the office of the director of medical services had suggested it should be located—a body named the Advanced Depot of Medical Stores would be ordered to supply said hospital. Supplies and equipment appropriate to a pathology laboratory would obviate the necessity of sending samples to the already busy pathology sections of the army general hospitals.

The range of the letters and forms—the number of folders to which Naomi had to take recourse—was itself a measure of the seriousness of Lady Tarlton. If Naomi had believed that Lady Tarlton was going into the hospital business on a genial whim and as an amateur, her filing of the woman's letters—sent and received—dispelled it.

On a clear spring morning—when it seemed the entire width of the Channel could be seen with all its shipping and scampering destroyers—Mitchie and Naomi occupied a state cabin along with Lady Tarlton in a troopship on its way to France. They drank tea and were permitted by a lieutenant general—who touched his cap to the viscountess and with his staff made way for her and her two comrades—to descend the gangplank first.

As Southampton had offered so little of ideal Britain, the basin in which they landed at Boulogne offered nothing of France. Though a distant castle could be seen on a rise, it was a mere token. They were separated from it by a vast, squalid railyard, where troops who had arrived fully equipped on earlier ferries waited and smoked by companies and battalions amidst shuttling trains. Here, loneliness in crowds and expectation and fear seemed to create their own odor. Soot lay over all. The absolute khakiness of the mass swamped the few tokens of difference—a group of kilts here, a slouch-hatted Australian there. But chiefly masses of undifferentiated men in steel helmets. And all of them nutriment for cannon.

They watched from the pier as from a shipboard crane onto the wharf of their cross-Channel steamer descended the great white black Vitesse Phaeton with its driver, Carling, in a military uniform supervising and yelling extraneous advice to the English crew above and the French stevedores below. The Phaeton landed on the wharf with a small mechanical squeak. Carling opened its back door and ushered in the ladies. They sat within and waited for the bags to come—Lady Tarlton's great traveling trunk and the more modest luggage of Mitchie and Naomi. Carling—Lady Tarlton explained—had been Tarlton's batman in the Dardanelles. Tarlton himself, she said, had for a time served as a brigadier general there but had been recalled.

Now that Tarlton himself is hors de combat—his yeomanry regiments were wiped out, you know, poor chaps, and the War Office decided he should abandon soldiering—Carling has become my—as the Australians say—"offsider" and "rouseabout." No, offsider. You're the rouseabout, Matron Mitchie!

Naomi wondered what indiscretion committed by Lord Tarlton or what shock suffered by him had caused them to tell him he was no longer required to lead yeomanry into the face of machine guns.

All packed up, the Phaeton drove them out of the great railyard and past a fish market. Women in the ordinary streets of the lower town were cooking pancakes on charcoal stoves. Soldiers and children in sabots waited for their order to be finished. The Phaeton then rose uphill into the town proper—which now revealed itself to look like the France she had expected. There were tall old buildings from what she would learn to call the Second Empire period. Naomi noticed the words "Angleterre" and "Anglais" on stores and streets. And yet little looked English. A mere twenty-six miles across a stretch of water made everything look somehow not-England. You traveled twenty-six miles in Australia and nothing altered. Two hundred and sixty miles, ditto. Here, it was a mere ferry ride between strangenesses.

At a Second Empire hotel called the Paris Grand, their luggage was unloaded under Carling's direction and morning tea was—as Lady Tarlton said—"taken" in a high-vaulted lobby. The lobby was drenched with light from vast windows and seemed to exist in warless parallel to the business they were about to launch on.

And Miss Durance, said Lady Tarlton, shaking her head, as if it were a means of seeing her more clearly, what is your history?

I'm afraid I don't have a history, Lady Tarlton, Naomi said, unaccomplished at answering that kind of question. You know Australia, Lady Tarlton. I'd had a life—as people do there.

Lady Tarlton laughed—a fluting but genuine sound, with too much body to it for it to be merely patronage.

I like the directness of your answer, she said, looking with her left hand for stray strands of her auburn hair—there always seemed to be one.

Matron Mitchie said, Ma'am, Miss Durance took control of our raft. I think had it been left to a man, I might not be here.

Naomi felt powerless to correct this kind of palaver. But Lady Tarlton tossed her head and cast her hands eastwards as if the front line were only a block away. Well, we see what happens when things are left to men. Tell me, though, Miss Durance, did you train in the bush?

Two years in a country town, ma'am. Then the city.

Tell me about the obstetrics in the country town.

Puerperal fever was not unknown in the Macleay District, said Naomi.

She did not mention that much evidence for this killer of young mothers could be found in the cemetery just below the ridge from the hospital. Poorer people upriver were forced to depend on a dairy farmer's wife with some midwifery experience to deliver their babies. When things went wrong the women might be two or more days' ride up the valley. They were brought to town only after the fever had already taken hold.

Lady Tarlton looked intently at Mitchie. You see, Marion. You see! If we had had more time . . .

In the Western District, said Mitchie with forgivable pride, we had bush nurses visiting women all through their pregnancies. Any chance of a problem and the woman was moved to town. But . . . the whole thing has languished without Lady Tarlton there to look after the financial side.

To harry donations, Matron Mitchie means, said Lady Tarlton with a wink. If the Australians had not begged the secretary of state for the colonies to relieve them of my husband's presence, we would have put a scheme in place throughout the country so that it would have been normal and unassailable. But my husband can't tolerate the Labour prime ministers the Australians have the ill grace to elect. Tarlton refused to allow the election the prime minister asked him to call. And so it was—as a wag in the *Sydney Bulletin* wrote—"Farewell Lord and Lady Tarlton, Sprigs of a Noble tree, We cannot tell you how pleased we are to see the back of thee."

Yes, confirmed Mitchie. You were tarred with the wrong brush. Women don't count as much as politics.

Lady Tarlton and Mitchie had created a standard of frankness Naomi hoped she would not be called on to imitate, and indeed tea finished and she had not been asked to say anything of that kind. They made for the car again and drove through a countryside of hedge-rows which concealed small, bountiful-looking fields. They inspected a number of vacant châteaux in overgrown grounds abundant in spring flowers. But some had been rendered unhealthy inside by too long a closing-up. The owners were either too hard up to restore them, or else had made themselves patriotically absent in the West Indies or North Africa until the war ended.

Lady Tarlton argued with French agents in unembarrassed, high, nasal French. If the lower floors looked passable, she would lead ev-eryone upstairs—Mitchie included—and look for the promise of light and airiness and security against draughts. Occasionally she would ask, How many beds can we fit in here, Mitchie?

Twelve, Mitchie would say. Or two dozen for a vast room—a noble-man's former library, say.

So many?

Things were much more crowded in Egypt, and on Lemnos, Mitchie assured her. They could fit forty beds in the ballroom down-stairs. And the family chapel would provide a ward for at least a fur-ther fifteen—ideal for a recuperating officers' ward.

We must plan for a winter in which peace has not broken out, said Lady Tarlton—obviously skeptical of the military promise of the coming summer. Therefore the grounds must be extensive enough to accommodate marquees and huts. Then there were latrines to be dug. There should be woods nearby to moderate the heat and give the walk-ing wounded something to explore and the wheelchair cases bosky excursions through forests and by ponds.

Three châteaux had been inspected. Lady Tarlton was becoming pessimistic in her vocal way and began asking the French agent and Mitchie and Naomi questions which were not meant to be answered.

I mean, one is doing one's best, pottering around the châteaux of the minor and more cowardly nobility—or probably of craven bour-geois who bought these places for show and then abandoned their country in her hour of peril. But I keep telling this agent I don't want a jumped-up manor house. I need a big château, and something in good order. I need some decent plumbing too. I am *not* in the house restoration business.

She honked at the agent who was driving with them, *J'ai besoin d'un grand château. Très grand.*

The man lit up as if he had exactly the right grand château in mind. It proved—when they drove there—to sit on a low coastal hill in the direction of Wimereux. Its name was Château Baincthun. Even its av-enue lined by yews—when they drove up it—gave a promise of space. Its vistas were wide but its copses close. Its façade was white and ornamented and fluted. The capitals under its roof were topped by stone-carved faces of kings or counts or sages.

By the time she had inspected its main downstairs room, Lady Tarlton clearly wanted it. The light flooded the dusty boards upstairs in a most inveigling way. Rear and upstairs rooms must be inspected to accommodate staff.

Marion, warned Lady Tarlton, as if Matron Mitchie were the flighty one, imagine this not in today's relative splendor but with ice on the eaves and an Arctic wind trying to pick the locks.

Matron Mitchie found it possible to do so and still believe in the warmth of the boys—as long as there were stoves in the wards.

Well, of course, said Lady Tarlton.

After taking the proffered lease on the Château Baincthun to a notary in Boulogne—who claimed that his father had tendered his services to Charles Dickens, a frequent visitor to Boulogne—they dined in a private room at the Grand Paris to celebrate. Lady Tarlton pressed Bordeaux wine on them. Naomi managed to choke a glass of it down her untutored throat and struggled with its unfamiliar robust-ness. Like other colonials she found the aftertaste—the after-feel, as well—a matter of greater relish than the drinking itself.

The Racecourse
and the Château

I t was working towards summer now. The sky was yellow at the rims but arched to a dazzling maritime blue above the racecourse. Sally waited for Naomi at the agreed-upon time at administration huts near the arched entrance. Her sister was coming from two hours' drive away and delays were possible, and indeed a half hour passed until a great black-and-white beast of an automobile pulled up by the huts. A middle-aged man in a private's uniform got out of the driver's side and came and saluted Sally. Naomi spilled out of one of the rear doors after him. Her motherless co-conspirator, she thought at once. Her sister, orphaned by a dead mother, by a father who reasonably enough replied to their desertion of him by remarriage. But Naomi was smiling without reserve and that brought Sally up to the regions of light. I love her, it came to Sally. This revelation surprised her. I love her and want her to be well. They embraced heartily—Naomi so willing and reckless that it brought out a similar passion in Sally.

What have *you* got yourself into? Sally asked.

Forgive me, said Naomi. I said I'd come back and here I am in Boulogne, with you in Rouen.

Oh, I understand you had to go to Mitchie. And what's fifty or sixty miles?

Sally also found herself now confronted with a tall, auburn-haired

304

woman in a fawn dress trimmed with navy blue, and a straw hat atop a river of hair almost artfully unruly. She had heard in her sister's letter of a week past of Lady Tarlton. She'd expected a severe mien and no one as ageless as this—or so casual in finery—or so distracted from her own splendor.

Don't mind me, Lady Tarlton announced to Sally. I won't interfere between you and your sister. I'm on my way to beard the medical officer commanding Rouen. Not just beard him, as the Bard mysteriously says. I hope, in fact, I can frighten him. Come into the car.

Sally obeyed. The women settled themselves in squeaking leather and Carling closed the door.

It is a modest enterprise your sister has committed herself to, Miss Durance, said Lady Tarlton from her seat. If I let them, they will try to turn us into a mere rest home and officers' club. As your sister will tell you, they are dragging their heels on giving me military doctors to work with my young Scottish doctor—a woman, in fact—and my two young male physicians, both afflicted with bad chests. I would have all women doctors if I could. They are not as pompous as an army surgeon. And they're certainly better than boys just cured of their consumption.

She had a strange lack of reserve—a candor almost out of order. It was clear she had a disciple in Naomi. Her statement had produced a glow of purpose on Naomi's face. The middle-aged soldier-driver cranked the engine as Sally—like Naomi before her—accustomed herself to the opulence of upholstery and mahogany woodwork.

As they rolled forth from the arched gate, Lady Tarlton turned again to Sally, who was staring out of the window with the suspicion that the world would look different through the glass of this magnificent mechanism.

You are not tempted to join us, Miss Durance? At the château, I mean.

Apart from an instant thought of Lieutenant Constable and his obliterated face, Sally had a sense that there was something that could not be predicted in Lady Tarlton's scheme.

She said, I am very flattered by the . . .

Lady Tarlton shook her head. I understand, she said, with her strange laugh which threatened to overflow its limits. After all, sisters might love each other. But sometimes there's room only for one of them per hospital.

Not that, Lady Tarlton, said Sally. But the three of them knew it *was* that.

Sally and Naomi were dropped in the square of Rouen, with the Hôtel de Ville on one side and the stupefying complexity of the cathedral Charlie had taken her to on the other. As the enormous car drove off, Naomi and Sally laughed together like two girls recently interviewed by an eccentric headmistress. They went straight to a café—a little wooden place with tables set on the surface of the square. Naomi raised her face to the sun and the gesture made Sally feel gleeful too. It was the sort of day when even sisters with their history could sit together and think, If they could see us now—here on the timeworn pavement—drinking our ferocious black coffee and eating not cake but gâteau!

You know, said Naomi, it's peculiar. It seems to me we're happier now—at this second and here—than in our past lifetime *there*.

Lemnos, you mean?

No. *There*.

You said Matron Mitchie was back? asked Sally, to move the conversation on to safer ground. How is that possible?

Pure willpower, that's how. She's a single woman with hardly any relatives. She may be frightened that if she lacks a mission, she's at an end.

But we're single women too.

Well, Naomi conceded, a little younger, to begin with. And it may change one day too. Marriage doesn't seem an impossibility to me anymore. I think the further I've got away from the Macleay, the less astounding it looks.

Robbie Shaw?

I don't know. I've written to him and as good as told him no. But he still persists.

He wants to be your fiancé?

When I said the less astounding marriage looks, I'm not thinking of anyone in particular. I'm beginning to think Robbie Shaw's idea *is* impossible. I don't have the disposition for him. I ought to write to him again but I keep delaying. This is the problem: the further away I get from him, the more inconceivable marrying him seems. Whereas it's supposed to be the other way round. He is a good fellow, a positive fellow. But he thinks there's something definite in me, when really I am only covering a lack. That's a dangerous delusion, you see. He'd find out afterwards and never forgive me, and so a really unhappy twenty or thirty years would begin. I've got other things to do with the next twenty or thirty years.

But that's the way marriage works, isn't it? asked Sally. It's not possible unless the man and the woman are deluded.

They were silent. They did not want to apply Sally's thesis to their parents.

No, said Naomi. I think a marriage can be sensibly embarked on. But the other thing Robbie Shaw's deluded about is that they'll have him back here, when one of his legs is five inches shorter than the other. They had Matron Mitchie back. But I think now it might have been Lady Tarlton who worked that magic. Shaw doesn't have a Lady Tarlton. But listen, you said in your letter you'd met a soldier?

How astonishing it was to Sally that she didn't feel discomfort at this conversation.

The solicitor's son, Charlie Condon, she said. He's amusing and has a very lively brain, though I can imagine on a hot day his enthusiasm for old buildings might get a bit much. But he'll need a clever woman when the time comes. He is a good sketcher but intends to become a better one. He wants to sketch blackfellas, even. It's the whites in the Macleay he's not so keen on. He says . . . Well, he understands how things are in town. A person can say these things when you're so far away and it's all reduced to size. All that bush hypocrisy.

They contemplated the idea of the town shame and decided they didn't want to expand on it.

Charlie hasn't been in fighting yet, said Sally. And I wish he didn't have to be. A shell could cut the life of a fine soul like his in a second. It's done it to other fine souls.

Then she told Naomi how Charlie had visited her and ordered a table by telegram. Underneath was the thought—If this can be told, then all can be said. All must anyhow be said one day. The blame and the thanks.

There was one subject left—Mrs. Sorley. They had both got letters from her which were pleasant and sensible and careful of their feelings.

Naomi confessed, She has sure instincts, that woman.

So we have to go on being fair to her, eh?

It's beginning to look that way.

Each sister knew—and knew the other one knew—that what stood in the way of becoming daughters to Mrs. Sorley was their caution about liking this unchosen figure, in case it happened that they began to feel her more admirable than the mother they were connected to by sinew and blood and acts of awful kindness.

After their morning coffee, Sally took Naomi through the cathedral and showed her the things that Lieutenant Condon had shown her. Then, almost with relief at having got through the meeting, they saw the great limousine prowling for Naomi around the square. Sally waved to it as energetically as Naomi. In spite of their compact in Alexandria, they were still practicing being at full ease with each other. But this French reunion had gone well.

Captain Constable's pulse and his blood pressure remained those of a healthy young man—though one plagued by sleeplessness. Sally did not often see his eye closed, even at night, and he would frequently want to write something down. Only sometimes—and then in the dark hours—was there self-pity in what he wrote.

One night he remarked, This is more like an accident in a factory than a wound taken in a battle.

Sally whispered rigorously, taking no nonsense, What's the difference? This war is a kind of great factory. All I know is you're still a first-class man.

His mood quickly lightened.

He wrote, Oh yes? Where's the evidence for that?

I know you by the way you are taking *this*!

No choice, he wrote. If I tossed things in now, I wouldn't get through it all.

Thinking like that, she told him, shows the man you are.

And the exchange went on, as they passed the pad back and forth.

I would have liked to have found out whether I made a true soldier or not. I wasn't even at Gallipoli.

And where is Gallipoli now? she asked. Gallipoli is a boneyard

She handed him the pad back. Those men—the survivors—they know themselves now, he wrote.

She said, There are millions of men who know themselves without war. Millions.

He shook his head and wrote energetically. When he handed her the pad, it read, Yes. But once you become a soldier the whole point is war. The whole point of it is finding how you manage yourself in war.

He nodded after she had read it, and Sally looked at him with the bleak knowledge that he was right. A thunder came up to the east. It was massive enough to make them uneasy about its meaning and intentions.

Will you ever listen to that? asked Honora, coming up to Sally.

They went to the door of the Nissen hut—the tents were giving way to such structures—and parted the inner and outer air-raid curtains. The eastward sky was continuously and massively lit by pulses and changing emphases of light which moved up and down the horizon. It was bigger than Gallipoli.

Honora said, Bloody old Mars himself doing the scales.

Are *they* doing it? Or are we? Sally asked. It dwarfed nature and its fires and furies. If it were them making this, how could the front hold? How could the war endure? This was the war's summit, she was sure. Something must end and something be born.

The thunder went on throughout their daytime rest and into a second night and a second day, and so on. At midnight on the third day the regiments of wounded arrived in convoys of ambulances that choked the approaches to the racecourse. It was like Gallipoli—the mutilation had overflowed the forward stations. And so in the reception wards to which most nurses were rushed, men still wore the reeking uniform fragments and the regimental insignia that now stood for nothing.

Again—amongst the mass of these British—the nurses were faced by an astounding and unearthly lack of raucous complaint from men getting to know their wounds. Even some of the amputees had abandoned their screams in the regimental aid post or the dressing post and clearing station and were now left with mere crumbs of complaint which nurses went about soothing with hypodermics full of morphine.

Only after the turmoil ceased and men had been carried away to appropriate wards was Sally sent back to the post-operative ward or the gas or thoracic wards. It was a broad education you got in Rouen.

She was sometimes sent to the gas wards for night duty. Usually it was days since the men had inhaled the stuff, yet the taint could still be smelled on them and their eyes were still wide and alarmed—their eye sockets and lips blue, their breathing tormented, froth around their mouths. Orderlies came round with hypodermics and atropine sulphate solution and Sally injected them. A device named "the octopus"—many masks running from an oxygen cylinder—was designed to give simultaneous comfort to a number of men. Revisiting them before going off duty at dawn, she saw that it had little effect. The gas was still working on their hidden membranes.

The shelling and roar and night illuminations in the east continued but there was no conclusive news—it appeared that no climax had been reached and little had been won. When it was adjudged safe by the ward doctors, amputees were taken out to the hospital ferries at the port of Rouen. So were some thoracic and abdominal cases— and head wounds and the blinded and gassed. Honora said with some credibility that they were making room for Australians—for they did not doubt Australians had now been thrown into the furnace and were on their way. That was the arrangement—clear the Australian hospitals for Australian casualties. In any case—Sally reflected—in this hectic season, Lady Tarlton's hospital would not beg for patients. Such was the weight of daily arrivals.

On the strength of her *Archimedes* experience, Sally spent three nights in the theatre giving anesthetics—more precisely, ether—for the nerveless and level-headed Dr. Fellowes. Ether was considered safer and more mistakeproof when you had an occasional anesthetist, which Sally was. But her work became necessary because in suddenly warm weather and over a day and a half, convoy by convoy, the Australians did indeed arrive—up to a thousand a day. They were nearly too numerous—too smeared in feature and too blurred in endeavor and pain—for her to look for Charlie Condon amongst them and see if he had been punished for knowing so much about Rouen Cathedral.

The men arrived with a word on their lips—Pozières. It might have been a village but it was vast in their minds: the birthplace of their pain. The English newspapers had a name even broader than Pozières. The name of a bloody river previously unremarked in the earth's imagination. The Somme ran scarlet and was vaster than the Nile or Amazon now in the imagination of all those in France. It was the altar on which Abraham *did* sacrifice his son, and no God spoke out to stay the knife.

The name ran around the reception ward while, with an orderly's help, Sally took a fouled dressing off the groin wound of a weathered, young-old man, when his femoral artery began to gush. Just stop the bleeding, Nurse, he said reasonably, and I'll get back to the missus and kids. All the pressure she and the orderly could apply did not save him—this man they knew could hew timber and hand plough and be unwearied at the day's end. He shuddered and then yielded up his existence.

The name Pozières was uttered by a boy with a chest wound who told Honora that he was too tired to sleep. In the theatre—before he was etherized—he admitted to the theatre nurse and the surgeon that he was only sixteen. The walking wounded from his unit pronounced the name too, as, getting ready to be sent back to the front or on to England, they paid him a visit and brought him cigarette cards they had collected for him—comic scenes of bulls charging tigers, of parrots shocking maids with the viciousness of their language, of cowboys and Indians, of soccer players, and trout fishermen.

A newspaper in the nurses' mess declared: "Huge Losses to the Hun. 'Fritz Is Running,' Says General."

Captain Constable remained at Rouen through the melee and treatment and transfer of men that Pozières created. The name seemed to call up a private crisis for him. Sepsis had broken out at the edge of his wound, a peccant tooth needed to be removed under anesthesia and the pus drained. And so England and its promised round of face-remaking surgery receded for him. As thousands came and went, he remained fixed in place. For it was axiomatic that no work could be done in England to repair him until he had been free of sepsis for six months.

At the Château Baincthun, Lady Tarlton had just two surgeons and two ward doctors on the day the Australian casualties began to arrive to join the small numbers of British officers of middling or light wounds so far sent there. Someone in the office of the deputy director of medical services clearly thought that a titled woman like Lady Tarlton should be confronted only by officers. But now Australians of all ranks turned up in motor ambulances.

The military had sent an apparently robust surgeon named Major Darlington. But he had a distant manner, and to Mitchie and Naomi it became clear that Lady Tarlton suspected he was a military reject— not for surgical reasons but perhaps for social ones. Immediately and unsuccessfully she set the Red Cross in London the job of recruiting another civilian surgeon—as if that could be done these days.

Darlington was a lanky man with a slight stoop that made him seem attentive but whose sentences sometimes were ambushed by thought and trailed off. But it was not long before he was seen as the essence of the place. Word of his competence came from theatre nurses. And from his side, he was pleased to be placed at an institution where he had control of his own pathology laboratory.

His junior was a young woman named Dr. Airdrie, a small-bodied and frizzy-haired volunteer with the Scottish Women's Hospital who was sent to Baincthun at Lady Tarlton's request. She too came to be considered a treasure of the place. But Darlington remained an odd treasure.

Mitchie walked the admission ward with Major Darlington, Naomi with Dr. Airdrie, and they directed where men were to be taken next. Airdrie still wore a little of her resentment at being sent here. She had been heard to say in her brogue, I didn't volunteer just so I could be a hobby doctor in fooking Boulogne. Her mind had been on the Mediterranean or Mesopotamia. But these ambulances grinding up the elm-lined drive of the previously undervisited Château Baincthun were changing her mind about Lady Tarlton being just a gentlewoman hostelier.

Soon Airdrie and Major Darlington became so busy in the theatre— and the two young ward doctors so overburdened—that Mitchie and Naomi became decision makers. They instructed the few newly arrived Australian nurses and others from the Red Cross, whom Lady Tarlton had gathered in to keep penciled records of wounds and treatment on sheets hung at the base of each man's cot—just as in the best-run hospitals. They announced dosages of morphine and other drugs and decided on the changing of dressings and irrigation of wounds. Naomi behaved with a confidence she had not felt at all on the *Archimedes*. She had learned somehow not to fret about decisions made in good faith. Men grinned up from the admission-ward cots when they heard her and the other Australian nurses talk. Could an accent be curative to those who shared it?

Naomi worked by timeless routine in which hours did not exist. Only the seconds of pulse measurement meant anything. There was no leisure to observe the larger areas of time their watches proffered. A convoy of ninety wounded from Pozières arrived and Naomi worked for more than a day without being aware of it—except through a contradictory lightness of her upper body balanced by a sense of the gravity dragging at her legs. As well as acting as a virtual matron, she had in a day and night herself dressed wounds and hauled oxygen cylinders for the nurses to administer to the gassed. The roster she had worked at in the Dorchester Hotel might as well have been a transcription of *Paradise Lost* for all the relationship it bore to the days after Pozières.

By early August of that year—the predicted year of triumph, 1916—the wards were crammed with Tommies and Australians and a few Indians. Another young ward doctor—a rejectee of the Medical Corps for some reason of health—arrived. So did a squad of voluntary aides summoned from London—of course through Lady Tarlton's airily deployed influence over the Red Cross.

My husband is hopeless, she hissed at Naomi and Mitchie one morning as they drank tea—scalding their mouths—in the mess room. He doesn't like my doing this and my being importunate with some of his chums. So he tells me he lacks any power. He's a whisperer, that's what he is. He can undermine, but he can't build.

And then—being herself a woman of action rather than whispers—she went to see what the volunteer English women were making for men's breakfasts.

It was easier for a man to get to Blighty from Baincthun. Major Darlington was kept busy making these assessments, which came on top of his surgery and work in the pathology lab. Dr. Airdrie and the ward doctors joined Darlington in their reluctance to send a man back to the front until he'd had at least a little Blighty leave. Rhetoric about shirking had no impact on them. Except in the rarest and most blatant cases of recovery—or in the face of furious insistence by a soldier that he should return to the fighting, they sent all who could travel—including the battle shocked—by ambulance to the ferries. And recuperation at the Australian Voluntary was no idle business. In the summer garden, Lady Tarlton used men to dig drains or stoke boilers or milk the three dairy cows she had acquired so that the wounded should have fresh milk. Carling was their inexhaustible foreman.

Those military satraps still hate us, you know, Lady Tarlton announced as a boast to all her staff.

The young Scots woman, Airdrie, had a melodious laugh and clearly admired Lady Tarlton. Since she was freshly minted as a physician, the Australian and English nurses muttered that she lacked a mentor to turn her into a fully accomplished surgeon. She was not haunted by that. The wounded Tommies and Australians who came under her knife all said—those who could—that they trusted her for her lack of airs. Men found the presence of a woman surgeon a strange thing only once they had outlived the pain of wounds and surgery.

Baincthun People

Naomi worked—according to need—as theatre nurse and anesthetist for both the surgeons. Mitchie's Australian and Red Cross nurses became the sort of fast learners and expert dressers that she and her sister had been—under necessity—a year before. Mitchie nicknamed the Red Cross women "the English Roses," but some of them were from the women's suffrage movement, of which it seemed Lady Tarlton had herself been a member. Many were from what the British called "better families." Their accents were not so far removed from that of Lady Tarlton. Their parents probably knew and trusted her as a mentor for their daughters. Others of the English Roses were not nurses and insisted on being cooks and scullery maids—a form of rebellion against the cosseted lives they had led, an assertion that women were equal in the moils of the earth and were all subject to the same condescension from the male world. Naomi and Mitchie's group delighted in telling them that Australian women had had the suffrage for—how long was it now?—twelve years. But they could not pretend it had delivered women from care—from being aged beyond their years and strength by labor and concern.

Major Darlington's slightly dazed belief in the uses of pathology was unshakeable and he promoted it even—or perhaps especially—in conversing with nurses and orderlies. He had quarreled with his superiors over the wearing of face masks in the treatment of wounds. The Australian Voluntary and its little pathology lab—which he equipped at his own expense—was his chance to manage experiments on the issue. To it he summoned nurses and orderlies and took swabs from their throats. He ordered that in certain wards nurses and orderlies dressing wounds should wear masks—a prominent placard marked MASKS was placed at the doorway of two wards. A NO MASKS sign was posted at the door of the other two. The wards in the newly built huts in the garden were not included in the experiment because that might make the numbers too hard for him to get his work done, either as pathologist or as surgeon. He came around the wards—himself wearing a mask—to take samples of wound tissue. He put them in a glass dish and bore them away. As he worked he told nurses in wafting and often broken sentences that he suspected streptococci in their throats were a peril to wounds. Not that, he laughed—in one of those near-silent laughs uttered with lowered chin and like a series of nods—their having streptococci was in any way a jailable offense. Streptococcus likes us, he told Naomi and some of the other nurses. He likes to take us dancing.

At this he uttered coughs of laughter.

His lean face—sallow on his arrival, and watchful and sour—then composed itself into an expression of calm purpose.

The masses of wounded and gassed of the bloodiest and most chemical-doused summer in human knowledge continued to arrive. They were at least two-thirds Australian—to justify the establishment's name—but frequently more. The hospital did not receive the shell-shocked, even though there were men with wounds who woke at night hyperventilating or screaming. But the Australian Voluntary was not equipped with alienists.

At the Voluntary there were separate messes for officers and men who were well enough to sit at tables. As summer progressed the tables were sometimes put out on the pavement in front of the château, where officers and men began to mingle as they had in the battles which brought them here. At Lady Tarlton's insistence a glass or two of wine was served with dinner for anyone fit to desire it. She had put together a subcommittee in London who put up the money for such delicacies. These seemed to be placed democratically on the tables without discrimination—preserves and condiments and shortbread from Fortnum & Mason were made available to the officers and men alike. It honored the reality, Lady Tarlton said to Naomi one day as they looked across the terraces at the walking wounded and recuperants at the sunny tables, of a citizen army in which some privates were schoolteachers, religious ministers, and journalists. She did not mention the hard-fisted country boys and the worldly innocent children of the slums. Yet—contrary to normal military credos—the firmament did not crack open when Lady Tarlton permitted this mingling.

Faster than Naomi could have believed, the days began to shrink and leaves reddened and withered to warn generals of their failed summer. The wildflowers of the hospital grounds of the Australian Voluntary Hospital—hyacinths and primroses—closed up. The sky turned a stubborn gray and descended on the château so that it seemed within reach of the gray slates of the roof. The mornings were misty with vapors the sun could not always burn off. Heaters were moved into the wards. The rain grew colder and even more slanted than on Lemnos—driven before a wind that swept in from the Channel and froze puddles overnight on the doorsteps of the château and in murderous little patches on the pathways to the huts. An English nurse broke her ankle in a journey between the reception wards in the garden and the house. Another scalded herself carrying cocoa across an open stretch. But the volunteers did not leave—as they had every right to. Lady Tarlton was a magnetic figure and the English Roses proved strongwilled young women who stuck. And where else would they go on the Western Front to see their suffragist principles in practice?

In the first onset of cold—the rehearsal for the winter that would ultimately take the unconcluded war to Christmas and into 1917—the young Scottish surgeon Dr. Airdrie would visit the wards in a wool-lined skin-and-fur jacket of the kind worn by officers and men. She sported stylish stalking boots which seemed to imply that she was ready to go hiking or hacking or hunting stags in the Highlands. Penelope was her first name—so it emerged—but no one used it. Perhaps because she had not encountered many other women doctors and had contempt for the hauteur of male physicians, she was familiar with the nurses and seemed to talk to them as if no veil of wisdom separated her from them. When—if ever—the war's giant wheel ceased to turn, she would be taught how to behave—at peril of her career—in a civilian hospital.

Naomi came to see that Airdrie had no other choice than to chat over tea with them. For she was in many ways the most isolated person in the château—potentially separated from nurses by her university education, but inevitably seen even by the distracted Major Darlington as a medical anomaly. She told Naomi and others that she found the two former consumptives who worked as ward doctors very plain company. They were the sort of men, she said, who'd studied their wee medicine rather than grow up and become human beings. Mammy so wanted her little boy to be a doctor! she mocked.

She liked to gossip and that was always welcome. Lord Tarlton owned half of Banffshire, she claimed—his grandfather, an English interloper, as described by Airdrie, had cleared out the population of the estates to Australia and New Zealand.

My uncle knows the present Tarlton remotely, she said, and a cousin was his land agent at some stage, though I haven't bothered Lady Tarlton with that news. As for Lady Tarlton herself, her name is Julia Henning and she's English—Manchester-born in fact. She owned her own millinery shop in the West End, with very blue-blooded ladies as her customers. But still, in the eyes of that group, a hatmaker—however fine a hat she might put together—is subhuman. My mother says it was murder for them when they married. Lady Hatshop, everyone called her. You see, there was many a mammy with a plain daughter had her eye on wee sawney Lord Tarlton. So there was an unco scandal when he bespoke beautiful Miss Henning. At first glance he might seem attractive—in a bit of a dither like Major Darlington—but there are no depths behind it. A high Tory messenger boy.

I mean, she continued, even the army dispensed with him. And I believe he didn't cover himself with glory in your country either. His wife's politics helped drive them apart from the beginning. So why did they marry? Well, a title's a title and a beautiful hatmaker is a beautiful hatmaker. And Miss Henning might have thought she could influence him and make something of him. But no sooner did he have her locked up than he started tomcatting his way around London. They have no children but he has bastards everywhere—I know one he's supporting in Putney. Though the Australians hated him, he has a certain charm and has wee bastards there as well—the daughters of the big graziers. He made himself persona non grata with all the big . . . What do you call them?

Squatters, Naomi supplied.

Yes, them.

You must be exaggerating, Doctor, Naomi suggested.

I don't think I am very much, said Airdrie after a pensive assessment. I would say that Lady Tarlton is the woman with the best excuse in the Empire for taking a lover.

Taking a lover? asked Naomi.

Taking a lover? asked the English Roses. Who?

Well, said Airdrie, let those with eyes to see . . .

Naomi was surprised by how quickly the initial shock of the idea faded in her and was replaced by annoyance at Airdrie and her supposed knowledge of Lady Tarlton.

You're a good, loyal girl, said Dr. Airdrie with conviction not mockery. You're standing up for Lady Tarlton, aren't you? Defending her repute? I don't think you need to. In my eyes, her repute stands.

Even then, Naomi saw some of the English Roses avert their eyes as if they knew something Naomi didn't.

And I thought you were being tolerant too, Durance. Of this Lady Tarlton and Major Darlington matter. Good luck to her, declared Airdrie. Funny though, that she goes for those slightly dazed sort of fellows. But you didn't know? Don't be ashamed. It speaks well of you.

Naomi set to in her mind to remodel the Lady Tarlton she knew to the possibility Airdrie was right. It was easier to do than she had thought. She would have been shaken a year or so ago—or, say, before the *Archimedes*. Now it was such a small matter. The front dwarfed all.

Airdrie approached her as she left to go back on duty.

I'm sorry, she said. I was mischievous in general but it was not aimed at you. You probably think I am a mere gossip too, and I am. Love it, I do. Can't help it. Forgive me.

Naomi walked away and didn't care what Airdrie thought of people who were brusque.

That evening she got an apologetic note from Airdrie, inviting her to lunch in Wimereux—they could get a lift in there with Carling the following Saturday. This would of course be dependent on a convoy coming in. But *moules* and *pommes frites* were a specialty of the Pas de Calais, wrote Airdrie with gusto. Yummy! And all you say to me—I swear—will be kept secret.

When it did snow in the meantime, an unusually early fall portending a bad winter, Mitchie's few Australian nurses danced in its cleanness—never before encountered by them—in the garden. They were watched with amusement by the English Roses. Naomi had by now heard a lightly wounded Australian officer murmuring the news that Major Darlington was getting on a treat with her ladyship. But even the Australians—with a taste for ribaldry—were careful how they displayed their amusement at this. Envy must not be confessed to, and so the male code was to reach for mockery. It would have been more open if Lady Tarlton and Major Darlington had not grown to be so worthy of esteem and veneration. There seemed to be a strong and informal agreement amongst the increasing number of those who knew of their affair that it should no longer be a matter of comment. A trip by the walking wounded into Boulogne, where they talked to other soldiers, proved that rumors that the Australian Voluntary was an eccentric and slapdash place were common. Knowing what they knew, they resented that image. As well as that, the affair had not distracted

Thomas Keneally

Lady Tarlton from keeping the meals plentiful and the wards warm in the huge spaces of the château—a house which, as she had feared, invited in a gale each time the main door opened.

Penelope Airdrie and Naomi went into Wimereux for their lunch and were pleased to take shelter in a restaurant from the windy promenade on which—for a freezing half hour or so—they inspected the long stretch of tidal beach and the murky whitecaps of a dismal sea.

Never one for the seaside, me, confessed Airdrie.

A fire blazed in the restaurant. They ordered mulled wine. Then a huge bowl of *moules* and another of fried potatoes was brought to their table. They donned large bibs and—after opening and devouring the *moules*—rinsed their hands in bowls of water. Dr. Airdrie looked out through the lace curtains.

Never pretty, never pretty, this time of year.

This gave her an opportunity to ask Naomi details of Australian weather, Australian skies, Australian strands. It was peculiar that weather brought out a tendency to patriotism in a person. Storms and murk were forgotten. Summers were described and frosts unmentioned. As she expanded on the subject of humid days generating thunderstorms, Dr. Airdrie raised her hands to cover her face.

You're not feeling sick, are you? asked Naomi.

I am not myself, said Dr. Airdrie. Listening to you, I am not myself. I believe I am in love.

Naomi thought this was worth at least rinsing her hands and ceasing to eat. Oh. Who is the most fortunate man?

That's the thing. I'm not of the fortunate-man persuasion. I love you.

Naomi felt riveted to her seat and something like an electric pulse moved upwards through her body. It was her turn to cover her face. This could not be taken in. It was not a matter of moral bewilderment. It was too strange.

Please say nothing, Airdrie softly urged her. I have studied you and the way you go about your work. This combination you have of intelligence and reserve and grit.

Naomi decided she would flee the restaurant. A kind of panic drove her. The words intelligence and reserve and grit had done it. Her haunches began to move without reference to her conscious mind. She could have been on the street before she knew it. But she knew on some calm plain of her soul that Airdrie would be back at the château by the evening and need to be worked with. She had heard a matron at Royal Prince Alfred warn of "Sapphic tendencies" which sometimes arose in nurses' quarters and were to be fought and—please, girls!—reported. Yet after all—after Lemnos and Freud's rape and all the rest—she was more stunned by Airdrie's gush of affection than by the idea that the doctor was somehow reprehensible and immoral and, as the matron in Sydney had urged, reportable.

She had been in love—or had thought she was—with the French teacher at the high school in the Macleay. A sunny younger woman who broke girls' hearts by marrying a traveler and moving to Sydney. In her imagination Naomi had imagined kisses exchanged with the French teacher. But that had been a girl's fantasy and had not lasted to become the currency between a woman surgeon and a nurse.

Please, Dr. Airdrie said—seeing at once she had been too rash. I shouldn't have said anything.

Naomi knew she didn't want Airdrie. But she also did not want Airdrie shamed—and that in spite of the woman's recklessness. This is why she talks to the nurses in that fevered way, she thought. She's uncomfortable with her desire. The "Sapphic tendencies." They make her chatter away.

Naomi reached and held her wrist—just as a woman would the wrist of another who had suffered a loss. Airdrie's voice became almost inaudible.

I am not enchanted by men, she confided, though I like their company. I am enchanted by women. I'm enchanted by you.

Listen, said Naomi. You're a good surgeon and the men respect you. And so they should. But I don't want you to be in love with me—if you are in fact in love, and not just lonely. Saying what you said bewilders me. It shames me too.

Airdrie's brown eyes showed a flare of anger.

You're shamed by love? If that's the case, I pity you.

Maybe you're right to.

The fury died in Airdrie. It had been perhaps just a product of the rebuff and of her discomfort. Both of them took off their ridiculous burghers' *moules*-eating bibs. Their meal was finished.

We can work together, said Airdrie flatly, whatever you think of me. That should be a given.

Of course, said Naomi. We'll work together as usual.

Any edge of complaint in Airdrie had now been utterly blunted and more as exposition, she murmured, If a man declares love for a woman, that's romance. But if a woman declares love for a woman, the heavens fall in. It's worse still for men who love other men. But I'm of normal Presbyterian stock and I fear that in the eyes of most people, and in yours, I've committed some crime.

No, no, said Naomi. I know by now that all the crimes are up at the front.

It would actually be easier to deal with my feelings of the moment, Airdrie confessed, if you were outraged. If you picked up your skirts and called down God's judgement and flounced out.

Once I would have condemned you to hell. Because I didn't know the scope of things.

Airdrie sighed. So, you won't give off an air of contempt when we're working at the Tarlton convent, eh? You won't flinch when I appear?

Don't be ridiculous, said Naomi. It was difficult when Airdrie—a surgeon who was meant to maintain remoteness—behaved like some anxious schoolgirl. It was also endearing.

They picked up their glasses of wine. Naomi looked her in the eye as if it was the best method of rebuff. She saw that though this doctor was a year or two older than she was, in some ways she was clearly younger than that.

Did you know I have a sister? Naomi asked. I have a real sister just down the road in Rouen.

You do? said Airdrie. You are not offering her as a substitute sacrifice, are you?

That's not worth answering.

Younger than you?

That's right. And we never got on until this war. It is stupid and vain to think that all this . . .

She waved her hand to imply not just the restaurant but the fiasco out there in the gale, where men stood in streams of water beneath parapets waiting to go on some useless patrol or for a stupefying barrage to descend on them.

It's stupid to think of this, Naomi persevered, as if it was a machine to make us true sisters. But that's the way it's happened. It won't be any consolation to the wives and mothers of the men. I may one day have a husband—though I can't exactly imagine it. But if I don't have a husband, I'll have my sister. Perhaps we'll get old living in the same house in the same town. It is possible now where it wasn't before. While we were at Lemnos we used to say that France and Belgium couldn't be worse than Gallipoli. But it is worse by multiples! We're so accustomed to dreadful things now that we might need to live together because no one else will understand the things we've seen.

The two finished their wine as equal partners, and beyond the window the malicious gale—mirror to the conflict itself—refused to abate.

After Naomi had rebuffed Dr. Airdrie—after her relief at surviving the lunch with something like aplomb—it was nonetheless as if through Airdrie's proposal Naomi's own loneliness had been proven. Her room was at the back of the house. It had been a little too warm through the summer—it missed the sea zephyrs and picked up any hot breeze from the south. Now it was so cold that it needed a stove, but she hesitated to ask for one because there was always a shortage. She used canvas from a torn tent to plug the gaps between the window and its frame. But the cold still seemed to her not a condition but a diabolic presence—like her own solitude made flesh.

As she lay there at night she began to understand that what Dr. Airdrie had spotted in her—and seen as an opportunity—was this unrealized need for warmth, for a body to interpose itself between her and the ruthless cold. Lady Tarlton complained that in the unheated offices overnight, hospital fountain pens broke open when the ink turned to ice. The water pipes froze, and nurses had to melt ice to make cocoa for the patients. And when the cold—despite blankets and a military long coat, army socks, long underwear, even a balaclava—threatened to split Naomi open, she understood the need to be held, flesh on flesh and blood against blood. The past freezing nights had brought her to this conviction—that she might meet Airdrie partway. There might be closeness without passion—embrace of one kind and not of another. Each morning she was pleased she had not yielded to this idea. Each night—under extracoarse blankets—she feared the entry of the perfidious cold into her core.

Someone could see her on her way to Airdrie's room though—that would be the trouble. Or Airdrie would be called on to operate at some frigid hour while Naomi was there. But one night her coldness could not be endured alone anymore, and she took to the corridor. She had excuses if encountered—she was on her way to a particular storeroom where perhaps there were spare hot-water bottles. She rehearsed the contract she would make with Airdrie.

But as she got close to the surgeon's door and stooped to knock secretively, she heard conversation inside. It was nothing too loud but was definite discussion of some kind. She could hear the piping voice of a particular tone and rhythm. It was one of the English women—one of Lady Tarlton's elegant young suffragist women of good family.

At once Naomi lost all sense of cold. Astonishment created its own friction in her blood. Surprisingly, she was amused. This was Dr. Airdrie's version of love! She had grieved Naomi's refusal—if at all—a week at most. Or maybe she was just cold too and had found another girl who possessed the desire for warmth. But if Airdrie had been in love with Naomi, she had found new consolation pretty quickly. Alone and in an army coat and socks—unlovely and freezing and shamed and amused by her own innocence in believing Airdrie—she turned around. Remorse and hilarity had both begun to warm her and to prickle along her veins.

Though she was grateful to reach her room and be taken in by its particular freezing air, once she lay down in cold sheets the idea she'd been infected by after the *Archimedes* came to her again with new certainty. I am not a complete or sealed person. If I was, why did I set out for Doctor Airdrie's room? Why did I find cold unbearable then and now find it tolerable? I am a string of recoils from circumstance. It was a matter of a mere filament whether I went to be warmed by Airdrie or not. If I had stayed in my room I would not have known why. And I don't know why I went.

So there was the Naomi who stayed in her room with the threat of ice, and the parallel Naomi who crept down the hall to be warmed by a surgeon. This was simply an echo of her suspicion that there was the Naomi who fell deep down with the *Archimedes* living in the same flesh as the Naomi who refused to. And so—with her parts and actions scattered all over the atmosphere and cold earth—she could not but deny the glacial night and fall into a profound, accepting sleep. There are men in frozen trenches tonight, she mumbled as a last conscious reproach. They all lacked an Airdrie.

Casualty Clearing

Major Darlington became exercised by the number of men at the Château Baincthun taking up beds in summer and winter because they had been disabled by trench foot or frostbite. Around the bed of a trench-foot–afflicted Australian private who had lost toes to surgery, he gathered Dr. Airdrie and all the nurses—both the half-dozen Australians and the English Roses.

Cripes, a man might as well be onstage, the Australian mumbled as they all gazed at him.

Here is a case, Darlington told them, of quite needless damage—though not, I hasten to say, through the fault of the man involved.

He addressed the Australian, who was clearly embarrassed by this jury of nurses.

Not your fault, eh, old man?

I wouldn't say so, said the soldier. I mean, sometimes a man got distracted with everything that was happening. Gas was more important. And no use changing your socks if your legs are likely to be blown off pretty soon.

I am sure, said stork-like Darlington, nodding and nodding again. Now, if we want to prevent this sort of thing, we simply must provide a dry, warm place in the trench where men will attend to the problem, have leisure to rub whale oil into their feet and change their socks and—if necessary—boots. For want of such precautions, this will happen, he said, nodding to an orderly, who removed the private's dressings and exposed the scabbed stumps and blackened flesh of his feet.

Did you use whale oil, my good man?

Everyone just gives up on the whale oil, the private told him. Five minutes after we do it, we're back up to our hocks in mud again.

You see? Darlington asked his audience. You see what happens?

What puzzled Naomi and the nurses was the question of what—at this distance from the front—they could do about the issue except adopt a stance of impotent protest. But Darlington had not finished.

On the front line, he intoned, men are allowed to stand for days in glutinous muck. Until a chap inevitably becomes a casualty. And sometimes staff officers in clean socks and polished shoes want to punish men, you see, to punish and harangue them for their functional disablement, for a condition which is the fault of the generals. But this, you know, this disablement takes beds from other wounded. No offense intended, old chap. But obviously someone must bear responsibility for the condition of the trenches.

This is not so much a military matter, declared Darlington, as an industrial outrage.

But, Major, asked Airdrie, in what way could we do anything to amend the mistakes of the front? We seem to be a wee bit removed from it.

Major Darlington was in no way aggrieved but raised a finger in the air.

Well, Doctor Airdrie, I intend to frame a letter on the matter which I would be obliged if those of you who felt so inclined could see your way to sign. The letter will assert the necessity of a boots-and-socks officer, to whom a section of men in every company will be assigned with the objective that they will deliver fresh boots and socks every two days to the men in the front. I admit that this might seem at first glance a comic suggestion, or one which is uneconomic. Well—if so, let them come to the rear and count the beds devoted to this curse. What will be done with the boots and socks replaced? Let our chaps throw them at the Huns if they care to. Money can be squandered on high explosive but not—so it seems—on footwear. Ah, now I think I have reached the end of my peroration on the matter. I must thank you for your attendance. And a round of applause, please, for our demonstration soldier.

All felt compelled by Darlington's zeal and gave a spatter of applause.

Mitchie murmured to Naomi as they left, None of that is as mad as it seems. Can you see any of the young lieutenants you know wanting to be appointed boots-and-socks officer though? Doesn't sound heroic, does it?

Naomi saw a second's contact between Airdrie's hand and the wrist of a handsome English Red Cross nurse whose name she was uncertain about. She would not have welcomed such a touch herself. So why was there a second's strange envy?

In the autumn Sally heard rumors running around Rouen that nurses might be put in casualty clearing stations located in the region of peril called "up the line." These were not quite believed at first. Yet the matrons came around the wards that November asking for volunteers for such places. Nurses had not been permitted to work in them before. So there were many applications. Sally, Honora, and Leonora Casement nominated themselves and were accepted almost automatically because of their long experience of wounds. There was the attraction as well that appointment to a casualty clearing station brought with it an immediate ten-day leave pass for England. This—pleasant in prospect—did not count with Sally. In so far as she understood motives, she realized that there had arisen in her a curiosity like Charlie Condon's before he knew what it would be like. Women too—she realized—might want to be sucked closer in to the fire.

The news had to be broken to their long-standing patient Captain Constable. Sally and Honora still worked regularly on the crater of his face, the screens drawn around to save him embarrassment. Yet he

was ambulatory now and sometimes went out for walks bandaged—
moving at a processional pace but without a stick along the streets
of the Australian general hospital. The matron had at first an eye out
for the growing friendship between Slattery and Sister Durance and
the unreplying Captain Constable. But it was as if his injury was considered to have unmanned him. Since it was reasoned a nurse was
unlikely to be infatuated by a faceless and wordless man they were
permitted to become his friend. And they knew that as they were going
elsewhere, so was he—earlier perhaps than they. For the wound—
considered purely as a wound—was healing over. Easing the packs of
gauze out of the mess after one dressing, Honora said, You're as clean
as a whistle these days.

Honora, however, was chary of telling him they were going. Sally
did it straight out.

Honora and I have been appointed to a casualty clearing station.
We'll be leaving the racecourse.

Constable shook his head a little in spite of his massive wound.

Honora told him, You'll be off to Blighty yourself soon—I'd say
within a week.

He reached for pencil and paper. "Clearing stations are too close
to things," he wrote.

He passed it to Sally since Honora had the irrigation syringe suspended in her hand. Well, that's part of the attraction, Sally told him.
You know what I mean.

He wrote and then displayed. If you had seen me there—when I
first came in, filthy and all—you would have left me for dead.

No, said Sally with genuine conviction. I would have seen your
eye. It is a fine eye. As for you, I was looking at a book in the mess
on maxillofacial surgery. There are charts of how thoroughly they can
remake your face. There are photographs of other men . . . You just
wouldn't believe it.

He scribbled, "Do you think I could see this book of yours? Or will
it give me the willies?"

She read this and answered, It's been rubber-stamped on the title page NOT TO BE REMOVED FROM OFFICERS' MESS. But I'll steal it.

She would too, said Honora, safely back on the whimsy track. Light-fingered, this one.

There was an amused grunt from deep in Captain Constable's throat.

The tome contained graphic news that some might think a patient should not be burdened with. A matron would not have been amused to see Constable skimming such a volume. To save the chance of being detected by day concealing the heavy, glossy-paged manual in her clothing, Sally brought it in one night after dinner. Advancing through the tobacco fumes emitted by recovering men, she came to him and put it in his bedside locker.

Look at this tomorrow, she said, when we put the curtains around you. Honora and I will leave you alone then to consider it. I have marked the places with paper. I know you. And I believe you'll be encouraged instead of depressed.

That was how it happened—he kept the manual conscientiously hidden in his locker and, after studying it behind screens, gave it back to Sally the following night. He wrote, "I see they'll take skin from over my ribs."

Yes, she said.

He wrote, "God made Eve out of a rib. The surgeons will make me. Flaps of skin, they talk about. For a while I'll look like someone's rag doll."

Sally read this. Then he wrote, "The surgeons seem pretty impressed about what they can do. I notice though that the book doesn't ask the patients what they think."

Sally regarded him earnestly. You can't let me down by getting sad about the book. I gave it to you because you're the sort of man who can deal with the brass tacks.

He wrote again. "Brass tacks it is!"

Honora and Sally saw him leaving the ward the following morning, escorted by an orderly because of his single eye and the problem it might give him between there and the ferry. They had time for the briefest exchange of sentiments.

On a streaky winter's day they were driven through tranquil open countryside until they came to a dank tent near a crossroads. Here they were hastily fed and received a day's instruction on the operation of a clearing station. Put bluntly, a medical officer told them, patients arrived, and within two days, and with a few exceptions, they had either succumbed or had been transported back to base hospitals such as Rouen or Boulogne or Wimereux. The nurses would be presented with a range of cases and with such suddenness that—as the first rule—they must never let themselves feel as if things were out of control. We want women, said the medical officer, who will not be put off, either by the frequency of unfriendly aeroplanes or proximity to shelling.

The clearing stations were anomalous, the medical officer told them. They were close to the front, five to seven miles back, yet sufficiently hard to reach via the communication trenches that sometimes, as an instance, gas gangrene—the buildup of gas in the tissues—had already struck by the time the patient reached them. And particularly so if the wounded man had been retrieved from No Man's Land after lying out there for a time.

He unscrolled a chart and hooked it onto a tripod. It was a pleasing chart in its rationality and design. The ambulances came to the admission ward and those who did not die there would be taken in a fanned-out pattern to a series of huts or wards beyond—medical, resuscitation, preoperative, chest, minor wounds, or gas. Patients in the preoperative surgery were taken quickly into X-ray and on to the operating theatres. Those in resuscitation would need surgery—but must first be made stable. A further diagrammatic arrow led into the postoperative and evacuation wards from which the gas and minor wounds cases would have been early transported to the general hospitals of the rear. All this rationality in the diagram seemed to contradict the medical officer's allusion to possible chaos.

Now, look here, he said, at the ward marked "Resuscitation," for those suffering wound shock.

They listened to him talk quite graphically—and even with narrative force—about how in shock the peripheral vessels of the body could not contain fluid; about violent variations in blood pressure; about coronary embolus; about the rapid pulse that then became almost imperceptible. In the worst cases a transfusion of isotonic fluid and blood plasma could be given. Or direct donations could be made by a paraffined glass tube between a donor vein and the recipient vein. Each orderly, each nurse, each doctor would be blood-typed at the clearing station pathology lab in case of the need for a transfusion.

Indeed, glass transfusion devices—needles, bottles, corrugated tubes, the latest gear—lay on a table by the diagram waiting to be demonstrated by the matrons. But staff engaged in resuscitation—the medical officer continued—should be prepared for death to occur in patients without warning and despite the best efforts.

As the Rouen women left the tent for their buses and took their minds off wound shock to contemplate their leave, they saw Freud talking to another woman. Freud had volunteered from her hospital at Wimereux and now greeted them with her usual careful intensity. She was still a grave personage. The theatrical Karla Freud remained hidden. But she joined Honora, Leo, and Sally at a table in the ferry from Boulogne to Dover.

So, said Honora, there's ten days of muck up and then we're chucked in the deep end.

As long as a person can keep afloat, said Freud, the deep end's the right place.

Freud's eyes glimmered with the promise of pride.

So I'm very happy, she announced. And I'm happy to see you too.

She seemed almost like the old Freud, and was pleased too when they met up with her again in their London hostel—the grand Palmers Lodge at Swiss Cottage. The location was stimulating—Piccadilly and Green Park just a short train ride away, with Fortnum & Mason and its fancy tearooms, and then a stroll on to the theatres of the West End!

An English officer with sleeve ornamentations—which showed he belonged to an ancient British regiment that probably fought at Waterloo, if not Agincourt—had spoken to them before the show and insisted on bringing them champagne at the interval. This gave him the indulgence to wink at his companion officers and ask, This is a British show, this one. Isn't it?

They were attending a performance of *Chu Chin Chow*, a phenomenon of the stage, it was said. They had let build in themselves a nationalist radiance at their connection with the most famous show in the West End—for the author and leading actor–singer was Oscar Ashe, an Australian. This was the show men were advised they had to see in case they were killed before their next leave. The War Chest Club across from the Australian Headquarters on Horseferry Road had bought up the tickets and sold them cheaply to those on leave. The only disadvantage to visiting Horseferry Road with its ugly barrage balloons floating in its grimy sky was that yellow-faced munitions girls—pretty despite the tinge the picric acid in the shells they made gave their complexions—waited around there to make extra money out of the young Australians emerging with their leave pay. But the benefits of Horseferry Road and the War Chest Club included the cut-price delight they were now enjoying at His Majesty's Theatre. They behaved like girls who hadn't seen the apocalypse. That was the way the soldiers behaved too. They shared a box of chocolates between them—Freud and Honora and Sally, Leo having been taken out to a dinner by Captain Fellowes. They absorbed the fantastical shifts of light and scenery and let the music reduce the world and its clamor to a string of gloriously vacuous tunes and primitive sentiment.

And then, this champagne in the interval. Honora rebuffed the offer of supper from a young officer. Lionel Dankworth—the angular and kindly soul from Lemnos—was due for leave and would come and meet her in London. This put her in hectic spirits.

And so the enchantments of the evening played themselves out and the officers took them to supper collectively—all on the strength of their sharing a continent of birth with Mr. Ashe.

Freud joined them again the next day for a meal at Mrs. Rattigan's Anzac Buffet in Victoria Road—Mrs. Rattigan kept a separate dining room for nurses but made officers and men mess in together. They were all sitting in the lounge afterwards to discuss whether they ought to take the ferry up the Thames to Hampton Court when they saw Sergeant Kiernan across the room engrossed in a copy of the *New Statesman*. Except that Kiernan was now an officer, with his hat and swagger stick on the chair beside him. They moved en masse to greet him, though Sally noticed that in approaching even decent fellows a darkness—something other than complexion—came forth in Freud's eyes.

Well, said Honora. What's a Quaker doing dressed up as a lieutenant?

He rose. He looked well in his uniform—plain as it was and issued by a quartermaster. It was certainly a variation from those of the men they'd met last night. It owed everything to standard issue and little to Bond Street.

Ah, he said, with lowered eyes and a smile which was not quite apologetic. I've joined the respectable classes.

He raised his face then and looked directly at them in turn. He said, All the women of the poor old *Archimedes*.

All the poor old women of the *Archimedes*, Honora corrected him.

Nonsense, he said. You all look marvelous. Have you sung for the mess, Nurse Freud?

I've lost the knack for singing, Freud told him, closing off that subject.

Sally asked him how he had been elevated to this eminence, a first lieutenant. *Two* pips on his shoulder. Would you call it a battlefield promotion? she asked him.

No, he said, I'd prefer you didn't. I was working at a casualty clearing station at Pozières and we all ran out of equipment and dressings. Everyone cursed the supply officer and there were complaints that he left the regimental aid posts and dressing stations even worse off. I spoke frankly to a surgeon about it. Next I knew they sent me on a two-month course in England. Here I am. Medical supply officer for a casualty clearing station.

They wondered aloud which one, and he told them.

What bad luck, said Honora.

Theirs bore a different number.

But maybe you could come across to us someday and give us lessons in French history or something else as grand.

I'll be too busy with my stores. All those lovely bandages, all that potassium manganate.

The tail of his coat bubbled and seemed a little short on him as he murmured with laughter.

My boat train leaves this afternoon, he said. Yours, I take it, doesn't. You don't look like women about to go back.

He gathered his hat and the unaccustomed stick. He didn't make a convincing officer. The others went out into the vestibule with surprisingly little comment.

He asked Sally, I wondered where your sister was?

It's a simple address, she said. The Australian Voluntary Hospital, Château Baincthun, via Boulogne.

She spelled Baincthun for him.

That afternoon—probably by the same boat which would then return Kiernan to France—Lionel Dankworth was arriving in London. He had booked a room in a hotel near Victoria Station and had written to Honora asking her to invite them all to come as his guests to a supper for which he had reserved a private dining room. So the afternoon

ahead lay glowing with possibility. Amidst a horde of Australian and
Canadian soldiers, they prowled Westminster Abbey looking for the
tombs of the renowned. The busts and elegant slabs and the remembrance plaques didn't seem to them to be a promise of death, but
called up ideas of an amiable world—one balanced between life and
an appropriate vanishing remote from the disorder and imbalance of
where they came from.

They got to the hotel in Victoria around six o'clock. Lionel Dankworth was already there—waiting for them in a tearoom and accompanied by two friends. Honora ran up and as he rose gave him an
intense, unembarrassed, almost motherly hug while his hands wan-
dered uncertainly around her shoulders. They all went off then to the
private dining room, where a massive table was set amidst walls heavily padded with velvety scarlet wallpaper. Lionel distributed his two
fellow soldiers amongst the women. They were lieutenants from his
company. It didn't take too many seconds of slack conversation for
their eyes somehow to wander off as if they were all at once reminded
of something they had to do the next day and which mustn't be forgotten. After the soup—a lobster bisque—Lionel was urged to his feet by
Honora, who sat beside him. As he did it, she merrily tapped a knife
against a glass to call for order. He was tall but had filled out at the
shoulders, a man of obvious command yet one who was nonetheless
nervous for the moment.

Ah, he said.

There was a gap during which he looked at the table setting in front
of him.

I take this liberty, he continued, or at least Honora told me to take
it, because she was of the opinion that the speech ought to be delivered now instead of after the beef.

He coughed.

This means she wants her life settled on course earlier than it
would have been if we had followed the normal pattern and waited for
one more dish to be served.

They all gave an anticipatory laugh.

As she rightly said, we Australians don't tend to follow the set-down pattern. So I just wanted to announce on my own behalf but above all that of my very beautiful friend here, Miss Slattery, that we are from this moment engaged. And therefore doomed to marriage. Or at least I should hope we are.

He produced a ring from one of the huge pockets of his uniform jacket and lifted her hand and put the ring in place. Everyone in the room stood and applauded. For Honora could look after herself in a marriage, Sally believed. Honora radiated a sense of achievement and raised herself as high as she could and kissed Dankworth's mouth through closed lips. This kiss seemed to signal the end of all furtiveness. It also exposed Dankworth's mashed but functional ear to their gaze, but there was chastity in those closed lips. The two were mobbed with warm wishes and congratulations as, one by one, their friends came up to them. Honora began to weep.

After the beef, Honora ate her flummery left-handed so that the ring could be seen and to enable her to hold on to Dankworth's hand with her right.

At the end of the evening—after they had waited in the lobby to allow Honora and Lionel a little while on a secluded ottoman to exchange a few sentiments and further embraces—Honora went back with them by cab to what she called Hardtack Castle—Palmer's Lodge was named after Samuel Palmer who, with Mr. Huntley, produced the tooth-breaking biscuits consumed at the front.

At the Peak of All Mad Things

These were even more bitter days at Château Baincthun as—with less hope than the previous year, but with a few shared and dutiful toasts offered in the messes, and one uttered in Erse by Doctor Airdrie—1917 began. It became apparent quite suddenly that the work and the winter were wasting Matron Mitchie. Her presence as well as her frame had thinned. Naomi saw her display irritability at the English Roses over wounds that had not been dressed for two days. It was partly a sense of impotence, a flare of frustration. Mitchie could not get around all the wards in a day. The gardens and paths between the house and the hut wards were so frozen that only sure-footed nurses and patients could walk there. Sometimes in the bleakness and transfixing cold, honest snow fell and consoled the earth—but blocked Mitchie further.

In this dim light and under the breath of what everyone said was the worst winter in this modern century, nothing had color and everything was demanding. And in the midst of such an undistinguished day, as Naomi supervised debridement and irrigation and the massage and anointing of lamed men, an orderly came to tell her there was a telephone call for her downstairs.

Access to the telephone seemed less strictly regulated under Lady Tarlton's regimen than it would have been in general hospitals. Here it was taken as a given that boyfriends on leave could briskly inform this or that frost-nipped, red-cheeked young woman of the Red Cross or this or that Australian nurse that they were in the locality. But when Naomi descended to the august telephone in the hallway, she feared for Sally. She had got a note about the casualty clearing station business from her sister and it sounded safe only by a margin.

Hello, Kiernan here, said the voice she heard. You might remember me? I am a most accomplished ship's newspaper editor.

Sergeant Kiernan?

His voice had that old color in it and the spaciousness of a translucent ocean.

Are you well? he asked.

Yes. A little cold.

Of course. Are you overworked?

Everyone here is. But you?

Things have changed a little with me, he told her. And your sister does not approve. I met her in Horseferry Road, and she and her friends were very judgemental. You see, I have accepted the King's commission. But I'm totally unconvincing in the role, so maybe that excuses it.

He told her that he was on his way to be supply officer at a casualty clearing station. Sadly, a different one than Sally would be attached to.

But, he continued, of course nothing is distant from anywhere else here. Did you know the entire British line is barely more than a hundred and twenty miles? Melbourne to Beechworth?

A great deal of slaughter in a little space, she agreed.

Just the same, the roads up there are impossible. So in effect that makes distances greater. I'm in Boulogne right now with most of the officers and men of my unit. What we're waiting for, I don't know. But I wondered if I could come there and take you for a picnic? It may need, however, to be indoors.

There was no clearly viable picnic place inside or outside the château. It was agreed they would meet in Boulogne. Somehow she switched shifts with the most senior of the Red Cross women. When Lady Tarlton was asked to ratify the matter, she insisted on providing the big black-and-white car Mitchie and Naomi had once been so overwhelmed by. And—of course—the middle-aged Private Carling to drive it.

Naomi dressed in every item of her gray-skirted, gray-jacketed and overcoated uniform she could put on. Her gloves were ungainly but necessary. She regretted her button-up shoes would leave her feet a little cold. But to such a meeting—to which she looked forward so much—she could not wear gumboots or borrow cavalry ones.

Kiernan was waiting at the British Officers' Club in Boulogne. Carling had a hard time getting there since fog had blotted out the country roads that led to it. The occasional wagon with its hunched farmer atop would appear out of the mist to test Carling's braking and heart. But once in town the aged private knew precisely where the club was. He said he would be waiting for her from three o'clock, but she was not to hurry. For, he said, she'd worked too hard and was entitled to a little time to herself.

Kiernan was sitting in a chair in the lobby of the club and reading a small, leather-bound book from the club's library. He put it in one of his jacket pockets—they were baggy enough to serve as a traveling library. As he had promised, he had all the looks of a man who'd been promoted from the ranks, including an awkward uniform. And his greatcoat—when the elderly Frenchman behind the desk fetched it—was the normal, graceless Australian army greatcoat.

Would you like a *moules* and fish place? Or would you prefer beef?

In this weather, said Naomi—of course remembering her meal with Airdrie—I suggest beef.

My exact instinct, he said. I've asked the concierge about a good place. Can you stand a walk?

Out in the dim day they spent their time further informing each other of their careers since they had last met. The phenomenon of Lady Tarlton figured large in Naomi's account.

I have nothing to tell you in return, said Kiernan, that isn't banal. But are you engaged yet to that pleasant fellow—Shaw, was it?

Of course not, she said.

That "Of course not" emerged from her barely without thought. She knew at once she didn't want any idea of engagement to Robbie Shaw to make Kiernan too respectful or distant. So now it was apparent. How criminal that she hadn't told Shaw himself definitely yet! How criminal if she didn't do it as soon as she was back at the Voluntary.

He said, I'm sorry if the question was an intrusion.

The restaurant recommended by the porter at the club proved a long walk past bleak parkland. He apologized maybe once too often. But she emphasized she was happy. And she was. They saw the sea and the wet beach stretching out to a barely visible tide. A Blighty boat making its slow way out there was rendered black in outline by the uncooperative light of the day. This was all no better climatically than the day Dr. Airdrie had taken her to town. But it was different in every other aspect.

They reached a hotel she knew from her French experience could be called "Third Empire" and climbed the stairs to the warmth of its restaurant. The windows were opaque with mist but a fire raged in the inglenook and the light was warm. There was a surprising crowd of people here. Many but not all were soldiers. She and Kiernan were taken to their table by a plump, confident, full-bosomed woman who seemed part of the room's grace. Naomi felt a sudden enthusiasm for conversation that the day outside had not encouraged.

So you've gone from the ranks to first lieutenant, she remarked as they were seated.

Oh, yes, your sister noted that too. But it was thought that a supply officer must of necessity have a certain authority.

Do you like it? Military rank in itself? Be honest now.

Do you like being a matron? Sally says you do.

I am only a matron by default. My rank is still that of staff nurse.

He thought a while. Actually, I do like a little rank, he decided.

For its own sake?

Almost certainly. Vanity of vanities . . . Quite a confession that is, isn't it? But the eye of God doesn't penetrate this mist.

Has your rank changed the way you talk to people though?

I always thought we talked well. But it's true that rank changes things a lot. That's why some men reject it. Better men than me have done so.

They may know they won't have power over shrapnel and the rest, whether they're commissioned or not, she argued.

Yes, but they have power before the bullet hits.

Look, she said, relenting, Don't let me tease you. I know why you took your commission. So you have more power to do sensible things. But what interests me is whether you'd have asked me to lunch without those two pips on your shoulder?

Well, I wouldn't have had the easy means to call your château. I would have had to get a lift out there. Or walked. But I would certainly have come.

This skirted the edge of a particular kind of intention. It was—she was surprised to find—a not unwelcome one.

But now, he said, I must splash around my lieutenant's pay while I have it. It is an honor to flash it around on such a lunch as we are— *Deo gratias*—about to receive. And—this is not only understood but normal—my shout!

Naomi nodded. I'll accept, she told him, because we don't often get paid out there at Baincthun. They want us to come to Boulogne to sign for it.

Maybe you should call into the pay depot this afternoon, he suggested, winking.

When had winks joined his repertoire?

A man came with a board of special dishes but they ordered the soup and then the pork with cider. A specialty of Normandy, the waiter assured them.

The Normandy beyond the windowpanes today looked as though it totally lacked specialty.

Would you like wine? Kiernan asked. I am afflicted with teetotalism.

I believe I can get through lunch without Bordeaux, she said.

They ordered Vichy water. The waiter left.

I was delighted to meet your sister in London, Kiernan told her. Because you have been on my mind since I left the hospital ship in Melbourne. That article you wrote remained with me. It showed . . .

He gestured, looking for a definition.

It showed a spirit, he decided. A humane wisdom.

And then you went and got it published in the *Herald*, she complained.

And the *Age*. But that wasn't me. Maybe it was one of the chaplains.

But you know I hate praise.

I do. You always say, "I'm a cow-cocky's daughter!" As if it gives you an exemption or something.

It ought to, she assured him. So before we get on to all the flattery men seem to think a meal in a restaurant requires, let me warn you off. It's obvious to me that you are an educated man. You are far above me in every aspect. I am—apart from nursing—untutored. "Humane wisdom." My God! Please, don't *you* start on all that stuff.

She was halfway joking—or being serious in a way that sounded falsely stern. She both meant what she said and feared driving him off. There *was* a kind of flattery she wanted. But she couldn't define or imagine what it was.

He spotted the emphasis in "don't *you* start."

Other people have started on what you call "all that stuff" then?

Not many. But you ought to know better. I can see you're still working yourself up to the usual stuff men go on with at the sight of a menu. And I don't want you to. That's straight. You are a friend. Be a friend and don't carry on.

I am a Friend, he said. With a capital *F*. Lady Tarlton's family—the Hennings—were Quakers too. Did you know that? What she's doing is typical Quaker work.

I'm not sure she's Quaker anymore. I've seen she likes gin.

I speak of a tradition, he said. The Society of Friends is a very broad church and sometimes it takes in gin. But—getting back to the start— you must face that what you wrote about the *Archimedes* gave honor to those who drowned. Apart from that, I know you are a good nurse. These things are *not* nothing. They are *not* a vacancy. And I know you don't like it, but there *is* reserve. It is a reserve of temperament, I know. But it also comes from experience. So that's about it. You can start chastising me again.

She smiled—delighted with what he said—and shook her head.

About Robbie Shaw . . . I seem to have been maneuvered into saying half yeses to him. I've been weak about it. If a person could re- main engaged forever and satisfy a fellow, that's what I'd do—as a pure favor. Of course, when he's present—and he has a strong presence—it all comes close to making sense. But overall it makes no sense at all.

Their meal arrived—served with a certain incomprehension on the waiter's part that anyone would eat such a dish without accompanying wine. But Boulogne was used—as a Channel port—to dealing with eccentric and wrongheaded British behavior. They ate with a winter ravenousness and went on to *sauce anglaise* and then had coffee. Out- side, the day drew in haggardly upon itself. Carling would be coming soon.

Naomi tried to get to Boulogne to see Lieutenant Kiernan every two or three days during the next ten while he and his medical unit remained there. Since she didn't want anyone remarking on her journeys, she would often wait at the gate by the road of frozen mud for a French farmer driving his wagon of produce into the city.

Allez-vous à Boulogne, Monsieur? she would ask. She did not even know if she had the phrase right. On the last of her three visits she was given a lift by two Tommies, who appeared out of the mist driving a khaki tractor. Glowing with anticipation in the freezing air, she arrived in town standing on part of its superstructure.

During their meetings thus far they had not touched each other except to shake hands. At this farewell meeting she agreed to walk with him in weather still not suited to it. For privacy's sake they stayed outdoors and spent an hour and a half standing at the sea wall above the high tide, listening to the waves slap and rattle the shingle below them. Utter craziness—to stand and talk in such a grim bowl of half light above a grim ocean. Yet it was also perfect. They had the opaqueness and the cold to themselves. Their shoulders in overcoats touched—there was a degree too of half-intended pressure involved on both their parts. When contact with a man was managed at such a pace—a shadow of a quarter-inch at a time—it seemed it would take a lifetime before there was anything like an honest holding. Things must be moved along, she concluded for the first time in her life. Kiernan could not be trusted to do it at the pace the times demanded.

Before she could he gave her further motive. He said he was un-sure—as everyone was—about future leaves. But—though it was not his business—he would come back and find out how she stood with her prospective fiancé.

I'll be posting a letter on that matter, she said.

To me? he asked with all the teasing leisure of the implicitly cho-sen man.

If I'm to write to you, I'll need your address.

"Third Australian Casualty Clearing Station" would find me, he as-sured her. Oh, and you'd better add "France." Though we might be in Belgium for all I know.

I'll be telling Robbie Shaw, said Naomi out into the fog, that I've decided I can't condemn him or me to all that misery and disappoint-ment just because of some sense of honor.

Ah, he murmured—and coughed.

Stuck for words are you? she said. Usually you fellows want to make all the declarations and use all the adjectives.

There are many adjectives I'd like to use. But you've warned me off.

Well, then, I'll do the job. You are a noble soul, Kiernan. I would in fact go nearly anywhere for you. I don't mean where you're going now. I mean generally and for good.

He coughed. Good gracious, he said. Give me a moment. I'm out-flanked and flustered.

He kissed her cheek and she turned and kissed his—a kiss far more rationed on both their parts than she would have preferred.

Gosh, he said. We've still got time to have champagne.

This is enough, she told him. Anyone could have champagne!

They listened for traffic on the promenade. Since there was none, they crossed it clamped close by held elbows. They came again to the apartments, hotels, restaurants, and shops along the front. He kissed her on the point of the cheek and at greater length.

It *is* quite a changed world indeed, he told her, in which women have the courage to say what must be said.

She had to return to duty. He signaled a cab that emerged from mist. They traveled together through its opaque grayness to Château Baincthun. The cab would need to take Kiernan back to town, and she told its driver to stop at the gate. Kiernan seemed to understand she did not want to take him further. She wanted him to be secret yet. She chose to arrive alone at the château—she knew mist would protect her as she approached it up the frozen driveway under the en-hanced murk of the elms. He went a few steps with her and kissed her again in a way she considered more satisfactory and which promised less cautious experiments eventually. He murmured, There is nothing a person can say at a moment like this.

Lingering around is hard, she agreed. But wait a minute anyhow.

She contemplated his face.

I wish I was French. Then I could pray to the Virgin for your safety.

Sadly, it hasn't helped the French. And, as you know, I am a man of the rear.

You almost sound as if you wish you weren't.

Young men feel the pull of self-immolation. If they didn't, none of this would be happening and the château here wouldn't be full.

Well, maybe you should go now, she said. Because the conversation's straying.

You must let me know when you hear from Captain Shaw.

The last contact was the best. She felt the pressure of his arms and the potential pressure and mass of his body. The only way to deal with this pleasure was—when it ended—to give him a small and playful push. He vanished into the cab, and she saw him go. He looked at her through the near-opaque oval rear window of the taxi. Mist consumed the vehicle but then she was held in place by its receding sound. That soon vanished from the air and she walked on crackling ground up to the architectural grimness and cold corridors of the château.

Her letter to Robbie Shaw—already written and addressed to his barracks in Brisbane, but not sent for lack of moral courage, waited amongst the pages of Baroness Orczy's *A Bride of the Plains*. The letter read:

Dear Robbie,

I should certainly have taken up a pen to write this earlier than now. I have very much enjoyed our long exchange of letters but—as you see from mine—I have resisted all ideas of a formal engagement and have warned you of my misgivings. Yet I have also delayed from cowardice in telling you this—that I cannot convince myself of the image of me you've manufactured in your head. Since I think we are such different people, you and I are setting ourselves for a great blunder which could ruin both our lives. I will certainly fail you and you will be embittered. Even were we amongst other people on social occasions there would be a problem. You are so at ease—you showed that on Lemnos. Whereas I'm edgy. People would say I was aloof and partly blame you for it. I know above all that we must step down from these delusions we both have.

I have to tell you—and I know a man of your cleverness would realize this—my decision has nothing to do with your injury which makes you look valiant anyhow and a true hero, and adds to your style.

As for the rest, it's my devout hope that you've come to the same conclusion as I have . . .

Towards the end of their England leave, Sally persuaded Honora and Leo that they should visit Eric Carradine at his hospital in Sudbury in Suffolk. They did so in the same mist which had hidden and aided Naomi in Boulogne. Freud decided to come too. They traveled in a gritty train in blind countryside and walked a mile and a half from the railway station to the gates of the military hospital. It was—like all such places—surrounded by therapeutic grounds and gardens. But the cold had driven everyone into the central fortress of the hospital itself. They were shown into a sitting room by a British army nurse, and anticipated they would find Lieutenant Carradine better than when they had last seen him in Egypt nearly a year before. When he was brought in in a wicker wheelchair with a blanket over his knees, the four of them stood and automatically smiled. But there was no smile on Lieutenant Carradine's lips.

Elsie? he said in a high-pitched voice. Are you Elsie's friends?

They said they were and introduced each other. They mentioned that they had met in the convent hospital in Alexandria. He seemed to take all this in. Please, he said, sit and pull your chairs closer.

A little puzzled, they all sat. Closer, he ordered them. And when they'd done it whispered, This is a terrible place, you know. You mustn't give them a thing. An inch and they take a mile. Where's that bitch Elsie anyhow?

Don't you remember? asked Sally, trying to hide her discomfort. They sent her to Australia. But she intends to get back to you as a volunteer.

Taking her sweet time about it, he said, and howled. How's a man expected to endure France after this? But I thought Elsie might have *another* man, you know. Did I read that somewhere? I think I read it. The *Daily Mail* . . .

The British nurse—who had remained—said, Most days Lieutenant Carradine is quite a lot better than this. Sometimes you're fine,
aren't you, Lieutenant Carradine? He doesn't remember his bad
spells. But when he's better I'll tell him you were here. He won't remember, I'm afraid.

She saw them out, leaving Eric Carradine still sitting in his wicker
chair. Better not tell his wife you found him like this, the nurse suggested. Because he will improve in the end. He'll probably always have
an occasional bad day though.

The Australian casualty clearing station at Deux Églises lay on the
gentle western slope of a minute hill—streaked with snow and blind
to any approaching enemy. It was as yet a settlement of tents and huts.
A north–south road ran at its base, and its sides were bordered by two
others running east and towards the battlefield. The modest outline of
the village of Deux Églises—marked by two small spires above bare
trees—lay within sight to the north.

Closer to the village stood another clearing station—British. For
clearing stations had been envisaged as working like twins, and the
theory was that when one was full of its misery, the other one—empty
till now—would then begin to receive. They would breathe in and out
in alternate rhythm.

The noise of guns was not simply a louder but sharper spur here.
You felt sometimes you could detect in the massed sound—like an
instrument in a band—the frightening malice of an individual shell,
nearer and more particular in its intentions. Sally noticed that not all
the nurses were threatened by the noise. They heard it as a clamorous
promise of what would come to harvest in the approaching season.
Once again—for them—*this* year was the year. But last summer had
cured Sally of looking for too much from the returning sun.

For Sally and for others preparing the station for business, doubt
came with the news that the tsar had fallen and Russia was as good
as beaten. Russia from where, said Freud, one of her grannies came,

and was pleased to do so. The tsar was not an admirable man in the book of the Freuds. Other opinion in the nurses' mess reasoned the Germans had still to keep their watch on the Eastern Front and that the Royal Navy had choked off German supplies for the west. Various soldiers they knew who had captured enemy dugouts said you could see how poor the supplies Fritz ate were compared to the good old days of the previous spring. And, said the This-Year-Is-It party, last year had indeed been bloody. But much had been learned.

A late winter letter from Charlie Condon found her. Charlie made no attempt to be prophetic about the war. He wrote a great deal about climate. The mud had frozen and the earth was suddenly ripe for sketching, he wrote, the black craters rimmed with snow. The air had cleared the week before, and an abnormal sun had appeared and the atmosphere had become vacant of gas—which cured everyone of the croaking tendencies they got from the usual lingering of the fumes. No slush lay in the trenches, which were frozen firm. Men had worked out that the regular puttees cut off circulation to their feet and caused frostbite, said Charlie. They were now using sandbags for gaiters. He liked these practical fellows, he said. Most of them had had hard lives. Yet one of them was a young Presbyterian minister who put up with the swearing of the others and did himself tend in that direction. There were some miners from the Hunter Valley who said they were communists and communism was the way of the future. The Irish— the Kellys and Byrnes and so on—were pugnacious and prideful but said the rosary like children every evening.

That was the sort of thing Condon wrote—not things to be embroidered on battle flags, or promises of an early close. Charlie defined a state of being and that somehow consoled Sally more than the hollow assurances she heard from others. The Kellys brawling and the miners arguing politics made the trench like something domestic and tedious. That was what—for Charlie's sake—she wanted it to be.

• • •

A convoy of Ford motor ambulances arrived outside the admissions ward on the very first evening at Deux Églises and before all was ready. Duckboards were not yet laid down in the big marquee t o make a floor. The question of how many cots were needed was still being debated between the chief medical officer, Major Bright, and the matron—a seasoned-looking, robust woman named Bolger. From the numbers of ambulances appearing that night on the frozen road outside, it was now clear that if this was the season to let the armies settle into their miserable lines and simply outwait the cold, the generals had not taken the message.

In the great bare-floored admissions marquee, the neatly made little man Major Bright, wearing a surgical coat, moved about energetically with the ward doctor and inspected the men laid down on cots or on the ground. Bright walked around the tent of perhaps forty stretchers giving brisk instructions for the disposal of the stretchers. He needed to clear the tent so another forty or more could be brought in.

For the early phases of arrivals, a large number of the nurses, including Sally as a ward sister, were there to deal with what must be dealt with at once—hemorrhage or agony or the coldness of shock. Other nurses waited in the wards beyond this great tent in which the needs of the harmed would be decided. So from their tables stocked with medical equipment—from dressings to opiates to hypodermics and sphygmomanometers for blood pressure, which in the stretcher cases who had survived the ambulance might well be diving fatally—nurses moved under the measured orders of Major Bright, calm Matron Bolger, and the ward doctor to inject morphine or to fill in names and conditions and dosages and the ward destination of each case. Orderlies carried the uniforms and kit taken from the wounded and hurled them into the tented gear room attached to the main marquee, which was drenched in electric light from a generator thundering outside.

Some men brought into the reception tents were found by this hard light to have died on their stretchers and were taken out to the morgue shed. The gray, ageless, unseamed faces of the chest or stomach wounded raised in Sally the ridiculous but angry question of why they had been carried so far to die, as if the surgeons further forward at the main dressing stations—and the stretcher bearers—had deliberately passed them down the line rather than deal with the deaths themselves.

A small mess annex opened out within the marquee. The walking wounded—wearing tags which said "D"—were given hot tea and cocoa. Men with "NYD(S)"—the "S" signifying not physical but psychic shock—pinned to their uniforms by dressing station doctors stood shuddering amongst the walking but could not be trusted with scalding fluid.

On the main floor there was an attaching of labels. Bright and the ward doctor moved about allocating "A," "B," and "C" to the stretcher cases—but other labels were also attached—with notations reading "Urgent," "Abdomen," "Chest," "Spine." Sally remembered having read such scrawled notes pinned to men arriving in Rouen. A nurse must admire the system, though it was one whose structure was under great pressure from the time the first raving head-wound case was laid on a cot or the ground and a deathly abdominal case was placed beside him, and staff nurses rushed in to stem sudden hemorrhaging.

Sally found herself taken back also to the *Archimedes*—the fetidness of uniforms or bits of them—and the stink from souring blood and that general stench of wounds turning towards sepsis or gangrene or gas gangrene. There was also the threat of panic in the air, lacking at tidier Rouen.

Supervising the movement of the nurses and having now the eminence of being a sister—the subaltern of a matron—Sally had asked to be appointed to the resuscitation ward up the slight slope towards the tent she shared with Honora and Leo and Freud. Her motives—apart from the fact that new methods were used there—were not fully apparent to her. As soon as men began to be taken there she would need to leave the admissions tent and go with them.

The night outside—when she left the admissions hut—carried intimations of madness. There were continuing barrages at the front and planes could be heard overhead. Sally had charge of two young staff nurses who walked with strange calmness beside the stretcher of a chest wound being carried by orderlies to resuscitation. His blood pressure had plummeted and they were in a hurry to get him into a place of floorboards and stoves. They laid him on a bed and piled on the blankets. Sally cannulated his arm while the young nurses set up a frame and hung from it a saline solution they connected by tubing into the vein. The orderlies then covered his body with a canopy to retain all warmth. A little double Primus burner with a metal dampener on top of it to give safety to its flame was lit by an orderly and placed in a concave space at the bed end. And now all else must wait. A ward doctor appeared and the canopy was lifted so that he could consider the man's pulse and ponder whether he would need to give the patient blood by transfusion. Plasma was promised, he said, but had not yet arrived.

Sally was busy in the resuscitation tent for twelve timeless hours. By then the numbers to do with wound shock—the expectations of anyone working there—had been established. There had been seven who could not be revived and eighteen sent on to surgery—where their fate would be a matter of margins. Four cases remained in the ward—their organs plugging along on the fuel of low blood oxygen.

She connected a healthy orderly's blood flow into that of a threatened case through a glass connector tube. She saw lesser wounded men turn up to ask reverent questions about some of those the resuscitation ward had handled. And then it all stopped. Nearly everyone except some thoracic cases had left for the base hospitals by ambulances. More patients might come that night. But until then there could be sleep.

The name that Sally began to hear this time from the walking and those with conscious speech left to them was Bullecourt. The parents of soldiers would not have heard of it. A month before, soldiers themselves would not have heard of it, or that the village of that name had been subsumed into the great defensive line named after Prussian General Hindenburg. Nor was Bullecourt over swiftly. A number of crowded convoys had arrived at Deux Églises and been "cleared," the men sent off with their records and X-rays. But still three Australian divisions—amongst whose numbers were Lionel Dankworth and Charlie Condon—were in place there and ready to advance again.

There were other meaningless names she would hear from the shocked and the wounded—from that portion of them that was talkative. Le Barque and Thilloy, Bapaume and Malt Trench, Lagnicourt and Ecoust, Doignes and Louverval. Time accelerated at Deux Églises. The passage of men, the evacuation of most cases by motor ambulances lined up in the lane or on the road to Deux Églises—all that had become a rhythmic phenomenon. The relief came on nights when there were fewer arrivals, or even from the closure for a day or so of the station.

Nurses were in the meantime rotated ward to ward—the aim being that they would learn all the medical functions of this endless war. Freud clung to her theatre work—assisting a Captain Boyton from Chicago who had become a member of the Royal Medical Corps to honor his British mother and who had somehow ended up with the Australians.

Outside the mess, orderlies dug slit trenches in case of air raids, and a capacious bomb shelter. The bombers people called Taubes groaned across the sky at night and sought some site or town or artillery park suitable for an exercise of their malice.

Men now arrived clogged with the season's mud and in tunics rendered solid by it. It was a malodorous mud in which rats had feasts at corpses and which was saturated by gas. In the fields about the clearing station the flowers were not yet out, and the screen of trees which protected Deux Églises were only beginning to leaf. So all the vaunted European spring had to offer was this heinous sogginess. It was therefore out of the mire that a dread letter for Honora came.

His battalion adjutant wrote that Lionel and a section of his company had occupied a forward position—a sort of listening post—

overnight. They had got hemmed in there by machine-gun fire. The next day they were seen by the enemy, attracting artillery shelling during which Captain Dankworth was killed with some of his men. Survivors returned by night to the Australian lines. They brought back his pay book. He had been gallant and affable and universally liked, the letter said.

It was at least two days before Honora gave the others the letter to read. With set lips Slattery had continued her work—levelly and without any irascibility. Now she was dry-eyed and rather dismissive of friends such as Karla and Sally when they tried to find the condoling words. There was an unspoken ban on them paying her any added tokens of comfort and concern than were usual in an average crisis. There were living and barely living to be attended to. So get out of my way!—that was Slattery's implied message. For I have a job to do in public and a shrine to tend in secret.

Major Bright had her to his office. Bright told her that there was an office run by a young Australian woman in London. A Red Cross volunteer—the daughter, in fact, of a former Australian prime minister. The woman's office was called the Australian Casualty Information Bureau. It would investigate the details about Lionel Dankworth's fate to the best of its ability, said Bright, and report back to her.

Both Major Bright and Honora wrote off to the bureau as the spring really did become spring and hollyhocks and foxgloves grew in the fields between the clearing station and the village. This was a time when on rare free days picnics could be attended—for Major Bright was a great picnic man and organized one for most Sundays, whether he could join it or not.

While Honora waited for an answer, certain delusions afflicted her. One mealtime she told Sally there was every hope Lionel was alive. She had written to his battalion commander who had assured her Lionel's body had been intact. He had not been blown apart—though chunks of shell had entered his body. The Germans—who had advanced the next day—might have found and tended him. For despite all the guff,

she assured Sally, they were as humane as we were. And they could
have brought Lionel round. But since the men had returned his pay
book, and because the identity disks did not always stand up to the
heavy conditions of the front, the Red Cross beyond the German lines
might not know who he was and would not know whom to tell. Or
else, Lionel might be suffering from amnesia or cerebral inflammation
from the concussion of the shell. So Honora now took on at the same
time the weight both of grief and of hope. In fact, hope gleamed in her
like a fever. Sally and Freud watched this with frowns and mumbled
words of caution. But she could not be dissuaded from the likelihood
of something having saved Lionel.

There was a new recklessness in her too. In speech, the barriers
which had existed now broke down. They had been lovers, Honora
said. She had succumbed to the argument that God would understand
if those who were tagged for death took a few hours to love. You can
depend on a nurse to know the proper precautions, she told them
frankly, but my period is regular only in its absence—what does that
do to us, I wonder? But I wouldn't want to know a God who would
judge. I'm even a little saddened by the care we took. We should have
let things happen as they may. Because up there where the men are,
things happen without anyone's permission every second of every day.

Just above the nurses' tents—amongst the wildflowers—nurses off
shift sat in deck chairs with their faces southwards towards the sun.
Here Honora wrote a further letter expounding her theory to the Australian Casualty Bureau. But the same day she got one from the young
woman who ran that office.

We have received an unofficial report from a man in the infantry
battalion to which Captain Dankworth belonged. The informant
states that on the early morning of 14 April Captain Dankworth
and the patrol he was leading were discovered and made to take
shelter in craters in No Man's Land. Captain Dankworth was
killed by a shell which landed on the edge of the crater in which

our informant also assures us—and you can take comfort in this, perhaps—the death occurred in an instant. Also killed were Lieutenant John McGregor and Corporal Sampson, whose pay books were also brought back to the Allied lines. May I assure you that the Red Cross is active in German hospitals and prison camps. But they have not discovered the presence of Captain Dankworth or of any wounded Australian carrying his name or description. Thus, for your own sake, you should not entertain hope.

Though the informant and his comrades brought back Captain Dankworth's pay book, they left on his body, which was still identifiable, not only his disks but a letter from you on which he placed great value and which was addressed to him in full by rank and first and second names. These between them would serve to guarantee him an individual grave, rather than the fate of being buried as an unknown soldier.

Nothing in the letter—which Honora willingly showed Sally—seemed to affect Honora's level of belief, or—for that matter—her work. But she was more subdued and a muted presence at the mess table. The idea of her letter in the enemy's hands was something to which she returned very often.

I don't know how I feel about my letter being read by Germans, she confessed. Oh yes, it means he will get his burial—if the woman in London's right. And I have to say she seems to be an honest woman. But there were tender feelings in there. I hope no bugger of a German intelligence officer laughs when he reads them. If *he's* lucky, he's had some poor German woman write similar stuff to him . . .

Still, at other times her idea was the letter would be read not by some German, or once Lionel Dankworth had been respectfully buried, but rather when he lay stunned in a German general hospital and recovering from oblivion an atom at a time.

Spring and All Its Follies

And now, along with the leafing of the trees, the day sky over the clearing station seemed to break out in aeroplanes. They saw German biplanes flying high and tentatively westwards and grinding at the firmament. Antiaircraft guns people called "Archies"—now moved in at the crossroads outside the village—fired at them from sandbagged redoubts either side of the large crucifix which stood there with its back to the battle. Smaller aircraft called fighters came low over the slight rise. They broke on the view like birds harried out of a copse. They coerced everyone's attention and tore away with it.

One morning a German Taube—or whatever species it was—appeared so low that those who were then in the open swore they could see the pilot and observer looking down. Sally was walking the path between her tent and the gas ward to which she had now been rotated and saw a pilot lean out of his socket in the air and wave at her. He wore a young man's larrikin grin. The observer in the other cockpit took no notice of her. But there were lethal reasons the pilot flew low. He was hunting for a target and hoping to find an installation that was not blessed with a red cross—as was the roof of the main admissions hut. Flying on, the young pilot saw the Archies, heard their first thunder, scudded by them and pushed a lever to drop two bombs—for reasons hard to explain—on Deux Églises. This was surely an error of war. There were no military columns in the streets. Deux Églises might as well have been Bungendore or Enoggera—offering nought that endangered the German Empire. While Sally flinched at the explosion, over her shoulder three aircraft wearing British insignia and with mysterious letters painted on their wings came at a predatory rate and raced low down the road to intercept the German who was still foolishly circling for evidence of his bombing success. They went at him—one higher, one level, and one lower.

They were all so close to the earth as to give Sally a sense of their impossible speed. The German aircraft now headed northeast. But it took a little time for its pilot to achieve his full, desperate pace. She heard the British machine guns prattling away loud and harsh. The German turned and dived—trying to lose himself in terrain or the trees along a canal—and the three British planes clamored on his tail. And then came a detonation that vibrated the rural air and was distinct from the artillery background. Beyond the village a cumulus of black smoke arose. The grin of the young fellow who'd waved at her was consumed by fire. Some orderlies grabbed an ambulance and raced away to bring in the two Germans, but they were both dead. And just as well—for their faces would have been smashed to fragments on impact by the coping of their cockpits and the butts of their machine guns, and the rest of them burned.

The meeting of eagles above Deux Églises—the fact the man had waved, gallant and amusing while seconds from death—showed her yet again that Charlie Condon, who possessed grace and style of a much higher order, must surely be in someone's sights. It was possible to deny it during hectic duty. But she could become immobilized for an instant on the pathways and distracted by anxiety even when entering the wards.

I have been deluding myself, Honora all at once confessed to her companions that evening at their dinner of army stew and beans and good bread. Would they search the body of a putrefying man?

Her use of the word "putrefying" shocked them. They would not have believed Honora would admit putrefaction to the catalogue of her possibilities for Lionel Dankworth. It is very likely, she said, he is buried with my letter still on him. There's something of me, of my hand. It means that he has a little monument in his pocket.

The nurses looked at each other.

Yes, said Leo, whose beloved Fellowes was working at a clearing station thirty miles off. And he'll have more monuments in the end.

At this time Germans were being brought in. Some walked. One of them—Sally would remember amidst the flux of cases—had a pitiable bayonet wound to the sternum. It crossed Sally's mind to wonder if Honora might be vengeful with them. But from what anyone saw she was businesslike and attentive in a normal sense. Why would you expect otherwise? Sally asked herself. But then she noticed that with the German walking wounded Honora sometimes briskly removed their jackets and exhaustively searched their pockets—almost as if there might be something sewn in the seams. She did not ask their permission, and they submitted to her search with a frown. She would obviously search the entire German army—all without hatred—to find the one who had her letter and thus knew Captain Lionel Dankworth's place on or beneath earth.

Naomi had not expected or wanted a reply from Robbie. But one arrived, in a Comforts Fund envelope from which she could tell it had come through the army postal services in France. Her impulse was to leave the thing unopened, but there was a sense in which she was too busy to develop any habit of delay.

> *Miss Durance,*
> *Your letter followed me from Australia from where I was finally despatched to France to be an RTO—Railway Transport Officer—and where I hoped to visit you at your posting. To say that I am disappointed is to put it very light. What I am most disappointed in is your delay in telling me to give up hope of your affection. I can only believe you when you say that my damaged gait has nothing to do with it. It is that you put off so long letting me know where*

I stand that I can't respect. You always seemed to me to be made of more forthright material. You did warn me that when I saw something in you I was fooling myself. So I can't say that you missed out on telling me to use caution.

But I must say once more—so many months! On the transport I daydreamed how we would meet up in France. Well, I was a fool. And you were not genuine with me. Since there is nothing more to be said,

I remain,
Robbie Shaw (Capt.)

There was first a rush of shame when Naomi read this. It was followed by anger at Lieutenant Shaw's moral haughtiness. He wrote as if she had as good as been engaged to him. That was his delusion. She walked the wards directing the work of the English Roses but rage would take her in the midst of sentences and she would forget their purpose.

What dosage did you say? an English Rose would ask, and Naomi would need to begin again.

But within a mere handful of hours, she was overtaken by a sense of reprieve. She had sidestepped the obvious but most lethal marriage. Kiernan had helped her do it.

As Naomi savored freedom from poor Robbie and anticipated a letter from Kiernan, Matron Mitchie had caught a cold which developed very swiftly into pneumonia. She gasped and became distressed about some jangled, fearful terror of childhood or girlhood. Or even of the *Archimedes*. The *Archimedes* must be there, Naomi was sure, in Matron Mitchie's delirium, since Naomi hadn't been able to eradicate it from her own dreams.

Doctor Airdrie was the one who diagnosed Mitchie's condition. Major Darlington also visited Mitchie and took her vital readings and weighed her general condition. Lady Tarlton sat by her bed reading softly to her while—in her own fevered privacy—Mitchie rattled away at phantoms. Even while levering herself about on walking sticks, Mitchie had mesmerized them into the belief that her energies had never been diminished. After this, Lady Tarlton muttered to Naomi, she should be sent at least to England to be built up. She should then go home, wouldn't you say?

Lady Tarlton looked like a woman due for a collapse herself. Her face had been pinched to thinness by the winter. The spring had not yet fully restored her. She remained recklessly devoted and palely beautiful. Her gloriously disordered hair flowed from the French mountaineer's cap she wore for warmth. Her arguments with generals had still taught her no subservience. She was talking about starting an Australian Club in Paris this coming summer. Because whenever the boys went to the capital from the trenches, they had to hunt around for accommodation. They were left to the mercy of the YMCA, she said, and hung around on the pavements outside estaminets and the tourist sites trying to convince themselves they were having a good time.

Lady Tarlton had been to Paris looking at buildings, seeking help from generals and making small progress. Her contempt for some of them was probably mutual, but her certainty she would override the generals of the rear was still girlish and bracing.

Floating about the wards, she was willing to talk about her battles with generals in front of anyone, and the Australians loved it—all her lambasting of the heroes of the desk. You'd think, she complained one day in that airy, nose-high, chin-jutted way of hers, I had asked them to open an Indian brothel.

Darlington remained her helpmeet. Not only did he serve his long hours in wards and perform surgery as sepsis bloomed in wounds or limbs were deformed in their healing, but he filled in forms, wrote letters, and then spent time examining tissue from the living and the dead in his pathology laboratory downstairs.

Naomi continued to meet now and then English nurses in Boulogne or Wimereux who had heard of Lady Tarlton's Australian hospital and thought of it as an amateur affair run by eccentrics. The place was rendered more laughable because gossip of the rumored love affair between Lady Tarlton and her senior surgeon was no longer confined to the château. The fact was that their own surgeons and doctors encouraged their nurses to believe Château Baincthun a farce. A nurse she met in Boulogne asked her, Isn't there a crackpot doctor there who wants you to wear a mask all the time?

It was the sort of question which called up instantaneous loyalty in Naomi. I'm sure it would be interesting for you, she said, to see his figures on sepsis.

But it had to be admitted he had the cranelike gait and the fixed eye of at least a highly argumentative fellow. He and Lady Tarlton shared that same air of having to push down walls to make the world see the self-evident things *they* saw.

Soon after Airdrie's diagnosis, Matron Mitchie's breathing grew very labored and her temperature went to a hundred and four degrees. The struggle reached a level where she should have surrendered—but of course she would not. This did not mean at all—Naomi knew—that she would live. It meant only that she was willing to endure a terrible death. There would be no sliding forth beneath an easeful cloud of morphine for Mitchie.

By the end of May, her pneumonia had broken. Now she appeared elderly. Her wrists were purple and thin and her fingers trembled as she reached for a teacup by her bed. Naomi could not be spared to sit by her for long. She was now their chief ward sister and—in fact if not in title—their matron. The idea that she should be in receipt of a matron's instead of a staff nurse's pay fortunately amused her rather than rankled. All industrial unease of that sort had been somehow washed from her soul. The reward of being prized by Lady Tarlton and trusted by Major Darlington—that's what she looked for.

At last, a letter from Kiernan!

You must forgive the delay—or at least I hope you might. I received your news about Robbie Shaw with a delight I won't disguise. I feel a devotion to you that is total. We were in the mist but utterly identified each other. Is that your impression too? If it's not, please ignore me. Here I am talking to a woman who has just liberated herself and I'm suggesting new shackles.

He then nominated dates on which he would have leave in Paris.

If my letter is not an utter mystification, would you consider the following: that we undergo a betrothal ceremony—the first step to marriage should you desire that—at the Friends' chapel in Paris? There is one, as it turns out. You may seek some other secular gesture we could make, and if that is what you would like then that is what we shall do. But the reason I suggest the Friends is because the process is thoughtful yet not binding, sensible and not loud. It strikes me that those qualities suit you. You are not a Friend, nor need you to be, nor am I attempting to make one of you. You are dearer to me than that.

If this letter is craziness in your eyes, don't feel you need to reply . . .

It was instantly apparent to Naomi that what Kiernan wanted was what she wanted. She believed in that formula—"thoughtful yet not binding, sensible and not loud." It was easy to tell Lady Tarlton she wished to meet her fiancé (the term "boyfriend" was fatuous) in Paris and that it was important to his religion that there be a ceremony of betrothal.

You have a fiancé? asked Lady Tarlton.

I've just received the suggestion by mail, said Naomi.

A ceremony? Is he Jewish? asked Lady Tarlton.

He's a member of the Society of Friends.

Quakers, she said. How fascinating. My family, of course, were Friends. I, however . . . I'm afraid I let it go. But, though human, they're not given to as much hypocrisy as the others, you understand.

Naomi took the afternoon train from Boulogne to Paris and found her way to the British Nurses' Home, which was an ornate place facing the ordered spaces of the Champs de Mars. For the purpose of betrothal, Lieutenant Kiernan had been given one day's leave and collected her—as a telegram had promised—at nine o'clock on the Sunday morning from the front of the nurses' home. She felt the unsullied and irreplaceable joy of seeing him. There was no sense in her of being conscripted for some alien ceremony. He wore a brown suit—it was the first time Naomi had seen him in civilian mode. So dressed he seemed a novelty and—even more—as if a dimension had been added to him.

I wouldn't impress them if I turned up in uniform, he told her.

Should I have worn something else?

Oh, no. Nurses are obvious noncombatants.

Their cab took them across the river. It was starting to be a splendid, still morning and the river swept away silver-green as the taxi made for the region named Montparnasse. The cab driver was not certain of which alley off the Rue de Vaugirard to drop them, but at last a point was selected and Ian helped her forth onto the pavement and paid the driver.

I think it's just along here, he reassured her when the cab was gone. This is it, I'm sure, he said, pointing down a cobbled entryway. My informant told me a double wooden door painted black.

They found such a wooden door where Ian Kiernan had expected it to be. But the rooms above it showed no sign of life. Naomi was content with the hour, and delighted simply to occupy the place beside him. They smiled at each other. She took off one of her leather gloves just because it was a warm enough day, and he lifted her bare hand and put his lips to it.

Be careful you don't catch anything, she said.

Right you are, he said, but shook his head. It's very Australian, he said, to debunk a man's kiss. I hope you won't feel obliged to do it in subsequent instances.

A spry little man of about sixty years, wearing a good-quality alpaca suit, an upright collar, a somber tie, but with kid gloves on his hands and a fashionable cane under his arm, came down the alley. He had already seen them and adopted a smile and increased his pace.

He looks like Billy Hughes, she whispered to Ian.

Sedgewick, the man said as introduction. You must be Brother Kiernan. How amazing that there are Friends in a place like Melbourne.

Naomi thought the same could be said for Paris.

I am the registering officer and the clerk for today's session. We have perhaps twenty-eight members. But sometimes we have surprise arrivals—Red Cross people who are Friends. There are also some Quaker ambulances . . . You have both brought your records? Good. Perhaps you wouldn't mind my keeping them until after the meeting.

Sedgewick unlocked one leaf of the double doors and they followed him up a steep staircase to a bare room where benches faced each other. There was no altar, no pulpit, and no enforced or pious silence. Sedgwick continued to converse. I'm afraid most of us are French, so the meeting will largely be in French. But the Committee of Clarity are all Anglophones, and obviously I include myself.

And this Committee of Clarity? asked Naomi.

Kiernan put a reproving hand to his forehead. Heavens above, he said, I didn't explain that.

He turned to Sedgewick. It sounds like the Committee of Public Safety in the French Revolution.

Sedgewick uttered a small sequence of sounds that added up to a laugh. It is a group of three, he said, who ask you merely if you are interested in each other as partners for life.

The other Friends began to arrive—modern-looking men like Ian, some older men, a number of women soberly but not unpleasantly dressed. Women's hands were kissed in the French manner. Men kissed each other on the cheek. They all welcomed Ian and Naomi in that manner and sat them on facing benches on either side of the room. Thus Naomi expected that when the service began the other women would be separated from the men. But men and women were mixed on the benches. In hers and Ian's case it was therefore a symbol of apartness—their betrothal had not become formal. There was to be a ritual distance between them.

Suddenly—and by some signal Naomi did not see—there was a silence for inner prayer.

O great God, Naomi intoned within herself, who is far beyond the battlefield, too kind to be close to it, too far to be blamed for it, take my thanks that I've been brought here by this noble man.

Someone began to speak in French. It was a man, but not Sedgewick. He went on praying for peace and brotherhood in a calm voice. A woman took up immediately after him. And then another woman— and so it went. Apart from hymn singing, she had never heard women make so much noise in church. An hour passed and betrothal had not been mentioned. At last Ian was nudged by Mr. Sedgewick and rose to progress to the middle of the floor, holding out a hand for Naomi to join him. She did so. She felt that her face blazed before these strangers.

Sedgewick stood and stated that Monsieur Panton, Madame Flerieu, Monsieur Gosselin, and he himself were the members of the Committee of Clarity on this matter. The committee swapped seats with others so that they could all sit together on a single bench. Allow us a second to study your papers, said Sedgewick.

Madame Flerieu—thin and fine boned—started a robust discussion about something. Mr. Sedgewick answered, gesturing like a Frenchman and adopting that throaty Gallic seriousness. The two other men had their say as well. At last Mr. Sedgewick looked up at the two candidates.

The question is, he explained apologetically, whether your work, Mr. Kiernan, could be seen as redeeming lives or preparing them for further military demands.

The woman—Madame Flerieu—was clearly the one who had taken this line. So, thought Naomi, this committee business is more serious than old Sedgewick implied.

I have had the same doubt myself, Ian said. I provide medical supplies and surgical equipment. There are Quaker ambulances from America working in the field and what might be said of me could be said of them as well. It is the ancient question of trying to do a small good in a devilish world.

Sedgewick appeared happy with that answer, but Madame Flerieu said in English in a reasonable but intense voice, Members of the ambulances of the Friends do not hold military ranks.

I confess that is a question to discuss, said Ian.

And Mademoiselle Durance holds a military rank. Do you not, Mademoiselle?

I work in a voluntary hospital. I believe the Australian army has forgotten me.

Sedgewick held up his hand and shook his head benignly like a man quelling unease.

And you intend to marry?

As far as Naomi could tell it was the first time anyone had actually used that verb aloud.

She said, Yes. If Ian intends to marry me.

Of course, said Kiernan. Of course I do.

At times convenient to you both, are you able to meet again with the Committee of Clarity? asked Sedgewick.

I'm sure we will make the arrangements, said Ian.

Sedgewick asked, Does Miss Durance have any concern about such a requirement?

Naomi said she did not. But—as she told them—given her duties at the Voluntary Hospital it would take some skill on both their parts to make their leaves coincide.

So it is your will before God, Ian Kiernan, to take Naomi Durance as your betrothed with a view to marriage?

Exalted by her re-creation as a woman betrothed, she heard him agree. Then Sedgewick asked Naomi the same question and afterwards she could not remember having given an answer.

So the betrothal is initiated, said Sedgewick. And may God turn his face to you.

Naomi felt in that second that the solemnity and casualness of the ceremony gave it unrivaled hope, and a sense of liberation, not of bonds. Here—in this room vacant of all but two dozen residents of France—lay a definition of marriage so particular as to mark Ian and herself off from the bad luck and ill will of other alliances. She was sure of it.

The clearing station had quickly spawned its own graveyard, which lay across the shallow valley and a few steps north towards the village in a field one side of which was a farmer's ditch. Night duty was a time when young men yielded up their souls. Orderlies carried bodies to the morgue hut from which in the morning they would be placed in coffins and carried across the Deux Églises road to the site where a padre from a unit resting out of the line—and a burial party ditto, along with a bugler or bagpiper—would give them their final rites.

Everyone seemed to take this growing crop of white crosses as a given and nothing to distract a person. Only sometimes—as the summer came on—did Sally notice in temporary shock that amongst the hollyhocks the place had grown new suburbs. Farmers and their wives ploughed and planted in the fields all about and were as indifferent to the raucousness of the front and to the field of crosses as were the nurses and orderlies.

Dr. Bright's Sunday picnics—held in a field on the slight ridge above the casualty clearing station—had grown since the spring and included English doctors and nurses from the British casualty clearing station across the road to Bapaume. Almost inevitably a surgeon from the British clearing station had brought a cricket kit. Thus Test matches— Australia versus England—were played. Nurses and middle-aged doctors leapt to catch hook shots at square leg and crouched to fumble at snicks in slips. But at least they had encountered the rich, dark soil and the irrepressible grass. Sally, however, took a big catch in the position she believed they called square leg.

Sister Durance, called Major Bright, take the slips with me.

For he was standing near the wicketkeeper.

I don't understand, said Sally.

Slips, here. I'm first slip, you be second. I see you're a good catch. Advance Australia Fair. Come on!

She moved grudgingly to take up the position and saw Honora was profoundly asleep under the tree on the ridgeline and was not engaged at all in the game but seemed in fact sedated by it.

You see this young chap? Major Bright asked Sally confidentially, pointing to an Australian gunner they'd found in an estaminet in Deux Églises and recruited for their team. He's a leg spinner. So be ready for a catch. It won't be fierce. Ball off the edge of the bat. A lollipop catch.

The English orderly at the batting crease met the Australian's less than distinguished delivery and belted it across the field so far that it disappeared over a hill.

My God, said Bright, they're taking it seriously. That's a bit rough.

He stood straight and inhaled.

I hope you don't mind my asking, Sister Durance, he murmured as beyond the fall of land Australian and British orderlies and two nurses searched the grass for the cricket ball. But I *would* be grateful if you kept an eye on young Slattery there. It seems to me that the word of the bureau in London, and of course of our glorious military authorities, is uniform. And she is the only dissenter.

Yes, said Sally. But her work stays solid.

Of course. But she writes too often to the bureau, and she continues to do so, even though they have nothing to tell her. She seemed to be over the loss, but she's reverted. She needs a long leave, and a chance to find the means to accept that her fiancé is dead. I am not asking you to be a spy. But there are so many letters to that bureau, I assure you—nearly daily. More—I confess—than I have actually sent off.

There were rumors Major Bright was more affected by Honora than that. There did exist, however, fifteen or more years' difference.

Please keep an eye on her. Just to see signs of stress or of the . . . the abnormal. She refuses to leave here; I have no grounds to make her. But she should be observed. In case . . .

Sally said she would do her best in this matter. On the rim of the slope a nurse had found the cricket ball, and this was a pretext for jubilation and cheers.

A Summer of Stubborn Matrons

In the garden on a suddenly blazing day when men sat in scattered light by oaks and elms and read books and magazines—with Matron Mitchie dozing in her wicker wheelchair—Lady Tarlton took Naomi aside.

Our friend Matron Mitchie, she confided, has had an X-ray in Boulogne at Major Darlington's insistence. There are damp spots on her lungs. She is suffering from tuberculosis. It's urgent that she go to a sanatorium down there in the south, and take ship to Australia as soon as she can healthily do so. I am trying to recruit an experienced sister or staff nurse from Étaples or Wimereux or Boulogne to special-nurse her. Because you notice that three of our volunteers left during the winter to return home? But I can hardly blame them.

Naomi thought that given the rigors of the work and of the château as a building three departures was a modest number. At the news of Mitchie's consumption, she thought at once of the sinking of the *Archimedes*. It was as if *that* cold and shock had caught up to her at Château Baincthun.

Not to put too fine a point on it, Lady Tarlton went on, she is refusing to move. A tear emerged in the corner of one of her eyes.

I fear she might have no family back there. And yet out of English reticence I don't ask. I think you can ask her. And use your best endeavors. She must go, says Major Darlington, if she is to see her senior years.

374

That night Naomi intercepted the volunteer who was carrying a meal from the kitchens to Matron Mitchie's room on the first floor. The girl was masked, according to the strictures of Major Darlington. Dr. Airdrie had told everyone that Darlington was about to publish an article in *The Lancet* on the connection between bacteria in nurses' throats and sepsis, and on the whole issue of masks on or masks off. This—everyone felt—would validate the Voluntary and Major Darlington and Lady Tarlton and themselves.

I'll take that meal to the matron, Nurse, Naomi said.

Would you, Sister? asked the girl in an elegant, tired voice. She was a sturdy young woman who had once well-meaningly said to Naomi, Your soldiers are extraordinary in their patois. And Naomi had said, I doubt they'd know what patois was.

Naomi took the meal from her but did not don a mask. How could you have a heart-to-heart with Mitchie through a mask?

The matron's room—into which she was bidden after knocking— was a little larger than her own. The French owners who had fled the war had at least left their thick curtains behind—and in Mitchie's room they were drawn. But the room was simple apart from that—an iron bedstead, a dresser, a lowboy of painted pine, a little bookcase made of pine. Matron Mitchie in bed wore a mobcap and her hands were folded across her stomach, her bedclothes neat, her prosthesis with its shoe on its false foot beside her bed. The matron grinned unambiguously and broadly at seeing Naomi.

Come, she said. You can put down the food and tea there. I'll have the tea first. As for the rest, my appetite is not . . . But tell me—your visit to Paris?

Naomi found herself without embarrassment relating their meeting with Mr. Sedgewick and the other *Amis* in Paris.

When she was finished, Mitchie declared, I always liked that Kiernan. He was a good egg from the start.

I am so sorry to hear about your problem, said Naomi.

Problem?

Well, that you have some consumption.

Some? asked Mitchie, mock sneering. That's not a very accurate medical assessment, Staff Nurse Durance. I wouldn't mind betting that blabbermouth Lady Tarlton told you all about it. And sent you to plague me into going to Marseille. I simply won't. I am better than Major Darlington and Lady Tarlton think.

Naomi said, You argued you were better than you were to get here in the first place.

Mitchie said, Is there soup on that tray? Place it there on the little table. I might have some.

Would you like me to feed you?

I'm neither a baby nor in my dotage, thank you. If I go to Marseille, they'll have me on the Australia boat before you know. And so to a sanatorium out in the Dandenongs. I am not a sanatorium dweller. It's not in my nature. Besides, what is so precious about me that I should be taken out of France? The countryside is weighed down by young men who need to be sent home. I'm tethered here by the same things as you are. So let's have no argument. I really mean it. Let's have none.

Namoi set her up with her soup.

Good soup indeed. Some of those English Roses can actually cook.

It's none of my affair, said Naomi, but I wondered if you had a family to look after you in Australia?

Here we go! said Mitchie in disgust. A family? I have a brother in Tasmania, since you ask. But he's totally unsuitable as a tuberculosis nurse. I wouldn't call my brother a relative in any meaningful way. I am as good as forgotten *there.* Anyhow, it seems that I have been here forever. Even Mudros is distant—and Egypt's distant beyond belief. This is my home and I won't be thrown out of my home. Lady Tarlton owes me her loyalty on this, rather than going around enlisting you all to evict me.

You should never have come to France in my opinion, Naomi said. But I know you'll argue otherwise.

So would you if you were in my position. You wouldn't want me to have missed out on meeting Major Darlington and all those well-bred English gels? Would you? Truth is, there is no rest for anyone until it's all over. Unless it's the sort of final rest they dish out in Flanders and on the Somme.

She handed her unfinished soup bowl back to Naomi. Naomi put it on the tray. The tubercular cough set in and Mitchie covered her mouth with an old towel. The spasm built to a paroxysm and then composed itself.

Don't gawk at me. I'm not spitting blood yet. Well, not much.

I won't gawk, Naomi promised.

But do not raise this business again if you want to be my friend. I say this not only to you but to Lady Tarlton too. So enough of it now! Remember this—in helping that woman out, that *Lady* Tarlton, I hacked all around the bush in third-class carriages and on bicycles and the back of trucks and by horseback. Setting up bases for our bush nurses and visiting them so they didn't feel lonely and leave us and go back to the big towns and cities. Lady Tarlton did not want any praise for the scheme, but it was her name in the newspapers. Well, her name deserved to be. But I was the one on the bike. I was the one who got saddle sore. And now I deserve her consideration too. I am not to be shunted off to the south. This end of France is where the war and the grief and my friends are, and this is the end I'm staying at.

Matron Mitchie sipped her tea and her lips curled and she frowned. It's gone cold. I made too long a speech, damn me!

I'll get you more, Naomi offered.

You're too busy, Matron Mitchie ordered. Have one of the gels do it.

Naomi said, I'll get some more. For now, have plenty of rest.

That sounds like condescension to me. "Have plenty of rest, dear!"

For God's sake, don't be so sensitive, Naomi told her smiling. A person would think you were a Durance.

• • •

Under the spur of her concern for Mitchie, Lady Tarlton thought about a villa on the cliff top at Antibes—between Marseille and Nice—owned by her husband's family. It was staffed by servants Lord Tarlton's brother-in-law had been too distracted to let go for the duration of the war. An entire domestic establishment down there thus awaited a convalescent Matron Mitchie. The proposition Lady Tarlton kept bluntly running with Mitchie was that in the south—where there was a North African sun and North African breezes—she would get better. Here she would die.

When Naomi visited her room, Mitchie complained of this further attempt at clearing her away from the Château Baincthun. The disease was eroding her and turning her pallid, thinning her skin to tissue, sharpening the bones at the points of her cheek, and narrowing her nose to a blade.

She thinks I want to stay out of pure vanity, Mitchie complained. I want to stay because this is the place and there isn't any other.

It seemed to Naomi that Mitchie had the talent and force of temperament to make a community wherever she went—and in the south of France no differently than anywhere else. Lady Tarlton had already found a reliable and pleasant Red Cross nurse to go to the marvelous, all-healing south with her, and had also organized some orderlies to travel with them to Paris and transfer them to the train down to the south. But it seemed that to Mitchie the supposed date of her departure hung over her like an ax and distressed her so much that one night Dr. Airdrie had to sedate her with lithium bromide.

By the evening before the departure Matron Mitchie had become a plaintive shadow of that figure Naomi had once seen on sticks and a prosthetic leg rising up the gangplank of the Melbourne-moored troopship, bent on Europe, the cockpit, the center of all matroning. Naomi began to wonder if the threat of leaving the château was not doing Mitchie more harm than good, and she went searching for Dr. Airdrie. She found her writing case notes in her office. Her handsome long nose was red at the tip from cold, and her hands mittened, though it was meant to be spring.

You must talk to Lady Tarlton, Naomi urged her after greetings. This going-south idea is doing no good at all.

That may be so, Airdrie admitted and reached for a cigarette. But convincing the boss lady is another thing. Look, Mitchie will be hunky-dory once she gets there.

It makes good sense medically, said Naomi. Except Mitchie has a real dread.

What is there to dread? asked Airdrie. I wish she were sending me.

Yet Airdrie could tell Naomi would not let the question rest.

I'll go and see Pretty Polly myself, Airdrie sighed. But you come too.

They went down the corridor and knocked on Lady Tarlton's office door. The young London Red Cross woman who worked as her secretary opened it. Lady Tarlton was at the desk frowning over documents. The office looked cluttered at first view—there were piles of paper around the walls, for example—but it did not take long before you saw they were organized, that each individual suburb of paper beneath the citadel of the desk had been deliberately assembled by the secretary and put in folders by alphabetic order and held in place by paperweights. Here were bills and requisitions, rental agreements, invoices for repairs and food and heating fuel and linen—some supplied by the military, some supplemented by her own purse and that of the London committee to whom she must send proper accounts. She looked up and greeted them with her normal flustered warmth.

Naomi and Airdrie did not sit. Naomi frankly made her point about Mitchie. When she was finished Lady Tarlton sighed a long, musical sigh. We must go and see her then, she said at last, dropping her pen and fetching up a shawl to wear in the corridor.

The door of Mitchie's room was opened by the English nurse meant to accompany her to Antibes. Mitchie greeted them with something like sullen disgust. Here we go! she said, casting up stricken eyes. The bailiffs have arrived!

She began to cough horrendously. Lady Tarlton sat on the chair by her bed and took one of her hands. Mitchie grudgingly permitted the grasp.

What's the trouble, old friend? asked Lady Tarlton. I have only your welfare in mind.

That's a fine excuse for torment, said Mitchie.

I feel I'd be guilty of murder if I did not send you off, Mitchie. Everything's so damp and changeable up here.

Mitchie's cheeks flared an angry, tubercular red. She tossed her head wearily.

If I were lying on a stretcher with my intestines hanging out, you'd have some idea of what to do for me. You'd listen to all I said. I am not in that condition and so I'm shorn of a voice of my own. I'm patronized and patted on the head and told I'll be taken—by orderlies!—to a train, and put on it like someone who's overstayed her leave.

The other thing, Mitchie continued, breathless but unlikely to stop, the other thing is that I am considered to be simply stubborn— like an old woman, or a four-year-old. I can be cajoled and humored, and treated with force if all that fails.

My dear friend, said Lady Tarlton. There won't be any force.

I'm glad to hear it. In that case I won't be going.

Lady Tarlton was silent, and her eyes looked bleak.

I have potent motives to remain here, Mitchie reiterated, believe me. Just because I don't blab them, it is no reason to consider me a pigheaded old biddy. For example, will I get the official casualty lists at this Antibes place?

No, I hope not. For you, it'll be as if the terrible ruination here doesn't exist.

But this is all that counts. This is the world. The ruination, or whatever.

For dear God's sake, Lady Tarlton honked. You've done more than anyone else could in this snake pit. You are an amputee with consumption. And even at the risk of offending you, I will not be guilty of your particular murder, my dear friend.

Mitchie slumped and began to weep with an obvious, chastening rage. That quelled them. That quelled Lady Tarlton too.

Damn you all! she yelled, and then lay panting. I have a son. I have a son who arrived here last spring. I have a son about to turn twenty-five years and he tried eighteen months ago to be taken as a soldier and at last, to hell with them, they did take him. His battalion is in this push. And I'm to sun myself somewhere in the distance? Damn you! Damn you all over!

Her tears stopped now as she realized she had seized a small corner of Tarlton's authority and sureness.

Oh, it was all a mess in those days. There was no chance of marriage. I had to leave the little boy, you see, with my mother. But now my son knows I'm his mother. I met him in Boulogne and he was . . . he was just such a template of a boy. And I won't leave him now. I won't be dragged away by your orderlies or by provosts or any other bugger.

They were all silent. Nothing more conclusive could be said. Lady Tarlton looked at her two companions.

Major Darlington would be angry with us, she said. He will have us all wearing masks around you if you stay here.

I wouldn't mind that, said Mitchie. I would rather stay here with masked friends than down there with barefaced people I don't know. And . . . my boy!

Naomi swallowed. She knew it was all settled now. Lady Tarlton had given up Antibes.

I'll go and get you some tea, Naomi said.

Good girl, said Mitchie—but like a reproof for having extended her duties to the menial. You go and do something like that. Bullying doesn't become you.

Well, said Lady Tarlton as Naomi left the room yet could still hear. It looks as if we must cancel the travel plans. On the other hand, Mitchie, you must damn well promise me not to die.

If *he* lives, Mitchie told her, then *I'll* live.

Making the tea, Naomi absorbed the revelation. She had thought of Matron Mitchie as a universal aunt. That she should be directly maternal hadn't occurred to her. She returned to the room tentatively with the tray. For the anger which had been in Mitchie was unfamiliar and full of risk for emotional novices.

When she got back to the door there was silence inside. Lady Tarlton and Dr. Airdrie had obviously retreated. Mitchie called for her to come in and her voice retained no trace of anger. Once Naomi was inside and had poured the tea, Mitchie ordered her to sit down. Naomi saw that the matron was drying new tears. But they did not seem to be the tears of helplessness.

The father, she said, is a surgeon. At *that* time he had recently arrived in Australia from Edinburgh. Newly minted, newly lettered. Fine featured and very gifted. He was sure of what he knew but didn't bully people with it. He was also certain of what he didn't know and did not try to move into those areas. So he seemed a fine man. Men can be fine in all areas except one. He had arrived in Melbourne as if he was a single man and was rather quiet about the fact he was already married and his wife was waiting for their child to be born and to mature a little before she too took ship with it. And to be honest I wanted to believe he wasn't already taken. He never told me straight out he was. He seemed too . . . young and singular and new made to be a married man.

Afterwards, I went home to Tasmania, pretended to be a widow and gave birth to the boy in Hobart. My mother—she was a brick, a true woman. My father pretended it wasn't happening. But my mother stuck close to home and wrote to friends that she was the pregnant one—what a surprise! She was forty-five but one never knew! And we stayed together all through it and when the boy was born in a hospital she took him home with her and raised and presented him as her son. And so I became his much older sister, as far as the world was concerned. And my son believed it. The whole arrangement was a sort of cowardice on my part. But the other thing is—I wanted to save the boy from the stain of being a bastard. And when I went away to work and left him with Mammie . . . it was for him but it was for me too. Whenever I saw him it was a joy and a reproach, and I didn't like reproach as a full-time business. You see now what sort of girl I was. How stupid and how shallow.

When I met the boy in Boulogne early last spring and I told him the facts, he was angry—he stormed out of the café where I told him, and I went back to my billet in town. But he sought me out later in the day and he had this forgiving sort of frown when he saw me and he put his arms around me and began to cry. What a dear boy! He was still dubious about it, I could tell. Trying to switch his whole compass around so that the needle pointed to me. But if I went to this Antibes, he wouldn't be able to visit me down there. And if anything happened, I wouldn't be in reach of him.

Naomi put out her hand and—after hesitation—laid it on Matron Mitchie's.

I think Lady Tarlton is convinced now, she said.

I'll tell you what, said Matron Mitchie. She'd bloody better be! Nor do I care who in the hell she tells anymore!

Mitchie could have been talking about an enemy.

In May a flood of men came down to the station from the morass. Nurses noticed the wounds had altered subtly—they were an hour or two older, since the front had gone forward. There were rumors that the casualty clearing station too might be moved some further miles northeast.

The terror of the front these days was borne in on Sally by the hollow-eyed stretcher bearers, who sometimes came directly from the line to the clearing station and then found a tent or hut and took a cup of tea and were felled by sleep on the fringes of some ward. The bearers had extracted men from the mired trenches and carried them against the traffic of food supplies and ammunition boxes and wire coils. The stretcher bearers with their burden of maimed soldier tottered on narrow duckboards, which felt like a raft at sea—or so one of these men told Sally. If pushed off the path, they and their wounded man might sink into muck that seemed to stretch to the earth's core.

There was a new gas now—mustard gas. It did not cripple the membranes and crimp the alveoli. It burned all membranes instead. It burned the eyes, the face, the mucous membranes, and the walls of the lung. The mustard victims arrived at the gas ward stripped naked by the orderlies in reception and carried on a clean stretcher in a clean blanket. For the oily vapors of the chemical yperite which had entered their clothing could burn them through fabric.

Sally—now rostered in the gas ward as part of the earlier-proclaimed broad education—supervised nurses and orderlies here as the victims' entire bodies, even groins and armpits, were sprayed with sodium bicarbonate. Other nurses hurried to them with steaming bowls of sulphates and sodas to inhale. If men could still not be comforted, and believed themselves drowning in their own lung fluid, the orderlies and nurses rushed oxygen cylinders and masks to them. The nurses did what could be done to help the naked and blistered, gasping men to gargle out the poison, to wash it from their noses and eyes. But the bodies of the gassed themselves exuded the poison, and every quarter of an hour nurses must go outside and take the fresh air and cough their throats clear of the communicated venom.

Bright remarked to Sally one night on a hurried visit that the pain in the head of a mustard-gas patient was as though acid-laced water was invading his nasal sinuses not once but continuously. This sense of drowning caused the wide-eyed distress she saw everywhere.

In the end they might be given chloroform or morphine to ease their burning membranes and their panic. The ward doctor more than once told Sally to cut open a man's arm to reduce the volume of blood crying out for oxygen. When a man's heart failed from edema—that inner drowning—Sally and her nurses reached for syringefuls of reviving camphor and pituitarin to revive the fellow.

One evening when the motor ambulances arrived and the transfer of patients from the admission hut to the gas ward was in progress, she was walking behind a victim, accompanied by an orderly with a Tilley lamp. She had visited admissions to assess how many more men they could expect in the tented ward. The sounds of the night were the normal background symphonics and shouted commands. The huge penetrating noise came from above in an instant. She heard the plane descend as if it were intimately dedicated to her, and she opened her mouth to warn the men. But all voice and hearing ceased—or was absorbed into something vaster—and the air was taken from her and she was thrown backwards with a ruthless force. She tumbled without dignity or hope—taking breath in the middle of her flight and having it jolted forth again as her hip crashed to earth.

She lay on earth where time was canceled. All lamps out, all lamps out! she eventually heard an orderly sergeant yelling.

The turning off took a little time. She could see the shattered lantern she had been following lying some distance along the gravel path and an arm and hand still holding it. It had been hooded with a metal flange but somehow the night flyer had seen it and taken to it in the utter bliss of attack. Parts of the first bearer and of the patient they had been attending to were scattered in gobbets of flesh in a crater beyond the dying lantern. The second orderly had a cut to his face and sat dazed where he had landed. He and Sally had been leaves blown in a happier direction.

She got up amidst a rain of grit and in a terrible acidic stillness which wasn't like quiet at all but which assaulted the air and rang in the ears. She could hear more planes close above. Was it virtue or fear that sent her running towards her ward? The shadow of the Church of England padre—who officiated regularly on the hill and worked in between as an orderly—emerged from it through the double black-out curtains and grasped her.

You must find shelter, Sister, he shouted.

The suggestion made her furious.

No, she said, I have to stay in the ward.

Jostling past both of them from within, Honora Slattery went towards the trenches with a blanketed patient over her shoulder. That seemed absurd. But Sally lacked the mind to be sure whether the sight was odd or normal. She ran into the usually dim-lit ward—bright now, since one of the Tilley lamps had shattered and set fire to the flooring. She fetched a blanket, and she and the ward doctor smothered the flames. Some men who should not have sat up were doing so and looking about with piteous eyes and shouting. The bombardment had jolted their system into life and activated their breath. Further detonations not so far away showed that planes were probably trying to destroy the barrage balloon depot—since pilots hated those contraptions.

I'm with you! she called to the patients, though she could not quite hear herself and would later think the declaration melodramatic.

Go to the door and see what you can see, the ward doctor dementedly told her.

She rushed to the door and pushed through its two flaps as if she could read from there the intentions of the planes, their number, and the likelihood and path through the air of more bombs. In the open night between the ward and the trenches, perhaps a dozen weeping men staggered about the yard and along the paths. Others knelt or cast their arms wide and raved or screamed. NYD(S).

She saw Honora emerging now from the thoracic ward—why had she gone there?—with yet another man on her shoulders. What are you doing? Sally—clearheaded now on the subject of Honora's lunacy—called out to her.

I am putting patients in the trenches, she shouted back. I put the first one in and he turned out to be a German. Imagine that!

She had mad purpose in her eye—she would carry every man in all the wards into slit trenches if she could. From within the gas ward Sally's own orderlies began helping their patients past her and to the shelter of trenches and dugouts.

Honora ran on. Sally turned back into the gas tent and passed the remaining wide-eyed nurses and orderlies, who were aware something momentous and ill defined had occurred. The ward doctor was with the gas cases who could not safely be moved. Two nurses were going about placing basins over the heads of the patients. It was a half-way rational idea to save them from shrapnel and it possessed for the nurses the comfort of acting to defy events.

The ward doctor told Sally something had happened near the theatres. They could smell the chloroform, and mixed with it was the penetrating stench of ether. If there was a fire out there then all the gas cases would need—whatever the results—to be moved.

Sally joined a nurse who was already at the rear door of the tent. From the hut steps they saw the surgical theatre hut begin to burn. The air was anesthetic from the shattered bottles of chloroform but it was the ether supplies that were burning, releasing vapors that the fire instantly sucked back into itself.

Sally heard people lamenting. Someone shouted, The hoses aren't working! A bucket line of nurses and orderlies attempted to stanch the flames. Were surgeons, theatre nurses, patients caught in there? Water wouldn't do anything, she knew. Earth or sand was needed to quench blazing ether. It was now that she reachieved her reason fully. She turned back into the gas ward and shouted without reference to the ward doctor that nurses and orderlies must hurry all possible cases into slit trenches.

You go, Sister, said the ward doctor.

No.

You *go*! he roared. I've sent off all the other nurses.

All right, she said. She would be a free agent once she was out in the night.

As she stepped forth she heard another inhuman impact some distance off, but it was not close enough to bear her mind away. She began pushing and dragging demented, howling, praying men towards trenches they did not want to enter. She thought of the thoracic ward and crazed Honora.

A Klaxon which had not rung at the start of things to warn anyone sounded now to reassure everyone. Silence all at once finally manifested itself like the clap of a great hand and stunned the earth. Voices and even yells were minute within it. The air was full still of the stench of the theatre fire and the embers seemed to fall like an incandescent snow.

Sally heard men's plaintive voices from a half-collapsed tent. Inside, Honora was lifting patients back onto beds, one bleeding from the ears from a nearby detonation. Am I too? Sally wondered, and began to help. Orderlies arrived to readjust the tent poles. At last, according to some dazed, unspoken accord between them that their job was done, she and Honora left the restored tent. The remaining heat of the theatre blaze wafted across the station. Sally set out back for the gas ward and skirted *her* crater—the one which held unscannable fragments of the gas case and an orderly. She saw Freud and Leonora coming from the lost fight with the fire, walking towards her and the untouched thoracic ward as if no shock had overtaken them and as if on normal duty. They stepped carefully but without amazement around obscure body parts that covered the paths and other spaces. As Leonora reached Sally, she said, An orderly told me. They blew up the morgue. What a triumph, eh?

Some NYD(S) were still wandering the station—quivering and dazed or making speeches—and it turned out an orderly had chased one down on the Deux Églises road. Orderlies retrieving such men were leading them back to their ward by the hand and shoulder, brotherly to a degree which caused Sally to shed tears as she returned to the gas ward. She wondered how it had been in the resuscitation ward during all the noise and fire and with the bombs making their random and absurd choices.

When day broke there was time for the nurses to return to their mess, glimpsing beyond the wards—more clearly now—the two-thirds-burned-out theatre hut. By accident—so Sally understood from Freud—it had been near empty at the time. The surgeons were in the admissions hut. Two orderlies had been blown wide.

At their mess table the women bolted down sugar-laced tea and ate bread which they doused in Queensland treacle as if to reembrace their dear, safe, sleeping home continent. Major Bright came in after beating on the door and told them with a mannish innocence and irrelevance—almost touching—that he had recommended them all for Military Medals. Those who stayed in their wards or had worked at the fire or had mercifully dealt with others or had placed tables or basins over men to make them feel safer or had put others on the floor and beneath their beds—even as orderlies yelled at them to get into the trenches. But, he said—as if it were a great concern arising from that mad night—it was a military lottery that would define who got the decorations.

They listened because he was such a good man. But military ambition burned very low in the women. It was amusing to Honora that the man she had carried from the chest ward was not after all a German but an English captain—and not only an Englishman but a German-speaking, renowned novelist named Alexander Southwell, the nephew of one Lord Finisterre who had been formerly a British cabinet minister. It was idly assumed that if there were medals they would go Honora's way. But the chief remark her act attracted was wonder at how a woman of five foot six inches had—in the fury of the moment—carried a six-foot man, limp and awaiting chest surgery, from his ward to the trench.

It was an issue which did not delay Honora in the least as she went back to duty immediately after breakfast. She was all business. The mere sentiment of compassion had left her. She pursued it all in a fierce, mechanical way. There was something to do with Dankworth mixed up in it.

Let her go, Matron Bolger said. I'll fetch her back for a rest in an hour or so.

Sally went back to her ward too but returned to the mess for a cup of tea before collapsing. Most of her gas cases had been moved to evacuation ambulances. Now it was up to the base hospitals to soothe and save them. Rest lay ahead since nothing could happen until the surgical theatres were resupplied. Honora returned with Matron Bolger—you could hear their chat before they reached the tent.

Karla Freud also arrived. She had been helping in the evacuation ward that morning—attending to men as they were loaded on rear-bound ambulances. Entering the tent now, she saw Honora and Sally and a few others—Leo too—and stood contemplating them. Honora was writing something on the card table—they all feared it was to that bureau and that the blasts of the night had unsettled her again.

Look, you've probably heard of my surgeon, Karla Freud stated. Boyton. He's an American from the British Medical Corps transferred here. Well, you can stop speculating. It's all true. I'm letting you know in case anything happens. Both of us might have been incinerated together last night, and weren't. That means there are two reasons why my friends from Lemnos can stop thinking, "Poor old Karla."

Then she sat down. Sally did not know whether she was supposed to congratulate her or be silent. Are we all suddenly mad? she wondered.

That's good news for us too, said Leo—exactly the right answer. I hope you have a happy life.

All right then, said Freud. Thank you.

And so? asked Leo. A few more details, please.

His mother's English, father's American, his practice is in Chicago. He's not Jewish and that means lamentations will be uttered in Melbourne. But in Chicago I won't hear them. Only thing . . .

She winked here.

It's the end of my dreams of the stage. Women are fools. We can't help offering ourselves up. Living sacrifices. That's us.

She turned to Honora, who was back-on at a side table writing her fluent letter.

Honora, she called in a frank but soft voice. Honora, dearie! Listen to me. He's dead, that kind picnicker from Lemnos. He's dead. He doesn't deserve to be, but he is. There aren't any more theories you can make up. No more letters, for God's sake.

Honora ceased writing but sat rigid and without turning. Freud moved to her and put her hands on those stiffened, raised shoulders. But a particular sound—of air being shredded—arose again. The Klaxon began to wail. The planes had returned and could be heard, low and fast. Sally stiffened to withstand the first jolt of a dropped bomb. The women rushed outside—they could not help themselves. When the reverberating explosion came—though it must have been a kilometer along the road—it threatened to loosen Sally's bladder. An orderly sergeant came yelling, Dugouts, ladies. Not wards! Split trench and dugouts!

But Sally ran to the resuscitation ward to see how many of last night's cases were too damaged to be moved. There was nothing to be done for these men, but she wanted to know the numbers. Two pale-faced staff nurses were there, looking startled but steadfast. They had been tending perhaps four cases of whom any informed assessor would say at least three would die. The way the girls stood—so professionally, with their hands half folded in front of them—reminded Sally of Karla Freud's phrase. "Living sacrifices."

Yet she too was willing to lose herself.

At her suggestion the three of them did the basin trick—the near-comic business of covering the patients' faces. It was ridiculous, an exercise in flimsiness and capable of adding to damage. It would be laughed at later. But it seemed a serious duty now. Anything more—to move them beneath their beds—would certainly finish them. For these were men too far gone to survive the journey to the remaining operating theatre, let alone the anesthesia once there. But the idea they would die without nurses present was abhorrent. Meanwhile the

Archies provided the continuous rhythm like minor instruments, the screaming descent of those explosive cylinders adding in the symphonic climaxes.

Sally uselessly took a hand of one of the patients—gently, as if feeling for a pulse. As she stood she saw Major Bright in the doorway. Will you, for God's sake— he yelled. But an explosion along the road made him repeat it. Will you, for God's sake, go to the dugout? Sister Durance, set an example, for God's sake!

Her two young women stared at him without comprehension.

It is General Birdwood's order, he roared. She waved the two girls to follow him. She wanted urgently to urinate and feared that if a bomb came near she might be concussed into this indignity.

Bright ran at their side, shepherding them to a slit trench, helping them jump down and leading them along the trench to a dugout—a covered structure Sally had never entered before, a dark pit thickly roofed with timber and loads of sandbags. As she went in, Bright held her elbow. His face was red. You have years of training and I have years more. How dare you risk all that!

There were a number of nurses inside sitting on benches. Honora was one of them. There was Freud, who had so recently tried to cure Honora of her delusions. And Matron Bolger.

Honora cried, Matron, this is an absolute bulldust order. The men hate us going.

These are today's men, the matron told her. Who will nurse tomorrow's men if you get blown to shreds?

Honora looked sullen. The matron took out a book from her pocket. She patted it with her hand and yelled against the continuous but blessedly distant explosions of bombs. If you do not come here when the Klaxon goes, she told them, it is very likely they will move us out of the casualty clearing stations. The general says he will not have us in danger and will move us if we expose ourselves to the Taubes. You understand?

She waved the book in her hand. For now, she announced, I want you to pay your mess bills. Don't tell me you don't have money on you.

She opened her book and began to go through the amounts each nurse owed for sherry or lemonade or ginger beer or wine or brandy, and made arrangements for payment—whether or not she received it then and there.

A titanic detonation of the surface above their heads occurred—as these things did—without introduction. They were jolted against each other by the brutal and bullying sound and then drew together and found themselves half deafened. But the matron continued to read.

Slattery, eleven shillings and sixpence. Freud, twelve and eight-pence. Casement, eighteen and seven pence—a lot of extra chocolate bought there, Casement . . .

The Klaxon declared temporary safety had returned long before the matron was finished. But in successive days the sound of aero-plane engines made daytime sleep hard and a woman could not take sleeping draughts at night for fear ambulances would arrive. After the sun had set, the enemy's aircraft traversed the sky indiscriminately—unable in darkness to tell a baby's cradle in Deux Églises from the enormous British gun now rumored to be emplaced a few miles west.

There was nothing worse on those summer nights than abandoning the startled, wide-eyed boys—those conscious of the raid but unable to be moved. But nothing was secretly and guiltily better than lean-ing inwards to listen to that older woman—the matron, the plausible aunt—reading her sums above the varying racket.

These Abnormal Days

These abnormal days Sally breakfasted after night duty in ten minutes. Then she slept till perhaps half past ten in the morning, when a sense of urgency woke her and sent her back to her ward. But at one of those dawns of rushed breakfasts she was interrupted. There's a fellow here asking for you, a staff nurse told her.

At once she knew. Charlie Condon. If it were him he could annul all the awful days and nights—though that this would happen was merely a notion. She went outside and on the path by the resuscitation hut saw him. He was leaning against the building and a bike was propped up near him. She noticed first that his face had grown somehow older. The features had hardened. It was the face—she thought straightaway—of a knowing warrior. She sensed that he could not only suffer anything imaginable but that he might do it too. It was a greater surprise to see him in this new form than it was simply to see him. He is another man, she considered, as I am another woman. Can we still converse? She dearly wanted to.

Oh, he said, almost as if he hadn't expected to see her. This has really turned out well. I'd heard you'd been bombed and—I've got to say—I was pretty worried. Since we're in a rest area just now, I borrowed this bike and rode down to see if you were all right.

"Down," she noticed. That must mean he'd traveled from further north.

Charlie, she said. So kind of you. We're all top of our form, except not a lot of sleep.

Yes, he said. That's the way it is up there too. Makes a person a bit crazy, doesn't it?

But you . . . you look . . .

What? Uglier?

Are you still an artist?

I'm a sketcher still, he reassured her. Do you know, a kiss would give my talent wings. But not possible here, I suppose.

Come and have tea, she told him.

If no ambulance convoy came in before full light they would be able to have a decent talk. And these plain words—these words of no merit at all—seemed the best ones to exchange with a man who must have the terror of the front fixed in his brain. And who had ridden a bike—how many kilometers?—to check if she was safe.

They went into the mess hut.

I can get you whisky, she offered. If you'd like it.

In fact, whisky, stout, brandy—they were all there for the having these days. Nurses could decide that a given patient needed something, and it was there in the pantry. They had begun to use a lot of it in the NYD ward. In a sane world whisky or brandy should not be administered with opiates. But in this world a quick effect was more important.

He said, Whisky would not go amiss by far.

Wait a second, she said, holding up a finger knowingly. She went and fetched him a tin mugful and brought it back. This simple function delighted her beyond measure.

If the matron should come in, she said, pointing to the mug she put down, we can pretend it's tea.

She poured herself tea and offered her cup towards his.

Your very good health, she said.

She assessed him again. She dared not think that—after all this—he looked like a man who might come through. But that was the case.

He always gave her that impression when she saw him, though not when he was away.

It's a great relief to clap eyes on you, she said.

Relief? he said.

Of course a relief. Here we only see the wounded. It seems— though it can't be true—that all men must be wounded sooner or later. But tell me again—the sketching . . . ?

I'm doing a bit in the rest areas. But there's nothing to sketch up there now. A limited palette, you'd say, for painting as well. Black and brown and slimy green-yellow. Not the stuff of aesthetics. The whisky is very good.

Tell me. How far did you cycle?

I don't know.

He pointed vaguely northwards. It was good for me. And I won't insult you by saying I haven't thought of you a lot.

I've been concerned for you too.

He smiled into the mug of whisky. Come on now. Aunts can be *concerned*. And you're not my aunt. I will accept something such as, I've been thinking a great deal about you too, Charlie. Or else, I haven't given you a blessed thought.

It's so hectic here. But I fear one of the men on stretchers might be you. You're on my mind a lot.

Ah! said Charlie, who had wanted to hear that. On your mind a lot. I'm pretty gratified to be told that, Sally. That'll suit me.

She was aware of nurses moving busily about them now—fetching breakfast plates and giving the banal nods and winks. Would there be more winking amongst them—and smart-aleck rolling of eyes in her direction—when Charlie Condon was gone again? Well, of course. That price must be paid.

I have a belief that if I think of you too much something will happen to you.

Well, no fooling you clearing station girls. You know enough to know there are some days a man can't believe he'll live. And nights, ditto. And if you live through the day and night there's another impossible day and night to come. Yet . . . there I was this morning. On my bike. You can't overstate how important this journey was to me.

It brought Sally herself a kind of exaltation to hear a sentiment like that.

I'm pretty impressed myself, she assured him.

The tent was near empty now. The others had got over their whispers and decided to give the two of them a time to themselves. Charlie reached for her wrist and she wished something more vigorous would happen. But it wasn't possible there.

I'll need to be back by seven o'clock this evening. That means I must set out on my bike about half past three. Just to be sure. The roads get a bit chancy towards dusk and there's a lot of traffic.

It was as if he were explaining why the hand on wrist would have to do her for now.

It's a pity, he laughed, a photographer from the *Macleay Argus* doesn't come in now and photograph us. The two brave Macleay warriors.

She said, It's hard to believe the Macleay still exists.

But unfortunately its waters now suddenly flowed back into her, washing along on their surface the still not fully absorbed ending they'd given their mother. It had all come back sharply, as she knew it must. No quantity of massacre could reduce it to a small taint. And Sally knew Charlie must be told about it if he intended to take the more energetic journeys she wanted him to take to keep tracking her down in the French or Flemish countryside.

Oh, I'm sure it's still there, she heard him say. It's determined, you know. The earth maintains a great indifference to what we do. When you come back to an area of fields like the ones round here, you understand that the mire up there is just waiting to break out into pasture again. It won't happen this year—it mightn't happen for another ten. But in the end the tendency won't be repressed. There's greenness waiting under all that slime.

The matron appeared briefly and said, Good morning, Sister; good morning, Captain. It was then Sally saw the nuggets of insignia on his straps which showed him to be that. A captain.

He whispered, Don't be impressed. The way things are just now there are fifteen men to a platoon and sixty to a company. But they are building us up with new blood. Forcing old hands like me up in rank.

New blood? she asked in horror.

I could have chosen better words, he conceded.

They decided to walk to town past the cemetery and a barley field which a farmer—gambling against a movement of the front line—had bravely planted. The road entered the town from the south. A two-storey official building near the *mairie* had a shattered roof, but people moved normally in the streets. Big-bosomed farmers' wives shopped and talked to each other in the open day.

I love these little towns, Charlie told her. I keep sketching them. But don't worry, I won't be sketching today.

He held out a hand towards the landscape on the edge of town.

You know, I look at all this, so very nice, very ordered. Farmed for thousands of years. And it does call up by contrast where we're from. I mean to say, what a valley, the Macleay! It's a valley that deserves a great painter. It's a place that almost defies a person to become a painter. It says, Come on, have a go, you useless hayseed! And it would explode Cézanne's palette. He'd have to go reaching for the tubes of paint he doesn't use here. That's what we've got, the Australians. We've got the place but we just don't have the artists. Up here, gloom and—admittedly—subtlety. And artists? My God. They've got wonderful artists to burn. I had leave, by the way, and went to all the galleries.

We saw the Louvre, said Sally. But we didn't see enough. We didn't bring the right eyes to it. Look-and-laugh sort of stuff.

Well, said Charlie, grinning, look-and-laugh isn't bad. I would be happy if in fifty years girls looked and laughed at something of mine. What amazes me is that up there at the front, you have . . . Well, you know what's up there, you deal with it daily. Then just fifty miles southwest down the road, acre after acre of pretty astounding rooms. Then the Salon—and someone took me to the Salon des Refusés—the paintings that before the war hadn't been accepted for the Academy. That was an education. Even the rejected are brilliant. In fact—as someone mentioned to me—it's the brilliant who *get* rejected. It all has a funny effect on your ambitions, you know. Part of you thinks, all right, all *you're* fit for, Sonny Jim, is to go back home and illustrate the covers of adventure papers and boys' magazines. And another part thinks, I can do something like that!

She said, From what I know, at least you'll give it a great shake.

If she was sure he would exist to take what he had back to Australia and try to see where it fitted in the fabric of the place, she didn't care too much what difficulties he had fitting it.

I want to give it a shake, he said. Yes, I'd like to. Mind you, one of the war artists I met took me to see some of the new schools—even this crowd called the Vorticists—who are full of a kind of dread, as if everything is going down the gurgler. That seems a reasonable enough idea for these times. But what confuses me is how to take any of it back to Australia. It's all so different from here. It's not Europe. It's non-Europe. And always will be.

They turned into an estaminet of paneled wood and dim glass windows. A townsman and his wife drank together at a table. They were not handsome, but they provided Sally with a parallel to the joy she felt at sharing a table with Charlie. Charlie ordered red wine. She would drink it too, so that they experienced simultaneously its rough strength against the roots of the palate.

Two farmers came in. Both saluted them informally—giving them the credit for being defenders of the township.

Charlie took a deep draught of his red wine when it arrived. She also took a mouthful of this fluid, still mysterious and acrid to her.

Of course, he continued, there's no substantial difference between us and French people, except in us a kind of innocence. But do you think those farmers over there are giving a hoot about Verlaine or

Seurat? They're just cow-cockies too. So I think the day's going to
come for Australia. Just a bit of a wait, that's all.

It was a tender hope and she smiled at it. She thought then—as he
finished his glass—something so alien to her and as utterly surprising
in its arrival as the Taubes. Yet Honora had said it once about Lionel.
If I had his son, he could not be lost entirely. And then, if he weren't
lost, there'd be two of them. Men with glittering spirits.

She said, Do you have leave soon?

He lowered his eyelids secretively.

There's a big stunt on. But . . . I think by November, maybe some
leave.

She noticed they had both drunk their raw red wine down. She had
unconsciously kept pace with Charlie. He called for more. With the
recent whisky and now this wine, he had become a drinker. It was said
they did drink at the front—it was taken for granted there were things
best done when a man was part soused.

Listen, she said, I don't know who Seurat is. I would like to go to
Paris and see the paintings with you.

Sally, he said, his face reddening as if he knew she'd read him too
accurately—his zeal and desire. I would be so delighted to take you if
we could make our leaves coincide. I'll lecture you mad, the way I did
in Rouen. I've become an even more obnoxious know-all.

Suddenly it was time to order some stew and bread. When it was
eaten they strolled back out of the town. At the crucifix at a shaded
corner—the one before the Bapaume Road—he pulled her to him
urgently and precisely as she'd hoped and in gratitude she took up the
full vigor of the kiss and reimposed it on him, meeting him six-tenths
of the way to show that he could hope for something reciprocal. It
went on so long as to have the feeling of being a solid entity. If a farmer
had appeared on a cart, or a British truck driven down the road with
whistling Tommies, it would not have let itself be dissolved.

But there came up again that almost automatic feeling of temporary disqualification from joy. The closer she got to him, the greater the

demand to tell him the size of what she'd done. She didn't disengage herself so violently as to puzzle him or disappoint him. She simply turned her head to one side—as if for breath.

I am on duty tonight, she told him. And you have a long ride.

But we'll go to Paris?

I hope so, she said. For she did hope so still. Despite the care she had taken not to leave him confused, she could see he was a little confused. But it would not be a jaunt. He would be tested there. She would be.

Well, he told her. It's back to the bike for now.

He mounted the framework of the cycle and put a boot in one of the stirrups. She could tell once more she'd confused him. So she said, Charlie!

He looked at her and was expectant.

There's no question, she said, that you're a man amongst men.

What does that mean? he asked, smiling. Because it doesn't mean much when you're in an army.

Well, she said, it means my love, that's what.

He grinned madly. It was what he had cycled all the way in hope of.

Well, he murmured. That's a big admission for a girl like you.

Malice Without Ceasing

Freud confided in Sally. She believed that unless Honora now fell apart there would be no putting her together again. The collapse came. Honora was sleepless and working a continuous shift. Then she entered the phase when she would prop herself powerless against the door of a ward and look at the beds with an anguished frown and be stuck as if paralyzed. It was as if all the wounds appealed so equally for her care that she could attend to none. Her overcommitted body smelled of stale summer sweat. This or that nurse would come up to take her by the elbow and fetch her back to the mess tent. But she was hostile to help and would shake herself free.

At last Major Bright himself came, and on his restrained authority she left her ward in the hands of Sally and Leo, who had washed her and packed her things for her. Sister Slattery was being sent back to Rouen for a rest, Bright told them. When her bag and valise were ready, he helped her to a car. She moved like someone elderly but was half dazed with barbital. Freud, Leonora, Sally, and the matron kissed her good-bye through the car window.

The revelation was that Bright intended to travel with her and then be back by evening for the hours when convoys generally came. He was going around to the car's far door when he met Sally.

I am no mind doctor, he said to her, but it is not just the matter of her fiancé. What happened to him has been made graver by what she's seen here.

To Sally it seemed as if he thought he must defend her from people who thought the best of her in any case.

Bright climbed into the car's backseat and adjusted a travel rug across Honora's lap. He had the demeanor of a servant. Could the scale of her grief have entranced him? After the car had disappeared, Freud said, He wants her well—amongst other reasons—so that he can talk to her. He doesn't want her mad grief to put her forever inside the walls—a nun or a lunatic.

Bright was back by the evening. And the convoys did come. This late summer and early autumn assault—gambits designed to bring peace by Christmas and consecrate the numbers 1917 forever in the minds of the human species—were said to be a success. Yet it was hard to judge it that way from the wards of Deux Églises. If these bodies equaled success, one could not imagine the formula of defeat.

But then there arrived suddenly a night when the earth froze again and this time the war appeared to pause to mark the change of climate. Summer now seemed to have lasted mere days, all its chances quickly squandered. In the resuscitation ward—to which Sally had returned—she and the nurses wore balaclavas and the cap comforters the soldiers wore, and had hot-water bottles placed for them on their trolleys to warm their hands before they touched a patient. When the hot water from the bottles went cold and threatened to freeze, it was boiled again for cocoa or Bovril.

Her third winter of war was established now. Amidst the wetness of days and the iciness of nights a letter from Charlie Condon arrived. It nominated the dates of the leave he believed he could get to meet her in Paris. She was grateful the letter did not have to chase her. For there were more rumors their clearing station was to be moved northeast into Flanders towards that curious town named Ypres—which officers pronounced "Eep" and soldiers "Wipers."

She took the letter out of the mess—where it had been delivered to her—and read it standing under a pewter sky on a frozen ground. Of course—observing herself as if from a distance—she took the luxury of weeping in the usual plain way. Tears were a necessary river in the case of her and Condon.

But there were other reasons for these tears. He'd come through again—just a few coin-sized bits of shrapnel near the shoulder blade, he wrote, and a few on the hips. Metal had, he said, kindly avoided his spine. She knew spines metal had chosen to enter.

And so it was set. It must be said to him. The plan to murder a mother was not diminished by the plans to murder divisions of men. Trustworthy Nurse Sally Durance had pilfered rescue, designed it to seep all the way to her mother's heart—her gracious and unsated heart. But Condon would not be told the Naomi part. I planned murder, she'd say, and would have done it. That's what I'm capable of.

Under the frosted, sullen sky, Sally understood that part of her still belonged to that sickroom twelve thousand miles away. That it was as close as the resuscitation or gas wards. And thus she could not prance around galleries with Charlie as another girl might. Even if—when she told him—doubt would afflict him and she might find herself back safely and terribly on her own.

For three minutes the hope and uncertainty of the coming meeting kept her out there in the cold. Then exhaustion and shivering drove her inside and to her bunk. It lay in the new-built nurses' hut, divided into rooms for three or four women set on either side of a central corridor. Even here she had stuck with Freud and Leo. To hell with being called cliquish. She slept profoundly through artillery and aircraft grinding their way to the sky's apex and then rose to savor Charlie's letter and its promise of grace. Until a four ack-emma clanging signaled a new convoy had arrived and the sharpness of self was submerged again by busyness.

Later in the day she spoke to Matron Bolger and wrote back to Condon with the dates offered her by that sturdy woman.

In the first days of December they were told the clearing station *was* being moved—with all its instruments of operation and mercy—away from Deux Églises to a place not yet announced. Sally had her trunk packed in case the move occurred while she was in Paris. She took a smaller bag to the capital to meet Captain Condon. She caught a truck to Amiens—one of the eight-tonners that supplied the clearing station. In the train from Amiens to Paris she slept—but woke in time to team herself with two Canadian nurses as unwilling as she was to negotiate the Métro with their luggage and willing to share a taxi fare from the Gare du Nord. They had time to compare notes briefly. The Canadians worked in a hospital near Arras and had had a tedious journey down to the train. Their faces looked a little hollow—they had the drawn look of women overworked. Do I look like that too? Sally wondered.

The taxi took them to a Red Cross hostel for nurses in Rue de Trévise—one of the Canadians was from Montreal and could thus tell the driver in French that it was close to the Place Vendôme. And—she confided under her breath to the others—the Folies Bergère. Charlie would not arrive until the following morning, so Sally accepted their invitation—as they were being given the keys to their reserved rooms—to join them in the plain dining room that night. They'd hit the town tomorrow, they said. After a needful rest.

Arriving in the dining room a little after six she saw her companions were already at a table. Its linen was fresh and solid-cornered with starch. There was one other woman at the far end of the room and—alone at her table—she seemed well advanced on her meal. Her back was to them. Even so, her shape and the way her shoulders moved minutely at the duties of devouring bread and casserole were acutely familiar. Sally was shocked but immediately filled with a sense of intrusion. It was obviously Naomi sitting there, maintaining the downcast, chaste gaze of a woman eating alone in public.

She must first tell her new companions and excuse herself. She crossed to them and said, I'm a bit astonished. My sister happens to be over there. She hasn't seen me yet.

They wanted to know where Naomi was working.

In Boulogne, said Sally.

You're welcome to join us, said one of the Canadian women, but we understand if . . . Not a lot of chance sisters get to meet and talk about home.

That's what we'll do, Sally thought. We'll talk about home. We'll talk home squared or to the power of three. We'll get it settled.

Naomi had by now heard the voices and risen from her table. Sally felt a gust of affection at the solemn, peaked, mature features.

I have leave, Sally told her stupidly. Naomi clasped her arms around Sally and Sally did the same in return. It was so much easier now.

Naomi led her by the elbow to a seat opposite her own place and then—overcome with the hilarity of the coincidence—bowed her head down onto Sally's shoulder like a confiding schoolgirl.

Well, said Naomi when they had sat opposite each other. *You* obviously need building up—a tonic.

I was thinking the same about you.

Oh, everyone works themselves too hard at the Voluntary.

I've got a week's pass, Sally told her. What about you?

Two days, said Naomi, waving at one of the Red Cross volunteers who served as waitresses at the hostel. A pity it's so short.

I'm meeting up with Charlie Condon tomorrow. He's going to show me the galleries.

That's wonderful, Naomi said.

What about you?

Ian Kiernan's coming tomorrow and we're going to see our Committee of Clarity.

Sally had never heard of such a thing and shook her head.

I'm sorry. I presumed I'd told you about it. It's the committee that's overseeing our engagement.

Your engagement?

Yes, I told you in a letter.

I didn't get it, complained Sally, though she knew she sounded rancorous—especially at the postal corps. Then of course the true force of the news struck her.

He's someone worthwhile then? she asked, anxious that her grand sister might be eroded.

Naomi laughed. You know him, she said. You know the man he is.

Yes, Sally admitted. A sturdy sort of bloke all right.

And . . . despite its highfalutin name, this committee's job is to make sure we're . . . genuinely keen on each other.

Sally watched as Naomi laughed at her own use of slang. Naomi was very happy. How could she manage to be so simply happy with Kiernan and their engagement when she'd used the hypodermic that night? If they could talk about it, Naomi might be able to instruct her. Sally could not eat her soup when it came, though she inspected it at considerable length.

What's the matter, Sal?

Do you ever think of our mother? Sally challenged her. I mean, think of her as more than the dead we see each day?

Of course. I forget for an hour. But she returns. I was with her when she went. Many would think that grief. But it was also a privilege.

Enough of that, Sally decided. You heard of Honora? she asked.

I did. And I think any of us could end like that, with a bit of bad luck.

But it was back to the main question. Will you tell your Committee of Clarity that you gave her the injection? Sally said. Or wouldn't they understand?

She looked up now and saw what she thought was confusion on Naomi's face.

And have you told Ian Kiernan about it? Sally asked.

No, said Naomi. Sally . . .

I'm going to have to come clean with Charlie . . . I can't have him not knowing. That would poison us. I'll take the blame for planning the business. No mention of you. Because I always intended the whole thing even if it was you who stepped in—purely out of generosity. I've never thanked you—I couldn't manage it till now.

Naomi was doing a good act of mystification.

You've got nothing to be grateful for, Naomi said. My God, you should see how you look, Sal—like the starveling coming home. Please eat that. You're scarecrow thin.

What does that matter? The thing is, I love you and I hate you for taking up the burden. For doing it.

Hold hard there, Sally. Doing *what*?

Sally lowered her voice. Killing her! *Killing her*. I know you found my little treasure of morphine. You knew what I meant to do. You took it on yourself to do it and you ground up or poured out what was left. That's a reason I started behaving as if I couldn't decide whether I should love you or hate you—be near you or stay clear.

Just wait a second, murmured Naomi. And by the way, the Canadians are staring at us a bit.

Do you care about that? asked Sally in a whisper—though a fierce one. And bile did rise now. Such a stupid small thing? You and I killed our mother, and you're worried about bloody Canadians!

There was a demonic fury in Sally because all Naomi did was lower her face. No sudden rising from the table. None of the outrage Sally had foreseen and now wanted.

I did nothing, said Naomi calmly. She had taken Sally's hand again. Our mother just died. That's all. I don't know why it was that night of all possible nights. But—pure and simple—she died.

That can't be true. You took the weight of it off me.

No. I came on your secret supply amongst the linen—it was exactly where I'd hide such a thing. And I could have used it if I had your bravery. And your love—let's not deny that. But she just died. And when I made my fire that morning, I ground in the morphine with the rest—with the rhubarb tonic and the bromide and every other bottle and useless cure.

At this claim Sally covered her face with her free hand. Naomi said with a sort of unanswerable emphasis, Listen to me. I told you the way she died and that I was there. I'll tell you again. Mama died, pure and simple.

Sally began shuddering. It was like the shaking out of devils in camp meetings.

My God, I should have told you, Naomi admitted. I didn't know how it weighed on you. I could tell you stories . . . a kid who collided with a tram . . . The thing is, they insist in certain cases we maintain life whatever the pain—as if that isn't a sin and taking action is.

If their mother died—just expired of her own free right, the organism itself renouncing further pain—Sally was not an accomplice except by desire. That awareness—if Naomi could be trusted, of course—shrank the tumor. It did not excise it though.

Have you ever thought of doing something like that here in France? asked Naomi.

But these men are strangers.

One of your closest friends—I won't say who—told me when I was at my lowest on the *Archimedes* that she solved a fatal hemorrhage on the operating table with a lethal chloroform dosage. It's easier to do than with ether. I've *often* thought of doing something like that here. But amongst all the damaged boys we're faced with, I've never had that certainty I had back then with that case involving the tram . . .

Further down the room the Canadians had got up from the table. They called a cheery good-night. They realized, of course, that something of moment had been argued between the sisters. They wanted to let them know it didn't matter to them and also to reassure them falsely that it hadn't been noticeable. When they left, the Durance sisters also got up and clung to each other. They grabbed each other's shoulders with the pressure of crimes committed or projected and now confessed.

Later—when they were going upstairs themselves—Naomi helped Sally along and held her by the shoulder as if she were an invalid.

Now, Naomi ordered her, put your mind on the normal things. Go round town with Charlie Condon, have a meal, have a drink. Would you like to sleep in my room tonight?

No, Sally told her. She could think of nothing worse than fitting her new set of confusions and certainties into the one bed with her sister. They stopped in front of Sally's door.

Sally said, I think I believe you.

Naomi took her by the chin. Have no doubt about it, she commanded in a lowered voice. There *are* only two choices, you know. Either die or live well. We live on behalf of thousands who don't. Millions. So let's not mope about it, eh?

In the end Naomi went in and sat with Sally until she was asleep.

Yet when Sally woke in the morning and found herself alone and weighed whether she would flee from the capital, she found that even more she wanted to meet up with Charlie on any terms. The things Naomi had told her altered to a near-tolerable level her *own* truth and her accepted version. There was no doubt that something had healed in her during her profound night's sleep, as she lay deeper than the *Archimedes* for hours on end—looking up to a descending hull and horses and bandaged men from her finally ascendant angle. As she washed herself that morning she felt that she was simply one more woman of distinct crimes and valors. She thought, Yes, I *shall* have breakfast with my sister.

Charlie Condon—arriving from the Métro and presenting himself at the front desk in his trench coat—was much enthused to meet Naomi when Sally introduced her. He still had that look of unbreakability and had taken on the same kind of agelessness as Naomi.

I remember you, he said, when you seemed so much older and grander at school.

Again, plain conversation shone in the air. Charlie asked if Naomi and Ian—who had not yet arrived—would like to come with them to the galleries. First stop, the Louvre, he said, and then a few other places after lunch. We'll have buckets of fun.

Naomi explained that there was an appointment they had to get to. Charlie said then he had made a dinner reservation at a restaurant another officer had recommended to him.

He's good at reservations, said Sally.

Charlie thought he and Sally might go there and dine in the officer's honor, for the poor fellow had "taken a knock," as soldiers said—had been lethally wounded. Charlie sat down at a table just inside the door of the nurses' hostel, pulled out his fountain pen and wrote the name of the restaurant. L'Arlésienne.

Within walking distance, he said, scrawling the address.

He and Sally emerged into the street now. On the walk towards the Palais Royal and on to the Louvre, he told her, We're going to see the old rebels before lunch. After lunch we'll see the young rebels.

He hoped aloud that it was possible to get at least a sense of the place in three hours or so. Fra Filippo Lippi first. Titian and El Greco—Titian born earlier and a breaker of the mold. In this place Condon reduced them to something like acquaintances who happened to dispense their thunderbolts of color and light. And that was it, as he pointed out. Yet he had read a tract about art being tone and said he'd been annoyed by it and felt that if he'd followed it he would be hamstrung. But light. To transform color into light—that remained the chief doctrine.

They went to Velásquez and Goya. There was one more recent artist he loved—Delacroix. Sally did not tell him that—with other nurses—she had once walked past Delacroix with barely a glance. She wondered if she would ever get sick of his discourses. Why would she when she wanted him to have the chance to continue them for a lifetime? He didn't preach or lecture though. He carried his knowledge with a sort of boyish excitement instead of with vanity. He was an enthusiast. His eyes shone. If there was a percentage of vanity it was the appropriate one. The major percentage was of delight.

He took her to a room she had not known existed, and in it they found the world encompassed in the space of a small meadow. Entranced, Charlie pointed to the way yellow was applied throughout the compass of the huge Delacroix canvas called *The Women of Algiers.* She saw then *The Shipwreck of Don Juan.* It gave her pause. Yet it was somehow a consolation for the *Archimedes.* At the one time it reduced the *Archimedes* to the scale of other tragedy while expanding it to the size of the globe. Delacroix's self-portrait looked out at her with certainty and penetration. Charlie and Delacroix and the rest—she believed—were conspirators at the business of rescuing her as they had rescued others as well—unworthy and lucky people had walked this trail, salon to salon.

From them she was fortified for a momentous lunchtime.

At this hour of Sally's highest eagerness, Naomi and Ian sat again on facing benches in the plain Friends meeting house with Mr. Sedgewick and his committee members, the meeting having begun with the usual period of silent prayer and reflection. Was it that her sense of the world had swung so thoroughly in the same direction as that of Ian, or was it a genuine spiritual instinct of her own, which made her feel that she could inhabit this silence very comfortably and that God—who was not in the war—was in the silence? Other religions began with certainties and pronounced them from the start of their rituals. The Friends seemed to have no certainties and humbly waited for the voice to emerge. These people did not seem to anticipate or even feel sure that anything would grace them with a visit. That attracted her. She had never been in an uncertain church before.

It had then been like last time. Madame Flerieu spoke first, addressing God—as Naomi could now both sense and tell from the French she knew—and then beginning to discuss "these two young persons." Then Mr. Sedgewick spoke—also in French. He remained sitting with his face forward, his eyes placid and fixed on no one at first. Then his gaze settled wistfully on Naomi before moving across the room to take in Ian.

He said to Ian, Forgive us for speaking in French. Madame Flerieu wishes you to know that she does not ask these questions out of malice or judgement. She wishes to know more clearly than last time whether Friends are granted military exemption from conscription in Australia, and if they are granted exemption, then—so to speak—why you find yourself here?

Ian showed no irritation, though even Naomi could see there *had* been an edge to Madame Flerieu's earlier speech and was not convinced there was no judgement there.

He had made his religious position known to the recruiters, he said, but he must also make one other thing clear—he had not been conscripted. The Australian army did not have conscription as a policy. The idea of compulsory enlistment had been twice voted down by the people. So he wore this uniform voluntarily. He and Miss Durance, he said, had earlier discussed the question of whether they succored men who were finished with fighting and were forever on their way out of battle, or whether they helped repair them so they could be sent back into the field. The generals wished the latter. But the horror of wounds ensured that to a large extent their work was with the former—healing those who would never be able to soldier again.

He was not evading the question or the responsibility, he said. But many Friends were merchants, engaged in shipping and purchase and sale. Were they sure that all their contracts were with men not engaged in business to do with the war? In matters of business, any Friend would do his utmost to ensure the probity of their dealings, but it could not always be proven. Is the help that those Friends who are not in uniform give to the unfortunate throughout the world not influenced by the same uncertainty? That they might—by their compassionate service of food and other forms of succor—help strengthen soldiers for the fight and preserve unjust governments from the discontent of the populace?

Madame Flerieu had seemed to an anxious Naomi near unanswerable. But in the field of discourse—as strange an image as it might be—Naomi thought he was putting Madame Flerieu to the sword. And he was not finished.

Our work cannot always be perfected, he continued. Did I become a medical orderly from vanity? It is possible, since the vain always deny their conceit. But I became one as a Friend too. As for Miss Durance—though as shocked by war as I am—she was not a Friend when this war began and may not ever become one. She was not in her soul in 1914 subject to the same restrictions as I was. She operated within her conscience. What more can be asked?

She was shocked by the phrase, "She was not a Friend." She was shocked by his extolling of her conscience when she'd embarked on her war nursing not on principle, as Ian had, but with insolent self-regard. Sedgewick summarized what Ian had said for Madame Flerieu's sake in French which was more exuberant and swift than his careful English. A lot of Englishmen Sedgewick's age would have cleared out of Paris, she thought—during the Battle of the Marne so many months before. But he'd stayed here—in this capital which was never quite safe from the enemy's ambitions—with his Friends.

Madame Flerieu remained uncertain, it was clear. But it must be said that she looked at them with intelligent rather than rancid eyes. It was as if she had asked what vanities moved her? But in the end she did not seem to wish to be the obstacle, the religious harpy. If empowered by some more hating and embattled creed, one could imagine her becoming so. Hence the impulse arose in Naomi to tell Kiernan, To hell with Flerieu! Let's just get married by an army padre.

Mr. Sedgewick yet again consulted his fellow committee members in French. It was agreed between them that as was normal—when they could all next meet together—Naomi and Ian would merely be asked to announce their fixed intentions as a formality and could then be married by Mr. Sedgewick. On the same day, if they chose.

At the door Mr. Sedgewick seemed to want to let the others go on their way and keep Naomi and Ian back. Indeed the others did go. You understand, he said then, Lieutenant Kiernan, that you are not being subjected to some abnormal scrutiny? But you answered well, I must say. We can behave as perfected men and women in a perfected world. The perfected world seems far off now. May I take you for tea?

He led them two blocks to an apartment building and—having spoken jovially to a concierge—ascended three flights of stairs with them and led them into a large apartment with a view over rooftops to the Île de la Cité with the cathedral set on it. He said, as he brought them tea that Naomi considered to be rather pallid, It is as well, isn't it, that this is the war to end all wars? According to the American president you will never be faced again with the choice you faced four years ago.

That reminder of war's end combined with the pale tea became like intoxicants and she smiled across at Ian to hear this global promise uttered by their friend Mr. Sedgewick.

After Charlie and Sally emerged from the Louvre, they walked south to the icy river, which seemed to threaten to freeze solid, and stopped at a café and decided to sit inside by a window. The air had cleared to a silveriness beneath which Sally was sure many utterances not normally plausible could be made. They both ordered tea, though Charlie felt—like Naomi—that the French didn't make it properly. But Sally had suggested they wouldn't touch wine until that evening—for fear it would blunt the sight, she said. This seemed to be no problem for Charlie. He did not drink today as he had when he visited her at Deux Églises. Having delivered the tea, the waiter took their lunch orders.

Sally was ecstatic and frantic at the one time. As soon as the waiter left she felt she had to speak to him, as if it would be impossible once the table was cluttered with food, cutlery, cups, glasses.

There's something I have to tell you, Charlie, before we go any further. Because it'll change what you think about me. And it'd be cruel to wait till later. I will not put forward any special pleadings in all this—I'll tell you how things happened. My mother was ill. It was cervical cancer. Do you know the disease, Charlie?

No, he said. I haven't even heard . . .

It's a vicious thing.

Yes? asked Charlie. He looked confused. After all his certainty in the gallery, he was for the moment lost.

The simple truth is—my mother told me she wanted to die. It was something she repeated and that was very unlike her. In the end, when it had all got beyond bearing and she was pleading with God and me to let her die, to *make* her die, I stole enough morphine to put her to rest. But she died, you see, anyhow. Of her own accord. Without me having to use it. Just the same, you're with a woman who intended to murder her mother. I could say it was mercy. And others could say it too. Naomi says it. But that's it. How does that match up against Delacroix? Or how does it match up with whatever picture you have of me? But you must know if you want to know me.

He had been frowning through this.

What do you want me to say? he asked. Do you want me to stamp out of here in outrage? You want me to recoil in horror? Is that it? To flog you out of the temple or something?

I was hoping you wouldn't.

But you were a merciful daughter, for God's sake, he murmured.

Well, you had to be told, that's all. Because I am sure you've never even dreamed of doing what I had plans of doing in those days.

He shook his head. Then he started kneading his cheek as if he had a toothache.

O Jesus, he said privately. O Jesus Christ.

She didn't know what this invocation meant.

Let me tell you something, Sally, he said suddenly and in a colorless voice. She could see his teeth. They were not quite locked together but seemed for the first time ready to bite. And there was a rictus.

Imagine this. Imagine a man who went out on a patrol last night and got somehow stuck out there, wounded, thirsty beyond belief, in pain without morphine, hanging on the wire and calling to us in our trench. Calling, "I'm here!" Calling, "Help me, cobber!"

Say we go out before dawn and try to reach him, but we can't—indeed some of us are killed and wounded trying. And the enemy in their trenches lets the poor bastard hang there through the early morning and they call out to us in primitive English to come and get our friend. If we tried it, of course . . . Well, you can imagine. A feast for the machine-gun nests. And our mate out there is still calling to us. "Just need a bit of help," he might call. Do you think we let him hang forever? Do you think we don't do what I would like to have done to me if I were there crucified on the wire? Do you think we go on listening to him plead forever?

I'm sorry, she told him. It's shocking. Even so, I have to say this and you have to hear it. That man is not related to you by blood.

No, he insisted. She was suddenly astonished that he was close to tears. But he's the one we'll always remember. Even if we get to be old men, we'll never shake him off. And I say "him" even though it's really "them." So why shouldn't I be angry when what you are telling me is a . . . Well, not a little thing . . . but nothing done. An unfired bullet, for dear Christ's sake?

She watched his anger. In part, it fascinated her.

There may come a time, he said, when you will need to reassure me that what I have confessed was nothing at all. That it was compassion, not murder. For Christ's sake, you must take that same medicine now.

I told you because I can live with the thing if you can. The murders and the killings of mercy have both brought it down to size. But the size is still big. It can be borne though. I can be a happy woman for you. It's my ambition.

She was in fact feeling exalted. She barely doubted she could fly above the cold river.

He closed his eyes briefly. Opening them again, he said, All right, you've told me. And I've told you. There's an end to it for now. I can't guarantee what I've told you might not sometimes seep through and poison an hour. But it won't poison my life.

Nor mine, said Sally. Neither of our tales will.

Bitterly amused now, he said, If I'd known you were going into all this stuff I would have insisted on wine.

It's not too late. You could have brandy.

And then their croque-monsieur arrived. They fell to it with all the ravenousness of the redeemed. They said little as they ate, his head frequently down, though once he raised it and smiled broadly at her and shook his head just a fraction one way or another. Cognac, he asked the waiter then. It came quickly. He reached out and held her hand as he downed it. He shook his head.

I'm very slow, he confessed. You wouldn't have told me about all that unless . . . Well, *unless*.

He waved his free hand in the air a little, trying to define the word.

I'm so very flattered. That's what I should have said straight off. Instead of all that stuff about men on the wire.

He finished the cognac with a gulp. He smiled.

You'll come with me this afternoon then? he asked.

Yes. With a lot more ease than this morning. Not that I didn't . . .

I know. You liked it. This morning we saw the world as it would like to be seen. This afternoon we have the reality of the world. We'll see the world as it is and the way it will become. When you see some of the work of these new chaps, you'll wish you were born French or Spanish.

During their exhilarating afternoon at the Salon d'Automne and the Salon des Indépendants, whose motto was "No juries, no prizes," Charlie declared himself nervous that Kiernan would at dinner prove a temperance man and exhibit piety. Sally was able to reassure him. The dinner at L'Arlésienne went delightfully—with Ian himself drinking red wine for the special occasion. Sally and Naomi spoke to each other in an easy way that made Sally remember conversation between them could be blessedly ordinary. The acrid, murderous weight—capable of souring a lifetime—was gone in a day to be replaced by something that could be borne through a lifetime. None of them talked about their particular work—though Kiernan did digress into the organization of clearing stations. Some aspects, he argued, could be better arranged. The stores hut should instead be dug into the earth because without that . . . well, they got the message. One hit by a Taube and nothing for the wards. And in some of the stores there were—yes, even in these terrible times—signs that a few officials were in the business of war procurement, who were either asinine or had done special deals with suppliers. How rich some people were getting from all these dressings and pharmaceuticals and equipment! he said. How rich from syringes that sometimes fell apart.

But how far it had all progressed since Egypt and the *Archimedes,* Naomi asserted.

Under the influence of unaccustomed wine, it came to Sally as a fancy that the three of them had been cast into the sea and delivered just for this dinner and as company for glorious Charlie.

Meanwhile Naomi reported on the Committee of Clarity and the enduring suspicions of Madame Flerieu, and explained who "dear old Sedgewick" was.

Hungrier than she ever had been since she went to the clearing station—hungry as the reprieved always are—Sally ate liver and pork like a woman who might one day get plump.

Lady Tarlton's château was decked for Christmas and kept warm at least in patches by army stoves. Naomi and the nurses made up Christmas boxes for each patient—simple things such as chocolate and tobacco, shortbread, a writing pad. Symbols of homely renewal. She had bought Matron Mitchie some lace in Boulogne. This was one of those Christmases Naomi had read of—when joy is a simple achievement. Her sister now wrote to her weekly and Ian at least each second day. Yet even with the Americans now in France, no one dared speak anymore of the coming year as the conclusive one.

Two days after Christmas, Matron Mitchie got a telegram. Her son was in the hospital at Wimereux with gas inhalation and pneumonia. Mitchie struggled upwards without anyone knowing and was largely dressed and—with prosthesis strapped on—ready to travel when Lady Tarlton found her grinding her way along the corridor.

Lady Tarlton knew by now that she should not thwart Mitchie. She pressed an extra comforter on her and adjusted the collar of her coat and summoned Carling. He was to get the Vitesse Phaeton ready to go to Wimereux. When that was settled, Mitchie asked Naomi to come with her. With difficulty Mitchie was helped downstairs and into the vehicle. She had the idea, she told Naomi once they were inside the great car—where even the smell of the aging leather was a cold exhalation—that she might get her son transferred to the Voluntary once his symptoms eased.

When—through an icebound landscape and out on to the coastal road—they reached the hospital at Wimereux, it looked huge and deliberately ugly under a foul sky. Its grounds were littered with patches of dirty snow, the decay of a glittering Christmas snow of two days before. Carling left them in the car as he made inquiries as to where the boy could be found, and then they rolled down the long and frozen streets between huts—no boys brought out to be exposed to the sun today—until they arrived at the gas ward where young Mitchie was located.

Naomi watched for ice patches as she aided Mitchie from the car into the ward. It was at least warm in there. Nurses had insisted on the season and strung tinsel around the walls. They found Private Mitchie with pads dipped in sodium bicarbonate on his eyes. His skin looked reddish and the ward sister mentioned edema in the lungs and a temperature so high that he had been very deluded—even leaving his bed sometimes.

When Mitchie sat beside him he did not seem to hear the scrape of the chair. He had a square face that was slightly smaller than one would expect for the spacious head behind it. Mitchie began stroking his red, gas-stippled hand with one finger. To Naomi his situation did not look or sound good. Oxygen was wheeled up to him and the mask was put on his face and, for some reason—perhaps because of the way oxygen forced itself into him—the rasping of his breath seemed more intense now than it had before. A nurse took the pads from his eyes in the hope he could see and converse. But he seemed to recognize nothing.

When the young ward doctor came around, Mitchie identified herself as the patient's mother and calmly discussed his case further, raising the matter of a tracheotomy and warm ether vapor being pumped into his lungs by way of it. A nurse arrived while they talked and further bathed his eyes with the pads before replacing them with new ones. He flinched and waved his head. He had presented himself at an aid post later than he should have, the doctor told her, and had done so while already suffering pulmonary distress. The combination must have been an alarming experience. But—the ward doctor said—he had his youth and robustness to fall back upon. This was exactly the sort of medical commonplace Matron Mitchie would have uttered to parents in the same situation as she was now. Naomi noticed she invested her attention in every word as if it would need to be subjected to a later analysis—as if there were subtleties of meaning there.

When the doctor was gone, she had a further conversation with the ward sister, during which she suppressed her cough as best she could. The handkerchief she held before her face was doused with eucalyptus oil and she interposed the saturated fabric between herself and anyone else, in case they read the telltale pallor, rose-petal cheeks, the stain of blood on the lips, and sent her away.

From that afternoon Naomi alternated with one of the English Roses in accompanying Mitchie to Wimereux every second day. Naomi was with her on the third afternoon when Private Mitchie's temperature began to fall. He was sleeping when they arrived but woke when the nurse came to give him oxygen. Through cracked lips and with breath he did not really have, he said, Big Sister. It can't be you.

Well, it is, she said, standing up and kissing his blistered forehead. But you know, don't you, it isn't Big Sister anymore?

He frowned. There was no complaint there, however.

He said, Force of habit. I'm feeling better.

You weren't taking care of yourself up there, Mitchie reproved him.

I was, he said and then winked, but I gave the servants a day off and they left the gas on. Buggers!

He laughed—choking—and his eyes watered so that he needed to close them. Mitchie had been laughing with him—crying also—and the shared jollity threatened to strangle her too.

That doesn't sound good, said the boy, nodding towards her.

Don't you worry about me, she said. It's just a winter cold.

He fell asleep again and after a while Mitchie and Naomi left.

The next time they went there, Mitchie asked Naomi—with more apology than Naomi was used to—if she would mind having tea in the nurses' mess while Mitchie went alone to the ward.

Naomi sat there for an hour and a half, reading *Punch* and being interrupted by jovial questions from other mostly Australian nurses, who wanted to know about the Château Baincthun—of which they had heard all manner of rumors. That it was a club for officers really, and that it was somehow a *loose* place. They didn't mean her, but by and large . . .

By now Naomi had learned to talk like other gossipy women in situations like this—she became an imitation girl, even though she'd barely been able to handle such impersonation in her earlier life.

I wish it *was* an officers' club, she told them, and we were all club floozies. But it's like any hospital. It has all the normal wards and departments. The work is just as long-winded as yours. We have surgeons, ward doctors, nurses, and orderlies and a pathology lab. All you've heard is nonsense. As for Lady Tarlton, the Medical Corps *had* to build your hospital. But she built the Australian Voluntary out of pure kindness.

Ah, said the women of Wimereux, it's good to get that cleared up.

And then they began to decry the failure of the conscription referendum, which would have forced new men into the frontline. Naomi knew all the arguments both ways. Could conscripts be trusted? Could the unwilling? And the contrary arguments. The British and Canadians have conscripts. And conscripts would allow our fellows longer to recover and longer leaves. Naomi's secret argument in response was that all those who arrived would anyhow be fed into the furnace, without any break for the ones already there.

She was rescued by Carling's arrival at the door telling her that Matron Mitchie was already in the Phaeton and ready to leave.

She followed Carling, the ice crunching beneath their boots. The light was nearly gone, and a high wind rattled the slimmer branches of the leafless trees around the hospital perimeter. She found Mitchie in the backseat sobbing without pause and taking jerking breaths between furies of grief.

He began to choke, she said. It's unfair. The pneumonia's gone and now this bloody mustard gas! The doctor came—they used the hot ether device. It was horrifying. Poor boy. Breathing again though.

It will take him a day or two, said Naomi meaninglessly. Then he'll be all right.

He called out for my mother to tell him he'd be all right. His eyes were searching for her. He didn't call for me.

Naomi embraced her and pulled her into her own shoulder. He's still getting used to it, Naomi said.

Matron Mitchie could not however rest there in Naomi's caress. Coughs racked her, and she turned her head away. The coughing grew cruel—as was the norm for Mitchie. In her desperation she near shoved the eucalyptus handkerchief into her mouth—as if its vapors could choke her disease.

They were partway home, amidst meadows and copses where ice delineated every bare branch. As they entered a dip in the road quite close to the château, Naomi felt the iron fabric of the car take up a new kind of motion, a glissade which the wheels seemed to her to follow—as if the chassis would otherwise tear itself away from its axles. As she watched, the hedges on her right-hand side slid away at angles and almost graciously the limousine turned its nose into the hedge on the left, pitched itself on to its side with a frightful steel whack and then, with a terrible howling and grating, slid endlessly on its side along the road. The glass of the window below her was shattered and road replaced open air, and Naomi hung by a leather strap for an instant before she was flung forward and downwards beyond all control. In her own gyrations she saw Matron Mitchie flying also and at one moment Naomi collided—brow forward—into the heel of Mitchie's unyielding prosthetic foot. Then Naomi's head found a sort of permanent harbor in a fixed bolster on the seats that had been opposite her. Far too late the shrieking slide ended. At last—in stillness—she moved her head from between the seat and arm bolster, within which she had been expecting her neck to break, and looked at the skywards door and at that side of the car which had now become the roof. A grudging light was still in the low clouds and she yearned to climb out and greet it. But she turned her head and saw Matron Mitchie. Her feet—the true and the false—were both now unshod. She was head down to the shattered window and—through it—to the road. Carling climbed over into the passenger compartment. His face was bloodied but he was frantic to bring rescue.

He reached down past Matron Mitchie's disordered skirts and lifted her by the waist. Naomi helped him pull her upwards. There was copious blood, of course. But what was worse was that her brow had been flattened and seemed to have become part of her skull.

Do you think you could climb up there, Miss Durance? Carling asked, pointing to the sky, and push the door open? Yes, use the bolster to stand on.

It was the same bolster that had saved her head.

She dug her remaining boot—the other had disappeared—into a cleft in the wall of upholstery, and turned the door handle and pushed with as much power as she could from such a purchase. But the door was heavy and it reclosed itself.

We need to smash the window, she told him. He lifted and laid down Matron Mitchie according to the car's new alignment. She seemed limp still, but the damned war gave one a certain faith in medicine, in resuscitation. She climbed into the front seat and came back with the starter handle which was kept in its own cavity. She smashed the window thoroughly with a number of blows. Glass rained down on them. But it was a lesser peril. Then she hauled herself up and out and knelt down on the flanks of the Phaeton.

She had barely positioned herself on the side of the great auto when a military supply truck appeared and behind it an ambulance on its way to the château with a delivery of wounded. They slowed and stopped. Driver and orderlies got out and climbed up onto the wreckage. Naomi's hands were bleeding and unsteady, so as two of the orderlies clambered up, she surrendered to them the responsibility of getting Mitchie out of the car. She could smell their sweat and their hair oil even as they did it. They lifted Mitchie out and down to two men below. Then they lifted Naomi herself on to the road. The astounding Carling levered himself free and slid down the roof of the Phaeton to the ground.

Oh, he said to the ambulance driver. There's a lane back there. Go back and turn right and you can get your men to the Voluntary that way.

He came to Naomi wringing his hands and with his face bleeding considerably. He wept. Forgive me, he said. Forgive me. It was ice. It just took the Phaeton away from me.

My God, you're knocked about, Miss, someone said as the icy atmosphere bit her wounds. She saw Mitchie lying by the side of the road as the orderlies brought a stretcher.

Oh my God, asked Carling. Have I killed her?

No, said Naomi definitely because she couldn't believe in Mitchie's death. And, then, contradictorily, It isn't your fault anyhow.

It couldn't be thought that with Mitchie's motherhood unresolved and yet to be savored, she should suffer too lethal a mutilation.

There was an Australian piper at the general hospital in Boulogne. He had learned the pipes as a boy in Melbourne and he preceded the funeral party to the general hospital cemetery. The coffin was carried by six soldiers on leave who had been visiting their girlfriends at the hospital. Most were officers—for what that mattered to Mitchie!

Up the coast—at the other general hospital at Wimereux—young Mitchie was still too ill to process with the others and to honor the woman who had claimed motherhood over him. But a considerable cortege of nurses made their way behind the coffin and the bleating melancholy of the pipes to the pit dug in icy ground for Matron Mitchie. At the head of the procession walked Major Darlington and Lady Tarlton, behind them a brigadier general of the Medical Corps, and behind him Dr. Airdrie and Naomi. Naomi was on crutches from a sprained ankle. Her broken ribs stabbed her as she hobbled over the cold ground, and her head was still bandaged—she had somehow cut it on the glass of the window she'd escaped by. Life was so ridiculous, she knew, that it must be accepted and worshipped as it came. To be saved from the *Archimedes* as Mitchie was and to find her way back to the world of the walking through all that pain—and then to rediscover her friend Lady Tarlton and a son, and at that point to vanish from the world with her great declaration of motherhood more or less still trailing from her mouth—that was nonsensical! And all just because her skull touched the road during the car's skid when Naomi's had been jammed in the upholstery . . . Well, the absurdity spoke for itself. The disparity between their respective injuries was ridiculous. If God were praised it should not be because there was a plan to the absurdity but because there was a divine lack of one.

A Presbyterian padre read the prayer, the honor guard fired into the sky the Allies still possessed, and then—to some old Scottish dirge, by the piper who roamed in the Scottish manner amongst the graves of the heroes—they all watched Mitchie's grave filled until the coffin had been covered. With Lady Tarlton and Airdrie, Naomi wept while her side howled with pain from her ribs. Lady Tarlton put a calming hand on her shoulder as she had on Carling's on the night of the accident. Then she and Major Darlington, Naomi and Airdrie waited there to look at the mound. The brigadier came across to where they stood and confided in Naomi.

I feel great sympathy for you at the loss of your matron. We need all the good ones now. With the Russian Reds out of it, Fritz is coming, you know. Everyone understands that much. Fritz is coming. God knows where and God knows when. But certainly this spring.

He went. Lady Tarlton said, That was almost sensible for a brigadier.

They laughed lowly. Then they retired in the wake of the burial party of soldiers.

Naomi wondered, who would be unlucky when Fritz came?

Bureau of Casualties

Major Bright gave Sally a regular rundown on how Honora was progressing. She had begun working again, he said. She was not content with resting in Rouen. At the advice of a mentalist, she had done what all her friends had unsuccessfully urged her to—stopped writing to the casualty bureau.

In talkative moments in the nurses' mess, Leo took some minor enjoyment from Bright's visits to Rouen. He seemed to carry this boyish conviction that no one could see through him. Freud had a great deal of time for Major Bright and thought Honora—when back to herself—should be encouraged to seduce him. Freud had begun favoring words such as "seduce" again. It was as if—as in the old days—she wanted to shock her sisters out of sedater terms. She called couples "lovers" where others used terms such as "pairs." She had been witnessed having the sort of quarrels with her American—Captain Boynton—that were symptoms of an intense but difficult attachment. She had certainly won back her air of knowing and the casual ease which had characterized her before the outrage on Lemnos.

Yet sometimes Sally wondered if it was really ease. There was still a fever in it. She respected Boynton, though, for the fact that when Freud worked with him as a theatre nurse, he encouraged her to excise smaller pieces of shrapnel with scalpel and forceps—a setup anyone else would consider irregular but which Freud was skilled enough for. He thought she ought to start medical studies after the

428

war—though if the war lasted another five years, she might be forty before she finished.

The clearing station did not move until the New Year of 1918, when the wards had been emptied and snow covered the mounds in the field of the dead who were now being left behind. Trucks were packed with surgical and medical gear—even the X-ray machine, with its miraculous potency shrouded with a tarpaulin, was winched up onto the rear of a lorry. The women barely turned to look at the vacant huts and tents, at the pathways and duckboards—it would not do to look back for fear of being overwhelmed—but climbed on an old French bus to go up to Bapaume. They had on their balaclavas, overcoats, rugs, and whatever they possessed which could lend warmth as the bus slowly took on the temperature of outside. At one stage the engine died, but the driver and an orderly somehow got it going again.

Despite the scathing night, Sally slept—they had all learned to sleep with an ease soldiers were said to have—and when she woke again she could see a ruined town. They were in the sector black with ruin and rimed mud which had been prized from German grasp last autumn. They got down from the bus and went wandering in the ragged town of Mellicourt. Very few people still lived there. It was in particular the old who emerged to answer their rapping on the doors of cafés and estaminets. And they shook their heads—nothing to eat. Nothing warm to drink. The pipes were frozen.

The new clearing station—chiefly hutted and with plain canvas marvelously rare—lay on flat ground and closer to the front than Deux Églises. Its cookhouse was already pumping smoke and offered a guarantee of comforting fluids. Again ambulances arrived the first night. British gas cases, nearly all of them. All the normal comfort was extended to various and hectic traumas.

It was a matter of joy to Sally to know in the meantime that the Australians had either been put in a quiet sector at Messines or had come out of the line and were resting. They might be drilling for future dangers but were safe from present ones. She had, of course, therefore written to Charlie, telling him where she was now in case he had a bicycle available and was within riding distance.

When a note came back from him, it asked if she could by any chance be in Amiens on 16 March? "I'll visit the main entrance to the belfry near the *mairie* every half hour from nine o'clock. I believe it's still standing but even if it's shelled in the interim, people will still be able to direct you to where it was in its square. All in hope of seeing you . . ."

There was not enough time to get a reply back to him. She went to doughty Matron Bolger, who had once saved them from hysterical fear by recounting their mess bills. Reasonably enough she frowned. No one knew when an onslaught would come and the resultant flood of activity.

Are you meeting a fiancé? the woman asked.

It would be convenient to say yes since that would end two-thirds of the argument and the matron could add the word "compassionate" to "leave." But Sally did not share a name for what existed with her and Condon, even with the matron.

I had a very close friend named Nurse Carradine, said Sally. She is working at the fracture hospital in Amiens.

It was a good story—a story nearly true. If she were allowed to go to Amiens, she would indeed visit Elsie Carradine.

Because Amiens was full of what the matron called rough soldiery, she even used the telephone to make Sally a booking at the nurses' hostel—a converted convent. Sally traveled there the usual way—in an ambulance taking men from Mellicourt to Carradine's fracture hospital. Arriving late in the evening of the fifteenth, she asked the location of the belfry. An elderly French porter at the hostel convent drew her a map. It was a mile or so away, over a canal with ancient-looking houses along it. The great black shape of the overwhelming cathedral acted as her reference and she came at last to the bell tower standing in the midst of a square. A few less fortunate structures nearby had been damaged by bombardment. But the belfry Charlie had nominated stood ornate and unmarred. She went to a café at the edge of the square and sat there but visited the door of the tower each half hour until eight o'clock that evening—just in case he was early. Then soldiers approached her and asked her if she was waiting for someone. There was such raw appetite in their eyes that she gave it up. This—as she had already discovered—was a city of men. She had been told that it was the center of venereal disease for young Australian men—who innocently took pleasure here in whatever address and then passed the name of the house on to their friends in the line.

From the belfry she crossed the canal again to get to Carradine's place. It seemed to her that old men and women, harried-looking mothers with urchins, café owners, and one or two priests had stayed in town amongst the soldiers of many nations. She found the Rue St. Germain, of whose convenience to the hospital Carradine had boasted in a letter.

Sally rose up the stairwell beside apartments that had the look somehow of being shut up, and found the right number on the second floor. After she knocked, she heard Carradine tell her to come in.

Elsie was advancing across the living room in an apron tied over the azure dress of the Red Cross volunteer nurses. On the couch, to Sally's surprise, sat a drowsy Lieutenant Carradine—although he would now prove to be a major. He was wearing an army shirt and pullover and unheroic pyjama pants. His face looked thinner even than when they had visited him in England.

After Sally and Carradine had kissed and hugged—Carradine exerting a greater pressure than Sally could find it in herself to apply—Elsie stood back and said to her frowning husband, You remember Sally Durance, darling? She visited you in Sudbury.

And there it was—the bewilderment on his face. He did not remember.

Of course, he said. He was used to faking knowledge which the wound and its malign afterhistory had taken from him.

We were just about to eat. I was making shepherd's pie—with a dash of bully beef I'm afraid. You must be hungry after the trip.

Sally admitted she was.

And what a wonderful accident that you're both here at the same time.

Carradine put her arm through her husband's elbow. Come on, let's all continue this at the table. A separate dining room. Did you notice that, Sally? Wouldn't get a flat like this in normal times.

In the dining room, Sally and Major Carradine sat down at the table. While Elsie was fetching the meal from the oven, the major looked at Sally a second with eyes that were vacant of interest and recognition.

Was it hard to find this place? she asked.

Oh, we're subletting it from a notary's family, said Elsie from the kitchen. They wanted to go down south because everyone believes the Germans will take this city.

Do you?

Well, everyone thought they'd capture Paris once. But they didn't. Eric and the boys will keep them out.

Eric grunted.

The two women talked about each other's work while Major Carradine looked at his plate as if trying to work out what was sitting on it. Carradine shot him glances as she discussed her fracture ward a few kilometers away. At least with fractures you're not waiting for people to die. And the new splints and the traction . . . much better than the old ways. But I think it's the busiest work I've ever done. Do you have a headache, darling?

Eric said in a narrowed-down voice, Why does a man always have to have a bloody headache if he keeps quiet a second?

Now come on, she said, with the fixed smile of a woman who had had her hopes, but now couldn't predict anything. I'm just worried your dinner will get cold.

He picked up the wine and drank half a glass. If it were to get cold, he told her, it would not hurt it very much. Then he looked away and said almost as if he were disappointed with himself, Oh damn! I've done it again.

He got up, set down but did not fold the laundered linen serviette his wife had somehow provided, and left the room saying, Well, sorry, sorry, Elsie. Done it again. Any whisky in the living room?

Yes, she called. The usual place.

Carradine said, He's actually better after whisky. Can you believe that? They do everything on whisky and rum up there. Whether they're breeding a race of drunkards we'll know when this is all over.

Sally said, If you want to go and . . .

No. I shouldn't follow him straightaway. He'll get angry again. I know all the rules by now. But can you believe he passes muster at the front? He must be a different person there. The question is, will he ever pass muster anywhere else?

She put her elbows on the table, made fists and lowered her forehead on to her knuckles. She grieved for ten seconds but there were no tears. Sally got up and put her hand on Carradine's shoulder.

I've sent the longest telegram of my life to his father, said Carradine. If he was to get attention, he'd have to be forced into it by burly orderlies. But they have to take him home, I told his father. England's no solution. If we put him there, he'll be back across that Channel in no time, trying to go to the trenches. I know Mr. Carradine the elder will help—he's coming to England, you know. On a ministerial visit. The trouble is, Eric's going back to his battalion tomorrow. Surely his colonel sees that something is wrong? Eric's his adjutant, for God's sake.

Perhaps he seems normal up there, Sally suggested. Everyone's temper must be pretty edgy there.

And his colonel's a man of about twenty-four. In times of peace a soldier was lucky to command a battalion by the wise age of fifty. Now it's infants with little knowledge of the world. Look, I'll go and see him now.

Carradine rose. Her food was untouched. Her thinness was more apparent to Sally. She was not long gone.

He's asleep, she said—relieved—when she returned. Her voice was more like the normal Carradine.

There might be something pressing on his brain, said Sally.

Maybe. His temperature is normal. He doesn't have encephalitis.

Carradine was captured by a thought then, and said, as millions did, This bloody war! Surely it must be over within two years.

Earlier, Sally lied.

But Elsie returned directly to the subject of Eric. We went to Paris last month. Had a room looking out on the Tuileries. It should have been perfect. But there were headaches, there was anger. "I don't want to go and see those stupid tarts and their dogs in the gardens!" There was a scene in the bar with a British officer . . . A little hidden alcove in the dining room was the only place he felt safe enough to break his bread. Oh, if that bloody conscription vote had been passed, we'd have plentiful new drafts coming in. It would be easy to get fellows like Eric out of the line.

Perhaps, Sally ventured, though because they'd be conscripts, he might have to stay with them to hold their hands or keep them in place.

There was a slight flare of anger in Carradine. You sound like all those Labour people. They say even the ordinary soldiers voted against it—they didn't want their battalions sullied by conscripts. Well, that's all right, but they're all dying, that's the thing. Some battalions are so small now they have to be squeezed into others. I'm sorry if I sound cross. I'm bewildered. But not as badly as him.

They looked to the door which led to the bedroom.

Look, said Carradine, tonight's been dismal. But you don't have to go yet.

I won't, Sally assented. Let's have some of the wine.

•   •   •

Now, at Carradine's table on the edge of the spring of 1918, Carradine poured another measure of wine into both their glasses and uttered an opinion she could not have even given respect to a few years past.

Valor is complicated, she said. Sometimes I think the only brave ones are the ones who flee.

Yes, said Sally. Sometimes I've thought that too.

I hope tomorrow morning, Carradine whispered, there'll be a soft-speaking officer and some orderlies and provosts at our door to help him away to more treatment. Eric will scream at me if it happens. And hate me.

She shrugged.

Carradine was nervous about Sally walking back to her hostel in that town so on edge and full of soldiers. But Sally went downstairs and began the journey with relief and in a fever of anticipation for the meeting at the belfry.

The Great Experiment

The next morning at nine o'clock Charlie was a sudden apparition outside the door of the bell tower. She saw him before he saw her. His overcoat was undone, he had one glove off and was smoking anxiously. She could tell somehow—even by his movements—that he was nervous both about the chance of her arrival and the opposite. His skin was as harsh as a stockrider's, his face thinner and his features even more prominent. But he was clearly the same Charlie who had taught her about light and harbored doctrinal reservations about color.

As she got nearer he saw her and his body loosened, then he walked forward. He put out his arm swiftly and gave her an economic hug. Neither he nor she wanted notice to be taken here, with soldiers and officers coming and going. They both wanted to know about time. When was she due back at Mellicourt? When was he due back up there? It was little more than a day and a half in either case.

What will you show me today then? she asked.

But it's time I asked you. What do you want to show me?

Well, she said, if you would care to look up you will see a magnificent leaden sky.

Oh, he said, I've seen one or two of those recently. They're tending to proliferate.

Well, that's about my limit. I'm still learning.

You'll get talkative enough. After a time.

She liked that phrase, "After a time."

Haven't you noticed, he went on, that I always choose subjects on which I can be a know-all, and studiously avoid those on which I am ignorant? Viticulture, say, or stamps, or the workings of the internal combustion engine. I am not a Renaissance man. I play my limited strengths, that's all.

That's enough for me.

They both became aware that men were looking across the square at them—ravenous for a gram of their shared fervor.

There will be a great outbreak by the enemy, he murmured, and half the men we see here . . .

But not you.

Certainly not me. I've been sent down here to reconnoiter. In case we have to move when the Germans come. Now, I admit I've been studying up the cathedral *here* just to impress you. But it'll be damned cold in there. First let's find a café.

They walked across the square. Her distress rose all at once—with a sort of heat.

This coming onslaught . . . ?

Don't concern yourself, he said. We're in reserve for now. In any case, up there or down here, they won't hit us first off.

How do you know?

Because we're too good for them, he said simply, without a hint of bravado. They won't hit the Canadians or the British veterans, he went on. They will hit some poor, hapless British army of conscripts—kids just moved up, eighteen-year-olds with a few good old NCOs. That's one of the flaws of conscription, you see—men undertrained. Divisions that don't know themselves.

It was surprising to hear him talk like that—as a military analyst, a role he had never adopted before.

The likelihood of coming assaults was far from being the only cause of her fretfulness. There was as they crossed the square the gravitation of their two bodies. She knew he was aware of it as well—if he hadn't been, it wouldn't have been gravitation. They sat a little discontentedly in a café—a pause in their ferocious rapport that had to be gone through. He ordered brandy and drank it without coughing—the coughing at cognac was far in his past. Gone with the choirboy features. She drank the light-colored stuff the French called *thé*. He reached an ungloved hand across the table, and she took it in her open palm and felt the cold rasp of his. Again, the holding of a hand did not attract the attention of the deity here like it did in the Macleay.

You are the best of companions, he said. Do you *want* to see the cathedral? I mean, for your own sake. Not so that I can blather on . . .

There was something dizzying about cathedrals, something cleansing too. They were a sort of Gothic autoclave. But she had seen enough for now. She wanted to be with him in a way that did not have to do with architecture.

Charlie, it's a wonderful big shape. I don't know what to say.

Look, he told her, there's one thing I want to see in case it's pounded to rubble. Could you stand that? It's called the Beau Dieu—the handsome God. It's in the doorway. Do you mind . . . ?

So, she thought, he still has a fascination outside of the larger issue. Or was he nervous and the handsome God a means of delay? She told him, Of course not. I'd like to see it too.

They walked up to the cathedral of mismatched towers and found—between the doors—the smiling stone Christ trying to bring mercy to naked sinners who entered the maw of hell on the inner fluting of that great stone entry. Christ stood benignly between the doors, hand raised in the calmest compassion but also regret. It was not a god of omnipotence but of grief for his children.

And then inevitably they went in. She insisted by instinct—as if to let a kind of longing accumulate—that having seen the Beau Dieu they might as well finish the business.

It was not the exquisite experience of their tour of Rouen Cathedral. But that was not *this* cathedral's fault. Their minds were on a different order of meeting. They proceeded down the sandbagged nave and saw fire marks on some of the walls. All the stained glass had been removed. So too had many of the statues from the side chapels. But the altar pieces were still ornate. They both worked at being engrossed by this. But all this huge piling of artful stone, all this steepling, all those vaultings which had resisted the temptation of gravity for so long—these did nothing but delay the aims of this meeting.

In one of the side alcoves—made deeper and more shadowy by the extra heaped sandbags against the main wall—they seized on each other so instantaneously that neither of them could have sworn who was the instigator. There was as profound and languorous a kiss as the place would permit. She could smell the sugary potency of brandy in his mouth. Feeling she had passed through into unfamiliar country where the currency of normal self was not recognized, she said after a while, I was speculating on how long it would take before we reached this point.

He laughed low and close to her face. Not only did I wonder how long, he said, but I made provision, should you wish . . . I don't know how to say this. There's a place north of here. Few soldiers, if any, there . . . in Ailly-sur-Somme. There's a decent enough little hotel on the western bank. I've booked two rooms and have a driver bribed to take us out there—he thinks it's just for a dinner in the country. And indeed we'll have dinner. And then we can come back afterwards or we can stay there.

She rubbed his surprisingly smooth jaw. The same part of the face, she was reminded, that had been shorn off Officer Constable. She must fight that Durance habit still entrenched in her: everything that presented itself to be rejoiced in had to be matched up at once with something that must be mourned and feared.

Oh, we'll definitely be staying, she told him like a woman who knew what she was doing—the sort of woman she'd never suspected herself to be.

You said *definitely*? he asked with a sort of disbelief.

Yes. And if you lose so-called respect for me, I don't care.

Why would I lose respect?

It is only afterwards that conversations of this nature take on their character of ordinariness, of things said before by the millions—as if somewhere in the Book of Common Prayer or some less elevated document there was a prescribed exchange not only of the plain vows of marriage but of those of seduction too. Yet at their congress of two in the alcove, everything seemed new. Sally had an ambition to be a reckless woman—having seen and envied it in others. And now it was achieved, and she was loved by Charlie for it.

We need another café, he told her, as if he could absorb these new things only by taking a seat. Wait a moment, he said. No more for now.

They went out and found one and sat at a table not warmly placed. This time they had coffee.

Now look, said Charlie. His eyes were direct but she could see a color of embarrassment even in that climate-hardened face. This is a fatal or glorious thing I'm asking, he said. Because I've booked two rooms, but that's useless. The madame won't choose to be deceived. It's a very different case from the British, who—I believe, anyhow—can choose to pretend that adjoining rooms are proper enough. But that's beside the point.

She thought now that she might be more eager than he was but could not find a way to tell him that, to tell him to be easy about it. At the same time she liked his nervousness and was fed by it.

I didn't know that in the end we'd need to discuss all this tawdry stuff, he said. These cheap little deceptions. All this dancing with shadows. I'm sorry for it.

She held his wrist in a way which really suggested, Get on with it!

Why does it have to be like planning a crime? he asked.

Because joy is a crime now, she told him.

He laughed in gratitude but shook his head. His confusion wasn't allayed at all.

But it's worse than anything I've said, he insisted. There's a bogus marriage certificate . . . The French officers make them and sell them

to us . . . When I get there I can say, Madame, the two-room reservation is a mistake . . . My wife and I need only . . .

She held her hands up. You needn't tell me, she said. I leave that
to you.

But why does the world make such a rigmarole?

To make people think twice, she suggested.

But they don't think twice when they want to tear a young fellow's
head off. They don't think twice about artillery and gas. You can get all
that without jumping through hoops. No forgeries, no nods and lies.

That's an argument you can't win, Charlie.

He assessed her. He found it hard to believe in her acceptance.
Whereas by now she'd got over her own astonishment at her will to
go ahead.

If the driver who took them out along the river to Ailly that afternoon suspected their true plans, they did not care, and were pleased to
be dropped off by the door of the hotel which was out of the town, in
woods through which a path led to the river. Sally sat in a chair in the
little parlor and let Charlie conduct the business at the desk. She felt
far from abashed. She felt like a woman in possession.

The room was heavily curtained and lined with wallpaper crowded
with roses on a dingy background. The bed seemed concave—sagging
from the heavy ease people had taken on it over tens of years. It was
covered with thick shawls and its pillows were muscular. Sally coun-
seled herself that this was where it would happen. It was to be *that*
arena—that high bed which shorter-legged women would be forced to
enter only by unseemly gymnastics but which she could lower herself
onto. She felt nervousness—for his sake and hers. She had, however,
encountered something of the movements behind this rite in nursing
texts. She knew the physiology. She was not quite as ignorant as if she
had worked as a typist. She had certainly been untroubled by embarrassment when they signed in with the authority of their freshly minted
but faked document placed on the desk by Charlie as casual proof of

union. Now, here, he was still the one who was flustered because he thought she might be. He could not be argued out of the suspicion. It seemed he didn't know this was a test they must put themselves to.

He took off his overcoat and Sam Browne and uniform jacket and hung them in the great sturdy armoire. A meticulous fellow, he made himself busy about it and commented on the mugginess of the room, even at this time of year, and asked her permission to open the window a little. It was stiff and presented him with a test—a swollen window-pane in a warped and shrinking frame. He seemed to be delighted to have to struggle with it. Sally took off her jacket and hung it in the armoire. Someone knocked tentatively at the door—it was a moon-faced girl with a tray of white wine and some grapes and cheese and biscuits. Monsieur, she mumbled and crossed the room and placed her tray on a table by two heavily upholstered chairs. Then—keeping custody of her eyes—she left, waving her hand in negation as Charlie offered her a few francs hastily delved from his pocket. He closed the door behind her.

Would you like some wine? he asked. For the tray offered him another grateful delay.

She was standing waiting in the middle of the room. She had taken off her gray overcoat and jacket—a reasonable thing to do in a sultry room.

Later for the wine, she told him.

Would you like me to wear . . . protection?

No, our periods don't come. They did at Rouen. But they stopped again at the casualty clearing station.

But she was faintly willing anyhow to conceive a child in case Charlie disappeared.

She was aware now that she must dictate the terms. She reached for and caressed the side of his face. She had always undervalued touch except as a medical technique. She had discovered its spectrum now. He responded—all fears of cheapness dropping easily away. The wise, harsh, watchful face battle had given him was close. His mouth was of course tentative again at first, until he detected the frank invitation in hers. She uttered a sentence she could not have foretold. It was a sentence of no distinction but phenomenal novelty to her. It asked him to put his hand inside her blouse.

He did it. Again enthusiasm and certainty grew slowly within him. Touch my breasts now, she instructed. The touch brought a kind of convulsion in her stomach and at the spine's base, a weakness of the upper thighs. This is why a bed is needed, it occurred to her. The lovers are lamed.

You should undress, she instructed him. Behind the screen, if you like. I'll do my nurse's work with the bed. We won't need eiderdowns.

Again she had made him more sure of himself. You say undress? he asked. He seemed to want details on what this meant.

But you're an artist—you've seen all those paintings of love. What do you see there?

Well, nakedness, of course, he said like a schoolboy at last achieving the right answer.

And those army shirts are pretty rough when it comes to texture, she told him with an instructive smile. Unless they're tailored. And I don't think yours is.

No sense in getting them tailored, he said. Clothes get ruined up there.

So I've noticed.

And you? he asked.

I'll wear a shift for now, she said with this alien certitude of hers. I'm not an artist like you.

He went behind the screen. In the great ark of the bed she lay on her side in her shift, observing what she had read—in franker romances exchanged between nurses—that etiquette dictated she should not watch him as he emerged. According to these books, if you did not turn away a man might think you were assessing his person, his old fellow, his penis, his prick, his John Thomas—which in any case she was sure he would have covered for now with his hands. She turned to him though as soon as he entered the bed and covered himself with a sheet. Again, it was the question of pace which bemused him. He lay like an untutored log—or nearly so. She realized she might have the jump on him, knowing those technical diagrams from nursing textbooks. She dragged him by the shoulders. His hands with the terror of combats in them went around her as she waited in her shift. She could feel the calluses of his palms abrading her back. She could feel him at her thigh. At once an even more disabling flame and torture entered her body. She knew to part her legs. She never expected to have this instinctive willingness.

Then—as she wanted—he entered her, and that fury she'd been awaiting became possible between them. She had feared this penetration since she'd first been conscious it happened amongst humans. And here it was. It mocked all fear and she felt that marvelous irrelevance of outer worlds and outer populations.

Nonetheless, even now a large part of her mind stood above the bed. It waited just as the courtiers used to hang over the beds of young kings and queens, to make sure that nature—which took its course with peasants and farmers—took its course with Crowns. The point was that to Sally this was not only love. It was also an experiment on the future. This witness in her wished to verify that there was something here—some promise of becoming a single flesh, though not necessarily today. Because today ran the chance of being hit-or-miss. But in a longer run, over time and through regular exercise. He had acquired a more unified mind in the meantime. Large in ambition he now pounded himself into her. There was no end to the profane and delightful simplicity of Charlie as he moved and moved within her.

Oh holy God! he said.

Yes, Sally uttered—but even then she was still the witness as well as the participant.

She heard his magnificent helpless whimper—he could not achieve more than the uttering of animal sounds—and felt the gush of him inside her and heard that strange, boyish laugh as if something difficult had been achieved. Then it was a naked, sated child she held.

Oh holy Christ, he said, to think a bullet could deprive a man of you. Of your magnificent body. And of everything you've given me.

She smiled against his face. He kissed her familiarly and at length. All that caution he had shown before had blown away.

She told him with a prophetic certainty, You won't get any harm up there. Not now I've found you.

But she was full of fear nonetheless.

How can you know that? he asked, already three-quarters sunk in belief.

I don't know how I know.

He kissed her. You have become an oracle, he said.

Her witness—the inner assessor who had hung above this bed—was heartily pleased. Now she had no excuse but to give up mental exercises. Now the witness could withdraw and leave the participants to their chosen sport. Body to body. That, said the departing arbiter, was fine.

Charlie got up and poured some wine. But neither of them drank it. For need had recurred.

Thirty hours later she was in Mellicourt. The question was whether they would recognize the newness in her. But when she went into the nurses' mess there was another distraction. She found Slattery there—returned—chatting away with Leonora in an easy chair by the stove and giving a good impersonation of never having left.

Ah, Honora said expansively—seeing Sally and standing. She pulled her close. Sally was jolted by a surge of tenderness. Don't worry, Honora whispered, I know Lionel's dead. I've been working in a head ward at Rouen, and they take so long to die, poor chaps. In the scales of luck or of God's will, or whatever you may choose to call it, Lionel was lucky.

She said nothing of Major Bright.

After a convoy arrived at six o'clock the next morning, Sally and Honora worked together in the resuscitation ward as accustomed partners.

In that earliest phase of spring, the two great armies were gathered together with such mutual intent that they could not stop even for one night. Visits in force were made to each other across icy ground and thickets of wire. This was a test of blood—apparently the raiders won if they bled less than the raided upon. Prisoners were taken—or if they weren't, it was considered a failed ploy. And the guns had their own volition with that sound of unceasing hunger for flesh and membrane.

Just as they had over Deux Églises, at night the Taubes came looking for the town of Mellicourt and the ordnance supply depot beyond it. Sally and others knew that one night they would—by accident or malice—find the new clearing station, since it stood near the end of a light railway and close enough to desired targets. The very sound of these machines was a bruise to the soul.

But in daylight and free time, Major Bright and Slattery walked together down the thawing lanes to Mellicourt. Bright was a private man who had to overcome his edginess at being seen as a courter. So he tried to adopt the stiffness of the physician walking the patient. He had led Honora gently to the acceptance of the death of one lover and was probably a bit ashamed to find himself with ambitions to replace him. The sight of Honora and Bright strolling along struck the women as strangely sentimental—a scene from a time before bombardments.

Shirker

From Mrs. Sorley—Naomi could think of her under nothing else but her old name—the sewn parcels full of luxuries continued to arrive at Château Baincthun and lighten the dour cuisine of the Voluntary Hospital. According to a letter she had written the previous autumn, Mrs. Sorley was fretting. Her son Ernest had volunteered that spring and was aboard a convoy for France. It was, she said, not so fashionable to volunteer now that people knew something of the truth of things. "I have been so bold as to give him your address. He is not a bad boy at all. If he should call on you—and if you have the time—I would be very grateful if you could treat him as a relative as I have every confidence you will. I must say you Durances are fine-grained people and he is lucky to have you as a stepsister."

And so in the first days of spring Ernest turned up at Château Baincthun—a lanky, strong-looking boy Naomi half remembered from the Macleay. He told her he had walked from Boulogne—where he was waiting for the boat to London for leave. He had spent the winter campaigning but as was usual with men he gave few details. In fact, when she was called to meet him, she thought that what he had been through seemed to sit easily with him. Unlike officers he wore no gloves and not even the mittens the orderlies at the château wore. The cold, wet hike from town had not seemed a hardship to him. She took him to drink tea in the room that served as the nurses' mess.

Sorry if I'm a bit in the way, he said. He did do an impersonation of a clodhopper in his army boots. And when she introduced him to Lady Tarlton, he was shy and spoke carefully, like a questioned adolescent.

It's my mother writing every week, he explained to Naomi. "Have you seen the girls?" Not that I've got any objection to that. Except I know you're busy . . .

And he made a gesture to the east, that casual reference to the huge zone of mire and blood. He drank his tea thirstily.

Isn't it funny to think that after the war we will be stepbrother and -sister? I think it's a real bargain on Mum's part. I always thought you Durance girls had a kind of style. Well, as long as you can stand the rough Sorleys . . .

Have you had any wounds? she asked.

I had the gas a bit, he admitted. The stuff that hangs around and everyone's hoarse with it. But I wasn't bad enough to go to the regimental aid post. You know, it's a shock at first. You go into stunts where you don't think a fly would live, let alone a man. But somehow you go on fitting yourself in amongst the lumps of lead. We're doing pretty well up in Flanders. Showing them a thing or two.

When it was time for him to go back to the camp she had a motorcar—not the fatal big black-and-white one—brought round to take him. She did not want him to travel alone on foot in the cold.

They waited on the steps for the vehicle. She asked, Have you seen my sister?

No. But if she's at a clearing station . . . It's amazing who you meet here if you stay long enough. I'll wait till after Fritz is finished with this big push they say is on the cards. Then I'll see her.

Hey, you've got a lot of authority, he said, winking at her as the car arrived and he got in. The Durances *are* a step up for the Sorleys.

No. Your mother says that. But she's wrong.

She watched the car roll away amidst the skeletal trees. Now she had another child to be concerned for.

• • •

A strange thing was observed at the clearing station in Mellicourt. Sally became aware of military police arriving and taking away order-lies. Not all of them, but a sampling. They were not under arrest, she was told by the nurses. They were to be transformed into infantry—even if that left the wards shorthanded.

These events had their impact at the Château Baincthun too. Naomi received an urgently scrawled note from Ian Kiernan.

> I'm afraid I write this by grace of a provost sergeant major. I am in the old gaol at Amiens. It's a bit like a gaol out of an opera. They have gleaned nonessential men from the Medical Corps and ordered them to take up arms and go to the front. I have been con-sidered nonessential to the future of my clearing station. I realize my naïveté, in that I did not ever think this a possible outcome. Madame Flerieu was right. But having refused to obey the order, here I am.
>
> Dearest Naomi, I know you are busy until late at night. But could you write a letter to the deputy provost marshal, Austra-lian Corps, and tell him of your knowledge of my conscientious objection? Could you also ask Mr. Sedgewick if he could write and mention our meetings with the Committee of Clarity? I know this is tedious for you, my love, but I am pleased to be able to allay your fears. The provosts treat me with every sym-pathy. I just wish if possible to avoid ending up in a prison in Britain—who would not wish that? In the meantime, we take comfort from the fact that the Australian commanders still re-fuse to impose the death sentence for my sort of behavior. I hate to think there may be some poor British Quaker, or even Ca-nadian, who has been trapped in this peculiar way and could be executed.

She took the letter to Lady Tarlton. Oh my dear heavens, said Lady Tarlton after reading it. Would you like me to write too?

You'd consider that, would you?

Yes. You must go to Amiens at once and take a letter from me. As if anyone would want to *pretend* to be a Quaker.

Naomi did not comment on this curious compliment. Lady Tarlton quickly assembled all manner of warrants to allow her to travel. They both knew it would not be a comfortable journey since Amiens was at the very crux of the British position along the Somme and was known to be so by the enemy.

When she arrived in Amiens, after a journey of many delays, and found her way to a military office near the entrance to the station, she was told that the prison was five kilometers north and to the west of the river. No, no transport. She should try to take a taxi.

She went to a hotel and found a lazy porter and risked giving him a handful of francs to find her a cab. The cab driver was told to expect a similar bounty. So in the back of his taxi she set off across the canals and at last through the suburbs and out into the countryside. The prison rose up—a fortress—amidst the clouds of a dour plain and its cultivated fields. Arriving at its gate she tried to persuade the taxi driver to wait. But despite all offers of reward he pretended not to understand and drove off. It was no problem—she could walk the five miles back to town.

She went over cold gravel to the wooden postern and noticed a bell to one side that could be rung by hand. This she took to with a will. A British corporal opened the postern. She told him what she wanted and he seemed amenable and asked her to step inside. She found herself in a gatehouse which contained cave-like offices. First she had to sign in. She had to admit it was not exactly like the oppression of the Christians as depicted in Sunday School. The British NCO seemed quite sympathetic that she'd got herself involved with a shirker.

And you're the fiancée? a sergeant-major asked from a more deeply placed desk of the office.

Yes, she said.

Good of you to come and see him, said the man.

He said he'd have a word with the captain, and turned a handle on his telephone. He murmured into the machine very confidentially. Young lady here. Wants to see her fiancé—Australian deep thinker. Serving nurse, named . . .

He cocked an eye but then looked at the register.

Durance, is it? Durance, he concluded. He looked at another roll book on the table. First Lieutenant Ian Kiernan, Australian Medical Corps. Yes, sir.

He came out from behind a counter and escorted her into the yard and along its thick enclosing wall and through a door. They entered now a further room which was utterly enclosed and totally bare except for a deal table and two fragile-looking chairs. Here he left her.

Naomi waited five minutes and grew more and more depressed by the place, and overwrought by its air of punishment—not anticipated punishment either. But punishment already as good as accomplished. Then there was a noise at the door and two military police armed with pistols brought in Ian. He looked identifiably the same Ian as before, but he was inadequately dressed for the weather—no jacket. They'd taken his braces and his belt so he had to hold up his trousers with a fist bunched at his waist.

The guards took up their posts on either side of the door. One of them announced in a voice of triumph, No, no touching.

And no loud opinions, thank you, said the other in his own loud voice.

Ian smiled. He sat at the table. She wanted of course to hold him but when she reached for his wrist, one of the guards said, Miss . . .

If you're so keen on the war, why aren't you fighting? she said to the guard. She knew it was a doomed argument.

Please, Naomi, Kiernan pleaded.

I've heard that one before, Miss, said the provost anyhow. From nearly every shirker.

She realized she must concentrate on Ian.

They are so stupid to lock you up after all this time, she said.

Well, now that I am in prison, the Committee of Clarity has every reason to believe in my sincerity, he said. By the way, Lady Tarlton wrote and said she would use her good offices . . . They gave me her letter because they were impressed by her title. They're obviously going to use the same argument as Madame Flerieu. It served her and will serve them. If I was a conscientious objector, I shouldn't have been in the Medical Corps in the first place. Medical orderlies are ripe to be called on to become riflemen, and they are naïve if they enlist and consider that they will never be asked to pick up a rifle.

But the chief medical officer at the clearing station must know your sincerity.

Oh, yes. But there have been French mutinies and even British ones. And our chaps are making an art form of absence without leave. The authorities have to make a stand, you see, and they are not always exact about how they do that.

He turned his head and she could see a bruise she had not spotted before, running from below his right temple and over his cheek and down his jaw. He put his finger to his lips.

Inexact methods, he murmured. But that's over now. A rite of passage.

The military policemen maintained their silence.

The strict charge is mutiny, he told her. When I get to the court martial, would you find it possible, my dearest Naomi, to be a witness? If they knew that we were pursuing betrothal under the aegis of the Friends . . .

Yes, she said. You must insist they call me.

One of the military policemen said time was up.

She said to them, Can't you give him a jumper? It's cold today.

All the prisoners have a blanket in their cells, one of them said.

She stood as Kiernan was taken out. Alone in the soulless room, she was overwhelmed by a combination of desire and a feeling of revelatory force. The world was after all malign by its nature and not by exception. Or else it was established that it was wonderful but a madhouse. Young men were smashed for obscure purposes and repaired and smashed again. The Friends were thus the criminals in the planetary asylum.

The trial will be in Amiens in March, the sergeant told her on the way out.

On the morning before the trial, Naomi again left the Château Baincthun—this time she had been summoned as a witness and by an authority superior even to Lady Tarlton's. Lady Tarlton had declared herself ready to go and speak as to Ian's character. But since she knew Ian only remotely, she was not summoned.

At the end of a tedious railway journey she reached the Gare d'Amiens, just by the cathedral, and had a dreary walk through streets populated by soldiers to the nurses' hostel. Here she failed to eat a plate of lumpen food. A ferment of concern had her repeating in her head every argument for Ian's exoneration. The skein of reasons rolled and unrolled itself there almost by its own volition. Just a few degrees more of intensity and she felt she would be in the streets haranguing military men. In such a state—and occupying a shifting mattress—she failed to sleep. She knew that most of the Australians were up in Flanders and that coming down here to the trial in Amiens was probably an excursion the officers of the court martial welcomed. She hoped that would put them in a kindly frame of mind.

A room in the *mairie* had been requisitioned for the trial and in the morning Naomi walked to that august French republican building with its two wings which made a near-encircling square within which little leniency seemed possible. Mounting the steps, she presented herself to the Tommy provost at the counter. He signed her in and asked her to wait in a corridor. Sitting on a bench, she saw a number of disheveled British soldiers proceeding to trial in handcuffs, to be judged for crimes of indiscipline and inebriation and desertion.

At last she was fetched by an Australian provost who asked her what the weather had been like on her journey and led her down a further corridor and into the featureless courtroom.

She saw Ian first. He stood in apparently good health behind a wooden barrier to one side of the room. He wore a jacket but with no webbing belt. They must have given him braces for the day because his pants seemed to stay up without the indignity of his holding them. There were two officers seated at tables on the floor of the court and then—at the table set on a rostrum—sat three young-looking officers who were to be Kiernan's judges. She had expected older men. But many of the older men had been winnowed out. The contrast between the judges' smartness, as worn as their uniforms might be, and Ian, produced a peculiar dread in her. Her eyes fixed on them as she was sworn in by a military clerk of the court and told to sit. They—by contrast—still wrote casual notes and turned around in their chairs to mutter to each other.

Ian's eyes lay calmly on her a second, and then he looked to his front as if he had earlier been ordered to. He had a young captain for his counsel—a man with the sort of moustache grown in the hope it will cause him to be taken seriously. His military prosecutor was a major and seemed the oldest man in court—though barely forty years. Could these men all be relied on to judge Ian in their own terms? That was the tortuous question. Were there unseen superiors they would attempt to gratify? And though this room in the *mairie* was bare and lacked the atmospherics of the stage, the members of the court could have with justice appeared in any court-martial drama in any theatre. It seemed a gratuitous matter that a man's freedom should hang on a ritual like this, with the three immature priests and the acolytes putting on their amateur show.

She was asked to stand in front of the table behind which stood Ian. During swearing-in and all the rest she could not see him. The prosecuting major asked her to outline her own military and individual reasons for having presented herself. Did she know the accused, when had she first met him, under what name did she know him, and in what subsequent circumstances did they meet? He asked automatically and seemed to have no idea how crucial all these matters were. There was a different order of urgency in her answers.

Despite not possessing any breath, she began to give the summary of their long acquaintance which the prosecutor did not let her spend much time on—interrupting details she considered crucial. For example, how Ian had behaved after the *Archimedes* sank. How could she make this major assess the true weight of these matters? How could he be made to see that it was essential to the globe's sanity that he be acquitted?

So, he asked, you are now the fiancée of the accused?

She said that they had been betrothed according to the rites of the Society of Friends.

The Quakers? he asked.

That's what people call them, said Naomi. And then she said, in case the name were an argument against Ian, When I visited the Society of Friends in Paris with Lieutenant Kiernan, I did not see anyone quake. In fact, the reverse was true. It was all calm consideration on their part.

And you are not one of these Quakers yourself?

No. I am not. But I am not averse to them.

Then how would you say this war should be fought? By men like Lieutenant Kiernan? Should everyone be a surgical supply officer or a medical orderly?

One of the presiding officers did remark offhandedly that the prosecutor was being perhaps too zealous and that Staff Nurse Durance was not herself on trial.

You don't come from a background of conscientious objection to fighting, do you? the major asked her.

I do not, she agreed. But, mind you, the question never arose where I came from.

If you had a son, say, and there was a future war, would you let him fight?

I would try to stop him. I've seen so much mutilation . . . No mother would . . .

All right, the major said, holding up a hand and returning to his table. He sat and now Ian's young captain was permitted to ask his questions. She watched his face for the sort of moral force that might set Ian free.

Has Lieutenant Kiernan ever mentioned in your presence his objection to bearing arms?

She was pleased to report he had. Even when we first met in 1915. Once we had become friends, he said many times he wanted to look after the wounded and sick but that his religion prevented him fighting.

And you and Lieutenant Kiernan are survivors of a torpedoed ship, the *Archimedes*? How did Lieutenant Kiernan behave at that time? Was he at all cowardly?

I would say he was very brave.

How did he demonstrate that courage?

In the water he took control of our party. It was why so many from our raft survived. He kept us together and urged us not to let go. Some men did let go but it was not his fault. When we saw a ship, he let off our flare.

And sadly that was all Ian's lawyer wanted to know. Ian looked at her with a half smile as she was taken out of the court. She did not intend to go politely. She turned and said, Gentlemen, everyone who ever met him was told. That his conscience would not let him bear arms.

The young officer who had represented Ian intercepted her and whispered, If you wait outside, I'll tell you the outcome.

The humanity of this cheered her. She waited in a delirium on a bench in the corridor. Here, she surmised, in peaceful times shop-keepers and farmers had sat awaiting decisions on land boundaries and drainage. Her imagination swung between Ian set free and some improbable sentence of years or worse. There was no question but that she too was counted in whatever befell him.

She was aware as she waited of all the futile prayers, including hers, which filled the air—appeals to a deity who did not seem able to stand between artillery and this or that mother's son or wife's husband. She felt the uselessness and the silliness of adding her own. Yet it was an unstoppable impulse. She pleaded that the judges became drunk with wisdom and sent Ian back to his clearing station.

The young captain advocate came out of the court.

I'm sorry to tell you this, he said. It's fifteen years.

The stated span of time made no instant impact on her. Fifteen years? she asked. What does that mean?

It's the sentence, sorry to say. Everyone agrees it's rotten luck. But it had to be done. And of course it's better than . . . other possibilities. What you said about his bravery when your ship sank . . . that helped him.

The reality of this toll of years entered her now like a wave of heat. She stumbled. He caught her by both elbows.

Steady on, Nurse, he told her. The presiding officer said you could see the prisoner for a few minutes. Only this. it's best not to get him or yourself distressed.

Two military police officers took her to a small room where she could say good-bye to him. He was already standing with his hands cuffed in front of him. The officers remained there and seemed anxious above all—like the ones at the prison days before—that no touch should occur.

This is ridiculous, she said to him. Ian, what can I do?

He said, Would you thank Lady Tarlton? Not much she could say, since she'd barely met me. And my CMO—I'll write my first letter to him. You did wonderfully, Naomi. I'll always remember you. Could you write to Mr. Sedgewick and tell him the marriage will not take place? You should forget about me now.

She held up her hand. She was close to anger, in fact. How can I root out memory? she asked. Lady Tarlton and I have not even begun writing letters for clemency and sending them to all points of the compass.

She hadn't thought until now of that option, and it transformed her from demented girl into campaigner.

He said, with a small chuckle, you're going to bludgeon the top blokes into a pardon?

I am, she said.

But you have no obligation at all, you know.

That talk is rubbish, she told him. He smiled at her so plainly but, she thought, with a mass of meaning—an invitation and farewell at the same time. According to what she knew of them, men were good at mixed messages—even Quaker men.

And now it seemed that everything had been encompassed and she could not think of what to say. Ten seconds ached by.

All right, said a provost as if he wanted to end the silence. That'll be just about it, lady and gentleman.

And so—regretting her silence had signaled the meeting's end—she was escorted out. She found the main entrance. I won't tremble and weep, she promised herself. I'll annoy and agitate. Life would be made tolerable by that mission.

At the front door a guard said, Hang on, Miss, there's Gothas overhead.

She could hear the bombers now, in amongst the background thunder of guns, the Archies close by and the seamless rage of the barrage at the front. She waited a second and then placed her head in a groove between two stone moldings and began to shudder at the awful perversion of things—of sky not permitted to be sky, of air not permitted to be air.

Men Lost

Naomi could not have explained the exact stirring of resolve that sent her into the street once the Archies stopped and safety was howled forth by way of a Klaxon. But the moment came. At the road passing the mouth of the *mairie* she saw some young but worn-looking Tommies—their eyes vacant and their pace unsteady and some without their rifles—drifting past. Their uniforms were stiff with mud or dully gleamed with filth. They began milling around a mobile canteen serving tea in the street. These man-boys drinking tea, and standing about cadging cigarettes, were—though Naomi did not fully understand this—the hollow-eyed ejectees of a broken front. Here and there military trucks pulled up and soldiers jumped down with rifles and took up positions at the major corners to try to gather up any further tide of broken men and urge them to stand fast.

An elderly lieutenant wearing the patch of some administrative corps watched this unfold, shook his head, and turned and saw Naomi.

Well, it's on now, Miss, he said. The line's busted and we are for it.

A paternal interest came into his eye.

You should get on your way, if you can. The trains may well still be operating. The further northwest you get, the better, for now. Though we don't quite know where they're aiming for yet.

She thanked him and went on. At the ornate railway station a few blocks away things were more orderly and men got down from the

Boulogne train with their rifles and kits and looked robust enough to take a swipe—at least—at restoring the line.

She boarded the train for its return to the coast and shared a compartment with a priest and a middle-aged French couple. It would have made as much sense to try the husband for cowardice—with her and the priest as judges—as what she had seen that day. The priest read his office book and the French couple and she exchanged a few primitive sentences in English and French about their destination. They either said they were from Wimereaux or were going to Wimereaux.

The railway ran along the Somme and then curved north, and there was certainly a sense of escape to it. The priest—having finished his office—joined in the chat. He seemed to be delighted to know that Naomi was from Australia. *Les belles Australiennes!* he insisted. *Nos Australiennes!*

Her fellow travelers did not seem alarmed by the threatened assault on the heart of France. Perhaps they were not as aware it was to happen. The priest reached into his pocket and handed her a small medal. She accepted it in her gloved hands. Somewhere between Methodism and Quakerdom, belief and disbelief, she held a graven image in her hand. And yet to do so seemed of no great import and bolstered her sense of purpose in a way she would not once have believed possible.

The astonishment awaiting her on her return was that Major Darlington had gone, all in one night, and—said the English Roses—without a proper farewell to Lady Tarlton. A new chief medical officer was awaited. In the meantime, Airdrie and the weedy but obviously enduring young ward doctors did what they could. The nurses knew where Naomi had been—how could such news not get around the hospital?—and were awed and dared not ask her the length of sentence.

Everyone in the meantime watched out for Lady Tarlton. In the wake of Darlington's departure she had chosen to retire to her office. They wanted—not without feeling for the woman—to see how she would seem once she reappeared. At teatime she came out as usual to make the rounds of the wards and talk to soldiers. Her presence was as ever a powerful medicine as she leaned above them asking after their health in that most elevated accent which many Australians had not heard till they came here. The recuperating officers waiting to go back to the front—their shrapnel or bullet wounds or concussions now healing—were clearly and to a man enchanted by her.

But that evening the experienced could see a delay in her gestures and inquiries—a distractedness that was no more than a tremor, a pulse. The eyes laid on the patient might go blank for a second and then engage themselves again.

Come to my office, she murmured in contralto to Naomi at the end of rounds.

Naomi was secretly and with shame pleased to have a sister in misery. As she followed Lady Tarlton, the eyes of all the Red Cross women were on her, covetous of her closeness to Lady Tarlton. They and the Australian nurses watched them with that fascination which women in a crisis of love generate in others. As they walked, Lady Tarlton questioned Naomi about Ian. Naomi—still dazed from the day but sustained by a margin by her belief in her campaign—told her all the details and confessed her urgency to write and write again to General Birdwood and General Howse of the Medical Corps.

Lady Tarlton's office as they entered seemed as ever it was. Fresh piles of documents on the desk and around the walls gave no suggestion of slackening business. She motioned Naomi to a seat, went and got a bottle of cognac from a bookshelf—there was no concealment and it stood in plain view—and poured some in two glasses that were on the desk.

Men are very strange creatures, Naomi, she said. And when they're not, they get punished by prison.

She sipped the cognac.

We had a quarrel. A *quarrel*—no more than that. Yet he used it as the pretext. It wasn't why he left. I'll never believe that. It served him as an excuse, a casus belli, and he bolted.

She drank again. Mmm, she said as she swallowed. Perhaps from now on, the bottle shall be my lover.

Naomi privately thought the bottle was an unlikely destination for all the light and energy in the woman.

The Quaker and your mishap, she told Naomi. Mitchie and her surgeon, me and mine. They are all misadventures, you know. It's a wonder we put in the effort. It seems I made a fool, or tried to, of a cousin of Darlington's in Boulogne, some Pooh-Bah in the Medical Corps. I remember the man, and am rather amazed the major was related to him. I mean, the major is a man of genuine talent. But I believe that as a result said Pooh-Bah swore vengeance on Darlington as well.

She drifted off and looked across the room blankly for a while.

So that's the official story, she continued. But there is a real story. And it's a sadder one. But we are straying too far from your grief.

No, please.

Be assured—we are just beginning our campaign in regards to your man.

But you did say "sadder" . . . ?

Yes. To men in power any woman who tries to deal with them on their terms is ex officio mad. My husband thinks me mad and actually evinces the sympathy of his fellows over me for going native in Australia, for never having the entirely appropriate dress, for failing infallibly to tolerate the primates who pass for society's leaders as he envisages them. So there you are—I'm announced as mad. I've been mentioned in dispatches for it a number of times. And so, since I'm madly importunate with the Royal Army Medical Corps, and particularly towards Major Darlington's poor upset cousin, the major suffers, you see. They talk about how poor old Darlington took up with the mad woman. After showing such promise! According to them, I am supposed to have been certified in Australia and spent time in a colonial asylum! And here is a man with research he wants accepted by a larger world, with valuable arguments about sepsis—a brilliant man. Yet everyone he talks to is thinking not about his argument, but about his mad lover. You see . . . And that was why he went. He had to choose between eminence and me.

Even in her own present state of wretchedness and edgy fortitude, Naomi felt the pain of this story, but doubted she could make any soothing commentary.

Of course, said Lady Tarlton, you don't want to hear this. I have hopes that despite this show of a trial, in the end, soon, you'll prove to be a fortunate woman. And have your Quaker, if that's what you want.

But you deserve good fortune too, said Naomi.

Why ever would I? asked Lady Tarlton with a laugh.

Because you're beautiful and clever and have a mighty soul.

Lady Tarlton laughed. That's the very recipe—down to the last ingredient—for disaster. You know, when the war ends I might simply return to the old business and be a milliner. That would fulfill every worst expectation that ever they had. And indeed I love it. I loved constructing those confections that women put on their heads. To me the right sort of hat is far more interesting than anything hung in the Royal Academy.

Lady Tarlton began laughing and shaking her head, weighing the world as they all seemed to be required to do these days.

Darlington will now be treated with more seriousness, she admitted. From the point of view of antisepsis it is a day of triumph. Far more important than an adulterous affair. Except I did not think of it in those terms until now. Strange. In the midst of so-called sin we feel we are virtuous yet.

Lady Tarlton found this amusing. Naomi smiled too, within her intent to rescue Kiernan, and sipped the cognac. They sat in the silence of their unlikely companionship and the coincidence of their miseries.

The wounded enemy, captured and questioned, seemed quiet, grateful, and so pleased with the food—plain as it was—that it was clear rations were shorter on their side. But now their brothers were advancing to encircle the food of the west. British battalions appeared at Mellicourt and rested along the streets of the village and then marched up the road past the clearing station to the front to take up the line. Nurses and orderlies who happened to be in the open cheered raggedly as they went past. These men seemed eager in their mass and were placed at a distance from their inner, quivering selves by the overall militant tide running eastwards to meet a contrary current. There was a chance they were mere tokens of sacrifice, that the chief praise they would receive from all history might be those few thin cries of applause from the tired men and women of Mellicourt clearing station.

The patients at Mellicourt were cleared as hurriedly as they could be. No one knew what was to come, but it was clear the wounded and ill would be safer in base hospitals. Gas cases were removed in a day or so, and surgery was restricted to men who needed it at all costs. Any vehicle was likely to be used to move the injured—returning ammunition trucks were loaded up with the minor wounds. In a confusion of orders, two eight-ton trucks were packed up with stretchers and blankets, tanks of oxygen, and unopened cases of dressings and pharmaceuticals, all ready to be removed to safety.

Stragglers appeared—the crumbs of broken units—going west and mixed in with families on wagons or pushing the children and their goods in wheelbarrows. Even wagons hauling guns ground along the roads going west—seeking a new but rearwards position from which to pour down fury on the advancing enemy.

It was amidst all that flurry that somehow Charlie Condon appeared. It was beyond belief that in the great confusion of geographies and movements he could have located Sally. But having presented himself to Major Bright he was permitted to find her in her ward.

Go, go! said the Australian matron distractedly after Charlie appeared at the door of the only partly occupied resuscitation ward. The matron assumed that given the crisis he would not be staying long. Sally went towards him. She could not remember what was said when she got to him—the ordinary things, no doubt. Embracing was a dangerous indulgence to display to her matron and fellow nurses—they both knew that. But on the path they hooked each other's hand until they reached the mess and a sitting room at the end of the hut which no one was using at this furious hour. They sat together and hauled their bodies close on an old settee which seemed to offer them intimacy but—being where it was, where anyone could appear at any second—could not deliver it. She could feel the mass of his upper body half turned to her. Sitting together wasn't satisfactory. The whole of a body could not be brought in contact with the whole of another.

This is improbable, Charlie, she said. I'm not saying unwelcome. But it's so improbable you'd be here.

No, he said, it's probable. Remember how I was down here on reconnoiter. Now I'm with the advance party from Flanders.

They embraced again. Their mouths were so responsive and knowing of each other that it amazed her and gave her at a calmer level a sense of their destiny, and thus of safety. These seemed the most natural postures now—the postures of nearness which under the pyramids she had thought herself incapable of and had had no ambition for

Mustn't worry, he muttered. Our men have always been out in the open and bleeding. Now *they're* in the open and, God knows, we'll make *them* bleed.

She could tell he was convinced of this and his evoking of vengeance did not shock her. They were *his* enemy.

There's talk we'll be ordered back, she confided. Maybe Corbie, but who could tell? Perhaps the Germans will take Amiens itself, for all we know. I don't want to see you coming in on a stretcher anyhow. And if you try to turn up and smile at me from a prone position, I'll be very angry.

I have to go now, Sally, he said.

A high plane of a bed in a curtained room was clearly not going to make itself available to them. This was not the time, although their bodies claimed it was. He stood stooped for a while, since love was ridiculous too. Then he ran out to a truck waiting in the Bapaume Road.

His eagerness frightened her. She mistrusted such haste. She felt almost betrayed with the speed and eagerness with which he ascended into the cabin and slammed the door.

Soon after Charlie left, stretcher bearers arrived in ambulances with wounded and told of regimental aid posts and dressing stations abandoned to the enemy with the poor fellows still lying in them. Prisoners who had been put to work under guards making a new path outside the wards were now speaking to each other in very jocular German. They could foresee assured deliverance. Some Gothas overhead began dropping their bombs from low height onto the retreating regiments and French people on the road. At a nearby crossroads two Archies barked at them like toothless house dogs. Morphine protected the worst wounded from knowledge of events. But in many other faces Sally saw an added panic and unrest. For the front from which they thought their wounds had excused them was reaching west to encompass them again.

At four o'clock, when Slattery and Sally were working in resuscitation with eight young nurses—all in the normal attempt to make the patients safe for being moved—Major Bright entered the ward and announced, We have orders to leave. You should pack what you have. Assemble with your luggage in ten minutes. We have to walk to the station, half a mile. There'll be no one to carry bags so perhaps you will want to leave things.

Sally was appalled. She said she couldn't simply leave the patients.

Honora said, I'll stay with them. I am sure the Germans are not the barbarians we think.

Bright seemed impatient with this woman whom he was said to be infatuated with.

I've already made the same offer, he said, but it is not to be entertained. We are all ordered to leave.

Then you'll have to carry me away, said Slattery. I'm not going of my own will.

For God's sake, Slattery, don't be dramatic. I promise you that once we've drawn back, you'll be as buried as you want in a cascade of thousands who need you. But all I know is that we're going west of here.

There were more than thirty nurses—and a number of doctors and perhaps sixty orderlies—who gathered their lighter kit and set off on the clogged road. They hobbled along with their luggage in hand towards the local railhead. Here they had travel warrants to Amiens to present. An orderly led them by a side road to avoid the blocked main, arrow-straight Bapaume–Albert Road. A spur line came to the railway station near the village and as the clearing station's evacuees converged on it they met thousands of people—and a further vast and undifferentiated crowd of soldiers who had been attracted to it also. The side road they had taken had availed them nothing—this small station built to service local farms was now besieged by an overwhelming mass. There were men not so much in uniforms as in a carapace of muck sitting on windowsills and doorsteps, looking blankly at the commotion. Guards overwhelmed at the entrance gate to the station let the nurses through and onto the platform, where a rail transport officer who looked oddly familiar to Sally limped about blowing a whistle and pointing to the mass of soldiers and civilians waiting either side of the line.

The officer hobbled up to them and said, Ladies, leave your luggage here. The train is said to be due in twenty minutes. Matron, your women may need to fight their way aboard.

He took a whistle hanging from a lanyard around his neck and blew it to direct the guards to keep the rabble off the track. But the last vibrations of his whistle were overtaken by something profounder and more massive in sound. He blew the whistle again and screamed at the nurses. Across the line, everyone! Slit trench, far side!

Beneath the bombers they ran across the tracks and threw themselves into the trenches. They clung close. Slattery and Leonora were beside Sally, who had a brief view of Freud along the trench. Freud was hunched yet somehow looking detached from the peril. While the bombs could scare the deepest atoms within Sally, there was a part of Freud that could not be alarmed.

Above them were sounds more vast, she was sure, than anything that had been in their universe before—enmity that made the walls of earth shudder like a land in earthquake.

Their stocks of thunder depleted, the Gothas at last vacated the air. There were now hollow noises of lamentation from the earth above the trenches, and they climbed out, chastened. Major Bright and other doctors were traveling round in a spot where there were wounded and a mess of dead. Soldiers and men and women lay like winnowed stalks. Inspection showed Sally and the others that a mother and two small children—laid out neat as if for burial—had been killed by concussion. A regimental sergeant-major crossed the lines—a man still in control—and said the captain regretted to inform them that the rail line had been destroyed just a few hundred yards west.

I'm afraid that you'll have to leave your luggage in the ticket office, said the sergeant-major, which I'll lock. Then you'd better take off by foot.

They presented themselves to Bright and asked to be permitted to move amongst the injured. The curse was they had no equipment. Sally attended uselessly to a hemorrhaging boy with badges which declared Staffordshire Light Infantry. Some tried to treat with handkerchiefs and other oddments those soldiers who had been hit by shrapnel. In a kind of exasperation and clearheadedness Bright ordered them to get going and threw their bags into the ticket office at the station. They set off along the line—some with hand luggage and some with nothing. They were no longer separate from the beaten troops and the fleeing French.

They made relatively fast time the first mile and then—in a laneway by the rail—there appeared a string of five lorries, rocking over the mud which a few genuine spring days had mercifully hardened. All the nurses were to board them, said Bright. Light was fading as they climbed up as clumsily as they liked. No one expected athleticism from them now.

Many fell asleep under the canopies of the trucks and were woken after a while by stiffness. They alighted into a cold spring night at a crossroads where two British casualty clearing stations stood. The matron divided them into two parties and half were sent to the station north of the road to crowd in with the nurses there and half south.

Sally and the others sent to the south side waited in the nurses' mess as a brisk British matron had orderlies carry palliasses and blankets for them into the women's hut. As they waited they washed as well as they could, made cocoa and ate bread. Then they went into the hut—amidst the bedsteads of the British girls—and found their places on the floor and slept.

In the morning as they went from the tent to help in the wards, they saw a new battalion marching in the most splendid order down the road towards Albert. So used were they to disorder by now that the sight of hundreds of men advancing by company seemed a forgotten spectacle. The first time they had seen men move with more than training intentions had been in Egypt in eons past. Those men were immaculate and unsullied and accompanied by music. The nurses thought the music had been crushed by now. But these men gave off a similar air of solidity both as a mass and at the core of each component soul. British nurses standing amongst the huts and tents were telling them, It's your Australians!

The fact that these were of her tribe and looked unflustered seemed like a curative for the Allied retreat and evoked in Sally and the others a primitive urge for celebration. Hope insisted on rising as it had in the ill-informed spring of 1916. They started hauling out handkerchiefs to wave, unaware for now of this being a commonplace of war and a means to stoke martial purpose. They went running down towards the road swinging them—cheering ecstatically as if this column were not simply a fragment of an army or a mere stone thrown into the maw of a gale but a total answer.

Leonora yelled, Gidday, boys! to them, and the men said, Crikey, it's Australian nurses. And men roared out that they were going to go and get the dingoes. That they'd show Fritz he shouldn't have left his dugouts. They'd come down from Belgium (following routes Charlie might have had some role in reconnoitering) to do that. This energy and ferocious purpose they gave off sent the women into a further delirium. Yesterday—the pain of being refugees and powerless. Today—this, the antidote. Now there were trucks, and another battalion, and Australians yelling, *Fini* retreat, girls! They looked so fresh because they had just left the railway and were full of marching. And if they were maniacs and spat in the face of reality, then theirs was a mania necessary for the morning.

The last of the men and some horse-drawn guns vanished down the road. The madness waned in the nurses and there was sudden wistfulness. Had they seen mere chaff for the furnace? They drifted back across the meadow to present themselves again for use in the wards.

That afternoon many of the English nurses were pulled out towards Doullens but Sally and the others were pleased to be permitted to stay. No ambulances arrived, however, to deliver wounded—only ambulances to take yesterday's away. And the next morning—despite the dazzling gestures of advance they had seen the previous day—they were ordered back again and packed washed and half-dry undergarments in their valises, embarrassed for their unbathed bodies. But all their patients had at least been cleared off to the rear or to the cemetery across from the road to town—placed just as the one at Deux Églises had been.

Their new station at Corbie shared a crossroads with a British casualty clearing station. Easter had come and gone—swallowed by the emergency. At a church parade in memory of the landings at Gallipoli three years before, an Australian padre declared that this year Easter had a special meaning, given the deliverance of the British Army from annihilation due—he stressed this—to the heroism and Christ-like self-sacrifice of those two Australian divisions who were thrown into the hole—sixty thousand or more of Christendom's finest young men. Even Sally found him irksome in his trumpeting of Antipodeans as saviors of lesser beings. It seemed a simpleminded version to those who had nursed the survivors of almost undifferentiated battles. Behind her, Sally heard a well-modulated English girl mutter, Vainglorious old fool!

But above all, points about who had died and who had fled and who had stood—although the latter had certainly been the Australians they'd seen march by—seemed for the moment beneath arguing about. For this was not the hour for being prideful. They knew the Germans could still come and had not been infallibly stopped. They were themselves just ten miles from Amiens. That told you something of the enemy's recent territorial success. Besides, the war was not a football match. Points were not allotted. Even in success, points were lost.

At the mess table in Corbie a retreat-exhausted Honora Slattery told Sally she did not believe the rumor—though many people did—that the new influenza striking orderlies and nurses and sending men to the rear had been dreamed up in an enemy laboratory. This was to give them too much credit, she declared.

Just the same, she said further, a woman can't help wondering . . .

It seemed now that Major Bright had been forgiven by Slattery for tearing her away from her wounded at Deux Églises—prisoners though they may have become. Slattery confided in Sally that she and Bright now "had an understanding." He was a disbeliever but a better fellow than most believers, and her parents would just have to lump him—the fact that he wasn't some rosary-saying, beer-guzzling, bet-laying RC fool from the slums.

Freud—when told—took the news with her air of wise distance.

What, precisely, do you mean by "an arrangement"? she asked with an unnecessary coldness.

It means, said Honora, determined not to answer her plainly, that if there's ever peace, I'll wait until the prison camps and the hospitals have been emptied and if Lionel has not been found . . . Then, we'll see. That's the arrangement with the major.

Freud said, My God! He's a patient man.

Would you want any other kind? asked Slattery. Is your American a patient man?

Sometimes, said Freud. It all grinds along. It is a hard thing to sustain enchantment. Particularly with a difficult woman like me.

Sally began to wonder if Freud would ever recover from Lemnos. She achieved the appearance of steady purpose for long periods and—apparently—in the operating theatre too. But on other days she swung between content and cold mistrust at a pace no one could have considered normal. Yes, it was established. Her surgeon Boynton was a patient man.

At the Australian Voluntary the crisis at the front was visible in the men who arrived by ambulances. The hospital had at a stretch held two hundred and fifty, but now the demand brought in over three hundred. The reported Australian success had not been bloodless—the cocksure Australians the nurses had seen marching that operatic morning, brimful of self-belief, had paid by the thousands. Naomi supervised treatment in the preoperative ward on more than a dozen fractures, face and thigh and even serious thoracic wounds, and amputations which had turned gangrenous or septic and needed to be prepared for surgery. A new young military surgeon and Airdrie worked in the theatres, along with one of the ward doctors anxious for surgical experience and showing none of that nicety of conscience or concern about it that Hookes had once shown.

On a hectic morning towards what would prove to be the end of the military crisis, Lady Tarlton came looking for Naomi and found her directing the Australian nurses and the English Roses. As ever, when she arrived Lady Tarlton had an earnest demeanor. She had taken no more time since her consolatory drink with Naomi to lament Major Darlington. But without Mitchie—and in the light of their combined loss of their men—they spoke to each other like confidantes. Lady Tarlton was not immobilized by sadness and none of her fervors had stalled.

The name of the commander of the newly assembled Australian Corps, she told Sally, a huge one of five divisions, has just been announced. This general is planning to visit the general hospital in Boulogne on his way from a meeting in London back to the front.

I knew him in Melbourne, said Lady Tarlton airily. He'll be tolerant if I raise the vexed matter of Lieutenant Kiernan's imprisonment. And, Naomi, we should be strong in the matter—even to the point of offending our hosts at Boulogne.

After his trial Ian had been sent across the Channel and was serving his sentence in Millbank Prison in London with other Australian miscreants and supposed deserters. Millbank lay on the dank edge of the Thames. It sounded to Naomi a cage for pneumonia as well as harm dished out by guards whose natures had been changed by the place. It was always a solace therefore to be associated with Lady Tarlton's determination. Sentiments such as "even to the point of offending our host" gave Naomi a sweet sense of alliance.

Can we spare the time?

Appoint the sister in charge of the English Roses. You and I are not indispensable, you know.

On the morning of the general's visit, Lady Tarlton appeared in the front hallway of the château in a full-length fawn coat over her best cerise dress and her long, thin-ankled button-up boots. She looked superb—a true force—and there was no trace of the rejected woman about her. Naomi, of course, wore her dull go-to-town uniform. They traveled to Boulogne in the now faded, dented, imperfectly repainted but functional glory of Lady Tarlton's vehicle and arrived in time to walk along the graveled paths and visit the grave of brave Matron Mitchie. Where was her son now? In England, they hoped. Or along the Somme or Ancre Rivers somewhere—engaged endlessly in repulsing the enemy, as all the Australian divisions were said to be.

Carling drove them along the familiar road—going slow in the sump where Mitchie had been killed—and to the outskirts of the huge general hospital. The administration building had put out all the flags and bunting for the arrival of the Australian commander. The large shape of a kangaroo done in white pebbles served as a centerpiece of a bed of gravel in the square. Beside this great white image of a marsupial the matron-in-chief welcomed Lady Tarlton—with an air which said she wished there had been some way of stopping her being there. The matron was torn between showing contempt for Lady Tarlton's well-advertised insistence upon maintaining the vanity of her own private hospital, and the fact that this was British nobility and the wife of a former governor-general of that Commonwealth in whose name they were lined up today around the dominating kangaroo. As they aligned themselves with the honor guard at the main entrance, Lady Tarlton murmured to Naomi, He's Jewish—you understand—and at the same time a child of Prussians. He was an engineer and very high in the militia and the university senate when my husband and I were in Melbourne. His name escapes me. Excuse me a second.

And she turned to the matron-in-chief who stood beside her and asked, Matron, could you refresh my memory? The general's name again, please?

General John Monash, the woman declared coldly. Milady.

That's it, said Lady Tarlton to Naomi, the matron listening in. That's the name. Monash. Now at his command are more than one hundred and twenty thousand of the finest men on earth! Oh yes, some of them are rough-hewn or not hewn at all. But trees that stand. That's it. Bravo, General Monash!

The general's automobile entered the gates and orderlies with rifles presented arms. Young nurses saluted because here was their chief. Their chief and his men—it was said—would lead the armies of salvation and redeem the known world and avenge the sad retreat only now ending. Monash's men—it was believed especially by Australians—could save the bacon, the beef, the kingdoms of the west. This was the man who had in the emergency driven back the Germans through Villers-Bretonneux. No maidenly yell of approbation could be too strident for him.

He dismounted his vehicle—a middle-aged man heavy in the hips and yet somehow youngish and crisp in movement. He introduced himself to the chief medical officer and then walked along the line of nurses attended by the matron-in-chief. Soon he reached Lady Tarlton. Lady Tarlton! he said with enthusiasm, as they wrung each other's hands. You and your husband were so generous to me and my wife in Melbourne. I've heard of your Australian hospital. I'm afraid that like me it attracts its critics. But since I feel I know you, I say, good for you! Yes, good for you!

I might as well tell you, stated Lady Tarlton, my efforts seem to be an embarrassment to many. Enthusiasm is my great fault.

The general said, If that were a disease, I wish others would catch it. I wish it was of an epidemic scale. As for embarrassment, you know that I am a source of embarrassment too. A mere citizen soldier. And . . . well, the other thing. And on the other thing, I must again thank you for the invitations to Government House.

She introduced him to her matron—as she called Naomi. An interesting and complicated face, Naomi thought, an activity behind the eyes and an engagement in all around him—in her as well. None of the oafish oblivion of Lord Dudley.

If you have a moment, said Tarlton in a lowered voice, I must ask you about Miss Durance's fiancé. A medical supply officer, he has been imprisoned for refusing to take up a rifle. And yet he is a Quaker and made his pacifism clear when he enlisted. I am sure you of all people could not stand by and see such religious persecution.

Naomi could see—from a visible jolt in the general's eyes—that he was not too pleased to be distracted by such a reproach on a ceremonial visit.

Why do you say that *I of all people* . . . Are you referring to my Jewishness? If so . . .

No, no, not that. I mean you as a citizen and a progressive.

Naomi decided to care little for the embarrassment of generals.

My fiancé, General Monash, has been imprisoned in Millbank because he is a member of the Society of Friends and served the Medical Corps and has done so since Gallipoli. To be of service in that regard was his motive for enlisting. But the order that he take up a rifle . . . that was something he could not consent to.

There was a darkness about the general's brow. You realize we can't have people making choices, he told Lady Tarlton as if she were the relay point for Naomi. You must understand above all that our French and English brethren are outraged by our leniency towards our own men when they are so stern towards theirs. I have to say, Lady Tarlton, I wish this matter had been raised in another forum.

Lady Tarlton said, If I were sure, General, that we would share some other forum, then I *would* choose to raise it then rather than now.

I plead with you, General, said Naomi, aware that she and her patron Lady Tarlton were sabotaging the event but willing to do it if she could simply by those means engrave Ian's case on the general's memory. This is a man—Ian Kiernan—who has done good service and is no coward, but a sincere Quaker.

You said Quaker already, the general murmured with some coldness.

May we write to you? asked Naomi. Will you remember us?

Oh, said the general, I think it's pretty well assured I shall remember you.

Then, thank you, said Naomi. Thank you earnestly, sir.

Yes, thank you, Colonel . . . no, I'm sorry, General, said Lady Tarlton, with her laugh a little like a shaken chandelier. When we first met, you were . . .

Yes, said the general, a militia colonel when you first met me, Lady Tarlton. Things change and wars elevate us to heady heights.

And I rejoice in your appointment, General, asserted Lady Tarlton.

Thank you. Excuse me.

And he moved away to visit the rest of the line of nurses.

Lady Tarlton turned to Naomi. I think we did very, very well, she whispered—though the rest of the reception line were at least mystified at why the renowned general had spent so much time with the eccentrics of the Australian Voluntary. The matron-in-chief wore a face drained of all hope. This was to be a meritorious, pleasant, smooth day. She walked on fixedly by the general's side. But she knew the occasion had been plundered.

The Fever People Talked Of

At Corbie one afternoon Sally could feel what might be the onset of the flu everyone was discussing. At some clearing stations they said it had felled—at least temporarily—one out of three, and in a few, half the personnel. Sally suffered a shiver and a leadenness of the joints and throat ache. She took her own temperature and saw it had escalated in a few hours, which was said to be one of the marks of the thing—rapidity of onset. She presented her symptoms to the matron and was taken to a tented ward where twelve nurses who had caught it were tended by other nurses wearing masks.

One of them said to her, How ridiculous, to have a spring and summer flu when there was no real winter one.

She suffered high-fever delirium in which she was back in the cold-to-the-core water after the *Archimedes*. And up swam her mother with an unfamiliar smile and said, I can teach you to let go.

Mama!

She was later told she cried that. Were you dreaming about your mother, love? she was asked.

Her exchange with her mother involved gratitude. You knew I had determined to commit a crime and you died of your own will to prevent it.

She also encountered Charlie Condon—he was engaged in painting the wall of a trench yellow and wanted her to admire it.

When she was clearer headed, she saw Slattery wearing a mask.

She had come to see her and told her how there had been an advance of some miles and everyone was going partway back towards Deux Églises—the trucks of equipment were loaded again. Amiens and all things holy were saved for now.

A doctor said, I don't think you have the flu. Your symptoms are not quite right. Yes, you had quick onset, but you caught something else—something that crawled out of the trenches and struck you.

She was taken from the contagious ward and put in a separate room in a medical ward just in case, but soon was permitted to walk around—feeling limp perhaps, but confident of revival. A brief post-card came from Charlie to say he was well, and a long-delayed and redirected note from Naomi, which broke to her the news that Ian Kiernan was in prison in England. The length of sentence took her breath away.

The influenza struck Château Baincthun when one of the Red Cross nurses collapsed. The pathology lab run by Darlington had fallen into disuse and throat swabs had to be sent to the overworked laboratory in Boulogne so that the nature of the thing could be confirmed. The nurse was placed in a separate room and declined with a terrible rapidity, dying in the afternoon of the following day. She was a woman exhausted by work and very thin and the common wisdom was that this was an influenza crafted—like howitzers—to take the young in particular.

She was considered unfortunate, however, because medical reports from elsewhere declared the infection would be widespread but the death rate shallow. Some of the men in the wards—the healthy and the recuperating—caught it. Masks were now compulsory if one was to nurse anyone suffering from the virus. The heresy of Major Darlington was becoming an orthodoxy—at least in this case.

In those early days of this startling new outbreak, Naomi received a further letter—this one from Melbourne. Its letterhead said "Kiernan and Webster, Importers and Manufacturers, Industrial Machinery."

Dear Nurse Durance,

Our son Ian has earlier written to us concerning your process of betrothal. He admires you to a great degree, and we are pleased that he has met a woman who understands his high purpose and who shares it with him, albeit he is now in prison. He has the right to send one letter a month and filial duty caused him to write the first to us. But he wanted us in turn to write to you and tell you that he declares himself to be surviving well. It is a great pain to us as it must be to you to know where he is, in that dank place—I believe it was founded in the middle of last century when concepts of appropriate punishment were even more drastic than they are now. I am a prison visitor here to Pentridge Prison, and my visits have given me an added perspective—I judge the conditions there and wonder how they apply to Ian's position. Our chief hope lies in the fact that he has a sturdy soul, that he is endowed with spiritual resources, that he understands he is not a criminal, and that we have formed a group of friends—and indeed Friends—to pursue a letter-writing campaign on his behalf. We make what representations we can to ministers and indeed to the prime minister. But we receive nothing but pro forma letters from civil servants pointing out that, the populace having rejected conscription, the Australian army must be entitled to dispose of the services of its members as it sees fit. I hope the men who write these letters are logical and that therefore when the conflict ends, as it one day must, the shortage of men will no longer be an issue and the idea of punishing Ian for the way Australians voted in those referenda need no longer apply. But for the present he writes, "I think my punishment inevitable in the world as it is at the moment."

Ian insisted we reiterate to you his awareness that you are a young woman and that the responsibility of the young is to their very youth and vigor. He is worldly enough to know that you must not feel forced to become an external prisoner serving time parallel to his own. I know you have probably written to him, but it seems that his correct address is now Kiernan, 27537, Millbank Military, London. We are very proud of Kiernan 27537, for we know other young men in the Society of Friends who began as Ian did and who yielded to the pressure of arms.

Naomi had not yet passed on to her own father the news of Ian Kiernan, let alone news of the betrothal sessions or his imprisonment. She did not choose yet to explain the—by Macleay standards—oddity of it all.

Sally stayed at Corbie with the British nurses until a doctor decided she was well enough to take the rough journey eastwards to start work at Albert, where her normal station had fetched up. There were now—said the walking wounded she took to nursing again—remarkable advances accomplished not over months but sometimes in a day or a few hours. In the mess, the newspapers—when she had time to read them—were full of phrases about thwarting the intentions of the Hun, turning back his hosts, stemming his tides. Was all this true? For there had seemed all that spring and early summer of 1918 to be no lessening of the ambulance stream. The clearing station at Corbie felt as she imagined a factory might when orders could not be fulfilled, however industrious the laborers.

So on a warm morning she climbed into the passenger seat of an ambulance to go to Vecquemont, to which her clearing station had been moved. The station was held within the arms of a forked road, and was chiefly a place of tents—a nascent institution. After a reunion in the mess she found out that here too some men were suffering the three-day fever—as people now called it. Or else they said the Spanish flu. What the Spanish had done to deserve the honor of that name Sally did not know. A new ward had to be set up to contain soldiers who arrived with it and orderlies who went down with it.

Be careful, ladies, said Dr. Bright, visiting the mess. Eat well and rest as much as you can.

But Sally could see Honora, Freud, Leo, the lot of them, were all dazed from working day-and-night–long shifts—interspersed by an occasional six or seven hours of sleep.

It was perhaps three days later that Leo—blessed always by sunlight and sturdiness and pursuing the firmest line of destiny of any of them—fell on the floor of her ward as if struck by a blow. This was what the vicious fever did, like the attacks at the front—it fulfilled its purpose in an hour. It ambushed and it felled the sufferer according to its own frantic timetable.

This was considered the worst of luck since the doctors had all decided the influenza was waning. They carried her to the tent which had been set up to contain the earlier victims of the virus. Overnight she declined at a terrible rate into a vicious kind of pneumonia. Someone had whimsically called the first phase of flu—the one Sally had been wrongly suspected of catching—"Three-day Lady." But this lady raged at a quicker rate. Honora and Freud took turns watching Leonora by day—speaking to her through their masks, taking her temperature and pulse, washing her face, promising her recovery. Sally—considered to be recuperating—was advised not to approach the place. In any case, recovery was the one possible outcome for a young, dazzling girl like Leo, a girl whose life had advanced like a life in a novel, whose inevitable marriage—announced two springs ago—had been delayed by evil events, but was designed to be the long story in which this present condition was a mere few pages. Her development from childhood to affections which bloomed in time into a noble union of effectiveness—that was the life intended for Leo. Everyone could sense it. She would get better.

In Leo's periods of clarity she remarked that there was pain behind her eyes and in her back. But later the next day her face grew abnormally blue and Honora and Freud saw with alarm a foamy blood appear at her nostrils. Her urine stained her bed and they cleaned her briskly as she moaned and carried on some phantom conversation. Towards evening Major Bright declared that her symptoms had become hemorrhagic—hence the blood now showing at the mouth. She grew comatose and two hours later—while the message of her illness was still on its way to Captain Fellowes—she died.

As well as grief there was astonishment. This girl whose soul was not written on water but on solid foundations had been unable to keep a hold on the earth. This girl was now attached to the malign Somme eternally. She was carried in a procession of every nurse who could be spared from the clearing station, of every orderly, to a grave over which stood a squad of French territorials and one aged trumpeter—all in their helmets and blue tunics. Dr. Fellowes arrived. He wavered and smelled of whisky and mumbled his thanks for uttered condolences at the graveside. Not only was life short but so was ceremony, and the clearing station now demanded the nurses' return.

This sudden, galloping death of Leonora grieved Sally, who could utter only obvious things such as, "Poor, poor girl. So beautiful, so sensible and such a good nurse." It was an obvious case of the disrespect of viruses and war for every solid plan. In the civil world lives were foreshortened by accidents with horses or falling timber, by tetanus and peritonitis. You couldn't help but believe—because the belief took away your own fear—that these victims were the lesser characters of the human tale—Mrs. Sorley's shadowy crushed husband for one. But it was clear now the influenza had combined with high explosives, the machine gun, and the mustard gas to disprove these illusions. And the numbers who saw this awful affliction as the enemy's work were diminishing. Germans suffering from the influenza were captured as evidence it was willing to be an equal slayer.

Honora asked Sally one evening in the mess, Do you think this *thing* is a punishment on us all for allowing the war?

But most of the women—including Honora and Sally—had had considerable childhood instruction in the doctrine of free will. Man chose what to do. Whatever he chose to do, God tolerated it, but might punish it too.

Freud asked briskly, If he didn't step in to stop it, why does he step in only at the punishment stage?

There was great uneasiness in some about Freud's opinion. It challenged too much what they had absorbed in childhoods to whose roofs they wanted to return.

Leo's unplanned death evoked in Sally a horror at the certainty of Charlie's death—planned as it was, along with others, by the ambitious enemy. She had always been subject to spasms of despair and confidence on the matter, but now they alternated at a hectic rate. His eminence as a man saved him by some lights and doomed him by others. The extra element of this influenza now struck her with an enhanced alarm for him, from which she could not distract herself by the normal means—working to the point of exhaustion.

Major Bright called together a gathering of them around the breakfast table and read a letter from the general of the Medical Corps praising them for the "textbook" workings of the station. There was—it seemed—a formula for death rates in stations in relation to numbers of surgeons, doctors, nurses, orderlies. The equation had shone a meritorious light on them. Mathematics emphasized that numbers—and not a lone tremulous soul—were the issue. That too somehow made everything worse.

July arrived with poppies growing in every spare foot of earth and around the edges of the woods, and news of further developments at the front came to Sally as if they were family tidings—intimate to her. The strangely jubilant lips of the wounded told of a specially and cleverly designed battle fought at a village named Hamel. Here, the Australians and Monash had shown the British and the French how things were done with tanks and aircraft, artillery and infantry—all in the one glorious amalgam. She hoped it was true.

Time thundered in her head and she began to suffer migraines and yellow blotched vision. Major Bright prescribed a draught of codeine for her. On a day when the station was utterly clear of casualties because some administrative error had told the authorities it was full, or else because of some lull at the front—indeed on a day where no artillery could be heard for extended periods of minutes—Major Bright enlivened them by calling another picnic on the edge of the woods a few hundred yards east of the station.

It was a wistful affair at first, for Leo was not there, and hers was a dominant and absorbing absence. But the invigorating day and the poppies and hollyhocks and butterflies grasped hold of them soon enough. Nurses and surgeons and ward doctors sat down beside spread bedsheets fresh from the makers and not yet used in the wards and ate all the good French things delivered up to them by a grateful Amiens— cheese, bread, pâté. When hunger was satisfied the question arose of what people would do after the war. Various doctors announced their plans—returning to practices in bush towns or in suburbs. One said he intended to stay in London to study ophthalmology. Bright declared he hoped to return to the operating theatres of Australia where—he claimed—the standards of practice were at least as good as anywhere in Europe or Britain.

I speak facts, he assured everyone. These are not the words of a jingo.

Freud's American boyfriend, Boynton, made no special claims that he'd go back to Chicago—when he had volunteered in early 1915, the senior surgeons at Rush Hospital had been so hostile to the idea that he wondered if he would get his job there back, even though he would return instructed by the experience of war surgery. But there were other places he could try, he supposed, even San Francisco, where his uncle was a physician and a surgeon.

Without warning—and like a public announcement not of professional intentions but of the end of the alliance with Boynton—and without waiting for all the doctors to define their plans, Freud spoke up. Well, she said, should the war ever end, I think I'll stay on in Europe. The reports from Germany—all the illness brought about by the blockade—make me think I might go there.

Dr. Boynton regarded the surface of the sheet on which the picnic items were spread. He knew, Sally assumed, that Freud was wounded in some way and that her goodwill towards him fluctuated. The corners of his mouth turned up in a semirictus that combined regret, bewilderment, and embarrassment.

I am sick of seeing Europe in this particular way, Freud added. I feel I haven't seen the true Europe at all.

Honora surprised everyone—not least Major Bright—by agreeing it was a good idea. It was as if she did not see Freud's statement in its real terms but only in terms of a desire for peaceful tourism.

I reckon, Honora went on, that whenever it ends, a woman could live for a year in France on the savings she makes working here.

A glaze came over Major Bright's eyes too. Was Honora—after all those demented months of hers—unable to read what Freud meant? He had his career to pursue in Australia—he would not be permitted to pursue it here once there were no more wounds. Professional urgency would not permit him to sightsee for a year in France.

Freud got up suddenly from the picnic. Thank you, Major, she said. If you will excuse me, ladies and gentlemen.

They tried to start a conversation again in normal tones, but it could only sputter along as Freud descended the slight slope which led to the nurses' tents.

Boynton begged them to excuse him soon after.

Sally had made no pronouncements on her own future. If Leo lacked one, all the more might she. So an instinct of reticence—which would have kept her quiet in normal times—prevented her all the more now. The young wounded who reckoned the enemy was dished might carry a sense of communal triumph to the grave with them. Yet she could not feel it herself. And if it did ever end, she thought, I might simultaneously stop breathing. Only the chance to see the artifices of paint in Charlie's company gave her a glimmer of the afterlife.

As a mist rose, the Ford and Sunbeam ambulances arrived, full of young Germans—dirty faced and bleeding, deflated and staring. The field-gray somber walking wounded of the enemy advanced with extreme caution and—as if trained in medical etiquette—soberly visited friends in the resuscitation ward and on nurses' orders held up bags of plasma and saline and looked down at their sallow comrades whose martial ambitions were reaching a close.

A letter from England from Captain Constable—the defaced soldier—had chased Sally all over Picardy and now caught up with her.

I have the dressings on my face from what the surgeons say was the last of my reconstructions. What emerges once they're off will be the final version of me from now on. Naturally I hope to find out what that is and discover it is not as bad as all that. There is hope for all of us now, says the matron. My bandages off will be a sign to her—part of a great global scheme in her head. Though I doubt the future of my dial is a matter upon which princes and prime ministers and parliaments will spend much time.

Despite the complaining flavor of my words, I think always of the boys who've been dead two years here and there—all without the option of wondering how things will turn out. How is that Slattery girl I knew? I hope you can tell me she is still young and fresh and impudent.

Well, enough! Enough, I hear you say and a fair thing too. Whatever is waiting behind the dressings I'd happily show you and her because I know you'd recognize me. Others might have a harder time of it.

Constable and his ironic distance from his frightful wound and from the regimen of face-remaking operations that he had endured was as much a tonic to her and Slattery as they had once tried to be to him.

Unexpectedly but in view of a further improvement at the numbers brought up by the algebraic formula applied to clearing stations by headquarters, Freud and Sally and a few others received orders signed by Bright to take leave. Without Charlie, Paris would not offer enough.

So Sally decided to try to get to Amiens and north to Boulogne to visit Naomi at the Australian Voluntary before taking the Blighty ship. She had a hankering to visit Captain Constable and to see one of the fatuous West End shows. But on the way she wanted to talk to Naomi about Charlie, and the swiftness of Leo's death as a sign of the imbalance of things.

The truck journey to Amiens took two of her available hours, and the train for Boulogne left on time since it fed the arteries of the war. In the train she slept almost without interruption in a near-empty first-class compartment of comfortable velvet. She reached the Gare Centrale and signed herself in to the Red Cross nurses' home and found she could send a messenger by bike to Château Baincthun. Waiting to hear from Naomi, she walked towards the port and managed to reach a lookout on the ancient walls, from which she could see the entire drama of the place. Camouflaged troopships were arriving with soldiers and leaving with wounded and men on leave. Along the beaches bathing cabins weren't disgorging many swimmers but she saw a man with one leg emerge and hop across the wet sand, determined to encounter the late summer sea.

She made her way back to the hostel along narrow workers' streets where barefooted boys played rough games and looked up from their little brutalities to see her pass. Future poilus, she thought, who would be sent to fight for the right to their squalor.

By the time she got back from her walk Naomi was outside the hostel looking peaked and concerned. Her face was transfigured when she saw Sally, and the sisters embraced without any complications or reticence or subtle suspicion or begrudging. Now—with all distance between them vanished—they went looking for a café. Naomi, Sally could see, had been altered by the loss of Mitchie and Kiernan to something simpler, more intense and direct. Sally had once thought her complexity would baffle all science. Now Naomi carried on her face a look of the most straightforward joy at reunion, of happiness unanalyzed and unapologized for. She also looked older—or at least ageless—and still thinner. As much as any soldier, she too needed a peace.

I had an idea, said Naomi, once they had ordered their coffee. It's a beautiful afternoon and the hospital is just five miles inland. Are you well enough to walk?

Sally was tired, but nonetheless felt exhilaration at the idea of a hike. They set off with the sun high and mists of insects tumbling in the air above the crops of wheat and barley that the sisters would see through gaps in hedges and over farm gates. Fields of flax bloomed pale-blue and blowflies troubled the hindquarters of cattle. This country was not as flat as the battle areas—the hedgerows climbed genuine slopes that were steeper than the mere slight ridges for which tens of thousands had died further east.

It seemed to Sally it was a time as far off as childhood since they had walked like this together in country roads. She spoke briefly of Charlie and more of Leo and the untowardness of all that. Naomi talked of the campaign she and Lady Tarlton were engaged in for liberating Kiernan. The many eminent people they'd written to. He had now been sent to Aldershot Military Prison—the Glasshouse, whose inmates were considered unfit for visits. Still, Naomi was trying to organize one. Trying to imagine what his life was like plagued her imagination. What sort of men might guard and bully him? she asked Sally, not expecting an answer. Certainly men who gave him no credit for the *Archimedes* or Lemnos or service in France.

In any case Lady Tarlton had told her—as Naomi further explained to her sister—that it was likely that, should war end, civil lawyers could be introduced into the equation, men who could argue a case like Ian's all over again in a world where reinforcements were no longer the constant cry of generals. Lady Tarlton said she knew a number of such lawyers—fellows who'd represented suffragettes. How they would be paid, Lady Tarlton did not say.

Of course, I'm willing to spend my savings, Naomi continued, and Ian's father is—I think—affluent. And certainly devoted to his son.

And I've never found that Lady Tarlton makes a boast on which she does not come good. So I have champions and I have possible resources. Well, that's my rave and I apologize it takes so long. But now, your Charlie. What of him?

There was less Sally could say. She couldn't broach the adventure in the hotel at Ailly. And the rest was all tedious and uninterrupted anxiety. There was no earthly power to whom she could write on Charlie's behalf.

He never seems to be my Charlie, she said. First he's the army's. Then he's his own man. It's because he's unownable, I think, that I love him.

Naomi laughed. Well, now, she said. That's you, that's Sally exactly.

Sally stared ahead, shielding her eyes so that she could scan the road for potential perils. Naomi reached and enclosed Sally's hand in her own.

Look, she said, as if to distract her sister. It was along here—in that little dip in the road—that the limousine was thrown on its side and went careering. And poor Mitchie . . .

This kindly and shady summer stretch—with a slight kink before the trees around the château—hove into view. They both inspected the patch of road as if its tragedy could be reread and perhaps adjusted.

Naomi said, I had a visit from Mrs. Sorley's son. He seems a big, handy boy. Another one to worry about though.

Sally privately thought she would swap Mrs. Sorley's son for Charlie's safety any day. Of course there was guilt attached to doing the deal in her head—Charlie for the other boy. As if there was in fact someone to make the contract with.

It was strange when I met young Sorley, said Naomi. We were trying to feel as if we were stepbrother and stepsister—he made the bravest attempt at it, poor boy. He took the trouble to come here in the first place. I hope we can sit down at some time and have real conversations.

Sally took thought and then said, It used to take us Durance girls a long time to get to know people like that. But we're getting better at it, I think.

Yes. Taciturn, that's what they call us. Standoffish. Were you aware people called us that?

Not you, insisted Sally.

Oh yes, said Naomi. Me more than you. They never used the word "shy." Well, I suppose people think, why use a good word when you can use a bad. I think that on balance *you're* much better at being social than I am. I felt you got on quicker with girls like Leo and Freud and Slattery.

You must be really bad then, said Sally, and they laughed together at the affliction of their genealogy.

Sally stayed at the château for two days—meeting Airdrie and the English Roses and the military surgeon and the young ward doctors, and sharing Naomi's room. Sometimes she went with Naomi into the wards to do dressings and irrigations and to make beds. Otherwise she walked men around the garden. The English Red Cross nurses were awed to see an army sister descend to a menial level, and one said, You Australians—you'll do anything! as if the Durance girls were exceptionally free-spirited colonials.

As they sat in bed, Naomi told her the story of Major Darlington who—went the authorized version—had chosen between the respectability of base hospitals and the favor of other surgeons over Lady Tarlton's company.

She seems, said Sally, unshaken.

She can't be defeated. When all this started I didn't expect her to be here all the time like this. I thought she would just set it going, like God starting the world, and then go back to London to her accustomed life. But she's labored with us. And when she's not here, she's in Paris visiting the club she's got going there. She belongs to whatever she begins. But after the war—so she says—she's not sure she won't just go back and put up with Lord Tarlton and make an end to all the blather and mess of the whole love business. I doubt she'll be able to though. It's always going to be in her nature to do exceptional things.

Naomi took her down to the docks when it was time for her Blighty ferry. They kissed like two children reunited in play. An old French paddlewheel ferry painted in its war patterns of gray waited like a cross between a Dickens-style Channel packet and an antique battleship.

I'll ask at Horseferry Road if I can see Ian, Sally promised her.

It would be marvelous. I'm afraid you'll be refused, but please try if you can.

A line of soldiers stood back to let Sally—her travel warrant in hand, and Naomi as escort—advance to the gangway. A military policeman checked and approved her documents and she went up the plank, turning partway to see Naomi's face streaming with tears. So the entente proposed in a palm court in Alexandria three years before was in full operation. Cherishing her sisterhood, she saw to the west the promise of a long twilight in rouged clouds yellow at the edges. It felt to Sally a good and decent thing to live. Even now. Rapture could not be postponed until a more perfect day. Not when a person had a lover and a sister.

The Epsom Hospital in Surrey was enormous and branched out— in grounds that were once the private garden of a rich family. The grounds held a number of huts and a space where men in hospital uniform—the baggy, pyjama-like tops and bottoms with various-colored lapels—were playing cricket. There was something about the energy of the game and the way hands were thrown up when a man was caught out from whacking a ball impossibly high that made her hope Captain Constable had not been hurled with his one eye into the deep end of a game just yet. She followed the driveway to the main house, where they knew she was coming—Captain Constable and she had exchanged mail about it.

A volunteer was sent to fetch him and he came down the stairs wearing military uniform, his soldierhood taken on again. She saw the sutures across his jaw, the not-quite-formed nose, the unnatural glossiness and tightness of the upper lip and cheek. Though she could see something of what he might have been before, what was there was both little and at the same time an undeniable cure. The scale of his bravery regarding the damage to his face had driven her to expect more than this. The surgeons had forced his facial items back in place. The surfaces they had restored were correct in a technical sense but were somehow unmoving and incapable of expression. His visage was doomed to be an artifact rather than a natural phenomenon. Except for the left eye, this face was dead. It had taken two years to achieve this, and this was all that could be achieved.

Hello, Sister, he said exuberantly. I wondered, might I take you to tea in the high street? It isn't far.

She agreed. They set off on the gravel drive with her arm in his. Reaching the gate and walking down leafy streets he pointed out the grandeur of the distant race track.

That's where that suffragette threw herself under the hooves of the King's horse, he said. Just like the boys who've thrown themselves under the hooves in the last four years.

You needn't have dressed for me, she said. If that was what you did.

Oh, he said, after all this time, I'm sick of those rotten pyjamas. They look ridiculous with a slouch hat.

She noticed the wound stripe on the left forearm of his jacket. She thought it underexplained what he had suffered.

They're sending me home very soon anyhow, he said. So I've had to clean up the old kit.

She wondered if the mayor of his municipality would bestow honors on this drastically altered young man, and remembered her sister's story of the epidemic of suicide on the ship Naomi had taken home long ago. But he was too strong a man for that.

In a teashop in the high street they ordered tea and cream puffs. English cakes were sludge beside French. Yet this big, jolly lump of dough and sugar was somehow the right thing. The waitress did not seem surprised by his appearance. She might have become used to serving such men.

Do you know, said Sally when the tea arrived and the fragrant steam began to have its effect on both of them, if I had to give a prize for my best patient of all, it would be you. It would *really* be you. I'm not trying to butter you up. I doubt I could have borne what you have.

He laughed a rueful laugh and drank some tea. She wondered if there were nerves in those lips to feel the heat of the drink.

I'm not so good now as I was earlier, he asserted. I'm getting churlish. The thing's settled now. I've got what I'll have forever. I could handle the disease but I don't know how I'll go—if I tell you the truth—with the cure.

You are entitled to be a bit churlish, as long as you don't overdo it.

She could feel though, very clearly, that he was in a new struggle.

I've decided to stay in the old town. Narromine. I'll work with my father on the station—we run sheep and stud rams. People can get used to me, I reckon, in a small place, where there's only so many you can shock. That makes sense. To me at least.

But you could go anywhere, she said. I would hate it if you thought you must limit your life somehow.

No, I think I'll start out at home. I just want to shy clear of the pity merchants for a while. And any special medallions and speeches. The old man will need to fight all that off too—I've told him. I don't want any band at the platform.

They walked back under a pleasant autumn sky that was the color of duck eggs. When the northern European weather took it into its head to be subtle and yet vital at once, it was able to do it with extreme craft, with fifty or so variations of blue and a hundred of yellow.

And so, he said, it looks like it's going to be at an end—everyone's saying so, hard as it is to believe. Fritz's line's gone.

But he'll make another, Sally said. There'll still be no shortage of wounded.

He considered this and then began to stutter with laughter.

What is it? she asked.

When they ask me to write my war memoirs, they'll consist of one thing. Standing in the wrong place.

This sounded like self-pity at last to her. Though she did not believe he could avoid it forever, she was disappointed.

She told him, I came to England especially to see you. I have to say honestly that when I think of a hero, I think of you. And you know I would not easily say that.

But with me you're also satisfying curiosity, aren't you? he asked, half amused. We're old friends—yes. But you're partly a tourist, aren't you? See what the joker looks like now! I'd be the same in your position.

You could drive people off saying that sort of thing, she warned him. I'm far too busy to be a tourist and I'm in a constant state about an infantryman I love who's still in the center of the storm. And on top of that, I have to try to visit my sister's fiancé, who's in prison in Aldershot for mutiny. But, listen, if your position ever seems to be too much for you, you write to me and I'll write back and come and visit if I can.

And on that basis, back at the hospital they exchanged addresses. Sally wrote down her father's farm—Sherwood via Kempsey, Macleay Valley, New South Wales—and found it was an address she could not imagine herself ever having occupied or inhabiting in the future. But there a letter would find her.

They said good-bye in the lobby and she was already at the door when he called out to her, You're too thin, you know. You're much thinner than you were at Rouen. Don't let them work you too hard.

Beyond the gate there was a line of tall shrubs. She stepped amongst them and let out a cry like a crow and then stood there while the river of tears flowed out of her, a grieving torrent. After ten minutes of it, she was well enough again and composed herself and went off to catch the early evening train to Victoria.

At Horseferry Road, Sally visited the provost marshal's office. The clerk at the desk led her into the office of a middle-aged captain, who listened with an open face—neither pretending too much sympathy nor sour with condemnation—as she made her case to visit Kiernan in Aldershot. When she was finished he laid out his hands palm-up on his desk. It's no use, he said. Aldershot is a British camp, and they play by their rules. We agreed to that so they wouldn't keep pestering us to shoot our boys.

Numbed by failure, that evening she went to a West End farce with Freud and Freud's American doctor. At the interval, as Captain Boynton queued to buy champagne for them, Freud said, He's always taking it for granted we'll live in Chicago. I've even been foolish enough to argue the surgical claims of Melbourne with him, as Bright does. But it seems the end of the earth to him.

It is, said Sally. Believe it or not, it is.

It could be cause for a rift. Or I could make it that. No one need think I'm that desperate to have a man.

That's not a good reason to get rid of a decent one.

It was interesting that as always Freud would say "have a man" when others would say "get married." But when Boynton arrived with the champagne, there seemed to be no chasm between them. The American was more exuberantly entranced than Fellowes would ever have admitted to being by Leo. They all chatted briskly and honestly, bantering away.

Do you think the characters in this play know there's a war on? Boynton asked.

That's the charm, said Freud. They live in a play where there never was a war.

Sounds like America, he said. But these characters? Their heads are empty of history.

Sometimes, Freud argued, people need a history enema.

The playwright's succeeded then, said Boynton. He's a real benefactor of humanity. Give the man a prize.

Whatever in God's name that is, said Freud.

At which the American hugged her by the waist.

Listen to this kid! he invited Sally.

She was back at Vecquemont within five days. As well as Captain Constable at Epsom, in London Sally had seen at a superficial level sights missed last time. But getting back was what she profoundly desired. First thing, she went looking for Slattery and found her standing at the far end of the gas ward coughing and watching as two nurses applied blister cream to a soldier's flesh. Honora saw her and—her boots clopping on the board floor—moved fast to meet her.

Is there a chance for a tea? Sally whispered. As she petitioned Honora she leaned down almost automatically and adjusted an oxygen mask on the face of a soldier. His mustard-gas rash called out for ointment. But oxygen was more important. The patient frowned up at her.

It's the horses, he said.

The man in the next bed —not as desperate for breath—said his companion was right.

The way they begin to neigh and bray and plunge about once those gas shells come landing with a little *thud, thud.*

He was exhausted by this speech and for what the gesture was worth Sally drew her hand over his shoulder as if she had some power to command his violated organism to operate the right way.

Sally, murmured Honora, Major Bright wants to see you.

Honora led her out of the ward and along duckboards to Bright's office near the theatres. He was attending to forms and letters. He got up from his desk, and it was by his demeanor—not by Slattery's earlier—that she understood the news and feared her existence was now void.

It's Charlie, she said.

Bright held up his hand. Be assured. Alive but wounded. He was at Franvillers but they've moved him to the big hospital at Étaples.

But I've had my leave, she said. She realized she must sound like a schoolkid.

No. That doesn't matter. You can see him. It's been arranged.

What sort of wound?

Bright looked at the floor.

I'm afraid I can't say. I don't know anything further. I'm sure it's minor . . . He must have been well enough to tell them to reach us here.

So—in a lather and ferment this time—she made ready to travel again and without unpacking caught one of the buses that brought troops from the great depot at Étaples, which the soldiers—distanced by a language from the place—called "Eatables," up to the rear lines beyond Corbie, and returned with soldiers going on leave. She traveled at the front of the crowded vehicle with blinkered sight, refusing to start conversations, though the officer beside her did his best. She both expected minor damage in Charlie and mourned his death. They traversed through a countryside of townships still rubbled from the battles of March and April and in a landscape chiefly populated—it seemed—by the aged, by hungry children, and, above all, by soldiers. Sometimes as she endured her frenzy in the front seat, the driver would let himself be hailed down by soldiers with leave papers, and after long discussion they would be let aboard. They all moved along the bus and passed the desolate girl in the front seat without knowing that the driver's slow braking and slow starts made her murderous towards him.

It was late afternoon when they reached the hospital in the base outside Étaples. In the summer evening light—just as at Rouen ages back—German prisoners worked on erecting new huts with all the energy and attention of men brought in on contract. Beyond the hospital lay a terrible immensity of camp, and over all of it a dismal air—a feeling of something ugly getting out of hand. A general look of depression, she thought, was apparent in the guards and the off-duty orderlies walking the streets of the hospital.

She reported to a guardhouse and was directed to the main office of the hospital to find out where Charlie was. Now and then as she waited for the records to be consulted, hope surged in her, and then receded to leave desolation. Once an orderly was called on to lead her, it was a long trudge down laneways. She found the ward, climbed the few stairs, presented herself at the nurses' station, and asked for Charlie Condon.

Oh, said a young Australian nurse, I'll take you there.

Is it bad? she asked.

You're trembling, said the girl. She seemed viciously determined to keep Sally in ignorance. She led Sally down the aisle between beds. Before Charlie could be reached they encountered the ward sister to whom the nurse introduced her. Sally saw on her a particular expression, something, she thought, which did not suggest the utter worst.

The sister led her down the aisle and with a shock she saw Charlie amongst all the unknown faces. He was asleep with a slight frown.

Some shrapnel wounds in the side and hip, the sister explained. But gangrene has set in in the arm. He's due for surgery.

The arm?

Surely it would be too melodramatic—even for this mongrel war—for an artist to lose his arm? It was a coincidence suitable to the stage but surely not to real tragedy. But on top of that, gangrene.

The sister took his pulse and the nurse found a chair for Sally to sit on. Sally put a hand on his forehead and the pulse-taking woke Charlie. He looked at the ceiling, and then lowered his head and with a slight effort of focus saw her.

Sally, he said wonderingly. He asked the sister, It's not the fever, is it?

No, said the sister. She's here, all right.

Aren't I lucky? he said but without the boyish exhilaration which often took over young men with disabling but not mortal wounds. A Blighty wound, he told her, *and* the left arm. All I need to paint is the right. Best of both worlds.

His eyes were fevered from the gangrene.

I mean, he told her, I can open the tubes of paint with my teeth.

Sally leaned and kissed him on the mouth—a lover with a lover. The sister did not object.

The sister said, The surgeon has him down for a below-elbow amputation, but it depends on nerve and tendon and the ability to get a good flap. And on the infection. Either way, he'll still have a stub of wing to wave with, won't you?

Precisely, Charlie slurred.

She waited until he was taken away and they brought her cocoa heavily laced with sugar—the way at Deux Églises and other places she had fed it to the casualties. After an hour and a half Charlie was carried back stupefied and when the surgeon visited and inspected him, he murmured to Sally that they'd done an above-elbow amputation to save him from the threat of the gangrene. The state of the brachial artery and the tendons—together with the sepsis—warranted above the elbow, said the surgeon.

She sat with him into the evening as they fed him morphine as regularly as she would have and dressed and irrigated the wound, which she wanted to do but was not permitted to. She felt an abounding thankfulness. They were no less prompt or less expert than she would have been. He was an utterly standard case, except that he was Charlie. The nurses found a bed for her in their quarters and at last persuaded her to go to it.

Sister to Sister

Sally left Étaples the following afternoon, with everyone assuring her Charlie was coming on well and already showing himself a robust recuperant. His temperature was down. They boasted they had "caught" the gangrene in time. She would be contacted if there was any change.

On the way back by ambulance, she felt her own fever return—not gradually but in a rush. Her joints were in agony and by the time the ambulance reached the clearing station the fever had her bewildered.

But the poor thing had it earlier, she heard Honora say to Dr. Bright as she lay in the influenza tent where Leo had died. Honora and Bright wore masks.

It's unfortunate, said Dr. Bright helplessly, but her first one wasn't the influenza. Honora's dissatified eyes loomed above Sally. Her mother looked over Bright's shoulder. Her mother was unmasked and knew that her daughter had drowned in the *Archimedes* and showed a curiosity about Sally's process of sinking. Sally had enough mind left to wonder why it was always the *Archimedes* she ended up with.

Do you have the morphine I stole for you? she asked her mother. The idea was if her mother would give it back now, it would take Sally away into light and air.

It has all gone to young men, her mother told her. And Mrs. Durance put her hands to her own temples as if trying to puzzle this out—the lack of comfort available to Sally.

Sally could feel things happen at the gallop within her. She blazed. Her lungs were bleeding southwards, melting away. She was frightened. But Charlie might come and pour her the sweet wine of clear air.

She's such a beautiful one, said Slattery to Bright. And Leonora went too. It takes the beautiful.

No, said Dr. Bright. I trust that can't be true.

Masked Slattery knelt by Sally's bed at some hour. Her face became as large as a balloon. But she said nothing. My lungs are bleeding away, Sally in the meantime acknowledged, stealing the breath pledged to Charlie, and the delight of lungs filled and expelled. Her mother's wan good wishes radiated out but could not prevail over melting luck.

The rottenest of luck, said Bright.

Charlie knows my body, she stated. I have opened it to him.

All the Sallys of her acquaintance—the child, the country nurse, the Egyptian tourist, the seaborne nurse, the landlocked one—were torn away like leaves off the boughs of her fever. The thief, the murderer, the sister, the hater, the sinker, the swimmer, the lover, the unloved, the witness of light, the coward of dark, and the binder and rinser of wounds, the daughter fled and the daughter forever. What do I think you do to your friends on the wire, Charlie? Australian mercy comes from the mouth of the rifle. Where is Charlie and his wing, his docked arm? So busy up in a hospital. Not knowing to come once more for a visit and give me back the air.

When air was not returned to her, terror gave way to confusion and it was all dreams and much tumult. It was dreadful how fast the tumult faded, until she let go of all the strings and felt herself choke awhile in a serenity that was A1, first class, not so bad as all that. A woman who wanted to feel more than this serenity would want portholes in her coffin. Ah, ease! It was not hard, after all, to rise—and even Charlie was just part of a mass of people left.

As Sally struggled, the revived influenza struck the Voluntary. Patients and orderlies and English Roses caught the thing and were in a special wing. Naomi too all at once sensed it advancing within her, but for about six hours—from ten in the morning until four that afternoon— denied the symptoms. When one staggered in corridors and was unsure of where the walls were—and the differentiation between them and the floor—then it was time to pay the fever attention. Declaring herself to Airdrie, Naomi was permitted to take to bed in her own room—an isolation ward of one. Her joints throbbed, she vomited the clear broth one of the masked Australian nurses fed her. Through lack of breath she felt a hellish separation from everything, from even the simplest objects in her room—a cup, a book, a coat hanging from a hook behind the door.

An English nurse came in to look at her with arresting but overhuge eyes. She was followed by two masked orderlies manhandling a bed, and two more with a stretcher on which one of the English Roses lay. The girl was gasping hard and thrashed her head continuously, squandering strength. They might both have been the victims of membrane-blistering yperite. At some stage of her fever Naomi was sure they were.

Separated from herself in this plain room, she was aware that another colleague visited her and stood writing on a chart as well. You have stayed here—she wanted to say. No military authority told you. Lady Tarlton asked you and you stayed. Was it to give me back my breath?

Naomi descended from her airless space above the bed to the deck of the *Archimedes,* where men and women ran about in hysteria. But with an acidic grief in her belly she went looking for Kiernan and her mother, who were both there and not there, who had both stayed and gone. She saw ponies milling on the foredeck as it began to rise.

Shoot the horses! shouted a nurse.

No one is doing it, her mother declared with that wistful smile Naomi had seen in childhood.

Naomi felt the rage she had always had against her mother, who was crying, Nothing can be done, nothing can be done . . .

Something *can* be done, Mama! Naomi insisted. Nothing can be done? I killed you with morphine because you said that sort of thing. Sally had taken it from the cupboard in the *Archimedes*. Sally, the little thief, had put it in place for me. I found it and let the snake run into your heart.

The horses first, said Mrs. Durance, farm-bred and grimly practical, the corners of her lower lip tucked under the upper in resignation. So she went off to attend to those things—the neighing beasts who would not question her, who offered no chance to this victim who made no threats and was content with her own murder.

When the room returned to Naomi, there were still horses in it, raging and panicked. She had time to sit at a breathless table with the gaol governor and plead with him to let Ian out to save the horses. The man was stupid and could not see the urgency which grew in her, the greatest agony of her life. The ship pitched till she and the asinine gaol governor and the men and women and horses slid into the sea which felt of nothing. Thus she went down. Roaring for breath.

1918–1922

Since both the Durance girls knew, without knowing the other did, that there was the smallest membrane between alternate histories of themselves—between the drowning and the floating, between the fevered and the convalescent—it was somehow appropriate that two contradictory reports appeared in the Macleay Valley's papers—the *Argus* and the *Chronicle*.

The *Argus* read, "Mr. Durance of Sherwood has received the sad news that his daughter Naomi has died of a prevailing influenza while serving as a nurse in France. The *Argus* and all its readers extend their sincerest sympathies . . ."

The *Chronicle* read, "Mr. Durance, a well-respected farmer of Sherwood, has been informed that his daughter Sally (Sarah) has died of a congestive disease while serving our gallant soldiers as a nurse in France. The *Chronicle* and its readers extend to Mr. Durance their . . ."

A few days later Mrs. Durance (formerly Sorley) dropped into the newspaper offices. The names had been mixed up, she told them. But that seemed to create further confusion.

The *Argus* printed a report that said, "The *Argus* regrets its earlier notification that Nurse Naomi Durance has died in France. It was her sister, Sally, who regrettably succumbed to influenza. The *Argus* apologizes to the Durance family and again extends its sincerest . . ."

While the *Chronicle* declared, "The *Chronicle* regrets that it was mistaken in reporting the death of Sally (Sarah) Durance of influenza while she was serving as a nurse in France. It was her sister, Naomi, who has died in the service of our valiant young men and of Australia, which this paper chooses to see as a separate entity to the Empire. But, rising above politics, we apologize to Mr. Eric Durance of Sherwood and offer our most heartfelt . . ."

Thus from the start people were confused. When they mentioned the Durance sisters—as they did infrequently—they were uncertain which of the girls had gone under to the Spanish influenza. It was known that the other one had married a man from Sydney or Melbourne, a returned soldier. One of them had been involved with the Condons, but the Condons were gone from the valley—the solicitor to join his brother's more extensive practice in Orange. They could not be conferred with on the matter.

The new Mrs. Durance had in a way lost one of her children too. Ernest was not the same boy when he came back from France. He spent a lot of time drinking with other repatriated soldiers at the Federal Hotel and then wandering down to the railway station to chat drunkenly in the refreshment room with any train passengers who were survivors of the war and who happened to be having a meal there during the half hour the Brisbane Mail sat at the station. Ernest had vanished by the end of 1920—off to Queensland, it was said.

So which of the sisters died and stayed in French soil? It was a question anyhow on which people expended some interest, but not a great amount. Out of politeness, they did not ask Mr. or Mrs. Durance.

But taking into account the membrane between alternate versions—of which Sally herself had become so convinced after the sinking of the *Archimedes,* believing that though she had survived, there was a parallel world of chance in which she had not—we can venture to say that at the end of the Australian summer of 1922 wealthy businessman, part-time painter, and printer of fine books Eddie Horowitz laid on a gallery for an exhibition by Charlie Condon.

When Charlie and Sally had first returned from Paris, the going had been hard for them. Sally worked at Sydney Hospital to give Charlie the breathing space homecoming always required. Paris had been in its way difficult too. But the excitement of beginning there—at the epicenter of art—had intoxicated them for a time. It was strange nonetheless that the British painters, the Americans, and the few Australians lived almost entirely in their own clique. They got together often to talk English or take holidays on the coasts of Normandy and Brittany—and thus to shy away from confronting the great alps of recent European achievement. The Americans were fascinated by Charlie's missing arm—though rather than pin up his sleeve, he used a prosthesis and a glove over an artificial hand in an attempt to put paid to the issue. The British took missing limbs more for granted. So it was not out of false sympathy that Charlie had two paintings exhibited in the Royal Academy in 1921. This provided the modicum of validation needed for the artist to keep going and for his wife to continue in her original faith. He was also invited to exhibit at the Chelsea Arts Club. Though at that stage Sally had been offered a job nursing at the English Sanatorium in Paris, Charlie insisted that she should not waste her French experience on drudgery.

The parties they went to in Paris could become difficult. Spirits—particularly cheap spirits, which were all they could afford—made Charlie irascible. Then, when they got home to their one-room apartment, there were the sort of night sweats and dreams that all the women of the soldiers of the world endured at secondhand.

Painting French forests and seasides and pastures was an education rather than a career, Charlie began to assert. When it became apparent to him and Sally that the honest and essential thing was to go home, they knew it would not be an easy business. The English artists who went home had the certainty that they could swan back to Paris whenever they liked. The Australians had the greater certainty that their decision was a choice—very nearly—for life.

But within a few months of Charlie and Sally getting back to Sydney, Eddie Horowitz had given Charlie's French work a cachet and was now trying to do his Australian coastal landscapes the same favor. Cachet in Sydney was not like cachet in Paris. But it would have to do. With the weight of the congealed Australian summer's heat on them, they rented a flat by the sea in Bronte. As Charlie had predicted, the light in Bronte made Wimereaux and Boulogne look sick by comparison, but still there was a vacancy in the air above them. The imagination had not filled it to the same extent to which *those* atmospheres had been filled. But then the air of France was filled with the dream of war and mangling, as well as the dream of light.

When Eddie Horowitz first saw Charlie's work, he introduced him to the Society of Artists in Sydney and the Australian Watercolor Institute. He also tried to get him a part-time job imparting sketching skills to the students of the Teachers' College and he found him a studio in George Street to share with a number of other artists. The only thing Eddie could not do was cause his business partners—and the businesspeople he invited to the exhibition—to buy Charlie's paintings and make Charlie's name.

Charlie was sufficiently impressed by the seriousness of the night of the exhibition opening to have bought a new suit. He understood by now the impact drink had on his behavior and despite the stress of the occasion remained utterly sober that night. He had given instructions to Eddie that in no press—as little as there might be—were his war wounds to be mentioned. He did not want to be written up as a freak—the one-handed artist. I only started to paint properly after I lost the left arm, you stupid bastard, he had cried to an American artist at a party in Paris—and he'd had to be taken home.

So this event in a studio on the top floor of David Jones department store was the punishment and reward for painting. A number of men and women approached Charlie with their whiskies and gins in hand to congratulate him, in an amused but overcheery manner which told him they would not be spending anything tonight. Across the room

Mrs. Sorley and Sally's father were talking to some of Charlie's friends from the studio.

Standing near them, a man in a good suit seemed engrossed by one of the paintings and he reminded Sally of Ian Kiernan. Her eyes had picked him out because this exhibition was frightening to her, and she looked for echoes of familiarity in it. The man did not look like an associate of Eddie Horowitz, there to please him for business reasons. Sally wished she could have said to Charlie, who was talking to friends, See that man there? Doesn't he look like Ian Kiernan?

She had not written to Kiernan for at least six months and did not know if he was still in prison.

The man leaned to the painting, stood upright, turned, saw her, and smiled broadly. It was a smile of recognition, a smile from the *Archimedes*. He strode across the room towards her and Charlie.

Charlie saw him now. They wrung each other's hand, and Ian kissed Sally's cheek and stepped back and said, So much like your sister . . .

I thought, said Sally. I mean, I didn't know if you were . . .

We were all amnestied in handfuls, said Kiernan. Thank God, our government didn't have its heart in locking us away for good. I'm back working in the family business—it is still the family business even though the government tried to acquire it. Now I am totally respectable. All is forgiven.

Are you married? asked Sally, perhaps too quickly.

Oh no, he said.

She was strangely appeased.

He said, I must congratulate you, Charlie. The river over there.

He pointed to the painting he had been studying so keenly. It's not the Somme, is it?

The Yser, said Charlie, with a smile. And look, I've got Australian rivers in the next alcove . . . the Clarence is there.

Painting the Yser isn't an act of national dereliction, Ian Kiernan assured him. And if I were to acquire the Yser, I suppose you would think that it was out of friendship or regard for your wounds rather than for its inherent quality.

With a man who could speak Charlie's fears so accurately, his buying a painting was no trouble, and they all knew it.

Three were sold that night. Eddie declared that was remarkable in this philistine age. Ian stayed till the end and walked out with them as Eddie Horowitz led the way. Eddie was taking them all to dinner at the Hotel Australia—Charlie, Sally, her father, and the new Mrs. Durance.

On the pavement, in the pleasant warmth of a summer's night whose southerly breeze had arrived, Kiernan said in a lowered voice to Sally, I can never forget her. We were the perfect fellow pilgrims.

He squeezed her hand, shook hands with Charlie, and walked away up Elizabeth Street.

Charlie kissed her ear and said, Ducky.

Ducky had become his pet name for her.

Ducky, I think that went very well.

But the reality that is actually most inhabited and concrete is the one that counts—although perhaps by a mere whisper of a degree. And it was Naomi who occupied the observed world after her sister—through gravest ill fortune—went down. In that reality, Charlie Condon's first exhibition in fact occurred at the Athenaeum Gallery in Collins Street and was organized by Bernard Favenc, an art dealer and patron. Bernard had been generous to Charlie since Charlie had returned to Australia some months before, drawn to Melbourne by the National Gallery Art School. And even though Charlie had not yet been able to build up much of an Australian portfolio—most of the paintings were of the streaky skies of northern France, the rivers and village streets—better-off soldiers, said Bernard, officer types, might like to have on their walls a village, however rendered, where they'd fought or rested. Get on to painting the Western District later, said Bernard Favenc. There were some Australian landscapes in the exhibition, but Charlie was sure that if any sold, it wouldn't be those.

In Paris, two-and-a-half years after he had lost his arm and had been required to absorb the news of Sally, Charlie had become infatuated with a broad-faced Belgian girl named Estelle who also had ambitions as a painter.

She sat now on a chair on the exhibition floor by the tall upstairs windows and looked sulky—which was to an extent her normal look and was mysteriously part of her allure to Charlie. Tonight she drank sherry with a fixity which might well be nervousness for his sake. She had lived through a Melbourne summer with less complaint than he expected. They were hard up—though he was doing book and magazine illustrations and she had got work in a dress shop. They rented a little house in Coburg. Before Bernard's guests arrived, she looked unimpressed, as if the brutishness of the place Charlie had brought her to was about to be conclusively revealed.

Luckily the first to arrive was a Russian artist, an émigré named Peliakov who was a member by invitation of the Arts Society of Victoria. Charlie made sure he introduced him to Estelle—in Paris she had always been fascinated by the émigrés, by the fact that a Russian count might be serving drinks at the George V or attending diners stylishly as a waiter. Now Peliakov distracted Estelle for the moment from the question of what she would do here with her own art and whether the barbarians would buy any of Charlie's. As he watched her, he felt a sudden certainty that she would leave him, perhaps for someone like Peliakov, and it wouldn't mean as much to him as it should.

He let himself be distracted from grief and hollowness when some fellow artists arrived. They were half broke, doing teaching jobs or cartoons and book illustrations for irregular pay and were keen for the free sherry. They raised by their presence the question of whether Australia could support one artist, let alone a tribe. A young man and his wife, whom Charlie suspected from their faces to be Eastern European, came up to him, very well dressed, and spoke informedly about his paintings. He made sure Estelle met them and was prodigiously grateful to them.

All at once the gallery—which had been sparsely peopled an instant before—seemed crowded. Bernard Favenc now rushed up with a sweat of excitement on his upper lip. You have met the Castans? The most civilized people in Melbourne. They're Jewish, you see, and they understand these things. They're deliberately putting together an Australian collection—no other private person is. I really mean a collection, not just a scatter of things for their walls. And they've bought both your Western District paintings. You're in instant favor, my son. You must go home and pray that the Castans live a long and profitable life.

As he spoke he was pumping Charlie's real, right hand and then he turned away, and Charlie—he later told art historians—felt a great, prickling sense of being empowered and of having an Australian license to paint.

He was jolted by the sight of acute familiarity across the studio by the door. There—her face sleek and exquisite—stood Naomi like a version of lost Sally. She wore a dress of white and black and a fine cloche hat and seemed to be in such fullness of her beauty that it hurt him to see it. She was smiling tentatively in his direction as if he might not recognize her. The sudden power of his loss made the room and all its urgency recede.

Then, beside her, he noticed, stood Kiernan in a brown suit—no gaol pallor there. His face had obviously seen the sun of freedom in the recent summer. Feeling unsteady, he approached them. Naomi's arms were out. When he embraced her he could not help but realize that he was feeling the same sort of bush-bred, sturdy body he had too infrequently known in Sally. He heard her sob and would have liked to have done the same himself. When she released him, he saw her teary lashes and her smile. He shook Kiernan's hand then.

Ah, he said, you're free!

Naomi and Lady Tarlton argued them into it, Ian said. Once there was peace, there was even less sense in keeping us shut up anyhow.

I have a confession to make, said Charlie to Naomi. The sight of her renewed his spasm of loss. I hope it doesn't offend you. I have a girlfriend here.

Well, of course you have a girl, said Naomi.

I think *she* understands—unjust as it might be to her—there would never be anyone . . . Well, you know.

Sally never grasped her own value, said Naomi. And neither did I. Not sufficiently.

They all stood looking at each other, knowing that the most important matters had been broached. Now, said Charlie, I have to forbid you from buying one of these canvasses. Your being here is enough honor.

Dear fellow, said Ian Kiernan, laughing, Naomi does what she wants, didn't you know?

He had a sudden duty to introduce them to Estelle. Half turning, he called her name across the room. She advanced towards Naomi and Kiernan and Charlie with the remnants of suspicion on her well-made face. The three of them waited for her in unuttered agreement on the incapacity of things to provide the essential Sally.

Acknowledgments

Thanks go abundantly to my indomitable agent Amanda Urban, and to Judith Curr and Peter Borland, for giving the Durance Sisters a genial home.

At the same level of sincerity, I must state my gratitude to my wife, Judy, natural-born editor of first choice and—very handily for this narrative—a former nurse, though in a later era than that dealt with in *The Daughters of Mars*. My sister-in-law, Jane Keneally, is also a nurse and read the manuscript and gave editorial input.

And my brother, Dr. John Keneally, made a Member of the Order of Australia for his services to child anesthesia and analgesia during the writing of this book, took time in the midst of severe illness to do a very thorough medical and general edit of the manuscript.

Needless to say, no blame for any remaining errors in the manuscript attach to these generous people.

Further Reading

I would like to declare a debt to the following works:

A. G. Butler, *The History of the Australian Medical Services in World War I*, Volumes 1–3 (Sydney, 1938–42).

Janet Butler, "Nursing Gallipoli: Identity and the Challenge of Experience," *Journal of Australian Studies*, Issue 78, 2003.

Nurse Elsie Cook war diaries, Australian War Memorial, Canberra.

Stretcher bearer George R. Faulkner war diaries, 1916–17, Mitchell Library, Sydney.

J. M. Gillings and J. Richards (eds.), *In All These Lines: the Diary of Sister Elsie Tranter, 1916–19* (Newstead, Tasmania, 2008).

Marina Larsson, *Shattered Anzacs* (Sydney, 2009).

Peter Rees, *The Other Anzacs* (Sydney, 2008).

Bruce Scates and Raelene Francis, *Women and the Great War* (Cambridge, 1997).

Michael B. Tyquin, *Gallipoli: The Medical War* (Sydney, 1993).

W. C. Watson, *Narrative of Experiences in France, 1917*, war diaries, Mitchell Library, Sydney.

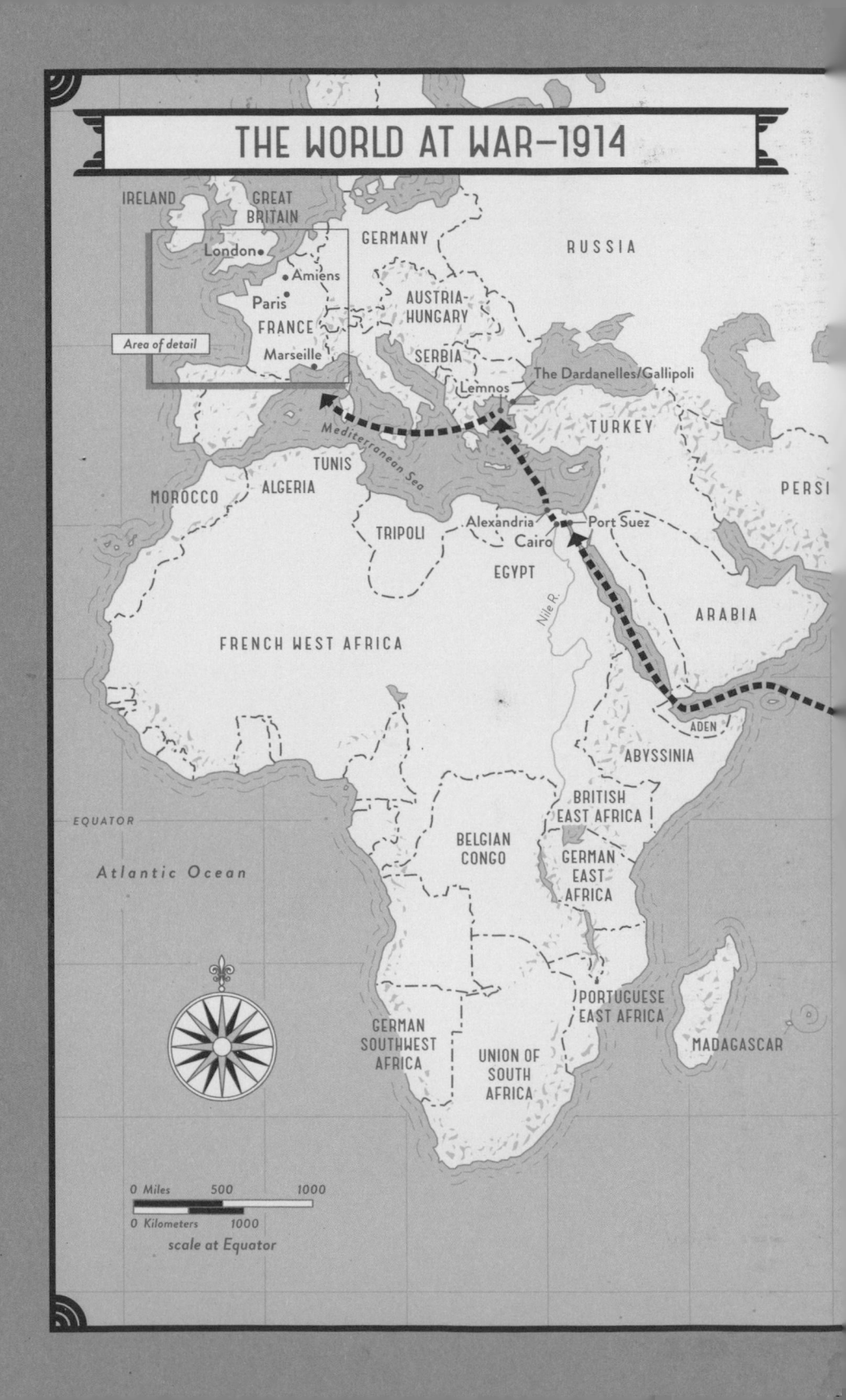

THE WORLD AT WAR—1914

IRELAND

GREAT BRITAIN

London

Amiens

Paris

FRANCE

Area of detail

Marseille

GERMANY

RUSSIA

AUSTRIA-HUNGARY

SERBIA

Lemnos

The Dardanelles/Gallipoli

TURKEY

PERSI

Mediterranean Sea

MOROCCO

TUNIS

ALGERIA

TRIPOLI

Alexandria

Cairo

Port Suez

EGYPT

Nile R.

ARABIA

FRENCH WEST AFRICA

ADEN

ABYSSINIA

EQUATOR

Atlantic Ocean

BELGIAN CONGO

BRITISH EAST AFRICA

GERMAN EAST AFRICA

GERMAN SOUTHWEST AFRICA

UNION OF SOUTH AFRICA

PORTUGUESE EAST AFRICA

MADAGASCAR

0 Miles 500 1000

0 Kilometers 1000

scale at Equator